"DAMN YOU, CASEY WALKER!"

Casey grasped Belle's wrists and brought them to her sides. "I'm only thinking of you and Tommy, Belle. How long can you keep running? You need someone to take care of you."

Belle pulled from his grasp, breathing hard, her eyes flashing angrily. "Are you suggesting you're that man?"

"Is that such an outlandish idea? We're explosive together, Belle!" Seizing her arms, he pulled Belle against him. "I didn't mean to upset you. I had to try one last time to—"

His lips came down on hers. And Casey's words were lost to her in the heat of his mouth and the melting strength of his arms. . . .

A LOVE TO CHERISH

CONNIE MASON

LOVE SPELL NEW YORK CITY

LOVE SPELL®

July 2002

Published by

Dorchester Publishing Co., Inc.
276 Fifth Avenue
New York, NY 10001

ISBN 0-505-52494-5

Prologue

Yuma Territorial Prison, Arizona
May 1876

"**T**his is the last time I'll be able to visit you for awhile, Mark. I'm leaving for San Francisco in the morning. Try not to worry about a thing. I've hired the best lawyer in the territory to get you out of this murder rap, so don't give up."

It nearly broke Casey Walker's heart to see his younger brother behind prison bars. Two months ago he had been convicted of murder and sent to Yuma Territorial Prison to serve his life term. Once a happy-go-lucky young man, Mark had aged quickly during his trial. His hazel eyes were shadowed with hopelessness and resignation. He was far too cynical for his twenty-four years and much too apathetic. Sure, Mark had always been a little wild, but he wasn't a murderer. He had shot that card cheat in self-defense, and the only witness to the shooting had fled to parts unknown before Mark's trial came up.

Mark raised defeated hazel eyes to Casey, looking as if he wanted to believe him but feared to get his hopes up. Casey's younger brother had never recovered after that day several months ago, when a gambler at the Dry Gulch Saloon had falsely accused him of cheating and drawn on him. Mark had been faster, his bullet going straight into the gambler's heart. The jury hadn't believed his plea of self-defense and the judge had sentenced him to life in prison.

"San Francisco?" Mark asked listlessly. "Does Allan Pinkerton have a job for you?"

"Yeah, one I can't refuse. The man who contacted Allan wanted the best detective in the Pinkerton Agency, and offered a bonus for finding a missing person." Casey grinned, revealing the deep dimple in his left cheek. "And since I'm the best man, and have need of the money to pay your lawyer, I've accepted the assignment."

The shadows in Mark's eyes deepened and he shrugged with a marked lack of enthusiasm. "You're wasting your money, Casey. You'll never find the man who can clear my name, so it doesn't matter how much you pay that fancy lawyer. I'm going to die in prison, I know it. I'm resigned to my fate, why don't you just forget about me?"

Casey drove strong fingers through his thick black hair, nearly defeated by Mark's apathy. He had to get Mark out of prison before it destroyed him. Unfortunately the money needed to offer a reward for the missing witness just wasn't available. Without the witness, filing an appeal was useless. This job had come at a time when Casey had nearly given up hope.

"Dammit, Mark, don't talk like that. I've tried my best to locate the missing witness. Before I leave I'm going to tell lawyer Levy to spare no expense in finding the man who was present during the shooting at the saloon that night. We can't reopen the case without positive evidence. Offering a substantial reward is a surefire way to bring the witness forward. Whatever it takes, I'll get the money for that reward."

Casey's strong jaw clenched with determination and his eyes, a curious greenish-brown flecked with gold, were incandescent with purpose. No one who heard him could doubt his utter confidence or sincerity.

His eyes downcast, Mark turned away. "It's all right, Casey, I know how hard you've worked on my behalf and I know you'll do everything in your power to set me free, but I fear it's out of your hands. No man could ask for a better brother. I won't think any less of you if you fail to find the witness. God knows you've neglected your job and run yourself ragged in my behalf these past few months. I really appreciate it. I haven't always been the best of brothers. You've put your own life on hold trying to clear my name. I know for a fact you've turned down assignments. I'm glad you've taken this one, for whatever reason."

If Casey could have reached inside the bars, he would have shaken some sense into Mark. The boy was far too accepting of his fate. Drawing himself up to his full, impressive height, Casey flexed his shoulders, sending tense muscles rippling across his broad torso. Somehow, some way, he was going to get the money to offer the kind of reward that would bring the missing witness forward. If he didn't do it, and do it soon, he feared Mark would lose all hope.

"I won't let you give up, Mark." His voice had taken on a hard edge and the chiseled planes of his rugged features were utterly ruthless with resolve.

"I'll get that money for the reward and I'll see you free again. Nothing or no one will stand in my way. I swear it."

Chapter 1

San Francisco
May 1876

"I'm Casey Walker, from the Pinkerton Agency. And you're Mr. McAllister, I presume."

Casey held out his hand to the owner of the McAllister Winery, a robust man with piercing dark eyes and thinning brown hair just beginning to turn gray. Though past his prime, McAllister possessed the vim and vigor of a much younger man. One totally obsessed with his own power. Intuition told Casey that and more about the wealthy businessman.

"T.J. McAllister, here," McAllister said heartily, shaking Casey's hand. "What took you so long?"

"It's a long way from Fort Yuma to San Francisco by stage," Casey said by way of an explanation. "Allan Pinkerton didn't elaborate on this assignment, so if you'll tell me who it is I'm looking for I can get right on the case."

"Sit down, Walker, and I'll tell you what you're

up against. I want you to find a woman. A conniving whore, to be exact. Belle Parker trapped my only son into marriage. She plied her trade at a local brothel, where she met my son. When young Tom announced his plans to marry the whore I flew into a rage. I tried to tell him she was after his money, but he wouldn't listen to reason."

Casey nodded sympathetically, committing McAllister's every word to memory. He'd met plenty of whores in his life, some schemers, some honest, but Belle Parker sounded like a woman who knew what she wanted and went after it.

"Tom went ahead and married the woman against my wishes," T.J. continued. "I promptly disowned him. Told him I wouldn't acknowledge him until he got rid of the conniving bitch. I made it clear that he was being cut off without a penny. The young fool had more spunk than I gave him credit for," McAllister allowed with a hint of admiration. "He got a job on a ranch and somehow managed to support himself and his wife without my help. By then the bad blood between us made it impossible for either of us to cave in. The little slut Tom married did a fine job of alienating my son and I."

"Is your son missing?" Casey asked, growing impatient with McAllister's rambling.

"I'm getting around to it, Walker," McAllister groused. "A few months after they married, Belle gave birth to a son. I refused to acknowledge the child, even though he is my only grandson by my only son. You have to understand how bitter I was over Tom's defection. I expected him to become disenchanted with the whore once he got his fill, but instead he had a child with her. I couldn't find it in my heart to forgive him."

"Begging your pardon, Mr. McAllister, but you still haven't told me the name of the person I'm to locate."

McAllister gave him a blistering look and continued. "My grandson is five years old now, and I want him. The tragedy in all this is that my son drowned on a trail drive over a year ago. Now my grandson is being raised by a woman unfit to raise pigs. To my knowledge she still plies her trade somewhere. Belle Parker is a money-hungry bitch who knows I'd do anything to get my grandson. She doesn't want the boy, I'd stake my life on it. She's just holding out for the right price, and I refuse to barter for my own flesh and blood, or give that whore a penny of my money. The law is on my side. I have every right to take the boy from his mother and raise him properly."

Walker thought it was rather late for McAllister to worry about his grandson's welfare, but maintained his silence. He was in desperate need of the bonus the man had offered and didn't want to risk losing this job.

"If the law is on your side, why don't you just go and take the boy?" Casey asked.

"I wouldn't need you if I knew where he was," McAllister countered caustically. "His mother got wind of my plans and took him away. They've disappeared from the face of the earth. I've been searching over a year for him."

"How old did you say your grandson is?"

"He's five, and old enough to know that his mother is a whore who sleeps with a different man every night. I have to get him away from her before she ruins him. The boy is the last remaining McAllister. There is no one else to inherit my fortune.

"Allan Pinkerton said you were a top-notch detective. I hope to God he's right. I want that boy, McAllister, and I'm offering an extra bonus of two thousand dollars in addition to your regular fee. The way I figure it, Belle will give up the boy with the right kind of persuasion." He gave Casey a searching look. "You're a good-looking man, I'm sure you've had experience with women. Find Belle, sweet-talk her, hell, bed her if you have to, promise her anything, if she'll give up custody of the boy without a fight. After you find her, if you fail to convince her to give up the boy peaceably, I'll be forced to do it my way. I have the law's approval to take my own flesh and blood away from a woman like that. Hell, she even has a whore's name."

Casey's heart pounded with excitement. Two thousand dollars was a helluva lot of money and he needed every penny of it. But something about the job stroked him the wrong way. Taking a child from his mother, whore or no, didn't seem right. If Belle was willing to give up the boy, she wouldn't have gone into hiding in the first place. Unless, he reflected, she *was* holding out for money, like McAllister said.

"You'd be doing the boy a favor by taking him out of an unhealthy environment," McAllister persisted when Walker hesitated. "Tell you what I'll do, bring that boy to me without creating a messy scandal and I'll increase the bonus to three thousand dollars. I'd prefer to take the boy without a fuss. I don't like the idea of dragging my name through the mud or digging up family secrets. Gossip can be cruel. I don't want the boy to go through life known as the son of a whore."

"Would you be willing to pay the bonus in

advance, Mr. McAllister?" Casey held his breath. An advance of that size meant he could send the money to Simon Levy right away. The sooner the money was in the lawyer's hands, the sooner he could post a reward for the missing witness.

"That's highly irregular, Walker. How good are you? My own men have failed to turn up a single clue to Belle's whereabouts."

"Good enough to be counted one of Pinkerton's best men. I haven't lost a case yet, or failed a client." Too bad he couldn't say the same about his own situation, Casey thought glumly. He'd spent months looking for the missing witness, to no avail. Perhaps the reward and Simon Levy would succeed where he had failed.

McAllister thumped his fingers against his desk as he studied Casey, thinking that he did indeed look like a man who seldom failed. His ruggedly handsome features could have been carved from stone and his eyes were coldly dangerous. Though he carried only one gun in his holster, McAllister suspected Casey carried another beneath his jacket, and that he was a damn accurate shot. "Very well," McAllister conceded. "You may have the bonus now. But I expect results, do I make myself clear? If you fail, the bonus is to be returned to me in full."

Casey raked him with his cool gaze. "You've made yourself perfectly clear." He uncoiled his lanky frame from the chair. "Give me the name of the whorehouse where Belle worked and I'll be on my way."

"Naomi's Pleasure Parlor. But you won't learn anything there. My men have already questioned the madam and all the girls."

An easy smile played at the corners of Casey's

mouth. "If you don't mind, I prefer conducting my own investigation."

Placerville
Two weeks later

Casey rode into the mining town of Placerville at midday. Originally called Dry Diggin's, the town's name had been changed to Hangtown in 1849 after a series of grisly lynchings, but in 1854 the miners changed the name to Placerville to satisfy self-conscience pride. Now Placerville was an important mining center, surrounded by mines taking thousands of dollars a day out of the ground. While passing through Sacramento, Casey had inquired about Placerville and learned that the town had a couple of respectable hotels, a Wells Fargo office with weekly stagecoach routes, a post office, and numerous saloons.

Since Casey had no idea yet where to find Belle Parker, he headed down Main Street, looking for the hotel. At No. 543 Main Street he passed a store whose sign, weathered but still legible, proclaimed that the J.M. Studebaker Company once produced the best wheelbarrows in California at that site. A few doors down, Phillip Armour's butcher shop and Mark Hopkins' grocery store sat side by side.

Casey reined up sharply before the next building, staring at the cracked, hand-painted wooden sign posted above the door. The name, Isabelle's Diner, captured his attention and he stared at it with interest.

After leaving McAllister's office two weeks ago, Casey had paid a visit to Naomi's Pleasure Parlor.

As McAllister had predicted, the madam and her girls had steadfastly refused to talk about Belle Parker. Casey thought their protectiveness toward the woman extraordinary. No one claimed to know a thing about the former whore. The only useful bit of information occurred when one of the whores let slip that Naomi hadn't received a letter from Isabelle in quite a while. The girl earned a stern look from Naomi.

But Casey wasn't a Pinkerton detective for nothing. He paid for the services of the curvaceous whore named Pansy and accompanied her upstairs. It had been far too long since he'd bedded a woman anyway, and he decided to satisfy his yearnings while gaining a bit of information. Pansy had been so beguiled by Casey's expertise in bed that his subtle questioning soon got her to reveal the location of Naomi's room.

After satisfying both himself and the woman, Casey plied Pansy with liquor, and while she dozed contentedly, he slipped out of the room. Spying Naomi by the front door, greeting guests, he stealthily entered the madam's room. In Naomi's dresser drawer Casey found a letter from Isabelle Henderson. Evidently Belle had taken on a new name and identity. The letter said little beyond the fact that Isabelle and her child were both well and reasonably happy. The letter had been posted from Sacramento by way of Wells Fargo in Placerville. Casey had both a destination and a name when he left the whorehouse a short time later. If McAllister's men had an ounce of ingenuity, they could have ferreted out the same information he had.

Now, standing before Isabelle's Diner, intuition told Casey that he was on the right track. Dismount-

ing, Casey tethered his horse to the hitching post
and entered the ramshackle building that appeared
to have been one of the first built in the gold camp in
1848. The lunch crowd had already dispersed, and
the large room set with trestle tables was empty but
for one man, who sat nursing a cup of coffee.

A woman came out of the kitchen and smiled at
him. "Can I help you, mister? It's too late for lunch,
but there might be a few leftovers in the kitchen if
you're hungry."

Casey returned her smile. Her voice appealed to
him. It was throaty and soft, surprisingly arousing,
and nothing like he'd expected. None of the whores
he knew, and he knew plenty, had voices that made
him think of bubbling mountain brooks and sighing
winds.

It was more than her delightfully dulcet voice that
made Casey think his intuition had failed him. This
woman couldn't be Belle Parker, the mercenary
whore who had coerced McAllister's young, naive
son into marriage. This appealing young woman
with rich brown hair, peaches-and-cream complexion, and wide brown eyes, was dressed conserva-
tively in a serviceable gray gown covered by a large
white apron. No woman who looked like Isabelle
Henderson could possibly be a whore. He had
expected to find a flamboyantly beautiful woman
servicing miners sexually, not someone resembling
the girl next door serving meals to them. Perhaps,
Casey thought, this young woman was merely an
employee, or not the same Isabelle Henderson he
sought.

"Anything will do," Casey said, taking a seat at
one of the tables. "Whatever you have to hold me
over till supper, miss."

"It's Mrs. Henderson," Belle said, sizing the man up as a stranger in camp. She didn't trust strangers. Being always on the lookout for her father-in-law's men was beginning to take its toll on her. "I can serve you up a plate of beans and biscuits."

"And coffee," Casey added. He knew it was rude to stare at the woman but seemed unable to look away.

Belle nodded and turned back to the kitchen. Casey continued to stare at her, stunned to note that she was limping. Though slight, her limp was nevertheless noticeable . . . and surprising. Men rarely were attracted to whores with deformities. Most madams would consider a lame whore a disability and bad for business. Either he had the wrong woman, Casey thought, or McAllister had lied about his daughter-in-law's profession. Casey didn't like being deceived. Unfortunately it was too late for second thoughts. He had already taken his bonus from McAllister and wired it to Simon Levy. Casey might not like McAllister, but he had agreed to do a job and he'd never reneged on an assignment in his entire career as a Pinkerton detective.

Belle peeked out the kitchen door at the handsome stranger while the beans were heating, gnawing her lower lip with even white teeth as she considered his strong chin and rugged features. He was handsome, no doubt about it. Those were the men she trusted least. Yet she couldn't seem to take her eyes off him. Shiny dark hair brushed the nape of his neck, and though she hadn't noted the color of his eyes, she knew they would be unusual. He was big; she could see his muscles rippling beneath his clothing. The man didn't look like a miner. Dressed in crisp canvas trousers, plaid shirt and leather vest, wearing leather boots that were scuffed but of good quality, his attire was too new to mark him as a miner.

Belle noted that the man wore one gun at his hip, a Colt single-action pistol. What Belle didn't know was that Casey carried an Underhammer "bootleg" percussion pistol beneath his vest. The gun was of small caliber but practical for personal protection when one wanted to carry concealed weapons.

A few minutes later Belle returned with a plate of beans and a cup of coffee, which she sat down before Casey. "I haven't seen you around before, mister. Going to try your hand at mining?"

Casey shoved his hat back on his head and smiled at Belle. "The name's Walker, Casey Walker. I'm just passing through. What kind of hotel is the Cary House?"

"The best, Mr. Walker. It was built after the Ruffles Hotel burned in 1856. Expensive, too. If it's too steep for you I can recommend another."

"I'll keep that in mind. How long have you been serving meals in Placerville, Mrs. Henderson?" Casey asked as he dug into his beans.

"Long enough."

"Is your husband a miner?"

"I'm a widow," Belle said crisply.

"Any children?" He tried to make the question sound casual.

Warning bells went off in Belle's head. "I don't believe that's any of your business, Mr. Walker. That's two bits for the beans and coffee."

"Sorry," Casey mumbled as he dug in his pocket for change. She's as skittish as a colt, he thought as he watched her limp away into the kitchen. Not that he could blame her. If Isabelle Henderson was indeed Belle Parker, she had good reason to be wary. She had to know that T.J. McAllister was breathing down her neck.

Gulping down the last of his coffee, Casey decided to get a hotel room and plan how to proceed with the young widow. Besides himself, the only customer left in the eatery was the man who had been sucking on a cup of coffee when he'd entered the establishment. From the corner of his eye Casey saw the man stumble to his feet and lurch toward the kitchen. Casey thought it rather odd but, then nothing about this assignment seemed normal.

Casey paused as he ambled toward the front door, wondering if Belle, or Isabelle, as she called herself, was plying her trade in the kitchen. It certainly seemed to prove that McAllister had been right about her being a whore. He was actually relieved. Knowing that McAllister was right made his job easier to swallow. He continued on his way. His hand was on the doorknob when a strangled cry stopped him in his tracks.

He whirled on his heel, listening, trying to decide if what he'd heard were cries of passion and he should mind his own business. Then it came again, only this time the cries sounded desperate and frightened and were followed by a crash of dishes. Raw instinct set his long legs into motion as he hurried toward the kitchen. He stopped abruptly in the open doorway and stared in consternation at the couple grappling on the kitchen table.

The woman had been shoved onto the table, which had been hastily cleared of dishes. Her skirts had been shoved up to her waist as the huge miner tried to mount her. The woman's small fists flailed at the miner but were as ineffectual as gnat stings against the burly man nearly three times her size.

"Aw, come on, Belle, be nice to me," the miner cajoled. "I got plenty of gold dust in my poke to pay ya for a little tumble. It ain't like ya ain't done it before. Ya got a son to prove it. I'll bet ya weren't even married, let alone a widow. Come on, Belle, open yer legs."

"Get off of me, Pike Dinks, you drunken oaf, unless you want Wan Yo to come after you!"

Dinks laughed gleefully. "That old Chinaman couldn't hurt a flea."

"You'll find willing women in any one of the numerous saloons in town."

Dinks gave Belle a sloppy kiss, shoved his knee between her legs and his hands inside her bodice. "Ain't enough whores to go around. I want you."

When Casey saw where the miner's hands were he flew into a rage. He couldn't recall when he felt so protective toward a woman, especially one who had been a whore before her marriage and was probably used to being mauled. Hell, maybe she liked it. But he didn't. It stuck in his craw to see her abused by a drunken, foul-mouthed miner. Upon further consideration, Casey decided she didn't look at all like she enjoyed being roughed up.

Belle shoved against Dinks with all her might, feeling like a bird trapped beneath his considerable bulk. She should have known better than to turn her back on Dinks. This wasn't the first time the miner had tried to assault her. She could smell booze on his breath and hadn't realized when he'd come in for lunch that he was drunk. When she felt his knee between her legs and his hands fumbling inside her bodice, she clamped her teeth down hard on his shoulder.

Dinks cried out, shaking himself free. "Ya little

bitch! You'll pay for that." His fist flew backward, but before he could bring it forward he went sailing through the air. He landed on the floor at Casey's feet.

"Pick on someone your own size," Casey said, baring his teeth in a feral smile. His eyes were luminous with anger and his face was the twisted visage from hell.

Dinks blinked up at him. "I don't wanna fight with you, mister."

"I can see that. You prefer to abuse women too weak to fight back. You're scum, Dinks. Get out of here and don't come back. Mrs. Henderson doesn't need your business." The air thickened with his anger. "And if you ever, I repeat, *ever* lay hands on this woman again, you're a dead man. Do I make myself clear?"

Dinks scooted backward toward the door, staring at Casey in abject fear. He wasn't a slouch when it came to defending himself, but he sensed something dangerously lethal in this man. Something about his eyes hinted of ruthlessness and a willingness to carry out his threats.

"I'm going, mister, don't get your dander up," Dinks said as he staggered to his feet and slunk out the door.

Belle hoisted herself from the table, still trembling from her encounter with Dinks but in full control now. She couldn't afford to show fear. She didn't know this stranger, and for all she knew he was of the same ilk as Dinks. Just because he had sent Dinks fleeing didn't mean he wouldn't launch an attack of his own once he had dealt with the miner.

During her years with Naomi, Belle had seen men of all sizes, shapes, and sexual persuasions. She had learned that good men were few and far between. Her own father, though he had loved her, had easily succumbed to the lure of wine, women, and cards. Tom had been the only good man she had ever known, and he was gone.

"Are you all right, Mrs. Henderson?"

"Yes, thank you, Mr. Walker. I'm grateful for your intervention. Pike Dinks has been pestering me ever since he came to town. The only times he's actually assaulted me, though, was when he was too drunk to know what he was doing."

Casey went still. "You mean this isn't the first time?"

Belle gave an inelegant shrug. "No, nor is he the first man to think he could take liberties."

"What in the hell is a defenseless woman doing in a rough gold camp with no one to protect her? Didn't I hear Dinks say you had a son? You must be crazy to stay here amid so much violence." Casey couldn't imagine why he was being so protective of a woman he hardly knew.

Belle's stubborn little chin lifted and her brown eyes darkened with anger. Casey thought her magnificent. He saw now that her hair wasn't really a true brown but a rich sable, so shiny it nearly blinded him. Except for her lameness her body was perfect. Slim and sinuous, she was also round where it counted, with a hint of long, supple legs hidden beneath her skirts.

"You're quick to find fault with someone you hardly know," Belle tossed back at him. "I've been in Placerville over a year and have managed quite nicely, thank you."

Casey gave a sarcastic snort. "It didn't look to me

as if you were managing. If I hadn't been handy Dinks would have raped you." His eyes narrowed and the searching look he gave her was almost insulting. "Unless I interrupted something I had no business interrupting. Are you in the habit of providing services to your customers after hours?"

Before she had time to consider the consequences, she lashed his cheek with the flat of her hand. "How dare you!"

Casey's jaw clenched. He supposed he deserved that. But something inside him had snapped at the thought of Belle selling herself to crude miners. He stepped closer, grasping her shoulders and bringing her hard against him. He was so startled by how good she felt pressed against him that he immediately pushed her away.

Belle tried to remain calm, frozen in place by the mesmerizing power of his strangely beautiful, mossy green eyes. Every part of him where she was briefly pressed against him had been hard and unyielding. Intuition told her that Casey Walker could be utterly ruthless. He was so honed and lethal, so swift and sure of himself, that it frightened her.

"I'll forgive you this time," Casey growled. "I had no call to say what I did." The urge to pull her against him again was so strong he had to consciously restrain himself. What in the hell had gotten into him? he chided himself. He wasn't about to stoop to the level of the crude miner who had tried to force himself on her. He was a professional, for godsake, and if he didn't act like one soon he was going to lose this job and be forced to return the bonus, which he no longer had.

"I find it difficult to believe you've managed on your own thus far. How many times have you had to defend yourself against men like Dinks?"

Belle flushed and stared at her hands. She'd had to defend herself plenty of times. "I've survived."

"What you need is a bodyguard."

Belle sent Casey a startled glance. That's *exactly* what she needed. Not for herself, but for Tommy. If T.J. McAllister ever found them he'd take away her son for sure. And the law would let him. All T.J. had to do was reveal her background and she'd lose Tommy to a detestable man who had disowned his own son and ignored Tommy until he realized the boy was the last living heir. It would be comforting to know Tommy would be well provided for, but it was not worth losing her son to his grandfather.

Belle eyed him with distrust. "I don't need a bodyguard, Mr. Walker."

Casey gave her a look that suggested he believed otherwise. He could think of no better way to learn everything there was to know about Belle Parker than signing on as her bodyguard. If he was to talk her into giving up her son to her father-in-law, he needed to earn her trust.

"Why not, Mrs. Henderson? You could use a bodyguard and I need a job."

Belle eyed him in silent contemplation. It was true Wan Yo, the faithful Chinese servant Naomi had sent along with her to protect her son, was getting on in years, and that McAllister was probably spending a fortune trying to locate her and Tommy. For all she knew, T.J.'s men were already hot on her trail. And Casey Walker looked like a man capable of giving Tommy the kind of protection he needed. But could she trust him?

"I don't need a bodyguard," she repeated.

"I think you do."

Belle considered his words and seemed to come to a decision. "I can't pay much. I don't need a guard for myself, it's for Tommy."

"Tommy?"

"My son."

"Why does your son need a bodyguard?"

"There are circumstances you can't imagine."

"Tell me so I'll know what I'm up against."

"All you have to do is keep a sharp lookout for strangers lurking about my establishment. You'll soon recognize my regular customers. Anyone else requires attention. I can pay you ten dollars a week and all your meals."

Casey nearly laughed aloud. If he told her the amount of money McAllister was paying him to find her she'd be appalled. "My hotel room will cost nearly that much."

"You can sleep in the spare room off the kitchen. Wan Yo used to sleep there, but he moved into the house to be nearer to Tommy."

"Wan Yo?"

"Wan Yo takes care of Tommy while I'm working. I've known him forever."

"Do you have any other employees? Running this diner is a lot of work for one woman." She wasn't a slouch when it came to work, Casey thought as he admired the cleanliness and order of the kitchen.

"That's all I'll tell you until we come to an agreement."

He stared at her, then nodded his head. "Very well, I accept your terms. Tell me everything I need to know."

"I still haven't decided a bodyguard is necessary,

but I will tell you that Sanchez and his wife Dolores help me in the kitchen." She grew silent for a moment, then said, "On second thought, hiring someone I know nothing about isn't such a good idea." She must be out of her mind to consider giving her trust so easily. She wasn't going to let anyone get close enough to her and Tommy to hurt them. "I know nothing about you. You could be a murderer, or rapist, or any number of things. I have Wan Yo, and I can protect my son better than anyone."

"Mama! Mama! A bad man hurt Wan Yo. Hurry, hurry!"

A small boy bounced into the room, clutched Belle's hand and pulled her out the door.

Completely forgetting Casey, Belle rushed out after Tommy. "What happened?"

Checking the position of his gun and removing the flap holding it in place, Casey followed.

Words tumbled out of the boy's mouth in a rush. "Wan Yo and I were walking to the store when a bad man started calling him names and pulling on his pigtail. I tried to help but the bad man pushed me hard and I fell on the ground. Wan Yo tried to help me but the bad man knocked him down and kicked his leg. Now Wan Yo can't get up."

Casey saw a crowd gathered around a small figure crumpled in the dirt. He sprinted ahead and saw a frail old Chinese man, wearing baggy black pajamas, writhing in pain on the ground. Was this the man Belle depended on for protection? Wan Yo was so slight of build Casey suspected a good wind would blow him away. His face had turned gray beneath his fragile yellow skin and his leg was bent at an unnatural angle.

"Who did this?" Belle cried, dropping to her knees beside the old man. It frightened her to think that Tommy could have been hurt as well.

"Bad man, Missy Belle, a bad, bad man. He no like Wan Yo's pigtail. Want to cut it off. No can do."

"Where is the man now, Wan Yo?" This was from Casey, who had joined Belle and Tommy at Wan Yo's side.

"Gone," Wan Yo wailed, "but Wan Yo not forget face. He tell Wan Yo Chinaman not welcome in Placerville. He tell Wan Yo to go to Chinese Camp with his own kind."

"Don't worry, Wan Yo, I'll take care of you," Belle crooned as she took off her apron and placed it under his head. The man was as dear to her as her own flesh and blood. He had become indispensable to her since the day she and Tommy had fled from her father-in-law. "Someone go for the doctor," she called out to anyone who would listen.

"I'll go." A man broke off from the crowd and headed toward the doctor's office.

"What were you saying about not needing a bodyguard, Mrs. Henderson?" Casey asked as he watched Belle fuss over the old man. "I'd say you were in desperate need of someone to watch over you and your son. Since I'm not interested in mining, I may as well make myself useful to you."

As much as Belle wanted to deny it, she couldn't. Wan Yo couldn't provide protection laid up with a broken leg, and God only knew what other injuries he'd sustained.

"Very well, Mr. Walker, you're hired. I just hope I don't live to regret my hasty decision."

Chapter 2

Doctor Lincoln arrived a few minutes later. A cursory examination confirmed that Wan Yo's leg was broken, along with three ribs. The rest of his injuries were minor.

"I'll send someone with a stretcher," the doctor said. "Can't have that leg jarred any more than necessary. You want to have him brought to my office, Mrs. Henderson?"

"No, I'll take him home," Belle said. "He'll be more comfortable there, if that's all right with you, doctor."

"I'll go back to the office then and gather up what I need to set Wan Yo's leg. Keep him quiet until the stretcher arrives."

"Does this kind of thing happen often?" Casey asked after the doctor had hurried away.

"People here don't like Chinamen."

Belle didn't say what she was really thinking. She feared someone had tried to kidnap her son and Wan Yo was injured in the scuffle. Had T.J. found them? Oh God, she hoped not. She didn't want to move again. She thought she'd be safe in Placerville

24

after a year had passed with no problems—except
minor ones with men like Dinks. Would she and
Tommy be safe from T.J.'s long arm *anywhere* in
California?

"Do you want me to find whoever's responsible?"

Belle turned and gave Casey an exasperated look.
Casey inhaled sharply as he felt the full potency of
her soft brown eyes settle on him. He felt as if he
were drowning in a sea of sweet, molten chocolate
that literally sucked him into its fathomless depths.
Right now those expressive eyes were filled with
contempt. "What's the use? No one will care."

"The sheriff . . ."

". . . Can't be bothered with something as trivial
as an old Chinese man. Just protect my son, that's
what you're being paid for."

Belle returned her gaze to Wan Yo, but not before
she saw Casey's remarkable hazel eyes darken with
some strange emotion she didn't have time to
interpret.

"Is Wan Yo going to be all right, Mama?" Tommy
asked as he hovered over the frail Chinese man.

Belle's eyes softened as she gazed at her son. She
couldn't lose him to McAllister, it would kill her.
"Wan Yo is going to be fine, sweetheart. And so are
you. I've just hired Mr. Walker to take care of you
and Wan Yo while Mama's working at the restaurant."

Tommy let his gaze wander up Casey's lean
length, tilting his head back so far he had to shade
his eyes against the sun. Casey noted that the boy's
eyes were the same warm brown as his mother's,
and his hair a shade lighter than Belle's mass of
gleaming sable curls.

"He sure is big," Tommy observed. "Do you think he can protect me against mean old Mc . . ."

"Tommy!" Belle's warning stopped Tommy's words in mid-sentence. She didn't trust Casey Walker enough to make him privy to her secrets. "We'll discuss this at home. Here comes the stretcher. I have to get back to the restaurant and prepare for the supper crowd. Sanchez and Dolores will be waiting for me. You go along to the house with Mr. Walker and Wan Yo. I'll see you later."

"But Mama . . ."

"It will be all right, you'll see," Belle cajoled. "Wan Yo will need you now that he can't do for himself."

"If you say so, Mama," Tommy said, not at all convinced that he should go with a man he didn't know.

Two men were putting Wan Yo on the stretcher now, and Wan Yo's pitiful moans turned Belle's attention from Tommy to the old man. She patted his hand in commiseration. The minute the doctor arrived, they started the slow trek down the street.

"I don't know where you live," Casey said. He had remained silent until now, watching and waiting.

"Tommy and I live in four small rooms connected to the restaurant by a breezeway. It's not only cheaper to live behind my place of business, but handy. There is a separate entrance, Tommy will show you. After I get Sanchez and Dolores started on supper, I'll look in on Wan Yo."

Looking decidedly worried over her hasty decision to hire a stranger to protect her son, Belle hurried off toward the restaurant.

"Well, kid, that leaves you and me," Casey said

somewhat uncertainly. "We're going to get along together just fine."

Casey couldn't ever recall conversing intelligently with a child before, certainly not one as young as Tommy. He felt like a bastard for what he had to do, but this assignment meant a lot of money to him, and the difference between life and death for Mark. Belle Parker might have been a whore at one time, but he could see no evidence thus far to suggest she was plying her trade in Placerville.

When Tommy made no attempt at conversation, Casey did not press him. Persuading Belle to give up her son to his grandfather without using force was going to be difficult, he reflected, and in order to do so he had to gain the trust of both Tommy and Belle. One day at a time, he told himself, and each day brought him that much closer to saving his brother from a lifetime of incarceration. He had already accepted McAllister's money, returning it was out of the question. His entire reputation rested on his ability to settle this case in McAllister's favor.

Belle worked silently in the kitchen, speaking only to relay orders to Sanchez and his wife about preparation of the evening meal. She usually fed close to a hundred men on good days. Even on bad days the number was impressive. She'd made a good living in Placerville, thanks in part to the money Naomi had given her when she'd fled San Francisco in panic.

She owed Naomi more than she could ever repay. Who would have thought that when Naomi found her all those years ago, a starving, injured urchin on the street, she would become the mother Belle couldn't remember? The Lord certainly worked in strange ways, Belle thought. Until today she and Wan Yo had been able to handle the rowdy miners who tried to take liberties with her. Now Wan Yo was injured and likely to be laid up for weeks, and she had been forced to hire a stranger to protect Tommy from his grandfather.

Belle realized that a man of Casey Walker's intelligence was going to want answers soon, and she still hadn't decided on the best way to handle those questions. She'd always found that honesty worked best, but could she trust Casey Walker with the truth?

The man had appeared from nowhere, and she knew nothing about him. For all she knew he could be T.J.'s man, though he didn't seem the type her father-in-law usually hired. She had seen some of the rough, uncouth drifters who worked for T.J. when he needed special jobs done. No, Casey Walker wasn't that type. He was almost too handsome, she thought. When he smiled at her she had been strangely stirred by that deep dimple in his cheek and those remarkable hazel eyes. Not green, not brown, but a mesmerizing combination.

"Should Sanchez cut more wood, senora?"

Belle gathered her scattered thoughts and concentrated on Dolores, the Mexican woman who helped her in the kitchen. Neither she nor her husband, Sanchez, were young, but they had needed work and were willing to accept the small salary Belle could afford.

"What did you say, Dolores?"

"Wood, senora. Should Sanchez cut more wood for the cookstove?"

"No, not now. I'm going back to check on Wan Yo and I'd prefer that Sanchez stay with you until I return. The town is teeming with riffraff looking for work or easy pickings, and it's not wise for a woman to be alone." She was thinking of Dinks and how close he had come to raping her. If it hadn't been for Casey Walker. . . .

Dolores nodded her understanding. "Si, senora, I will call Sanchez and you can see to Wan Yo. But Wan Yo will need a man's help with certain chores until he can get around on his own. Sanchez will do that for you. What about the little one? Who will protect him with Wan Yo laid up?"

"I hired a man today to see to Tommy's safety."

"Do you think the niño's grandfather . . ."

"I don't know. I told you about Tommy's grandfather because I wanted you to be aware of the danger once you started working for me. No one else knows, and I'd like to keep it that way."

"Si, senora, you can trust me and Sanchez. If not for you we would be living on the streets or dying of starvation. You can depend on us. Go see to Wan Yo and Tommy, we will finish the cooking."

"I'll be back before the customers start arriving," Belle said as she headed out the rear door.

Casey felt out of place. Doctor Lincoln had just left and Wan Yo was sleeping off the sedative he'd been given. Tommy sat by the old man's bedside, keeping watch, while Casey prowled the tiny parlor. When Belle said she occupied four small rooms behind the restaurant, she hadn't been lying. He felt like a bull in a china shop. Barely six paces in any direction and he'd be in another room. Wan Yo occupied one bedroom, which meant Tommy probably slept on the cot he'd seen in the tiny kitchen, and the other bedroom belonged to Belle.

Casey stopped pacing when he felt Tommy yanking on his hand. "When is Wan Yo going to wake up, mister?"

"My name is Casey, Tommy." He hunkered down until he was eye level with Tommy. "You're fond of Wan Yo, aren't you?"

"Aunt Naomi sent him with us. He takes real good care of me and Mama."

Casey led Tommy over to the couch. "Sit down and tell me about Aunt Naomi. Where does she live?"

Casey hated using a child's innocence to gather information but it was necessary. Long ago he had hardened himself against situations that pulled at his heartstrings. That's what made him a good detective. Ridding himself of sentimentality and remaining focused allowed him to solve cases others could not.

"Why do you want to know about Aunt Naomi?" Tommy asked, suddenly wary. "Mama said I shouldn't talk about her."

"If I'm to protect you and your mother, I should know what kind of danger to watch out for."

"Aunt Naomi is not dangerous," Tommy protested. "She gives me presents and writes Mama letters. After Papa died she let us live with her in her big house so that mean old . . . nevermind, I'm not supposed to say anything about him."

"Him?"

"Yes, the mean man who wants to take me away from Mama. But Mama and Aunt Naomi said they won't let him take me. There are lots of girls living in Aunt Naomi's house. It was fun there."

"Tommy! What have you been telling Mr. Walker?

How many times have I told you not to discuss family business with strangers?"

"Didn't you hire Casey to protect us, Mama? I was just telling him about Aunt Naomi and the girls."

Belle blanched. God, if Casey Walker was T.J.'s man, this was one more black mark against her already besmirched character.

"Go sit by Wan Yo, Tommy, he may wake up and need something."

"I'm sorry, Mama," Tommy said as he trudged back into the bedroom.

"I don't know what Tommy told you, Mr. Walker . . ."

"Casey."

"What?"

"My name is Casey."

"As I was saying, Mr. Walker, Tommy doesn't really know what he's talking about. He's only a child."

"He wasn't saying much, just telling me about his aunt. Do you have any other relatives?"

"I have no relatives, Mr. Walker. Naomi isn't a blood relative. She's just a woman who's been incredibly good to me and Tommy."

"If this woman cares for you, what are you doing in Placerville by yourself? I'd expect you to settle where you had someone to rely upon after your husband's death. What about your inlaws? Aren't they willing to help you?"

Belle stiffened. Dear God, this stranger was baring her secrets one by one without realizing it. "There is no one," she repeated.

Casey stared into the frightened depths of Belle's

brown eyes and could almost smell her fear. He was somewhat surprised at the guilt he felt at pressing her for answers, but she still hadn't told him everything he needed to know.

"What's the real reason you hired me, Belle?"

Belle was immediately alert. He had called her by her nickname. Where had he heard it? Her eyes narrowed and her lush lips pressed together into a flat line. "Why did you call me Belle just now? I told you my name is Isabelle."

Casey wanted to laugh. Didn't she think he had ears? "I heard Wan Yo call you Belle. And that man Dinks. I reckon there are others who call you by that name."

Belle plopped into the nearest chair and breathed deeply. She was becoming paranoid lately. But she had a gnawing fear that McAllister was closing in on her. If she lost Tommy she'd have nothing . . . nothing . . .

"I'm sorry," Belle said, trying to sound natural despite her racing heart. "I prefer Isabelle, but some call me by my shortened name." How she wished she could trust this man. She needed someone to confide in, someone to turn to for comfort. Lord, what was she thinking? She hardly knew Casey Walker. And she certainly didn't need a man. Damn few were worth the trouble.

"Why don't you take your things to your room, Mr. Walker? You'll find it off the kitchen. I'm going to stay here awhile with Tommy and Wan Yo. Tell Dolores and Sanchez you're the man I hired today. Since I usually feed Tommy at the restaurant, your services won't be needed any more today."

"You haven't answered my question, Belle. Don't

you think I should know the reason Tommy needs protection?"

Belle came out of the chair, her expression guarded. "Soon, but not now. I don't know yet if I can trust you. Just keep your eyes peeled and your ears open. If you notice anything suspicious report it to me immediately. If anyone tries to hurt Tommy, you're to protect him."

"What about you? Don't you need protection?"

"I can take care of myself. Surely you've noticed I'm crippled. Men are put off by women with deformities."

Casey gave a bark of laughter. "Says who? What about Dinks? Your deformity didn't seem to bother him."

She flushed. "He was drunk. You have your orders, Mr. Walker."

"Casey."

"Whatever. Just do the job you're being paid to do and keep your curiosity under control. If I think you need to know anything more, I'll tell you."

Casey gave her a crooked grin that deepened the dimple in his cheek and nearly made Belle forget her name. "Sure, boss, whatever you say. I'll see you later." He doffed his hat and headed for the door that led into the restaurant. Suddenly he stopped and swung around to face her, "Oh, by the way, what makes you think you don't need protection at night? Do you depend on your gentlemen callers to provide protection?"

Damn, Casey knew that remark was uncalled for, but somehow it had slipped out before he could call it back.

"Callers?" Belle asked.

"Forget I said that. I'm not being paid to dig into your personal life."

Hidden fires within her dark eyes flared dangerously. "I'm glad you remembered. I have no idea what you're talking about and I don't think I want to know. But if you have any doubts about taking this job, it's best you leave now."

Casey studied Belle's features, favorably impressed with her determination, her beauty, her protectiveness toward her son. Funny, he hardly noticed her limp now. Nor was he bothered by the fact that she had been a whore at one time. There were too many fascinating facets to Belle Parker to dwell upon something that had no bearing on her appearance or what she was now. She seemed to have accepted her disability with good humor, and he'd soon learn if she still practiced her trade.

Casey had nothing against a reformed whore, but he knew the courts of law would back McAllister in his bid for his grandson. Possession was nine-tenths of the law, and once McAllister got his hands on the boy no court in the land would give him back to a whore, reformed or not. As he left Belle's rooms, he had the unaccountable urge to run away from this case and everything it represented. He had the distinct feeling that his life would never be the same again as a result of his encounter with Belle Parker McAllister.

Belle watched Casey leave, admiring his broad shoulders and the way his trousers hugged his lean hips. Casey Walker was the first man since Tom's death she had looked at with anything but mild distaste. Tom's death had devastated her. He had been husband, lover, protector, and Tommy's father. Guilt had been her constant companion since the day she received notice of Tom's drowning. If he hadn't insisted on marrying her, there would have been no need for him to take a job that placed him in danger. He'd still be the apple of his father's eye, and he wouldn't have had to expose himself to life-threatening situations. It was her fault Tom was dead. McAllister had every right to accuse her of being the cause of his son's death.

Supper was well in progress when Casey walked into the diner and took an empty seat next to a group of miners. The menu posted on the door boasted of beef stew, dumplings, buttered peas, and apple pie. Casey's mouth watered just thinking about it. When Dolores set a heaping plate of savory meat and vegetables before him, he dug in with gusto. He had to hand it to Belle, she was a damn good cook. He couldn't wait to sample the apple pie. The men around him seemed as intent upon their meals as he was. It wasn't until he was sipping the steaming cup of dark, rich coffee at the end of the satisfying meal that he struck up a conversation with the man sitting next to him.

"I'm new in town, does Belle always serve such good meals?"

"Best damn place in town to eat," the man vowed. "And reasonable, too. Most of the miners take their meals here."

"I'm Casey Walker," Casey said, offering his hand.

"Bram London," the man said, shaking Casey's hand. "You a miner? If you're looking for work maybe I can help you out. I'm foreman at the Gold Bug mine."

"I might take you up on the offer one of these

days, but not now. I've just accepted another position. Besides, I don't expect to be in town long."

London did not inquire further. Out here a man's past was his own private business, and his comings and goings could be speculated upon but never questioned.

"How long have you been taking your meals at the diner?"

"From the first day it opened."

"Do you know Mrs. Henderson well?"

London shrugged. "As well as most."

"How well is that?" Casey's line of questioning had a definite purpose. He hoped to learn whether Belle was still practicing her trade while using the restaurant as a front.

London took exception to Casey's altogether too personal inquiries. "What are you getting at, Walker? Mrs. Henderson's personal life is no one's business, you ought to know that."

"I sure would like to know her better—a whole lot better," a leering miner across from Casey alleged. He had been eavesdropping on the conversation and decided to horn in. "Dinks said she was a sweet little piece despite her lame leg."

"Dinks?" Casey asked sharply, recalling the drunken miner he'd pulled off Belle earlier today.

"Yeah, he's a friend of mine. Works at the Big Cut. He's had the little widow plenty of times, the lucky stiff."

Casey was trying to decide whether to beat the crap out of the ugly miner or shoot him, when Belle happened to walk out of the kitchen. The chatter all but stopped as she traveled between tables, passing around a platter of dumplings. Casey wasn't at all pleased by the elbow-nudging and whispering among the customers for he knew exactly what they were thinking. He could read it in their hungry expressions. Each and every one of them wanted to bed Belle, and he included himself in their numbers.

"How do you suppose Mrs. Henderson came up lame, Wentz?" London asked the vulgar man sitting across from him and Casey.

"Who cares." Wentz gave a lascivious laugh. "She's like any other woman where it counts. It's not her legs I'm interested in, but what's between them." He licked his thick lips. "Dinks says she's good, real good."

London looked skeptical. "I wouldn't put stock in anything Dinks said. He's drunk more often than not these days."

Casey decided he liked Bram London and couldn't abide Wentz. "I strongly suggest you don't repeat anything Dinks says, Mr. Wentz."

Wentz gazed into the depths of Casey's hazel eyes, and the recognition of something ruthless and dangerous in them passed over his face. He instinctively sidled away from Casey, as if trying to escape some deadly peril.

"I don't know what business it is of yours, mister," Wentz challenged, "but if it will make you feel better, everyone knows Dinks is a liar." He rose abruptly. "I gotta go, can't sit around jawing all day."

"Me, too," London said. "See ya around, Walker."

Casey sat brooding over his empty coffee cup, knowing that Dinks' personal claims about Belle were false, yet wondering if somewhere in his words lay a thread of truth.

"Would you like more coffee, Mr. Walker?"

Casey looked up and saw Belle standing beside him with a coffeepot in one hand. Damn, she had the prettiest brown eyes he'd ever seen. And her mouth. A man could get lost staring into those warm brown eyes and thinking about what she could do to him with that sweet mouth. He blinked, startled by the direction of his thoughts. He couldn't afford to think of Belle as anything but a means to get Mark out of jail. Only a sentimental fool would allow himself to become enmeshed in her life, or involve himself in things that might distract him from his job.

"Did you hear me, Mr. Walker? Would you like more coffee?"

"Casey, my name is Casey. And more coffee would be welcome. Damn good coffee, Belle. In fact, the whole meal was excellent. Well worth the four bits you charge. Why don't you join me? The dinner rush is over and you deserve to relax a few minutes."

"There are still the dishes," Belle reminded him. But she sat down anyway, absently rubbing the kinks out of her lame leg.

Casey wished he could take over the chore for her, but he knew better than to risk touching her so intimately. He was smart enough to recognize his attraction for her and knew he couldn't afford to succumb to it.

"How did that happen?"

Belle gave him a wry look. "My lameness? It was an accident. I was very young and don't remember too much about it."

"Does it bother you much?"

Belle shrugged. "Only when I'm on my feet for long hours at a time."

"Which is every day," Casey guessed.

"I have to make a living." From the corner of her eye Belle saw Dolores gathering dirty dishes from the tables. "I'll be right there to help with the cleaning up, Dolores," she called out.

"Don't bother, senora, Sanchez and I can clean up tonight. You've worked hard enough for one day."

They were alone now, the last customer had left, and Casey poured coffee into a clean cup and set it before Belle. "Here, I think you could use this. I wanted to talk to you, anyway."

"Are you having second thoughts about taking this job? It's all right if you are, because I'm also wondering if hiring you was wise."

"Hell no, I'm not having second thoughts. I just thought it's time you told me the truth about why you and Tommy need protection."

Belle blanched. "I—you know all you need to know."

"I'm leaving now, Senora," Dolores sang out. "Kitchen all clean and fire banked. Sanchez is helping Wan Yo. Be sure and lock the doors."

"Good night, and thank you," Belle replied, unable to turn her gaze from the penetrating brilliance of Casey's eyes.

"Who are you afraid of, Belle?" Casey persisted doggedly.

Belle stared at her hands, startled to find she had wadded her apron into a hopeless tangle.

"I have to know who's threatening you."

Belle felt the distressing need to unburden herself to this strong man, but fought it tooth and nail. She had learned not to give her trust lightly, and until Casey Walker proved himself worthy she'd keep her own council. If he couldn't live with those terms then he wasn't the kind of man she needed to protect Tommy.

"You have all the information I'm willing to give," she stubbornly insisted. "If you'll excuse me, it's Tommy's bedtime. I think you'll find everything you need in your room. The outhouse is out back, if you haven't already found it. There's a bathhouse down the street and—"

"I've already explored the town, Belle. I'm fully aware of all its amenities. I'm sure the room will suit me just fine."

She stood. "Then I'll bid you good night."

She turned abruptly and her lame leg, weakened from her long day, caught in her skirts. She stumbled clumsily and would have fallen if not for Casey's intervention. Before she realized what happened, Casey had leapt to his feet and scooped her up into his arms.

"You can put me down now, Mr. Walker, I'll be fine. I'm not always this clumsy."

"If you call me Mr. Walker one more time I'm going to . . . kiss you each time it happens."

Good Lord, what was he thinking? He supposed it was having those lush lips so close that made him propose something so flagrantly outrageous.

"Mr. Walker! You—"

"I warned you," Casey growled as his lips hovered inches from hers.

She felt the searing heat of his mouth as it angled across hers. There was nothing gentle in his kiss. It was hard and hot and wet, and so arousing Belle felt a tingling sensation in places that hadn't felt arousal since Tom had last made love to her over a year ago. She nearly wept with the joy of the forgotten sensation. Then she recalled who was kissing her. A stranger. A man who could be a vicious gunman, an outlaw, or even McAllister's man.

She tried to break off the kiss, but Casey was enjoying himself too damn much to stop. He nudged her lips apart and thrust his tongue into her mouth, groaning with the sheer pleasure of her sweet response as she touched her tongue to his and stroked. Casey knew she was no stranger to intimacy and his first thought was that he wanted to explore that passion to the fullest. His final outrageous thought was to wonder if she'd learned all her tricks at Naomi's whorehouse.

He let her slide down his body until her feet touched the floor. He wanted to find the nearest bed and he wanted to find it now.

Belle felt the heat and strength of his arousal pressing against her thigh and realized where this could lead. Did Casey Walker think she was a whore? She was certainly acting like one. Was he like Dinks and his kind, who took what they wanted by force? She had hired Casey Walker for protection, not to fall victim to his charm.

"Let me go!" She pulled free of his arms, her face mottled with rage. "Don't ever do that again."

"Why not? You seemed to like it. Besides, I warned you what would happen the next time you called me Mr. Walker."

She swiped at her mouth with the back of her hand but his unique taste remained on her lips. She whirled on her heel, stumbled, righted herself and limped away, her shoulders rigid.

"Do you need help, Belle?" This time there was concern in his voice.

"There is only one thing I need from you, Mr.—

Casey, and that's your gun. There are people who want Tommy. Protect him from those people, that's all I want from you."

Her head held high, she disappeared into the kitchen. Casey thought her magnificent, and brave. And foolish. She didn't have a prayer against a powerful man like T.J. McAllister.

She didn't have a prayer against Casey Walker, Pinkerton detective.

Chapter 3

Belle was careful to avoid Casey in the days following the encounter in the dining hall. She couldn't believe he had kissed her, couldn't comprehend what had moved him to do it. She certainly hadn't provoked him, or done anything to even suggest that she wanted his kisses. She touched her lips with her fingertip. She imagined she could still feel the pressure of his mouth on hers, and was surprised at the tingling heat that pooled low in her belly.

Shaking her head to clear it of thoughts that were far too erotic, Belle dug her hands into the pile of bread dough on the counter and kneaded furiously. Why had Casey Walker come to Placerville? Anyone could see he wasn't a miner. He looked too prosperous to be a saddle bum or a drifter. He could be a hired gun, she speculated, or even McAllister's man. Yet if she believed that, why had she hired him to protect Tommy?

Obviously because he had defended her against Dinks, she decided. It didn't appear as if he meant either her or Tommy any harm, so she had recklessly hired him as a bodyguard. Dear God, why did he have to come to Placerville now? She touched her mouth again, thinking how wonderfully erotic Casey's lips had felt against hers. In the year since Tom's death, Belle had neither the time nor the inclination to think of another man in a romantic sense.

Not that men hadn't tried to capture her attention. But she just hadn't been interested. She had enough problems staying one step ahead of T.J. McAllister to consider a romantic relationship. Until Casey Walker had kissed her she was convinced she could live without love, without a man's arms and comfort, and was damn annoyed that Casey's kiss had made her feel like a woman again . . . a woman who had been without those things far too long. She wondered what there was about this man that attracted her. There were plenty of honest miners interested in her, but she hadn't given them the time of day.

"If you continue to punch the bread dough like that there won't be enough left to bake."

"Oh." Belle started violently. Swiveling her head, she saw Casey filling the doorway. His arms were crossed at his broad chest; the doorjamb supported one shoulder and his feet were crossed at the ankles. "You frightened me." He was smiling, and she was momentarily distracted by his dimples.

"I get the distinct feeling that you've been avoiding me, Belle."

Belle turned back to her bread dough. "That's nonsense. Is there something I can do for you?" She stopped abruptly and swung back around to face Casey. "Y—you haven't noticed anything suspicious, have you? Tommy is all right, isn't he? Why aren't you watching him?"

"Don't get your dander up, boss lady. Tommy is fine. He's sitting with Wan Yo. The old man is restless. He wants to be up and about but isn't strong enough yet."

Belle's relief was enormous. "It frightens me to have Tommy left unguarded."

Casey pushed himself away from the doorjamb and walked into the kitchen. "I haven't noticed that Tommy is in danger. I'm more apt to think you're the one who needs protecting. The town is teeming with men like Dinks. I don't like the idea of you being alone in the dining hall."

Belle limped to the cupboard for bread pans and filled them with the bread dough beneath Casey's watchful gaze. "I'm not usually alone. Dolores left after lunch to take care of Sanchez. He developed a fever so I sent her home. I don't really need her until serving time. I can't cook and serve both."

"Why didn't you tell me you were alone?"

"I didn't think it was necessary."

"Dammit, I . . ."

"Hey, Belle, you in there?"

Belle frowned. The diner was closed for another two hours. Casey tensed, recognizing the voice. He glared at Belle. "Are you expecting company? Is that why you didn't want me to know you'd be alone?"

Belle sent him a fulminating look. She was beginning to run out of patience with Casey Walker and his vile insinuations.

A moment later Dinks burst into the kitchen, followed in short order by two burly miners, all of whom reeked with the odor of hard liquor. Dinks slid to a halt when he spied Casey.

"What are you doing here, Walker? You plan on getting yourself a little, too?"

"Get out of here, Dinks," Casey said quietly.

"I don't think so," Dinks replied, leering at Belle. "I brought my friends Whitey and Curly. You might have seen Whitey at lunch today. He wanted to get a good look at you. Whitey has an incredible memory. He swears he saw you at Naomi's Pleasure Parlor five or six years back. It's the limp that gave you away. Tell them, Whitey."

Whitey, nearly as disheveled and drunk as Dinks, nodded his head affirmatively. "Yep, it's just like Dinks said. Saw this here little lady at Naomi's in San Francisco. Me and my friends figured if Belle pleasured men in a whorehouse she wouldn't mind doing it right here in the diner. Got plenty of money." He pulled out his poke and waved it in front of Belle's nose.

Belle blanched and moved instinctively closer to Casey. "I'm going to tell you one more time, get the hell out of here." This time Casey's voice held a hard edge that promised swift retribution if they continued to plague Belle. His hand moved reflexively over his Colt.

"Aw shit, Walker, don't go greedy on us. We're willing to share. Whitey and Curly ain't particular. They'll let you go first."

Casey's gun came out so fast Belle didn't see his hand move. When Dinks reached for his own weapon, Casey discharged a shot that came alarmingly close to his head. "I won't miss next time, Dinks. Take your friends and get out of here. You've obviously mistaken Mrs. Henderson for someone else. She's not now, nor will she ever be, interested in any proposal you have to offer."

Dinks wasn't satisfied. "Is that right, Belle? Ain't you interested in making yourself a little money on the side?"

Belle fixed Dinks with a malevolent glare and shook her head. She couldn't talk, couldn't even breathe. If she hadn't braced herself against the kitchen table, she wouldn't have been able to stand. She thought she'd be safe here from her past, but should have known that one day someone who remembered her from Naomi's would show up. Not that she was ashamed of those years. On the contrary, she had done nothing wrong. But she had Tommy to worry about now, and no Tom to protect them from the kind of malicious gossip that could ruin a young boy's life.

Casey cocked his gun. "You heard the lady. She isn't interested in your vile suggestions. In the future, if any of you make an improper gesture toward her, you'll have me to contend with. And I'm good, boys, damn good."

Evidently the men believed him for they backed out of the kitchen, stumbling over their own feet. Belle collapsed into the nearest chair, gagging. She was so pale Casey thought she was going to faint. Scooping her into his arms, he paused for only a moment before heading for the nearest bed. The one in his room off the kitchen. He laid her down gently and poured her a cup of water from the pitcher sitting on his nightstand. He held her head while she sipped. When she'd had her fill, he set the cup down and perched on the side of the bed.

"What was that all about?"

Belle shook her head, refusing to look at him. He wouldn't let her off that easily. It appeared as if this was the opening he'd been waiting for. Perhaps now was the time to convince Belle to give her son up to McAllister without a fight. Grasping her chin between thumb and forefinger, he forced her to look at him.

"Were Dinks and his friends right? Did you work at Naomi's Pleasure Parlor? I've been there a time or two, she runs a damn good establishment. Her girls are the best."

Belle's eyes blazed with unrelenting fury. "What do you know? You're just like the others. Eager to condemn a woman without benefit of an explanation."

"No, I'm willing to listen. Don't you think it's time you told me about yourself? Why do you believe Tommy needs protection?"

"Does my past make any difference in our business arrangement? Will you refuse to protect my son if you perceive me as something I'm not?"

"I'm not a man to jump to conclusions. Why don't you tell me and let me decide for myself?"

She tried to rise but his hands pinned her shoulders to the bed.

"How do I know I can trust you? How do I know I can trust anyone?" Her words spewed forth in a long, drawn-out sob.

"I think I've proven myself. That's twice I've been able to prevent an ugly incident for you. How many close calls have you had with different men before I came to town? As long as I'm around, I'm not going to let anyone hurt you or Tommy."

That much at least was true. McAllister didn't want to hurt Tommy, he wanted to give him all the advantages his mother couldn't. If Casey believed for one minute that McAllister would harm Tommy, he would never have accepted the assignment, money or no. McAllister merely wanted to protect the child, to prevent him from learning that his mother was a whore, or had once been one.

Casey no longer believed Belle plied her trade in the mining town. Her son was too important to her to risk his finding out about her former profession. Something about Belle moved Casey deeply and he tried to push it to the back of his mind. Sentiments had no place in his life, not now, not when his brother's life was at stake. He had accepted McAllister's money, and had no choice but to bring the case to a favorable conclusion.

Belle truly wanted to believe Casey. She was so tired of bearing the burden herself. So weary of looking over her shoulder for McAllister's men. She hadn't had a good night's sleep in over a year. Not since she learned T.J. McAllister wanted to take her son away from her, and that the law would uphold his claim.

Casey watched the play of emotion on Belle's features and could only guess at the kind of private demons she was fighting. "Belle, I'm waiting," Casey repeated. "Is there any truth in what Dinks said?"

After an inner struggle with her conscience, Belle seemed to come to a decision. She lifted herself up until her eyes were on the same level as Casey's. "What do you think?"

"I don't know. Why don't you tell me?"

"Very well. You wanted to know if I was seen at Naomi's Pleasure Parlor in San Francisco. Yes. Now are you satisfied?" She'd be damned if she'd tell Casey her life story. She didn't owe him a blessed thing.

For some reason Casey felt a crushing disappointment. After meeting Belle, he hadn't wanted to believe McAllister's claim that she was a whore, but the lady had all but admitted it. Or had she? Thinking over her answer, she hadn't exactly admitted that she had worked at Naomi's as a whore, only that she'd been seen there.

"Go on."

"There is nothing more to tell."

"I think there is."

"Damn you! You're fired. I don't need you digging into my past or meddling in my personal life. I don't need you at all! I'll take Tommy and go where no one can find us."

Casey gave an exasperated sigh. This was getting him nowhere. "I told you I wouldn't let anyone hurt you or Tommy. Don't you believe me?"

Belle's eyes went murky. "Tom was the only man I ever trusted."

"Tom is dead."

"Don't you think I know that? If he was still alive I wouldn't be running away from his father." Her mouth snapped shut and tears filled her eyes. "Oh, God, what did I say?"

"Now we're getting somewhere. Why did you run away from your husband's father?" Of course he knew one side of the story, but he wanted to hear Belle's version.

She glared at him. "It's a long story."

"I've got time. I'm not going anywhere and neither are you, not until I've heard the truth."

"You want the truth? Very well. Tom's father is rich, very rich. He acknowledged neither my marriage to his son nor Tommy's birth. It wasn't until Tom died that T.J realized Tommy was the only grandson he'd ever have, and decided to take him away from me."

"How could he do that? You seem like a damn good mother to me."

Belle sighed. They were right back where they started from. For Casey to understand, she'd be required to divulge her background. "T.J. has always hated me. He didn't think I was good enough for his son. He had a society marriage planned for Tom when we met and fell in love. T.J. forbade Tom to see me but Tom disobeyed him. I think that, more than anything, made T.J. hate me. We married against T.J.'s wishes and he promptly disowned Tom. He hoped Tom would abandon me and run back to him when he cut off Tom's allowance.

"Tom was made of sterner stuff and defied his father. I became pregnant almost immediately, and Tom got a job on a nearby ranch in order to support us. I was so proud of Tom. He didn't care about being disowned and disinherited. He had me and Tommy to love. Then he drowned on a trail drive and my world came to an end. T.J. wasted no time in sending word that he was coming after Tommy, and that he was bringing the law to make sure I complied with his wishes."

"What did you do?" Casey asked, having already heard most of the story up to now from McAllister.

Belle looked him straight in the eye and said, "I ran. Naomi took me in for awhile. She gave me the money to get out of town. I got as far as Placerville, saw this diner for sale, and bought it with what remained of Naomi's money."

"How long were you a whore before you married Tom?"

Belle raised her hand and dealt him a stinging blow. When she would have slapped him a second time, he grasped her wrist and brought it down to her side. "Bastard! You're just like the others. You haven't known me long enough to judge me."

"I'm not judging you. Tell me if I'm jumping to conclusions. Then again, what in the hell am I supposed to think when you admitted meeting your husband in a whorehouse?"

She turned her face away. "You're not supposed to think anything. It doesn't matter what you think of me."

He touched her cheek and she turned back to him, glaring. She looked so vulnerable, so defeated, he couldn't have stopped himself from kissing her if he'd wanted to. Lowering his head, his lips touched hers. She tried to push him away, but he was determined. He deepened his kiss, and she caught her breath and opened her mouth to the solid thrust of his tongue, whimpering.

His mouth was hot and wet, his breath tasting faintly of tobacco—a taste uniquely his. She loved it. His tongue grew bolder, rimming the inside of her lips then plunging deeply. He kissed her again and again, as if he couldn't get enough of her, until Belle felt his hands on her breasts and his fingers rubbing her nipples through the fabric of her dress. She was becoming aroused, and the sudden realization that she was succumbing to a virtual stranger brought her rising ardor to a screeching halt.

"Stop! Stop it! I'm no whore no matter what you think. I lived and worked at Naomi's but not as a whore!"

Casey went still. What in the hell had gotten into him? In his entire history with the Pinkerton Agency he had never allowed his emotions to rule his head. What was it about Belle Parker that made him forget duty and family? He sat back on the edge of the bed, staring at Belle as if she were the Devil. He was still so damned aroused it took several minutes of deep breathing before he understood what she was saying.

"What do you mean you weren't a whore? Do you want to explain yourself? Usually when a woman works in a whorehouse she—"

"Stop it, I say! That's exactly what T.J. thought. Naomi was the mother I never had. I was a child of ten when she took me in. I was living on the streets, abandoned and injured, eating from garbage cans and sleeping in gutters. One night I collapsed on her doorstep. I had no idea it was a whorehouse. The house looked warm and friendly and I could walk no farther."

"Where was your family?"

"I can't remember my mother. My father was a professional gambler. We moved frequently from town to town. Pa was killed in a saloon fight. No one knew he had a daughter. When the rent on our room ran out, I was evicted."

"My God, you must have been terrified, a babe in the woods. Why didn't you seek help? Did you have no relatives?"

Belle shook her head. "None that I knew of. I remember being frightened, too frightened to talk to anyone."

"And you were crippled besides."

"No, not then. I was struck by a carriage not long after I was turned out of our lodging. My ankle must have been broken, and of course I had no money for a doctor. It healed badly, and my ankle is deformed and my leg weak because of it. The night I crawled to Naomi's doorstep was the luckiest day of my life."

"She treated you well?" Casey asked sharply.

"Like the daughter she never had. I was a lame, half-starved waif who surely would have died had she not taken me in. I repaid her when I was old enough by working for her."

A nerve in Casey's jaw twitched. "In what capacity?" he asked suspiciously.

"How like a man to think the worst. Naomi wouldn't allow me to become a whore, nor did I even consider it. I worked in other capacities. I cooked, cleaned, and on busy nights served drinks to the customers."

"You never . . . not in all the years you were with Naomi?"

"Never. When men tried to buy my services, Naomi informed them that they couldn't afford me. They only wanted me out of curiosity anyway. They placed bets on what my leg looked like." Her expression gave Casey a hint of what she must have suffered because of her injury.

Casey wanted to strangle McAllister for lying about Belle. What else had he lied about? he wondered. Surely McAllister had known that Belle wasn't one of Naomi's stable of girls.

"How did you meet Tom?"

Reminiscence must have been sweet, for Belle smiled. "I served him drinks one night and we struck up a conversation. He was the kindest, gentlest man I had ever met. Nothing like his father, who came to Naomi's often. Tom kept coming back, but not for sex, only to talk to me. After several weeks he asked me to step out with him."

"What did Naomi think about that?"

"She encouraged me. And when Tom asked me to marry him, Naomi was ecstatic. It meant a different kind of life for me, one Naomi thoroughly approved of."

Casey had no business asking the next question but he couldn't help himself. "Did you love Tom?"

Belle smiled wistfully. "Yes. I loved him and he loved me. We were happy. When Tommy was born our life was complete, despite the fact that we were literally ignored by Tom's father. Tom's untimely death devastated me. Then, when Tom's father made it clear that he meant to take my son from me, I fled. I'd heard the vile things he was saying about me and realized the law wouldn't help me."

No matter what Casey thought personally, he couldn't let emotions interfere with his job. Mark was depending on him, and he had no way of paying back the money he'd accepted from McAllister if he bowed out now. He rose abruptly and walked to the window. He didn't look at her when he said, "Perhaps it would be best for Tommy if he went to live with his grandfather. It doesn't sound to me as if the old man wishes to harm the boy. Think of all the advantages he could give your son."

Belle's strangled gasp brought a flush of guilt to Casey's cheeks. He hated to deceive her, hell, he even sympathized with her, but business was business. As long as McAllister presented no menace to Tommy, he didn't see why a compromise couldn't be worked out.

She leapt from the bed and pounded on his back until he turned to face her. "You want me to give up Tommy to his grandfather? After all I went through to cover my tracks? I even changed my last name to throw him off the trail. Tommy is all I have. I would die before giving him up, and Tommy would be unhappy without me. I can't give him luxuries like T.J., but my son lacks none of the important things."

"What I'm suggesting is that you work out a compromise; both you and Tommy could live with McAllister."

Belle gave an inelegant snort. "The man wants no part of me. He thinks I'm a bad influence on Tommy. He told the authorities I'm an unfit mother. You have a poor grasp of the situation if you think my father-in-law will compromise."

Casey was inclined to agree. From his brief meeting with McAllister, he'd pegged him as an unrelenting and unforgiving man. One who blamed his daughter-in-law for his son's death. He'd do anything to punish Belle, and taking away her son was his way of avenging a perceived wrong. As far as Casey could see, all Belle was guilty of was loving a man whose father wanted to control his life.

Having said all she intended to, Belle turned and shuffled toward the door. Casey moved swiftly to reach her side and once again, Belle found herself in his arms. The pounding in her blood had nothing to do with exhaustion and everything to do with Casey Walker.

Casey carried her to his bed and sat her on the edge. Then he knelt before her and lifted her right leg until it rested on his thigh. "You've been on your feet for too long." He lifted her skirt and she squawked in protest, trying to pull it back down.

"What are you doing?"

"Looking at your ankle. Does this kind of thing happen often?"

When Belle heard he wanted to look at her ankle

she resisted in earnest, but he refused to release his hold on her limb. "I don't know what you mean. Let me go."

Casey ignored her. "You know damn well what I'm talking about. Does your leg give way beneath you often?" He didn't give her a chance to reply. "You shouldn't be working this hard. You're on your feet way too much."

He had worked her skirt up to her knee by now, and finally glanced down at her lower leg. He blanched when he saw the unnatural angle of her ankle, and realized the enormous stress the injury must place on the rest of her leg, which was whole and beautifully shaped. He raised his gaze to her face.

"If you've looked your fill you can lower my skirt, Mr. Walker. I don't need your pity."

Casey did so with alacrity, not wanting to embarrass her further. "I'm sorry. I didn't mean to distress you."

"Did you have a morbid curiosity to look upon my deformity?"

He rose and sat beside her. "It's not your fault. You have a beautiful limb but for that one small defect."

She laughed harshly. "Ha! Don't you think I know how I look?"

"You underestimate your appeal. Didn't you say men at Naomi's wanted you? And what about Dinks and his friends? They certainly weren't bothered by your lameness."

"That's because they didn't see what you did. They would have been repelled by my deformity. That's one of the reasons I loved Tom so much. He saw inside me, he didn't care how I was formed."

"You have a lovely form," Casey said, grinning owlishly. "Your breasts are perfect and I believe I can span your waist with my hands. And your mouth, God, I've never seen such pretty lips. So lush, so inviting, they're enough to drive a man wild. Would you like me to prove it?"

Belle opened her mouth to protest and suddenly found Casey's lips devouring hers and his tongue probing past the barrier of her teeth. Her breathless little sigh entered Casey's mouth, making him even more ravenous to taste her. She tentatively touched her tongue to his and he went wild, kissing and nipping, his mouth wet and hot and his tongue a sword thirsting for her sweetness.

Belle was thoroughly amazed, completely beguiled, by the suddenness of Casey's passion. One moment they were talking rationally, and the next he was kissing her with such fire she felt utterly consumed by him. She jerked reflexively when she felt his hands covering her breasts, squeezing them hard then tweaking the nipples, before sliding down over her ribcage to span her waist with his two hands.

When Casey finally released her mouth, Belle could do little more than touch her lips and stare at him. All her senses were alive, as if released from a long, drawn-out dream where all sensation had been suspended until this man released her. Her body tingled, her toes curled, and all she could think of was how much she wished Casey would kiss her again. What was wrong with her?

"Why did you do that?" she asked curiously.

"To prove to you that I find your body desirable despite having looked upon your so-called deformity. I was right, I could span your waist with my hands. You're a damn desirable woman, Belle Henderson, or whatever your name is."

"It's McAllister. Do you know my father-in-law?"

His lie was deliberate and he felt guilty as hell about it, but he had no choice. "No. I'm not from this part of the country. I hail from Arizona. Been traveling a lot lately."

"Do you have a family?"

"Only a brother."

"Do you love him?"

Casey gave her an exasperated look. Would he be here now, pumping Belle for information, if he didn't? "Of course I do. Why do you ask?"

"If you love your brother half as much as I love Tommy you'd know why I can't give him up to his grandfather."

"I can certainly understand your misgivings but—"

"No buts. That's the end of it. Tommy stays with me. Do you still want the job of protecting him or have you decided not to become involved?"

Damn! Casey already wished he hadn't become involved. But there was no turning back now. "I won't abandon you or Tommy. I'll be around should either of you need me."

Belle rose somewhat stiffly. "There's still work to be done in the kitchen. Dolores will be here soon to lend a hand."

"Belle." She looked at him, her eyebrows raised askance. "I wish . . ." He couldn't say what he was thinking, he had no right. "Christ, get out of here before I lose control."

Belle knew exactly to what Casey was referring. She had learned more than she wanted about men from her years with Naomi. When she married Tom, she went to him a virgin and had experienced passion for the first time. She could read desire in Casey's eyes, could smell his arousal, and after a year of celibacy she realized that her own eyes must reflect those same feelings.

Had she finally met a men who could take Tom's place in her heart? Could she trust Casey enough to place her safety and that of her beloved son into his keeping?

Chapter 4

Wan Yo was up and about now, hobbling around on crutches provided by the doctor. A perceptive man, Wan Yo was suspicious of Casey and voiced his suspicions to Belle one evening after she returned home from a hectic day at the diner.

"Wan Yo afraid hiring Mr. Walker not a good thing, Missy Belle," Wan Yo said. "He big mystery man. Missy Naomi tell Wan Yo to protect Missy Belle and Tommy."

"I know, Wan Yo," Belle said with a weary sigh. "I've considered that same thing. But I desperately needed someone, with you injured and Tommy getting to be such a rambunctious little scamp. And Mr. Walker was there when I needed him. If not for him . . . well, I won't go into that right now. Suffice it to say, Mr. Walker has proven to be trustworthy."

"Mr. McAllister velly shrewd man, Missy Belle must be careful," Wan Yo warned. "When Wan Yo's leg heals you no need bodyguard."

Belle didn't want to tell Wan Yo that the incident resulting in his injuries made it impossible to rely on a frail old man for protection. Especially in a town like Placerville, inhabited by miners, drifters, and unscrupulous men. Though she knew precious little about Casey Walker, she did know that he'd been helpful when she'd needed him.

"We will discuss this again when you're completely well," Belle temporized. "Meanwhile, we will both keep an eye on Mr. Walker."

Keeping an eye on Casey Walker was something Belle had done a lot of lately. He was dangerously and subtly intoxicating, and too attractive for her peace of mind. The quicksilver blaze of his hazel eyes consumed her, and the sound of his voice caressed her like sunlight. The way he had kissed her had sent hot blood pounding through her veins, and God only knew she had little information. Yet she trusted him, and that bothered her. She really should learn more about the enigmatic Casey Walker before giving him her trust.

Casey wallowed in indecision, and guilt was no little part of his dilemma. The more he learned about Belle the more he regretted taking this case. He should have dug deeper into Belle's background before accepting McAllister's word that she was a whore and an unfit mother. God, what was he going to do? Like it or not, he had become deeply enmeshed in the lives of Belle and Tommy. Hell, he admired the woman for her gumption to stand up to McAllister. If he hadn't already wired the advance to Simon Levy, he'd return the money and tell McAllister to find another man to do his dirty work.

Unfortunately he no longer had the money to return and he had promised McAllister that he'd find his grandson. Professional honor demanded that he either convince Belle to give her son up without a fuss, or tell McAllister where to find the boy. With the law on his side, McAllister could easily claim Tommy once he knew where Belle had taken him.

Casey recalled how close he'd come to making love to Belle that day he'd sent Dinks packing for the second time. He'd wanted to, oh yes, he still wanted to. She had a rare kind of beauty that no defect could diminish. Not just beauty of face and form but beauty of spirit. Her life hadn't been easy but she had persevered and overcome obstacles lesser women would have found daunting.

Time was running out; Casey knew he couldn't remain in Placerville forever. McAllister would be chomping at the bit, waiting for some word from him. Casey began to curse the physical attraction he felt for Belle. Despite the attachments he'd formed in this case, Casey realized sentiments had no place in the life of a detective, and that he had to resolve things soon. To that end, he paid a visit to Belle after the dinner hour late one evening. He found her in the kitchen, just finishing up the dishes.

"Belle, can I talk to you?"

Since Dolores was with her, Belle felt safe. She couldn't afford to succumb to Casey's charm again, or let herself drift aimlessly into the dark, mesmerizing depths of his eyes. She must never forget that Tommy came first in her life.

"Certainly. You can talk while I work. Tommy is waiting for me."

"Tommy is already sleeping. I just checked on him." He glanced at Dolores, who was eyeing him with distrust. "Alone, if you don't mind."

"You can speak in front of Dolores. She knows all my secrets."

"I'd prefer not to."

"Very well." To the Mexican woman, she said, "Go on home, Dolores. Sanchez should be through stacking wood now and you are both tired. I'll see you in the morning."

"Are you sure, senora? I don't mind staying."

"I'm sure. Mr. Walker is in my employ, I trust him."

Casey winced when Belle voiced her trust in him. He certainly didn't deserve it.

"Si, senora," Dolores said, clearly not convinced she should leave.

"Sit down, Belle," Casey said after Dolores had hung up her apron and left through the front door.

"Is something the matter, Mr.—Casey? Has someone aroused your suspicion?"

"There is something wrong, but it's not what you think." He paced restlessly. "I've given your situation a lot of thought and can see only one solution."

Belle stared up at him through outrageously long lashes. "I might as well tell you I'm not inclined to follow advice from someone I hardly know."

"Nevertheless, I feel obligated to offer my opinion. Ever since you told me about your situation, I've been racking my brain for a solution that will please both you and your father-in-law. Just try to remember that what I'm going to suggest is best for everyone."

Belle started to rise. "I don't want to hear it. I'm terminating your job, Mr. Walker."

"Sit down, Belle." His voice was harsh, commanding. "You can't go on like this. You hired me to protect your son, but surely you must know I won't be around forever. What if the next man you hire is unscrupulous? What if he tries to take advantage of you?"

Head held high in subconscious defiance, she glared at him. "I took a chance on you, didn't I? Do you consider yourself unscrupulous? I know nothing about you except that you have a brother in Arizona. In a moment of weakness I told you my story, I didn't ask for your advice nor do I want it now. I can handle it alone. What makes you think you're qualified to offer advice?"

Casey shrugged off Belle's questions. The less she knew about him the better. He abruptly stopped his pacing and paused in front of her, scowling furiously. "Forget me. I'm not hiding from someone, you are. Give Tommy's grandfather a chance to get to know the boy. Go to him. Work out a compromise. I'm sure he'll be reasonable about visitation and such. You *are* the boy's mother. Please, Belle, I implore you, stop running. McAllister will find you one day, and you could lose Tommy for good. I don't want that to happen."

Belle leapt to her feet and flew at Casey, pounding on his chest with clenched fists. "No! Never! How could you suggest such a thing? I told you T.J. hates me. He'd never let me see Tommy again. Damn you, Casey Walker! Whose side are you on, anyway?"

Casey grasped Belle's wrists, trying not to hurt her as he brought them to her sides. "I'm only thinking of you and Tommy, Belle. I don't want to see either of you hurt. How long can you keep running? You need someone to take care of you. You work much too hard in the diner. You need a man to pamper and love you."

"Are you suggesting you're that man?" Belle

made a disgusting sound deep in her throat, telling
Casey without words exactly what she thought of
that idea.

If it would convince Belle to give up Tommy to
McAllister without a fight, he'd tell her anything.
He feared McAllister would hurt her worse than
merely depriving her of her son. "Is that such an
outlandish idea? We're explosive together, Belle."
Truer words were never spoken. Tension rippled
beneath the surface of his skin. His eyes had darkened, his nostrils flared and his grip upon her wrists
had tightened. Even now his manhood defied con-
finement, provoked merely by her nearness.

Belle pulled from his grasp, breathing hard, her
eyes flashing angrily. "You and your suggestions
can go to hell, Mr. Walker. I will never, I repeat,
never give up my son. If you knew T.J. McAllister,
you wouldn't suggest such a thing."

"I'm sorry, Belle," Casey said. "Sorrier than I've
ever been in my life." Belle's refusal to compromise
left him with no choice but to contact McAllister.
But, dear Lord, could he do it? Could he actually tell
McAllister where to find Tommy? Regret, guilt,
shame, remorse, all those emotions made him feel
like the lowest bastard who'd ever walked the face
of the earth.

On the other hand, there was Mark. Innocent of a
murder charge, and depending on his big brother to
get him out of prison. A man didn't live who was
more torn or tormented than Casey Walker.

Belle stared at Casey and felt her anger slowly
drain away. If the expression on his face was any
indication, he was suffering his own private hell.
She had no idea what had brought it on, but

something inside her couldn't let it continue. Her soft heart made her reach out to him, touching his arm gently.

"I think I know what's best for my son, Casey. We haven't known one another long, so you can't possibly understand the situation. Or convince me that you're interested in me as a woman. I don't know the reason for your anguish, but there is no reason to pretend with me. You have to know by now that no man is worth the loss of my son. Not even you, Casey Walker."

If Casey harbored the hope that he could talk Belle into giving her son up to McAllister, it had died with her last words. Truth to tell, he admired her determination. Most women would cave in to the pressure being applied by McAllister.

"I didn't mean to upset you. I had to try one last time to . . ."

"To what?"

"To make certain you knew what you were doing," he improvised.

"I do," Belle vowed as she turned back to her chores.

For his own peace of mind, Casey needed to make Belle understand why he was concerned about her and Tommy. But what could he say that wouldn't send her and Tommy fleeing to only God knew where to escape McAllister? Misery flailed him unbearably. He couldn't ever recall feeling such gut-wrenching guilt. Seizing Belle's arms, he pulled her against him, trying to make her understand his position without words.

Belle had no idea what Casey was saying as his lips came down on hers. Words were wrenched from him in a low growl. Whatever he was muttering was lost to her in the heat of Casey's mouth and the melting strength of his arms.

"I'm sorry, Belle, so damn sorry. Had I known. Oh, God, had I known . . . Too late . . . Too late . . ."

Realizing the futility of his retrospection, Casey abruptly broke off the kiss and turned to leave.

Reduced to a boneless heap by his kisses, Belle was stunned by his abrupt dismissal. "Casey, wait! What did you say? I don't understand."

"No, I don't suppose you do. You never will. If you only knew. . . . I have to leave for a few days, Belle. I have business to take care of. Have Sanchez watch over Tommy if you can spare him in the diner."

His words had a chilling effect. "Where are you going? Are you coming back?"

"I'm coming back, Belle." He knew she would need him after McAllister took her son, even though she might hate him for his part in it.

Belle watched him disappear through the door, wondering if she would ever see Casey Walker again. She tried to tell herself it didn't matter. She didn't need a man, she only needed Tommy. It briefly occurred to her that Casey might tell T.J. where to find Tommy. But she quickly discarded the notion. She had never mentioned where T.J. lived. She didn't know much about Casey, but what little she did know convinced her that he wasn't the kind of man to pull so despicable a stunt. Surely he felt the same kind of attraction she felt, didn't he? He would never hurt her like that, would he?

Belle wanted to believe in the basic goodness of

man, but had learned the hard way to trust sparingly. Casey had done nothing to earn her distrust except for trying to convince her to give her son up to McAllister. However much she tried to convince herself that she could trust Casey, a small niggling doubt remained. She vowed to be extra vigilant with Tommy until Casey returned and she learned why he had suddenly left town. For her own peace of mind she had to believe in Casey. Had to trust that he wouldn't betray her to McAllister. It would destroy her to learn that Casey was like McAllister and men of his ilk.

Casey boarded the stagecoach at the Wells Fargo office the following morning. He journeyed the entire distance to San Francisco in brooding silence, though he knew it would change nothing. He'd lost the choice to back out of this assignment the day he'd taken T.J.'s money and sent it to Simon Levy. His strong sense of duty was in direct opposition to his sense of honor. Since when had he developed a conscience? Casey wondered. This was the first time he could recall allowing sentiments to interfere with duty. And all because of a very courageous, immensely appealing young woman named Belle Parker McAllister.

He'd met women more beautiful than Belle. Women perfect in every respect. Women without deformities. But he'd met no woman who engaged his fancy or defied logic or reason like Belle. If she possessed a modicum of sense she'd see the logic of allowing her father-in-law to raise Tommy, to give him the world, if he so desired. Perhaps he could act as mediator, Casey considered, and work out something whereby McAllister and Belle could share custody. The theory sounded entirely reasonable, which made Casey feel a helluva lot less like a heel than he had been feeling. If he put his mind to it, perhaps he'd find a way to make both parties happy.

Two days later Casey stood before T.J. McAllister.

"It's about time, Walker," McAllister said sourly. "Where in the hell have you been for the past month? I'd begun to think you'd taken off with my money."

"I always get my man, Mr. McAllister. I found your grandson, but there are some mitigating circumstances that need addressing before I tell you where he is."

McAllister's eyes lit up. "You've found Tommy? Good God, man, you *are* good! My men have been a whole year looking for the lad without finding a clue to his whereabouts."

"Yeah, well, as I was saying, there are still some things that need defining."

Instantly suspicious, McAllister asked, "What things?"

"For instance. What about the boy's mother? Do you intend to share custody with her? Or give her visiting rights?"

"Belle?" He gave a bark of laughter. "You've got to be kidding. The woman's a whore. She could care less about the boy."

Casey felt his temper rising. "How well do you know Belle?"

McAllister's eyes narrowed dangerously. "The question is, how well do *you* know Belle? Are you falling for the whore? I told you she was good. I warned you about her. Look how she snared Tom. Lame or no, that woman lured Tom into her bed then talked him into marrying her."

"Cut the crap, McAllister! I think you know the truth about Belle but are afraid to admit it. You're blind to everything but the need to salve your own conscience for Tom's death. You think you can do that by giving Tommy everything his mother can't."

"You weren't paid to pass judgment, Walker. I gave you hard cash to find my grandson. You've found him, I'm satisfied. Now, tell me where he is."

"You haven't answered my question. Are you willing to share custody with Belle? Or offer her a place in your home so she can see Tommy every day? It's only right, you know."

"Who in the hell made you my conscience? I want nothing to do with that whore. If not for her my son would still be alive. There will be no sharing of custody. I don't want Belle anywhere within my sight. And she's not going to get a red cent of my money, either."

He'd tried, sweet Jesus, he'd tried. Nothing in Casey's life had prepared him for something like this. He'd been accused of being cold, determined, and thoroughly merciless. Unfeeling. Even heartless. He'd had taken pride in his ability to do his job without becoming emotionally involved. He'd always brought in his man, always solved his case using whatever means available, and gone on to the next assignment with a clear conscience. Not this time. Oh, no, not this time. Something inside him balked at betraying Belle.

"I feel sorry for you, McAllister. Wild horses

couldn't drag the information from me. It will be a cold day in hell when I tell you where to find Belle and Tommy."

McAllister leapt from his chair, waving his hands before Casey like a madman. "What do you mean? You took my money! You accepted the assignment. I paid you in good faith. I was right, wasn't I? You've bedded the bitch."

Casey's clenched fists and white lips should have warned McAllister, but they didn't.

"How was she, Walker? She must have been damn good in the sack to get you so fired up. Go ahead and screw her head off, it won't change a damn thing. I paid you to do a job and you owe me. Give me the information I want."

Grasping McAllister's lapels, Casey pulled him out of the chair and halfway across his desk, giving him a vicious shake for good measure. "Go to hell! I wouldn't give you the time of day. You needn't worry about your money." Releasing McAllister, Casey grabbed paper and pen from the desk, scribbled an IOU and threw it in his face. "Here! I'll see that you get every penny I owe you."

Free from Casey's bruising grip, McAllister slumped back into his chair, his face mottled with rage. "Allan Pinkerton is going to know about this. I'm not without influence. I'll see that you never work again for the agency."

A vision of Belle appeared before Casey's eyes, her face tear-stained, her arms raised beseechingly as McAllister carried off her son. An instant later it was replaced by Mark's face, wan and pinched from his months in prison, pleading with him to set him free. He was being torn from both sides. And in the center was his honor, his very reputation as a detective. In the end there was no choice but the one he had already made.

"I said you'll get your money back and I meant it. You have my IOU. I'll deal with Allan Pinkerton. If he wants my resignation he'll get it. Good day, sir."

"Damn you to hell! I want my grandson. You won't get away with this, Walker. I'll hire a hundred men to find him if I have to. No one cheats T.J. McAllister. No one!"

McAllister was still raging when Casey left. He knew he'd made a serious enemy, and that his job was on the line, but he couldn't betray Belle, not for all the money in the world. He depended on his long association with Allan Pinkerton to stand him in good stead. When he left McAllister he went directly to the telegraph office.

As concisely as possible, Casey told Pinkerton he was dropping out of the case and that he needed a loan of three thousand dollars. Several hours later Pinkerton wired back, stating that he trusted Casey's judgment but expected a full report at his Chicago office. A bank draft would be mailed to him in care of General Delivery in San Francisco.

The next day Casey boarded the Placerville stage-coach. Upon his return he was determined to tell Belle about his association with McAllister and his reason for being in Placerville.

If Casey hadn't been so distraught, he would have realized that McAllister wasn't going to let the matter drop. Shortly after Casey left his office, McAllister hired two thugs to watch Casey and report on his movements. When told Casey had boarded a stagecoach, McAllister hurried to the Wells Fargo office and learned that Casey had purchased a ticket to Placerville. He dispatched his

two hirelings forthwith to Placerville, giving them
precise instructions and a letter that was to be left
for Casey Walker.

"Hello, Belle."

Belle's heart leapt with gladness at the sight of
Casey. "You're back!"

"Did you think I wouldn't be?"

She forced a smile. "It had entered my mind."

He returned her smile, though he felt little like
smiling. What he had to tell Belle was bound to
make her hate him.

"Are you going to stay, Casey?"

Casey's smile faltered. He had wired Simon Levy
before he left San Francisco and told him to contact
him in Placerville if the missing witness was found.
If the witness failed to respond to the reward soon,
Casey knew he had to return to Arizona and
conduct his own search. Mark was depending on
him and he couldn't let his kid brother down.

On the other hand, he didn't want to leave Belle
and Tommy at the mercy of a man like McAllister.
Refusing to tell McAllister where to find Tommy
was the most selfless thing he'd ever done, and the
most foolish. It did little to enhance his reputation
as a Pinkerton detective or endear him to the
agency. What it did was restore his honor. Did he
still have a job? he wondered. Almost every penny
he had to his name had gone toward lawyer fees in
Mark's behalf.

"Belle, there is something . . ." Christ, he
couldn't tell her. Not yet. Call him a coward, call
him foolish, but he didn't want Belle to think of him
as a betrayer. "I can stick around a while longer," he

finally said. "To make sure your father-in-law doesn't get wind of your whereabouts."

"Why would he? It's been a year since I left. I'd appreciate it, however, if you could stay until Wan Yo is on his feet again."

"I'll try, Belle, but I can't promise. There are things I haven't told you. Things that . . . You see, my brother is in prison for a killing he didn't commit. I'm waiting for his lawyer to wire me about a missing witness. As soon as I hear something I'll be heading back to Arizona."

"Oh, Casey, I'm so sorry." At last she was learning something about Casey Walker. "Is your home in Arizona?" she probed gently.

"Not exactly," he hedged. "I travel a lot. I promise to tell you all about it before I leave." And hope you don't hate me, he thought but did not say.

Casey had no inkling that he was staring at Belle with longing in his eyes until she started fidgeting beneath his intense perusal. He stared at her lips, recalling how sweet they tasted and how eagerly she had responded to his kisses. But after the way he'd lied to her about his assignment in Placerville, he didn't have the right to kiss her. He cleared his throat and looked away. "I think I'll go see Tommy now. I missed that little scamp."

He was almost out the door when Belle called out softly, "Casey. Thank you."

He turned back to her. "For what?"

"For coming back. I—I missed you. Trust is an awesome burden to have to bestow on someone, but I feel you've earned it."

"Don't credit me with virtues I don't deserve," Casey warned as he strode out the door.

Chapter 5

The burden of Belle's trust weighed heavily on Casey. Defying McAllister had been a difficult choice, but Casey was smart enough to realize that McAllister would use his resources to find Belle and Tommy, and he would succeed sooner or later. That could mean disaster for Belle. Tommy was her whole life.

Casey spent the following days trying to decide whether to tell Belle to take Tommy and run, or to say nothing and hope for the best. Since he had formally disassociated himself from the case, technically he had no further interest in what happened and he should leave. He had his own problems to solve. Unfortunately, extenuating circumstances, which consisted of a sable-haired, brown-eyed temptress and a winsome little boy, prevented him from leaving.

The cast had been removed from Wan Yo's leg and he was getting stronger every day. The old Chinaman had made it abundantly clear that he considered himself more than capable of protecting Tommy. Every instinct told Casey he should leave, but his conscience demanded that he tell Belle that McAllister was hot on her trail. Instead of acting upon either his instinct or conscience, Casey drifted into indecision.

He was in his small room behind the kitchen one evening when Tommy drifted in and sat down beside him on the bed, watching while Casey cleaned his gun by lamplight.

"Are you going to use that?" Tommy asked, indicating the gun.

Casey gave him a quick smile. "Only if I have to."

"Wan Yo is well now. Mama says you'll be going away soon. Are you?"

"I reckon I'll have to leave one day soon. Then it will be up to you and Wan Yo to take care of your mother."

"Do you think mean old McAllister has stopped looking for me?"

"The man is your grandfather, Tommy."

"He wants to take me away from Mama. I don't like him."

"Have you ever met him?"

"No, and I never want to."

"He can give you everything a boy your age could ever want."

Tommy's pointed little chin rose stubbornly. Casey couldn't help but smile. "I have everything I want. If Grandfather takes me away Mama will be sad. She's sad already. I hear her crying at night when she thinks I'm asleep."

Casey's hand froze on the polishing cloth and he stared at Tommy. "Your mother cries?"

"All the time," Tommy said solemnly. "She never cried when Papa was alive."

Casey set the gun aside. "Do you remember your father?"

Tommy gave him a wistful smile and nodded. "He played with me and took me up on his horse with him. Mama was never sad then, she was always laughing. I'd like to see her laugh again but she won't, not while mean old McAllister is looking for us."

"I'll bet you can make your mama laugh again if you try," Casey remarked.

Tommy's face lit up. "Do you think so? She's happy when you're around, Casey. Do you have to go away? Don't you like us? I like you, and so does Mama. Will you be my papa?"

Remorse gnawed at Casey. A child's trust was a precious thing. It bugged the hell out of him that he hadn't earned that trust. He liked Tommy a lot, and his mother too damn much. Tommy's plea for a papa had struck a responsive chord in his heart. Regretfully, he wasn't able to answer Tommy's question, however much he wanted to. He was visualizing Belle's reaction to his confession that he was a Pinkerton detective. But Tommy was undaunted. He simply repeated his question.

"Will you be my papa, Casey?"

Casey was saved from answering when Belle rapped on the door, then entered the room moments later.

"There you are, Tommy. I thought I'd find you here. Don't bother Mr. Walker."

"He's not bothering me, Belle. He's a smart kid. You've raised him well. I just wish . . ." He sentence ended abruptly. What in the hell was he thinking? He had responsibilities, he had no business wishing for impossible things when he was in no position to pursue them. Mark was his brother, his own flesh and blood, and he had to come first in Casey's life.

"It's time to go back to the house, Tommy. Wan Yo is looking for you."

"Do I have to, Mama?"

"It's bedtime, son. I'll join you as soon as I finish up here. I still have bread dough to set out."

Tommy left reluctantly but Belle lingered. "I hope Tommy wasn't telling you tales he shouldn't have. I know how talkative little boys can be. And curious."

"Tommy is a treasure. I can understand why you won't give him up."

"I was beginning to wonder, especially after you did your best to talk me into sending Tommy to my father-in-law. I was afraid . . . never mind. It was foolish of me to think you could be working for McAllister."

Casey made a gurgling sound in his throat. "Come here and sit down, Belle, I want to talk to you." He patted the bed beside him.

Belle considered the invitation for several long moments before limping to the bed and sitting primly on the edge. Just looking at Casey brought an exhilarating rush that began in her face and raced along every nerve ending. She shivered. If she responded physically to the sound of his voice and his gaze, what would she do if he touched her?

Casey noted her uneven steps, and could tell by her pronounced limp that she had been on her feet long hours today and was paying for it in pain. "Does your leg hurt?"

Belle shrugged. "I've learned to live with it. No need to feel sorry for me. I know most men are repulsed by deformities like mine."

"Dammit, Belle, that's not what I'm thinking at all."

Belle caught her breath, praying he wasn't thinking the same thing she was. She was looking at his mouth and wishing he would kiss her, like he did before. God, what was wrong with her? "What are you thinking, Casey?"

"That you're brave and determined and beautiful. Your hair is the color of rich sable. So shiny and soft I want to thrust my hands into it and let the silken strands slip through my fingers. And that I don't like to see you weary all the time."

Unconsciously Belle rubbed her lame leg. "I don't mind. I have to make a living for Tommy and me."

Lamplight caught the golden highlights in her soft brown eyes, and Casey felt desire thicken inside him. The thought that he wanted Belle sexually wasn't a new one, but never had it been stronger or more compelling than it was now. His hazel eyes glowed darkly as she turned her guileless gaze on him, and Lord help him, he wanted her.

Belle expelled her breath on a soft little sigh. There was no mistakiing the look in Casey's eyes, for she had seen it too many times on the faces of men who came to Naomi's house for sex. On the faces of other men, that look had disgusted her, but now she was enthralled by it, helplessly drawn into the heated center of Casey's gaze, lured by the promise of untold pleasure. Her eyes widened when his face lowered, his lips hovering scant inches from hers. He gave her sufficient time to turn away. When she didn't, his lips came down hard on hers, and his hands came up to tunnel through her hair, holding her head in place while he plundered her mouth.

"You're so sweet," Casey whispered against her lips. "You taste of honey, and smell of sugar and spice."

"I've been baking," Belle returned flippantly. She was trying without much success to diffuse a potentially volatile moment.

Casey's mouth converged over hers, parting her lips with his tongue so he could caress the inside of her mouth. Belle sighed, welcoming the heat and wetness of his passionate kiss through a haze of sensation that began with her lips and pooled in the pit of her stomach. She knew she should stop this now but it felt too wonderful to bring to an end. Casey groaned and Belle heard herself echo the sound. Then she was drifting down onto the bed, with Casey sprawled across her. She could scarcely tell when one kiss ended and the next began.

Wanting was clawing through Casey with talons sharpened by his hunger for this woman. He cupped her face, kissing her again and again, tasting her with his tongue, feeling the heat of her through her clothing. Shifting slightly away from her, he brought his hands down to her breasts, pleased with their size and shape. But it wasn't enough. He wanted, he craved, more. With practiced ease he found the buttons on the front of her bodice and worked them loose. The string holding her chemise together fell apart beneath his determination and suddenly he touched bare flesh. No corset, he dimly thought, and thanked God for that small concession.

Belle vaguely realized that Casey was touching her in places he shouldn't. Her breasts swelled beneath his fingers, and when he stroked and tugged at her nipples she felt her throat go hot and hollow. His lips left hers and she whimpered at the loss, until she felt his open mouth upon her nipple, sucking it into a hard little point then laving it with the rough pad of his tongue.

Belle arched upward into this mouth, splaying her hands against his chest; he was making her feel things she hadn't felt in so very long. She could feel his hot skin beneath his shirt, and his strength, his hardness, the pure masculine power of him. His muscles were sleek and solid as steel. The heat radiating from his body and his mouth fairly vanquished her. She was dissolving into a puddle and didn't know how to stop it, even if she wanted to. But she had to try.

She pushed against his chest. "Casey, no, this isn't right."

He gave her a cocky grin. "Feels right to me. Sit up, I want to rid you of this cumbersome dress."

"Someone will come in."

He rose abruptly and locked the door. When he returned, he lifted her to her feet and peeled her dress away with an expertise that left her wondering how many women he'd undressed in his life. More than he could count, obviously.

"Tommy needs me."

"Wan Yo can see to him." He bore her backward onto the bed. "I've wanted to do this since the first day I saw you."

He knelt at the side of the bed and flipped up her petticoats, baring her legs. Belle sputtered indignantly but Casey ignored her as he stared at her limbs.

She tried without success to push her petticoats down around her ankles. "What are you doing? Do you get some kind of perverse pleasure from looking at my deformity?"

Casey gazed at her twisted, swollen ankle and felt unreasonable anger at the uncaring people who must have seen the injured child and done nothing to help her. He touched the misshapen joint and he felt her flinch.

"You're not deformed, don't ever consider yourself lacking in any way." Grasping her leg gently, he began to massage the soreness out of her limb. "Obviously your husband didn't consider you unattractive."

His voice was low and coaxing, and Belle found herself relaxing beneath his ministrations, despite her embarrassment at having Casey view her injury. "Tom was one-of-a-kind. He thought me beautiful."

"I think you're beautiful." His hand moved higher, to the edge of her drawers, then down again to her ankle, gently massaging the length of her leg.

Belle moaned. It felt wonderful, but she didn't delude herself into believing that Casey actually thought her beautiful. She knew how she looked. There was nothing extraordinary about her brown hair and brown eyes. Her figure was passable but nothing to shout about. And she was a cripple.

"You must be blind." She felt his hand move higher, past her knee, pushing her drawers up to her thigh. "What are you doing?"

Their gazes met and embraced, her eyes wide and staring, his narrowed and hungry. His luminous hazel eyes were direct, pleading, compelling. Belle became lost in those bewitching depths, and for a moment almost believed herself beautiful.

Suddenly Casey looked away. He wanted to make

love to Belle but had no right. His hands moved back down to her lower limb, massaging the aches and pains from her calf and twisted ankle. "How does this feel?"

"Very soothing," she admitted, suddenly embarrassed by his impersonal tone. She must have been out of her mind to let Casey undress her and touch her body so intimately. "You're very good at this but . . ."

"I want to make love to you," Casey blurted out. He made a strangled sound beneath his breath. What in the hell was the matter with him? He had never known himself to be so utterly lacking in finesse. He felt like a schoolboy with his first woman. His unsubtle remark sounded crass to his own ears.

Belle's mind went blank. It wasn't as if she hadn't known Casey's intention all along. He had bared her breasts and removed her dress, and she had allowed it. Did that mean she wanted him to make love to her? The answer was not too surprising. Her body's reaction to Casey's hands and mouth was a shameful reminder that she wanted him as much as he wanted her. His kisses thrilled her and his touch captivated her.

"Belle, did you hear me? I want you."

Before she could form a reply, Casey began kissing her again, stealing her breath and her will. She knew that once Casey left she'd never see him again, but she couldn't deny the existence of her need, or the fact that she craved his kisses and whatever else came after that. She was a fully grown woman, responsible for her own decisions, and making love with Casey was something she wanted very much.

His kisses grew more frenzied as they moved from her mouth to her breasts, pulling aside her chemise to bare even more of her pale flesh. Only then did Belle become aware that one of his hands had begun a slow slide up the inside of her leg. Unerringly he located the slit in her drawers, working his fingers inside until he found her heated center. Belle moaned and arched sharply upward.

"You're so hot there. You're driving me crazy, Belle. In another minute you won't have a choice. If you're going to leave, do it now."

Belle couldn't move, she could only gasp and writhe as his fingers slid into her, creating a wanting more powerful than she could ever recall. Tom's gentle loving had been pleasurable and rewarding, but it hadn't provoked the wildness in her like Casey's loving. She grasped Casey's shoulders, begging him without words not to stop, that she wanted this as much as he did.

Reading the silent message in the burning depths of her eyes, Casey quickly removed Belle's drawers, petticoats and shift and sank back on his haunches to admire her. She was slim as a girl, her body perfect despite having borne a child. Her breasts, rosy from his loving, were high and firm, crowned with dusky elongated nipples. Her minuscule waist begged to be spanned by his large hands and her hips tapered down to long shapely legs. So captivating were her combined charms that Casey barely noticed her deformity.

Casey must have looked at her legs longer than Belle thought necessary for she tried to hide her twisted ankle beneath the bed covering. "I know it's ugly, please don't look at it."

Casey drew her foot out from beneath the covering, brought it up to his lips and kissed it. "Nothing about you is ugly."

Belle flinched when she felt his lips on her ankle, but when she saw he wasn't repulsed, she relaxed, enjoying the sensations he was creating inside her. She had thought that Tom was the only man not disgusted by her deformity, but Casey had just proved her wrong. He made her feel wanted, and sexy, and yes, loved, even though she knew there was nothing between them but pure lust. They hadn't known one another long enough to form an attachment, but that didn't stop her from wanting to make love with Casey. It certainly didn't stop her from wanting him as naked as she.

Reaching up, she tugged at his shirt.

Casey gave her a heart-stopping grin. "Does that mean you aren't going to send me away?"

"It's a little late for that, isn't it?"

"I hope so." With a minimum of effort, Casey shed his shirt. He paused a moment with his hands on the waistband of his trousers, and when Belle did not look away, he peeled them down his hips along with his cotton drawers. He flipped them aside then positioned himself between Belle's legs.

Belle followed the line of hair marching down his stomach to the dark triangle between his legs. Her breath caught in her throat when she saw the granitelike column of his manhood rising against his stomach. He was fully, overwhelmingly erect, a shiny pearl of liquid visible at the very tip of his erection.

"I can promise you nothing but pleasure, Belle," Casey said, giving her one final opportunity to back out.

"I didn't ask for promises. Tommy is my life. I don't need anyone else."

That's all Casey needed to hear. His body covering hers, he kissed her hungrily as his hands learned her body, finding all those places that gave her pleasure. He put into play all his expertise, using lips and hands and mouth to bring her to the brink of madness.

"I want to bring you more pleasure than you've ever known," he whispered into her ear.

"I've had no man since Tom died, and none before," Belle admitted on a sigh. "I'm not all that knowledgeable."

For some reason that pleased Casey. It made him more determined than ever to please Belle. He kissed a trail of fire down her body to her breasts. The end of his tongue tasted her nipple, circled it, then drew the crest into his mouth for a thorough tasting.

Heat shimmered through Belle, making her dizzy with delight. The varying textures of his tongue and mouth against her skin enthralled and enraptured her. She purred her pleasure as his hands slid down her body, shaping her breasts and waist and thighs, finding the burning, inner heat of her, sweet and yielding, with his fingers. Her whimpers told him what she wanted, and he eased his fingers through the tights curls into her slick passage.

Belle tried to speak, but her breath broke on a strangled gasp as she convulsed around his fingers, spilling warmth onto his hand. She thought she cried out his name but couldn't be sure. His answer was another penetrating caress that made her body weep passionately for him.

"Sweet Jesus!" Casey cried, feeling his body swell as it prepared to spill its seed. "I don't know what in the hell is happening to us, but it's making me crazy."

He pulled his hand away abruptly; Belle murmured a protest at its loss. Against her skin, he blazed a trail of wet kisses, down between her breasts, across her stomach, licking, touching, tantalizing, until his lips found her sweet, tiny nub. Then he did something so outrageous Belle's eyes flew open and she lost the ability to think. His mouth found the place where his fingers had been only moments before. Then he parted the dewy petals of her sex with his tongue and sipped hungrily of her sweet essence.

Belle finally found her voice, crying out on a note of shock. "Oh, no, you can't. . . . It's not . . ." She tugged at his hair, trying to get him to stop.

"Didn't your husband ever do this to you?"

"No, never. Please, I don't want . . ." Her sentence ended in a strangled sob as her body began to vibrate against the friction of his tongue.

Reluctant to do anything Belle didn't want, Casey slid upward along her body, settling between her slender thighs. He separated her soft portals with his blunt flesh, forcing himself to press slowly, despite his nearly out-of-control passion that demanded a swift release. She was wet and hot, sultry and welcoming, and he fought for the control he normally practiced. Sweat glistened on his body as he pushed deeper inside her, groaning when he felt her inner muscles welcoming him.

He rested his head on her forehead while he caught his breath. But it didn't help. His passion doubled and redoubled. "Oh, God, lie still or I won't be able to do either of us any good. I can't ever recall being like this with a woman. I have this violent need to thrust and thrust until I bring myself to climax, and I'm afraid I'll hurt you.''

Lying motionless beneath Casey's powerful body was nearly beyond Belle. She wanted to move her hips, to undulate beneath him, to feel his strength driving into her, touching her very soul. She wanted to reach for the stars and watch them explode around her. She wanted to find paradise with Casey. For a brief interval she satisfied herself with running her hands over his body, learning his bold masculine contours. But it was difficult to concentrate when the hard, pulsing length of his manhood was embedded deep inside her. She moved her hips the tiniest bit and it was all the invitation Casey needed.

He flexed his hips and began thrusting forcefully, nearly driving her off the bed with the wild fury of his strokes. He kissed her as if he'd die if he didn't. Blood squeezed hot and slow through his veins, flowing into his distended sex.

Belle's nails dug into the tanned flesh of his shoulders, crying out softly as she moved with him, bringing the shimmering pressure of his manhood deeper inside her. She felt her hips spanned and lifted by his big hands, felt her control slipping. She called out his name on a rising note of urgency. His answer was a thrust that went deep and hard. She was wet, soft and hot, and nearly as wild for release as he was. She came abruptly, shivering and crying as splinters of ecstasy pierced her, triggering Casey's own release as he poured himself into her sweet body.

When Casey could breathe again, over the lingering tremors of ecstasy rippling through him, he shifted his weight from her and pulled her into the curve of his body. "I'm sorry if I hurt you. I don't know what happened to me. I'm usually more disciplined."

Belle stared at him in fear and disbelief. How could a man she hardly knew make her feel this way? She felt irrevocably joined with him, sharing breath and body, bound together by passion. She had loved Tom, enjoyed making love with him, but she had never experienced this kind of frenzied, wanton, coming together. It made her feel . . . immoral!

"Are you all right?" Casey asked, concerned by her blank expression.

She managed a weak smile. "More than all right. You made me feel . . . wonderful. It was . . . quite extraordinary."

Casey laughed with genuine pleasure. "The pleasure was all mine, sweetheart."

They lay in silence, resting, gathering strength. Casey knew he should tell Belle his reason for being in Placerville, but couldn't bring himself to disillusion her after they had just made love so sweetly. But soon, he promised himself. He hoped she'd find it in her heart to forgive him. Especially since he'd left McAllister's employ rather than betray her and Tommy. As much as he would like to, Casey didn't dare think of Belle in terms of a longer relationship. He had no idea how long it would take to clear Mark of murder charges. Even if it took the rest of his life he would strive for Mark's release. Belle and Tommy deserved better than a man unable to lavish his full attention upon them.

Belle let out a long, drawn-out sigh as she snug-

gled against Casey. She'd expected no commitment
from Casey and received none. The words of love
that usually followed lovemaking were missing and
she felt the loss keenly. She sighed again and Casey
turned her against him.

"Are you sorry?"

She didn't even have to think about that one.
"No, are you?"

"Only sorry that we waited so long."

"We haven't known each other all that long. You
must think I'm a woman of loose morals. I've never
done anything this wanton or spontaneous before. I
made Tom wait until we were married."

"I think you're a warm, passionate woman who
needs a man to take care of her." He paused, forcing
the next words out even though he didn't mean
them. "Unfortunately, I'm not that man. There are
things you don't know about me. I've put this off
long enough but I think you should know . . ."

She placed a finger against his lips. "No, I don't
want to hear it. Don't spoil things now. Tell me
tomorrow, after I've had time to adjust to being with
you like this." She made as if to rise. "I really should
be going."

He pinned her against him with the awesome
strength of his arms. "Not yet. Let me love you
again."

He ground himself against her and she sighed,
half in longing and half in regret. She really
shouldn't do this again. But Casey made it difficult
for her to refuse. She felt the weight of him against
her thigh, the shape of him, the hardness and
length, and melted into his embrace. Recriminations
could come tomorrow, tonight was hers to savor
and enjoy.

He stroked and aroused her and she responded by initiating a few bold caresses of her own. He loved the feel of her, the hunger inside her when she responded to his caresses. Their second coming together was every bit as wild and untamed as the first time, but Casey reveled in the knowledge that he had been able to prolong their pleasure this time. He felt strength coursing through him, a power heightened and finally released by the woman striving with him toward a common goal. He stroked his thick length to the root inside her, and smiled as she whimpered and writhed beneath him. He bent and drank her small cries from her lips, thrusting and withdrawing, until her cries became piercing, urgent, demanding.

The sharp edge of ecstasy pierced them, then splintered into millions of tiny glittering pieces. The outside world did not exist for the lovers inside the small room. They had stumbled upon something precious, something too earth-shattering to suffer interference from problems that threatened their newly discovered passion. Unfortunately forces were at work that would shatter those feelings.

Chapter 6

⟡⟡

"**Missy** Belle! Missy Belle! Where are you? Big trouble."

Still flushed and warm from Casey's loving, Belle bolted upright in bed. "That's Wan Yo! Something's wrong. Oh, God, I've got to get out of here."

Casey leapt from bed, pulling on his pants and shirt before Belle had struggled into even one of her petticoats. "I'll go out and see what he wants while you finish dressing. Hurry." He placed a quick kiss on her lips, unlocked the door, and stepped into the kitchen.

"What is it, Wan Yo? What happened?"

Wan Yo staggered into a shaft of light and Casey caught his breath in alarm. The old man was staggering drunkenly, favoring his newly mended leg, blood streaming from his head.

"Big trouble, Mr. Casey, poor Missy Belle."

A coldness settled in the pit of Casey's stomach. "Where is Tommy? Who hurt you?"

The old man wagged his head from side to side, dribbling blood into his eyes. "Bad men break into house, hit Wan Yo, take Tommy."

93

Belle came out of the bedroom, heard Wan Yo's last words, and screamed. She would have fallen to the floor if Casey hadn't caught her. Regaining her wits, Belle shrugged away Casey's support and went to Wan Yo. "Sit down, Wan Yo, and tell us what happened while I place a cool cloth on your head."

Suddenly realizing where Belle had been and with whom, Wan Yo sent her a reproachful look. "Tommy wait for you, but when you not come Wan Yo put Tommy to bed. Wan Yo fall asleep. Didn't hear bad men come in through window. Then Wan Yo hear struggle and go to Tommy. Too late, missy, too late. Man hit Wan Yo in head and take Tommy. Sorry, Missy Belle, so sorry."

"It's not your fault, Wan Yo, it's mine," Belle choked out.

"No, it's mine," Casey pointed out. "I should have been more vigilant. Tommy's abductors must have known Belle was . . . not in the house. How long ago did this happen?"

"No can tell. Two hours. Three. Hit on head knock Wan Yo out."

Casey spit out an oath. "Go back to the house, Wan Yo. I'll take care of this."

Wan Yo turned to go, then paused. "Almost forgot, man leave letter on Tommy's pillow." He handed Belle a sealed envelope.

"This has your name on it, Casey," Belle said. Stark, cold fear seized her. Why would Tommy's abductors write Casey a note? What was this all about? Too curious to let Casey read the note himself, Belle tore open the envelope. Five one hundred dollar bills drifted to the floor as she unfolded the slim sheet of paper inside.

The message was brief and to the point. When she

finished with it she threw it to the floor and flew at Casey, pounding him with her clenched fists.

"Damn you! Damn your traitorous hide! You're in cahoots with my miserable father-in-law."

Her unexpected attack nearly knocked Casey off his feet. Bracing himself, he grasped her wrists and tried not to hurt her as he dodged her feet, which she used in place of her imprisoned fists. "Dammit, Belle, what is it? What did the note say?"

Belle pulled away from his grasp, picked up the paper, and shoved it in Casey's face. "Don't try to deny this. It's all here in black and white and it all adds up. The reason you showed up in Placerville, your eagerness to get close to me and Tommy, your betrayal. Oh, God," she sobbed brokenly. "It makes me ill to think that you used me to get to Tommy. You seduced me, you bastard! I hope you're happy. You've just ruined two lives."

Before Casey could answer to the charges, he wanted to know of what he was being accused. Though truth to tell, he could well imagine. T.J. McAllister was full of tricks. No doubt this was his way of getting even with Casey for defying him. He should have been more careful, Casey reflected bitterly. It was utterly stupid of him to let his guard down. He should have known he'd be followed. His fault lay in his eagerness to return to Belle and Tommy.

Casey read the letter twice before letting it flutter to the floor. In essence, it complimented Casey for being a good detective and thanked him for finding his grandson. He enclosed a bonus of five hundred dollars for aiding him in Tommy's abduction.

Casey cursed himself a thousand times over. He had allowed one woman to make him forget years of specialized training. He wasn't proud of himself right now, and he deserved Belle's contempt. He realized that her guilt over what they had been doing when Tommy was abducted was as enormous as his.

"Well, do you deny you were hired by McAllister to find Tommy?"

Hands on hips, facing him nose to nose, Belle's temper was nearly explosive. Casey could literally feel the heat emanating from the hot centers of her eyes. He could feel not just her rage, but her fright and hurt as well. That he had hurt her so profoundly nearly vanquished him. He was as devastated as Belle by the turn of events. For it to happen now, right after they had made love, made their loving seem like a tawdry affair. And he hated that.

"Let me explain, Belle. After I'm finished I hope you'll understand. I took the job before knowing anything about you and Tommy except what I'd been told. I'm a detective, Belle, a damn good one. I never expected to become personally involved in this case."

"Didn't you? Were you instructed to make love to me? Did you enjoy making a fool out of me? I'm the stupidest woman alive for believing you cared what happened to me and Tommy. I let your pretty words turn my head."

Realizing she was growing hysterical, Casey grasped her shoulders and gave her a hard shake. "Stop it, Belle! You don't know what you're saying. I meant everything I said. I wanted to make love to you tonight for myself, because I care for you."

Belle gave a snort of laughter. "You have a funny way of showing it. Pick up your money and get out of here. I should have sent you packing a long time ago."

"I'm not going anywhere. You're going to sit down and listen to me." He swept her from her feet, sat her down in the nearest chair, and dropped to his knees beside her. When she tried to get up he pushed her back down. "This won't take long. I want to tell you about myself."

"I don't want to hear it. I feel nothing for you but disgust. Nothing you say will change my mind. Do you have any idea how guilty I feel for not being with Tommy when he needed me?"

"Belle . . ."

"And do you know where I was?" she continued, too wound·up to allow Casey a word in edgewise. "I was in bed with a man, behaving like a paid whore." She suddenly ran out of words.

"Belle, I'm sorry. Please let me explain. I work for the Pinkerton Agency. I never know what a job requires of· me. Allan Pinkerton sent me to San Francisco at McAllister's request. I was summoned at a time when I was in desperate need of money, and McAllister offered twice the usual fee. No, don't interrupt," Casey said when Belle started to speak.

"I'd spent all the money I had in the world hiring lawyers to defend my brother. Mark was accused of murdering a professional gambler over a card game. There was one witness who could have testified that the gambler drew first, but he took off for parts unknown. Consequently Mark was tried, convicted, and sent to Yuma Territorial prison. He'll spend the rest of his life there if the witness isn't found and brought to testify. Mark's lawyer says he can reopen the case if new evidence is found. I needed money, lots of it, to lure the witness forward."

"And you went after a little boy who never hurt a soul," Belle charged.

"McAllister offered a lot of money, plus a bonus for finding Tommy. I was reluctant to take the job at first, but the money won me over. McAllister said you were a whore, an unfit mother, that it would be in Tommy's best interest to find him so he could be given a proper upbringing."

"So you decided to find out if I *am* a whore, and bedding me tonight proved McAllister was right about me," Belle blasted.

Casey shook his head. "No, Belle, it isn't like that at all. I'd only known you a day or two when I decided McAllister had lied about you. You're not a whore. You're a beautiful young woman who loves her son dearly."

Belle glared at him in disbelief. "Then why did you betray us? I trusted you. I gave my heart and body to you. You're a no-good liar, Casey Walker! All this time you've been working for McAllister. You're probably lying about your brother. And even if you're not, it makes no difference to me. Tommy is the issue here. A small, defenseless little boy who needs his mother."

Pain and guilt nearly defeated Casey, but he had to make Belle understand. "I didn't betray you. Do you remember when I went to San Francisco a week or so ago? I saw McAllister and told him I was off the case. I refused to tell him where to find Tommy. He became angry because I took his money and couldn't pay it back. I gave him an IOU and promised him full payment."

"When were you going to tell me you worked for McAllister? When it was too late?" she asked. "It's too late now, Casey. Tommy is gone and I may never see him again."

"I swear I'll get him back for you, Belle."

"You're responsible for his abduction, why should I believe you?"

"Because I'm a man of my word."

Her laughter was without mirth. "You're a lying bastard who would do anything for money. I hate you, Casey Walker. I don't need your help. I'll get Tommy back and I'll do it my own way. Clear your things out of here. I never want to see you again."

Casey grasped her hands and pulled her to her feet. "You don't mean that, Belle. What about tonight? Did that mean nothing to you?"

"About as much as it meant to you," she retorted. "Let me go, there's much to be done and so little time."

"What are you going to do?"

"I'm going to beard the lion in his den. Get out of my way."

"Are you crazy? McAllister's a dangerous man. He's prepared to go to any length to keep Tommy."

"And I'm prepared to go to any length to see that he doesn't."

"Let me handle this. Maybe I can convince him to share custody."

Belle gave him a look that told him exactly what she thought of that idea. "The old man hates me. He thinks I'm responsible for Tom's death. He'd never agree to share custody. Don't you understand? I don't want your help. I don't want you anywhere near me. I'm going to do what I have to do and nothing is going to stop me."

"Dammit, Belle!" Unable to think of any way to stop her headlong rush into danger, Casey did the only thing he could think of at the moment. Seizing her arms, he pulled her hard against him and kissed her. Kissed her with his heart and soul and body. It was not enough.

Belle wrenched herself from his arms and struck

him across the face. She was sobbing openly now, and Casey wanted to pull her back into his arms and comfort her. She wanted nothing from him. She wiped her mouth with the back of her hand, grimacing with distaste. "Don't ever do that again!"

"Something happened between us tonight, Belle. Surely you cannot dismiss it as if it never happened."

"Damn you! You used me ruthlessly. Coldly. Allowing me to think you cared. Don't ever touch me again." Turning on her heel, she stormed from the room.

Casey watched her leave, feeling lower than dirt. He hadn't betrayed Belle, but he faulted himself for being careless. He should have realized McAllister would put a tail on him and set a false trail for them. McAllister was smart, he'd give him that. And determined. McAllister had planned well. His men made their move at a time when both he and Belle had been distracted and vulnerable. They must have been spying on them for days, waiting for just such a moment.

Now Belle blamed him for Tommy's abduction. She was convinced he had seduced her simply to get her out of the way while her son was being abducted. Shit! He should have refused the job, should have let Pinkerton send a replacement, but he had been in desperate need of money. Well, he had the money and he still felt like a heel.

Belle packed her suitcase through a veil of tears. Tommy was gone and it was all her fault. If she had been with him instead of cavorting like some whore with that damn detective, he would still be here with her. The San Francisco stage came through the day after tomorrow, and she intended to be on it.

There was so much to do before then. She had to take what little money she had accumulated from the bank, turn the diner over to Dolores and Sanchez, and help Wan Yo prepare for their departure. The old man was beside himself with grief and remorse. He blamed himself for not protecting Tommy, and nothing she could say or do seemed to help. When they returned to San Francisco, Belle decided she would send Wan Yo to Naomi, and hope the madam could help him overcome his guilt.

Two days later Casey was on hand when the San Francisco stage pulled out of Placerville. Belle neither looked at nor acknowledged him. He did manage to speak with Wan Yo and explain his position, but didn't know if the old man understood or not. Casey waited until the stage had loaded its passengers and rattled out of town, before mounting his newly purchased horse and riding hell-for-leather to San Francisco.

Exhausted and grimy from her trip over dusty, rutted roads, Belle disembarked at the Wells Fargo staging area two harrowing days after leaving Placerville. Wan Yo was as pale as a ghost while he waited for Belle to arrange for their luggage to be taken to their separate destinations. Belle's was to go to the Fremont Hotel and Wan Yo's to Naomi's Pleasure Parlor. Belle knew she didn't have a chance in hell of getting custody of Tommy if she lived with Naomi, so she had chosen the best hotel in town.

"Tell Naomi I'll be around to see her soon, Wan Yo," Belle instructed as they prepared to part.

"Where you go now, Missy Belle?"

"I'm going to the McAllister mansion."

"Wan Yo go with missy."

"No, this is something I have to do alone. I'll be all right. He won't dare hurt me. I'm Tommy's mother."

"Wan Yo think hard about Mister Casey. Maybe he tell truth. Maybe he no tell McAllister where to find Tommy. You need help, missy."

"I'd die before I accept help from that gutless detective. No, Wan Yo, don't let Casey fool you. Money is his master. He'll betray anyone for a price. I won't forget how he used me. I'll be at the Fremont if you need me. Go along, now, I'll see you soon."

Belle hired a hack to take her to T.J. McAllister's fashionable mansion located on Telegraph Hill. She paid the driver and stood before the gate several long minutes, before marshaling her courage and forging ahead. The gate was unlocked, and she let herself into the compound. She had scarcely reached the front steps when the door opened and a huge, barrel-chested man filled the entrance. He was toting guns on either hip and looked mean enough to chew nails.

"What do you want?" he asked harshly.

"To see my son," Belle replied, tilting her chin in open defiance. "I'm Belle McAllister, I demand entrance."

"Sorry, lady, no one comes in here without Mr. McAllister's approval."

"He can't keep me from my son."

He sneered in derision. "I know who you are. The boss told me all about ya. He hired me to protect his grandson. The law says yer a bad influence on the boy. Go away, you ain't gettin' in here." He started to shut the door in her face.

"That's not true!" Belle cried, shoving against the door. "I'm a good mother and I want my son."

"Tell it to the law."

"Wait! Just tell me how Tommy is. Is he well?"

"The kid's fine," the thug allowed. Just before the door slammed in her face, his insulting gaze slid down the length of her. "Maybe I'll see ya at Naomi's. You can't be too expensive, what with yer limp and all."

Shaking from rage, Belle stared at the closed door with growing horror. Would she never see her son again? Tears misted her eyes and she could actually feel her heart breaking. Not for the first time she cursed Casey Walker. If not for him she and Tommy would still be in Placerville, living in relative safety. Her only hope now was the law. She walked the entire distance to the sheriff's office, needing the time to compose her thoughts before confronting the lawman.

Sheriff Rogan leaned back in his chair and raised his brow inquiringly. "What can I do for you, ma'am?"

"My name is Belle Parker McAllister and I need your help."

The sheriff's attention sharpened. "Do tell. You wouldn't happen to be T.J. McAllister's daughter-in-law, would you? I've heard all about you."

Tried and condemned, Belle thought despondently. T.J. had certainly done his utmost to discredit her. "Whatever my father-in-law told you was a lie. He's taken my son. Kidnapped him right out of his bed. What kind of man would do that to a five-year-old who's never been parted from his mother?"

"Mr. McAllister wants what's best for the boy. He was in here just yesterday explaining what he'd done, and why. He had an order signed by the judge giving him custody of the boy. If you make trouble I can arrest you for disturbing the peace."

Belle stared at him in abject horror. "Not see Tommy? You're as mad as McAllister. He's my son. He needs me. He's only five years old. What grounds did McAllister have for taking Tommy from me?"

"He's the boy's grandfather and has every right to take the boy away from an unfit mother," the sheriff stated. "You go along peaceably, ma'am, and there won't be any trouble."

"You're out of your mind if you expect me to go away and leave my son to a man he despises. McAllister cared nothing for Tommy until his own son died. Then he suddenly has a change of heart and wants his grandson. He can't have Tommy, do you hear me!" Belle cried, growing hysterical. "You haven't heard the last from me." Whirling on her heel, she beat a hasty retreat. But she wasn't going far, oh, no. Only as far as T.J. McAllister's office.

"Tell her I don't want to see her," a gruff voice called through the partially opened door.

McAllister's secretary closed the door and gave Belle a sheepish look. "I'm sorry, ma'am, Mr. McAllister is . . . he's too busy to see anyone right now."

Belle wasn't about to take no for an answer. Marching past the flustered secretary, she flung open the door and stormed into the office. McAllister looked up at her forced entrance, his eyes narrowed in outrage.

"What's the meaning of this, Myerson? I clearly stated I didn't want to see this woman."

"I'm sorry, Mr. McAllister," the secretary stammered, "she pushed right past me."

"Get out, Myerson, I'll speak with Miss Parker."

Belle turned on McAllister the moment the door closed behind Myerson. "How dare you kidnap my son! And my name is McAllister, as you well know. I married your son, remember?"

McAllister's lips thinned. "I never recognized the marriage. I had a society marriage arranged for Tom, it would have been perfect for him. Then he fell into your clutches and you saw a chance to better yourself. You may have a license declaring the legality of the union, but I steadfastly refuse to welcome a whore into the family."

Belle's temper exploded. "You have no right to judge me when you know nothing about me! You visited Naomi's when I lived there. Did you ever see me go upstairs with a man? Did you ever see me do anything but serve drinks and clean up after the girls?"

"I could round up a dozen men who'd swear they had you."

Belle could hardly credit his words. "I knew you hated me, but I had no idea the lengths you'd go to ruin me. But no matter how much you hate me, it still doesn't condone what you've done to Tommy."

"Tommy is better off without you. He's a fine boy. The sooner he forgets you the better off he'll be. He'll have everything money can buy. When he's of age he'll inherit my wine empire, and more money than he can spend in a lifetime."

"What about love? Can you give him love?"

"I'm not incapable of giving love."

"You could have fooled me. I'm talking about a mother's love."

"Tommy will have nurses, nannies, and tutors. He'll lack for nothing. Now if you'll excuse me, I'm expecting an important client."

Belle thrust her jaw out stubbornly. "I'm not budging from here until you let me see Tommy."

"Impossible." He busied himself with a stack of papers piled before him on his desk. "I have an injunction forbidding any contact between you and my grandson. Break the law and I'll see you behind bars."

"Have you no heart? No compassion?"

"Not where you're concerned." He leered at her, his expression one of satisfaction. "You're a whore and I can prove it. Where were you when my men broke into your house and took Tommy?"

Belle blanched and staggered beneath his hurtful accusation.

"You don't need to answer, Belle, I know you were screwing Casey Walker. He's a damn good detective, dedicated to his job. I hope the pleasure he gave you was worth the loss of your son. Walker was worth every dime I paid him."

It was a vicious, calculated blow, and Belle was nearly vanquished by it. Yet McAllister knew exactly what he was about. His henchmen had been briefed on the situation and had followed Walker to Placerville. They spent several days spying on Walker and Belle before actually snatching Tommy. Their orders were to keep a low profile and take the boy without the knowledge of either Walker or Belle. The men had waited for the right moment and were rewarded when, spying through the window, they saw Belle go into Walker's bedroom.

When they saw Tommy leave the bedroom alone, they assumed that Walker would keep Belle occupied for several hours, and they were right. There was only one reason a woman went into a man's bedroom, and McAllister's spies had reported what they had seen upon their return to San Francisco. Leaving the note had been a stroke of genius, and McAllister congratulated himself for thinking of it. Getting even with Walker felt good.

Beyond speechless, Belle felt the lifeblood drain out of her. Casey Walker! He had cost her everything she loved and held dear. He might as well have taken a gun to her. Without Tommy, she had no life.

McAllister knew he had wounded Belle, but thought it only just considering how she had taken his son and heir from him. If there were tender feelings between Belle and Walker, his lies about the detective more than paid the bastard back for taking his money and betraying him. Belle had no choice now but to believe that Walker had used her to get to Tommy, and that pleased McAllister. He had killed two birds with one stone. He had defeated both Belle and Walker.

"I won't let you get away with this," Belle charged when she finally found her voice. "Beware, Mr. McAllister. One way or another, I'll get my son back."

With all the dignity she could muster, she turned and limped from the room. The interview had left her shaken and demoralized. She was hopelessly out of her league. She had no weapons to use against a man like McAllister. He held all the cards and she was outmaneuvered. But all wasn't lost yet. There had to be some way to stop McAllister from separating her and Tommy. With careful thought, she would find it.

* * *

Belle knew she would soon have to find cheaper lodging than the Fremont Hotel, for she had far better places in which to spend her money, but for the time being it sufficed. After her visit with McAllister she had no appetite for food, but since she had to keep up her strength she ordered a light repast from room service. While she waited, she bathed, donned her nightgown and robe, and sat in silent contemplation. She missed Tommy desperately and wondered if he missed her. She dried her tears, aware that wallowing in self pity was doing neither her nor Tommy any good. She had to direct all her energy toward finding a way to get him back.

A knock on the door brought her from her reverie. Thinking it was room service with her food, she thoughtlessly opened the door. When she saw the tall man filling the doorway, she tried to slam the panel in his face. Casey shoved the door wide, stepped inside, and closed the door behind him.

"What are you doing here? I told you I never wanted to see you again. How did you know where to find me?"

"I want to talk to you. I went to Naomi's and Wan Yo told me where to find you. Dammit, Belle, what will it take for you to believe I didn't lead McAllister to Tommy?"

"Nothing. I'll never believe you. McAllister knows what you and I were doing when Tommy was abducted. He told me you'd deliberately seduced me. He says it proves I'm a whore, and that the law will never grant me custody of Tommy."

Casey groaned in genuine dismay. "The bastard. He said he'd get even with me for taking his money and quitting the case. I wrote Allen Pinkerton for a loan. It was waiting for me at the post office.

Tomorrow I'm going to pay McAllister every dime I took from him. Perhaps I can convince him to share Tommy with you. It's better than nothing."

Belle turned her back on him. "I don't believe a word you've said, Mr. Walker. Good night."

Casey was at his wit's end. Belle was unreachable. She hated him and he couldn't blame her. Acting on instinct and a need for her to understand, he grasped her shoulders and turned her to face him. "Dammit, Belle, don't you know I care for you?" Desperate to prove his words, he pulled her against him and covered her mouth in a soul-baring kiss. Everything he felt, all he was and would ever be was centered in that kiss.

Despite the hatred she harbored for Casey, Belle fought the pounding in her blood and the sharp edge of desire spiraling through her. Was it possible to love and hate at the same time?

Casey felt her lips soften beneath his, and something dark and wild, a feeling embellished by memories of their loving and subsequent loss, made him deepen the kiss. But neither the compelling pressure of his mouth or the tantalizing thrust of his tongue could make the terrible hurt he had caused her more bearable. He tasted the salt of her tears and stepped away.

Belle retreated, her eyes gleaming with cold brilliance. "If you care for me, you'll find a way to get my son back for me." The pain in her voice overwhelmed him.

"You'll get Tommy back, Belle, I swear it." He had no idea how he would make it happen, but somehow he must. He wasn't the best damn detective in the Pinkerton Agency for nothing.

Chapter 7

Casey found cheap lodging in a not quite respectable, somewhat shabby inn on the waterfront that catered to sailors. Though it was not what he was usually accustomed to, it fit his slim purse. He retired early, intending to get a good night's sleep, but thoughts of Belle kept interfering. He'd tried without success to convince her that he hadn't brought McAllister's men to Placerville and felt so damn helpless. What made it all so confusing and difficult to explain was the very fact that in the beginning he *had* gone to Placerville with every intention of separating Belle from her son.

There were times when Casey hated the type of work he was involved in, and this was one of them. Earlier this evening when he visited Belle's hotel room, he'd had a difficult time keeping his hands off of her. His fingers itched to touch her, to caress her cheek, to stroke her body as he made love to her. Belle wanted nothing to do with him, however, and that one brief kiss she'd allowed him had shown him a hint of paradise that would never be his. He'd

110

blown his chance with Belle when he withheld the truth from her.

Finally sleep did come, but it was fraught with dreams. No matter how hard he tried, he could not forget Belle's horror upon learning he had worked for McAllister. Only one other time in his life had he felt this defeated, and that was when his brother had been found guilty of murder. With any luck Mark would be free, but it would take more than luck to regain Belle's trust.

Casey awoke early, ate breakfast at a nearby diner, and went directly to McAllister's residence. Since it was Sunday, Casey expected to find McAllister at home. Casey was determined to see Tommy no matter what, and no gunman was going to turn him away.

McAllister's bodyguard answered Casey's knock. "What do you want?" he asked curtly.

"To see your boss."

"He ain't receivin' this morning. Don't you know it's Sunday? Save your business for tomorrow."

"This business won't wait," Casey said, shoving past the bodyguard. "I'm not a helpless woman you can intimidate with your brawn." His right hand hovered dangerously close to his gun. "You can try to make me leave but it will be at your own peril."

"State yer business and I'll see if Mr. McAllister will see ya."

"He'll see me. Tell him Casey Walker is here to pay his debt."

The man pinned Casey with a speculative look, then shrugged. "Wait here. Don't go gettin' nosy or you'll be sorry."

"I'm not going anywhere," Casey said, leaning against the door and crossing his arms.

The bodyguard disappeared down the hallway, and Casey cast a curious glance up the staircase, wondering if Tommy's room was up there on the second floor. Then suddenly he no longer had to wonder, for Tommy appeared at the top of the stairs, accompanied by a stern-faced woman wearing a starched uniform over tightly corsetted flesh that gave the appearance of being stuffed into her dress.

Tommy spied him and gave a whoop of joy as he bounded down the stairs. Casey sank down on his haunches and scooped Tommy into his outstretched arms. Huffing and puffing, the nursemaid bounced down the stairs after him.

"Casey! I knew you'd come for me. I told mean old . . . I mean, grandfather, that you'd come and take me back to Mama." He glanced hopefully behind Casey. "Where is Mama? Why didn't she come with you?"

T.J. McAllister walked briskly down the hallway, saw Tommy in Casey's arms, and sputtered with outrage. "Mrs. Grundig, take the boy to his room!"

"No!" Tommy cried, clinging to Casey with almost frantic desperation. "I want my mama. Casey is going to take me to Mama and you can't stop him."

"You're wrong, my boy. You're mine to raise now. You're never going to see your slut of a mother again."

Casey carefully set Tommy aside, rose to his full, impressive height, and turned his glacial stare on McAllister. He bared his teeth in a feral smile. "If you ever call Belle that again you're going to be very sorry." His expression was hard, implacable, his voice threatening.

McAllister recognized the cold fury emanating from Casey and sidled close to his hired gunman. "Your threats don't frighten me, Walker. One false move and my man will blow you to kingdom come. You're trespassing, it's no crime to protect one's home and family."

"I'm here on business, and to see that no harm has come to Tommy. You're a ruthless bastard, McAllister. What would it have hurt to let Belle see her son when she called here yesterday?"

"Mrs. Grundig, do as I say, take Tommy to his room. Now!"

"No! I won't go! I want to go with Casey." Winding his arms around Casey's legs, Tommy refused to be dislodged. "Do I have to stay here, Casey?"

His little face was so pathetically hopeful, it nearly broke Casey's heart to have to tell him he couldn't return to his mother any time soon. Dropping to his knees, he pulled Tommy against his chest and hugged him tightly.

"You have to stay with your grandfather for the time being, Tommy. The law appointed him your guardian. But I'm going to do everything in my power to change that. Be brave and remember that your mother loves you. Go now with your nursemaid. I need to speak with your grandfather."

The nursemaid finally succeeded in prying Tommy from Casey's arms. As he was being dragged upstairs, he turned his tear-stained face back to Casey and gave him a watery smile. "I'll remember, Casey. Tell Mama I love her."

"I'm not a monster, Walker," McAllister declared. "I've grown fond of the boy. I've already changed my will in his favor. When I die everything I own in the world will go to Tommy. Taking the boy from his mother is for his own good."

"If you had a heart you wouldn't cut him completely from his mother. You're a compassionless, vindictive bastard, McAllister."

McAllister's face hardened. "State your business, Walker. It's Sunday, I'm not in the habit of conducting business on the Sabbath."

"And I'm not in the habit of conducting business in front of paid gunmen."

"Kellerman said you mentioned something about repaying a debt."

Casey nodded. "Can we speak in private?"

"Very well. Come into my study. But let me remind you that Kellerman will be right outside the door. One word from me and he'll come in blasting."

"How comforting for you," Casey remarked dryly.

McAllister led the way down the hall, opened a door and motioned Casey inside. "I'm not going to ask you to sit down, because you're not staying long enough to make yourself comfortable. Now, about that debt . . ."

Casey removed a thick envelope from his vest and tossed it on McAllister's desk. McAllister picked it up, pulled out the wad of bills, and started counting. "It's all there. My debt is paid in full."

"Where did you get this much money?"

"It's none of your business. We're quits, that's all that matters."

"So it seems. I'm a busy man, Walker, forgive me for not seeing you out."

"There's one more thing."

McAllister smiled cynically. "I knew there might be, but I'm disinclined to listen. Good-bye, Walker."

"Let Belle visit her son," Casey pleaded. He hated like hell to beg. "What can it hurt? You're killing her, McAllister."

"Payback time, Walker, she killed my son."

"Your son drowned."

"He wouldn't have if he'd married a woman worthy of him. Belle dragged him down in the gutter with her and forced me to disinherit him. If he hadn't married the slut, he wouldn't have been forced to take a dangerous job and he'd still be alive today."

"Your son had the gumption to stand up for what he wanted. Can't you bring yourself to relent? You already have custody of Tommy, what will it hurt to let him see his mother?"

"What will it hurt? Will it bring back my son? Will it make the boy a better person to know his mother is a whore? There is no way Belle Parker is going to corrupt my grandson like she did my son. Get out of here, Walker. You've said your piece and I've said mine."

White ridges of anger formed around Casey's clenched lips. "I'm not going to give up. I'm a detective, remember? I'm going to dig into your past until I find something so discrediting you're going to be forced to relent. If not, I'll lay your entire past dealings before the world. There's a streak of cruelty in you, McAllister. A man with your proclivity toward ruthlessness must have hurt people and made enemies to get to the top. I'm going to find those people."

For a moment McAllister looked discomfited. No, more than that, Casey thought, more like frightened. There was something in McAllister's past he didn't want revealed, Casey decided, and he was just the man to find it.

"You don't scare me, Walker. Do your worst. Now get out of here before I call Kellerman to show you the way."

"I'll be back to see Tommy."

McAllister laughed. "Good luck."

Belle sat at the desk in her hotel room contemplating the options open to her with regard to Tommy. They were pitifully few, and most of them unworkable. There seemed no way legally to get custody of Tommy. The law was against her. That left illegal means. And she was desperate enough to break the law. She was considering the various methods available to her when someone knocked on the door.

Recalling how she had opened the door last night and found Casey on the doorstep, this time she wanted no surprises. "Who is it?"

"Casey."

Belle went rigid. "Go away."

Determined to gain entrance, Casey said, "I've seen Tommy."

Predictably, the door was flung open immediately. Casey had spoken the magic word that had assured his entrance.

"You saw Tommy?" Excitement colored her words. "How is he? Is he being treated well?"

Casey stepped inside and closed the door behind him. "He is well, Belle. He misses you."

"Oh, God," she sobbed brokenly. "I can't stand it." She would have collapsed if Casey hadn't caught her up against him.

"You have to be strong, Belle. I tried to get McAllister to relent, but he was inflexible. Don't worry, I'll find a way to help you. I need time, please don't give up."

"Don't make promises you don't intend to keep, Mr. Walker," she snapped. "Just tell me about Tommy and get out of here."

"Tommy seemed fine, Belle. Though I don't condone his despicable behavior toward you, I believe McAllister cares for Tommy in his own way."

"How did you get in to see Tommy when his own mother wasn't allowed past the guard?"

Casey patted his gun. "It took a little persuasion, but I managed to convince the man to let me in. Besides, I had business with McAllister."

Belle scowled at him. "Unscrupulous business, I assume."

"I returned the money I owed McAllister. And I tried to convince him to let you see Tommy. Unfortunately, the bastard wouldn't listen to reason. But I'm not giving up, Belle. It hurts like hell to think of the pain I caused you, despite the fact that I'm guilty of nothing but taking the case before I got to know you and Tommy."

"I didn't expect McAllister to change his mind," Belle said with resignation. "He's always hated me."

"Did you know McAllister changed his will in Tommy's favor? Your son is going to be extremely wealthy one day."

"Money! Ha! Tommy needs me more than he needs money."

"I agree."

She lifted her brows in honest surprise. "Isn't it rather late for that sentiment?"

"It doesn't have to be. We can work together to get Tommy back."

"If you have nothing more to say, you can leave."

He couldn't stand it any longer. This coldness was tearing him apart. "God, I want you." The sincerity of his agonized words was evident in the spasmodic tightening of his hands as they reached out for her, in the gentleness of his touch as he drew her closer, and in the incredible yearning in his eyes as he touched her lips in a bittersweet kiss.

Belle's eyes widened in dismay as his lips came down on hers. A shaft of sunlight pierced through the window, sharpening the edges of his rough-hewn face and making the regret in his dark eyes more pronounced. Her pulse rioted even as her mind screamed in protest. She did not trust this man. Would never trust him again. Casey Walker would only cause her grief, and more heartache than she could bear.

Belle had given herself to him because she cared for him, and steadfastly refused to fall victim to his sweet lies a second time. But with him kissing her as if he'd die if he didn't, the will to resist fled. Yet if she didn't stop this assault upon her senses she'd be lost forever. She couldn't allow herself to feel anything for Casey Walker, not after the way he had betrayed her trust.

"Belle, please don't send me away. Let me comfort you. We need each other now more than ever." He wanted to lay her down on the bed and make her his again in a way that was as wild and tumultuous as a summer storm, as enduring as the moon and stars, and as sweet as ambrosia.

"I don't need you, Casey. All I need is my son."

"Tell me you don't want me," he challenged, kissing her again and again, begging her with his compelling kisses to believe him.

With Casey's mouth on hers, Belle found it difficult, if not impossible, to think rationally. Beset by insurmountable problems and assailed by Casey's passion, she felt as if she had entered the eye of a storm and was being buffeted from every direction.

"You're very persuasive, Casey," Belle said when she came up for air. "But not persuasive enough." She pushed herself from his arms, finding it the hardest thing she had ever done in her life. "I want you to leave. I've plans to make and people to see."

Casey eyed her narrowly. "You're not going to do anything rash, are you?"

She averted her gaze, refusing to look him in the eye. "I'll do whatever I must for Tommy's sake."

"Don't do anything until you hear from me. Promise me, Belle. I haven't finished with McAllister yet."

"I can't promise you anything. I have to leave now, I told Wan Yo I'd stop by Naomi's to see how he's getting along."

"I'll leave, but I'll be back. I've got some ideas of my own to pursue. If you need me, you'll find me at the Waterfront Inn. Send someone around with a message."

She turned her back on him. "I won't need you." She didn't turn around until she heard the soft click of the door closing behind him. Then she whirled to stare after him, her eyes misty with tears.

Things could have been so different, she lamented sadly. If Casey had been what and who he'd claimed to be when they'd first met, she could have found happiness with him. He had made love to her as if he truly cared for her, and like a fool she had fallen for his charming lies. She touched her lips, imagining the sweet pressure of his kisses. The taste of him, unique and totally his, still lingered in her mouth. Heat throbbed in her belly. To make it stop, she bit her lip until pain brought tears to her eyes. Determined to forget Casey, she cast his image from her mind and heart. Then she left her room and walked the entire distance to Naomi's Pleasure Parlor.

Naomi welcomed Belle with open arms and tears. "Oh, honey, I'm so sorry about Tommy. I'd give everything I owned if I could restore him to you. You know how much I love the little scamp."

Belle gave her a watery smile. She loved Naomi like a mother. Plump and pretty in an ostentatious way, Naomi was no longer young and was content now to forgo physical pleasure and run her establishment profitably. She was fair to her girls and they appreciated her care of them. Her place was clean, orderly, and extremely popular.

"I'm going to get Tommy back, Naomi, or die trying."

"Don't talk like that, honey," Naomi cautioned, leading her into the kitchen. "Of course you're going to get Tommy back. With that big detective on your side, you can't lose."

"Forget Casey. You don't know him like I do. Are you aware that he lied to me? He was working for my father-in-law."

They sat down at the kitchen table, and Naomi poured Belle a cup of tea laced with a dash of whiskey. "Drink this, honey, it will make you feel better. Casey was here yesterday," she continued. "He wanted to know where to find you. He spoke with Wan Yo. If that Chinaman didn't trust Casey, he wouldn't have told him a damn thing."

"In the beginning, Wan Yo was the one who didn't trust Casey. It wasn't until Casey spoke with him shortly before we left Placerville that Wan Yo changed his mind about him."

"I know. Wan Yo told me everything. I even spoke with Casey myself. I tend to believe him. I'll admit I didn't trust him when he came here weeks ago asking questions, but he didn't know you then. He swore he didn't tell McAllister you were in Placerville and I believe him."

"You're too good-hearted, Naomi," Belle contended. "But I didn't come here to talk about Casey. I have a plan and I need your help."

"I'll do anything, honey. Just tell me how I can help."

"First, don't scold me because my mind is made up. I want to hire men to kidnap Tommy from McAllister's house, and I don't know how to go about it. Tell me where to find the kind of men who will do anything for money, and I'll do the rest."

Naomi stared at Belle as if she'd just sprouted horns. "You can't be serious!"

"Very serious. If you won't help me, I'll do this on my own."

"Come on, honey," Naomi cajoled. "This kind of thinking will get you into a heap of trouble."

Belle's jaw tilted stubbornly. "Are you going to help me?"

"Is there any other way? Can't I talk you out of this?"

"No, I'm determined. Once I have Tommy again I'll head to Mexico, or maybe take a train east. I haven't decided yet. Now, where can the type of men I need be found? I don't care how unscrupulous they are, as long as they'll do as I ask."

"I'll blame myself if something goes wrong."

"Nothing will go wrong," Belle said with more confidence than she felt.

"I don't personally know anyone like you described, but I've heard my customers mention 'Sydney Ducks.' They're Australians who have jumped ship at one time or another and hang out at waterfront dives. They're a lawless bunch and will do anything for a price. They can be found almost any night in any one of those low places where no lady should be seen. Let me send Wan Yo, or one of my bouncers, to pave the way for you. I'll send word around to your hotel when contact is made."

Belle shook her head. "No, I have to do this myself. T.J. McAllister is a vindictive man. He could ruin you. I don't want you or your employees involved in my problems. All I ask is that you find transportation out of town for me and Tommy. I'll let you know the day."

"Do you need money?"

"No, I've taken enough from you. I have a thousand dollars saved up from my business in Placerville, and I'm prepared to use all of it to get Tommy back."

"How soon are you going to act?"

"Soon, maybe tonight. The sooner I find men willing to carry out my plan the better. Tommy needs me and I need him."

"Let me send someone with you."

"No, that will only raise suspicion. The kind of men I'm looking for will feel threatened if they see that I'm accompanied by a bodyguard. I have to go myself. I'll keep in touch."

Naomi sat at the table long after Belle left, lamenting Belle's rash behavior. She should have hogtied Belle to keep her from rushing headlong into danger. She had to do something to protect the woman she loved like a daughter, but what? Then it dawned on her. Casey Walker. He had told her where he was staying, and she dashed off a note telling him what Belle planned and the danger it involved. She dispatched it with Wan Yo.

An hour later Wan Yo returned from his mission without having seen Casey. He left the note with the proprietor, along with some money to ensure that it would be delivered when Casey returned to his lodging.

Belle waited until well after dark before leaving her hotel room. Covered from head to toe in a dark, hooded cloak, she hailed a hack to take her to the waterfront. Tucked in her reticule were five one hundred dollar bills.

"Are ya alone, lady?" the driver asked, eyeing her with misgiving when she gave her destination. "It ain't safe fer a lady down there."

"I . . . I'm meeting someone," Belle lied. "If you don't want the fare I'll find someone who does."

"It's yer funeral, lady. Get in. I'll take ya wherever ya want to go. The waterfront it is. Do ya have an address?"

"I'll tell you where to stop."

The hack rattled off down the street and Belle

admitted that she was courting danger. Then she thought of Tommy, alone and afraid, and courage stiffened her spine.

The waterfront looked dark and sinister. Fog swirled along the ground and drifted upward to engulf the hack in a suffocating mist. The eerie note of a foghorn sent its doleful siren's song across the dark waters. Only the lights spilling through the windows of the alehouses and inns clustered along the street gave a semblance of welcome. "Stop here, driver," Belle called through the window.

"Are ya sure, lady?"

"Very sure." The hack ground to a halt and Belle stepped down. "Please wait for me, I won't be long."

"Not a chance, lady. I ain't waitin' fer no one in a place like this. If ya want my advice, you'll get back inside the hack and go back where ya came from."

"Thank you, but I can't." She handed him the fare and watched regretfully as the hack rattled off down the street. Gathering her courage, she surveyed the plethora of alehouses lining the street. Picking one at random, she marched resolutely toward the beckoning light in the window.

The acrid stench of smoke and stale spirits assailed Belle's nostrils as she poised in the open doorway of the Wayfarer's Inn. The room was crowded with men, some wearing seamen's garb and others dressed in the rough clothing of longshoremen. Many looked like fugitives from the law. Then there were women, if one used the term loosely. In various stages of undress, they were draped around the patrons, blatantly inviting their rough caresses. Though Belle had been aware of what went on at Naomi's, the lasciviousness of the scene before her reddened her cheeks. Naomi's was definitely a more refined establishment.

All talk ceased when Belle stepped into the room, and all eyes turned in her direction. Her features were obscured by the deep folds of her hood, but there was no mistaking the small feminine form wrapped within the dark cloak. Stiffening her spine, Belle limped her way to the bar.

"If ya want a room, lady, ya come to the right place," the barkeep said. "Where's yer man? If yer lookin' fer one, there's plenty here to choose from." He made a sweeping gesture with his hand.

Belle swallowed past a lump of fear. "I'm looking for someone. Someone willing to do a job for me with no questions asked."

The barkeep's eyes grew flinty. "Ya got money?"

"Enough to pay generously for the job. Do you know someone who will fit the bill? I was told men known as Sydney Ducks frequented the waterfront."

"So it's Sydney Ducks ya want, eh? You've come to the right place." He motioned toward two men at the end of the bar, who were leering at her with lewd appreciation. "There be two of them, lady. That pair would be right happy to take yer money, and anything else ya got to offer." He laughed as if from some private joke.

The vulgar way in which the men were staring at Belle was nearly enough to cause her to flee. Their eyes gleamed with wicked intent and their faces revealed all too clearly their lustful thoughts. But the knowledge that Tommy was suffering in the hands of his unscrupulous grandfather gave her the courage to approach them.

"Look, Ferdie," one of the men said, addressing

his friend, "if I ain't mistaken we're gonna get lucky tonight."

"Aye, she looks like a rum one to me, Joey."

Belle heard their remarks and ignored them. "Are you men interested in a proposition? You could earn a great deal of money if you are."

"Who do you want us to kill, lady?" Joey snickered.

Belle gasped, aghast at their callous disrespect for life. She could expect no less from men culled from the dregs of society. "I don't want you to kill anyone. I just want you to remove my son from a certain house and bring him to me. It won't be easy. The house is heavily guarded."

"Blimey," Ferdie said, "that don't sound hard. How much ya willin' ta pay?"

"Five hundred dollars," Belle stated emphatically. "The boy is my son; he's five years old. His grandfather took him away from me and I want him back. The house is on Telegraph Hill."

"Telegraph Hill, ain't that where wealthy nobs live?" Ferdie mused. His voice hardened. "We want the money first."

Belle was too smart to fall for that ploy. "No, you'll get the money when I have my son, not before."

"How do we know ya got that much money," Joey asked slyly.

"You'll just have to take my word for it."

"No thanks, lady." They turned away, their interest waning.

Belle was desperate. If all Sydney Ducks on the waterfront were like these two, demanding payment first, she'd never get Tommy back. Trusting them was out of the question. She feared they'd take off with her money without fulfilling their part of the bargain. "I can pay you and I can prove it." Their attention sharpened. "I have the money with me. If I show it to you, will you help me?"

"You have the money with you?" Joey said, sharing a knowing look with Ferdie. "Well, now, that changes everything, don't it, Joey?" Joey nodded eagerly. "Where is the money, lady?"

Belle's mouth went dry. She felt as if she was jumping from the frying pan into the fire. Did she have an alternative? The answer was obvious. "I have the money with me, that's all you need to know. If you'll turn around I'll take it out and show it to you."

Joey was actually drooling. "No, not here. There are too many people around. Come outside. Once we see the money you can tell us where to find the boy."

Belle cast a fearful glance out the window and swallowed visibly. Trusting these two greedy-eyed creatures was dangerous. The matter was taken out of her hands when Ferdie and Joey flanked her on either side and herded her out the door.

Once outside, Joey grinned at Belle and held out his hand. "Right-ho, lady, show us the color of yer money."

"Do you promise to follow my instructions? I don't want my son hurt, mind you. And no killing."

"We won't hurt anyone, will we, mate?" Joey said, winking broadly at Ferdie.

"Not bloody likely," Ferdie lied.

Too desperate to think past getting her son back in her arms where he belonged, Belle opened her reticule and pulled out a roll of bills.

Joey's eyes gleamed. "Ain't that sweet, mate." He

tried to grab the reticule from Belle's hands but she snatched it away in the nick of time.

"Give it to me," Ferdie snarled.

All Belle's senses screamed of danger. "No!" She started to run, but the men weren't about to let that much money get away from them. They grabbed Belle from behind and backed her into a dark alley. Joey tore the reticule from her grasp, while Ferdie pushed her to the filthy, garbage littered ground and fell on top of her. Filling her lungs with air, Belle screamed and screamed and screamed, until Ferdie smashed his fist in her face, sending her into a black abyss.

Chapter 8

❧❧❧❧❧

Darkness had settled over the waterfront when Casey returned to his lodging. He had spent most of the day reading through old copies of newspapers and going through records at city hall. A few times he'd thought he'd found something worth pursuing, then the lead fizzled out. But he wasn't giving up. At some point, McAllister must have done something he wasn't proud of. Unscrupulous men often left a trail of enemies, and Casey was determined to uncover McAllister's shameful secrets. If he could ferret them out, Casey was banking on the fact that McAllister wouldn't want them revealed, and would then be willing to listen to reason where Tommy was concerned.

Casey entered the Waterfront Inn, nodded to the proprietor, and started up the stairs to his room. He was nearly to the top when he was hailed from below.

"Mr. Walker, you have a letter." He waved a sealed envelope in the air. "I'd almost forgotten."

Casey bounded back down the stairs and seized the letter, hoping it was from Belle. "Thank you, Mr.

Lambert." Casey tore open the envelope and read the message as he climbed the stairs. Suddenly he stopped, spit out a curse and leapt down the stairs to the landing. "Who delivered this, Mr. Lambert?"

"A Chinaman."

"How long ago?"

"Late this afternoon. I hope it isn't bad news."

"It could be." He tried to contain his fear, but he knew it was there in his expression. He had cautioned Belle not to do anything rash and she had foolishly chosen to disregard him. Thank God for Naomi's warning. He prayed he would locate Belle before danger found her.

Casey made the rounds of the alehouses, saloons, and inns scattered along the waterfront. After visiting the first half dozen, he dared to hope that Belle had given up her ill-advised scheme. He entered the Wayfarer's Inn, saw nothing to indicate that Belle had been there, and strode to the bar to question the barkeep.

"I'm looking for a woman," Casey began. "The kind of woman not normally seen on the waterfront. She's small and exceptionally pretty. Oh, yes, she walks with a slight limp."

The barkeep eyed Casey warily. "What's it to ya? Is she yer wife?"

"Not my wife, but a friend. I'm afraid she may be in trouble. If you haven't seen her I'll be on my way."

"Wait! What's it worth to ya?"

His shifty eyes gave Casey a glimmer of hope. The man knew something, he was sure of it. Casey wasn't flush with money, but he still had enough to make the man's mouth water when he pulled two ten dollar bills from his pocket.

The barkeep's fist closed on the money. "Yeah,

she was in here. And if ya want my opinion, she was beggin' fer trouble. She left not five minutes ago with a scurvy pair of Sydney Ducks.''

Casey paled visibly. Whirling on his heel, he pounded out the door. He reached the sidewalk and came to a screeching halt, faced with the challenge of selecting the direction in which Belle had gone. Then he heard a scream, and another, and another, then silence, and he no longer wondered where Belle had gotten to. The screams came from the alley between the Wayfarer's Inn and another equally unsavory establishment.

Moments later he was standing at the alley's entrance, squinting into the swirling spirals of darkness and fog. What he saw froze the blood in his veins. There were two men. The one nearest him was rifling through a woman's reticule. And the other, oh, God, the other knelt between a woman's outstretched legs. He was shoving her skirts past her thighs as he fiddled with the buttons on the front of his trousers. The woman appeared comatose; she was neither moving nor protesting his rough handling. Intuitively Casey knew it was Belle and wanted to kill the two men hurting her.

Casey gave a roar of outrage and charged down the narrow alley toward the man straining over Belle, ignoring the other man in his haste to get to Belle before serious harm was done to her. Ferdie never knew what hit him as Casey lifted him off Belle and threw him against the side of the building. There was a sickening thud as his head struck wood, and then Ferdie began a slow slide to the muck-littered ground.

"Here now, what did ye do to me mate?" Joey thundered. He dropped Belle's reticule and reached for the weapon he carried beneath his jacket. He wasn't fast enough. Joey's hand had yet to reach his gun when Casey aimed his own at the thug's head.

"Drop the gun," Casey order brusquely. Joey did as he was told. "Now pick up the reticule and put the money back into it." Again Joey obeyed. "Now hand it to me." Joey held out the purse and Casey tucked it into his waistband. "Take your friend and get out of here. If I ever see you attacking helpless women again I won't give you a second chance. Move!" Casey ordered when Joey failed to act fast enough.

The look on Casey's face dissuaded Joey from lingering. He half dragged, half carried Ferdie out of the alley. "If you've done the lady permanent damage you can't run far enough or fast enough to get away from me. I'll find you no matter where you go."

Once the men rounded the corner, Casey pocketed Joey's gun and dropped to his knees before Belle. She was still out cold. Carefully he picked her up, gathered her cloak around her, and carried her out of the alley into the fog-thickened night. When he paused beneath a street lamp, he saw the dark swelling on her jaw and spit out a curse. He was sorry now he had let the bastards get off so easily. At first he'd thought Belle had merely fainted, but he saw now that she had been struck a hard blow. A moment later she moaned, and Casey turned in the direction of the Waterfront Inn.

Since his own rooms were closer, Casey did not even consider taking Belle to her hotel. Or to Naomi's. If her injuries were serious she needed immediate attention, and finding a hack on the waterfront this time of night would be next to impossible.

A few men sat in the common room of the inn when Casey entered, but they paid scant attention to the man carrying a woman up to his room. Things like that happened all the time on the waterfront. Only the proprietor appeared interested, and only because a second person in the room cost extra.

"If she's going to stay the night it will cost you a dollar more," the proprietor informed Casey as he started up the stairs.

"Fine, add it to my tab," Casey bit out curtly.

Once in his room he placed Belle on the bed and carefully undressed her. It was difficult not to become aroused by her nudity as he searched for injuries and he tried to think of anything but her soft white skin beneath his fingertips. He covered her quickly when he found no damage, and dipped a cloth in water to bathe her forehead.

Belle stirred and moaned, instinctively seeking the coolness sliding across her forehead.

"Belle, wake up. Speak to me, love."

Belle opened her eyes, blinking when a hazy image began to take shape. Casey! She started to rise, felt a sharp pain begin behind her eyes and fell back against the pillow.

"Where am I?"

"In my room."

Her eyes widened. "How did I get here?"

"Don't you remember?"

She started to shake her head then thought better of it. "No."

"Think hard, love. What were you doing on the waterfront? Who were those two men I found you with?"

Belle's brow furrowed. It hurt to think. And when she did start to remember, all she could recall was pain.

"Belle, if Naomi hadn't gotten a message to me those men might have killed you. What in God's name were you thinking to come down here by yourself? Thank God I found you in time."

Memory came to her on a rush, and with it keen disappointment. She had failed. Now she'd never see her son again. The anguish of that thought was unbearable. Huge tears rolled down Belle's pale cheeks and she doubled over in pain.

"Where do you hurt, love? Should I go for the doctor? I should have killed those bastards when I had the chance."

"I remember now, one of them struck me. I don't know what happened after that. I wasn't . . . They didn't . . . ?"

"I arrived before they got to you," Casey assured her. "You were out like a light. I brought you to my room because it was closer than your hotel. You have a bruise the size of a lemon on your left cheek and a black eye, but no other injuries that I could tell."

Suddenly Belle realized she was naked beneath the covers. "You undressed me!"

"I had to know if you sustained injuries elsewhere. Get some rest, love, it's too late now to take you back to your hotel. And I'm not sure we could find a hack this time of night. I'll take you back in the morning."

Belle nodded warily. It occurred to her that Casey had saved her from dangerous situations on more than one occasion. But she wasn't sure she trusted herself to spend the night in Casey's bed. And she sure as hell didn't trust Casey.

She started to rise but found she wasn't as strong as she had hoped. Her head throbbed and her body ached from Ferdie's mauling. She fell back with a sigh. When Casey chuckled, she sent him a sour look.

"You're weak as a kitten. Go to sleep, Belle, I'm

not going to ravish you. You'll feel stronger in the morning. Then we'll talk about how foolish you were to attempt something like this."

"Where are you going to sleep?"

Casey's gaze settled on the empty spot beside Belle on the bed.

"Oh, no," Belle protested. "I don't trust you."

"You've made that abundantly clear. Nevertheless, I'm tired. I've had a busy day and an even busier one awaits me tomorrow. We can share the bed. You're too weak for me to molest. When we make love again I want you fully awake to enjoy what I do to you." ·

He plopped down on the side of the bed and Belle scooted as close to the opposite edge as she could get without falling off. When Casey pulled off his boots and stood to shed his pants and shirt, she deliberately looked away. The mattress dipped and Belle heard the covers rustle and felt him settle down beside her. She held her breath, fearful of what would happen next, knowing that she didn't have the strength to resist him. Then he started snoring softly and she allowed herself to breathe again. Moments later she joined him in slumber.

Shortly before dawn the mist grew heavier, wrapping the night in a chilling embrace. Fog curled through the open window of Casey's room, enveloping the occupants in bone-numbing dampness. Belle shivered in her sleep and unconsciously sought Casey's warmth, snuggling against his back and twining her legs with his. Her warm little body tempted Casey from sleep, luring him into a dream-like state where fantasy nudged aside reality. Casey's body instinctively reacted to the knowledge that the woman he craved above all others was cuddled warmly against him.

He turned to embrace her, pulling her flush against him, her head resting in the crook of his neck. He inhaled deeply, savoring the sweet scent of her flesh. If he was dreaming he never wanted to awaken. Her body fit his like a glove. Inadvertently his hand brushed her breast and a breathless little sigh slid past her lips. When he tried to remove his hand, instinctively she sought it again, thrusting her breast impudently into his palm. He squeezed gently and heard her sigh again.

Casey was wide awake now, and fully aroused. He tried to ignore his pulsing erection but with Belle's body molded against his he could think of nothing but thrusting himself between her sweet thighs. He had every intention of pulling away and letting her sleep. Instead he raised on his elbows and allowed his fingers to glide over her cheeks and caress her lips. He ached to kiss her, just once, then he'd leave her alone. He leaned toward her and lowered his head, brushing her lips with the gentlest of kisses. His tongue slid along her bottom lip and he felt it tremble.

His mouth settled over hers in a light caress. He would end it soon, he told himself. Then he felt her lips part under his and her fingers slide into his hair, urging him closer, and the feather-light touch of her tongue as it mated with his.

He loved the way her body arched sharply upward to meet his, the way her round, ripe breasts pushed into his chest. She tasted of sunshine and sweetness. Her skin felt smooth as satin beneath his fingertips. Casey growled low in his throat as his control slowly eroded.

Belle was having the most erotic dream. Her body tingled and burned. Her breasts felt swollen and heavy, her nipples distended and tender. Her mouth was filled with the heat and taste of . . . Casey! Oh, God, was she sleeping or awake? When she felt the roughness of Casey's tongue mating with hers she knew this was no dream. He whispered her name and Belle felt her world spinning out of control.

"Casey, don't," Belle gasped. "You promised." She was acutely aware of his body, hard and aroused and urgently pressing against hers. "Don't," she repeated, not completely sure she meant it.

"Don't make me stop," Casey pleaded hoarsely. He filled his hands with her breasts, caressing them, working the peaks until they pebbled. He kissed her again, this time with all the longing that had been building inside him.

"I hate you, Casey." She kissed him back, making a mockery of her words. "I don't trust you."

He kissed her harder, deeper, his hands sliding down between her legs to caress her there.

Her small fingers sifted through the hair on his chest. He could feel her trembling, feel the heat of her body, and went crazy with wanting. He couldn't stop her now if his life depended upon it. She wanted him as much as he wanted her.

"Don't fight this, Belle. Trust me. I want to love you."

Then he was kissing her eyes, her nose, her cheeks, finally taking her mouth again and plunging his tongue inside. His hands grasped her buttocks, cupping them, kneading them, setting her aflame with his passion. His fingers probed her sweet sheath. Shivers sped through her body and a fever roared through her blood.

It was difficult to move, to think, trembling as she was. "Casey, you're too experienced for me. You could make a piece of wood want you. Please stop."

"I'm not making love to a piece of wood, love. It's you I want, and you want me, too. Open your legs, I want to come inside you."

Desire crested, became consuming. She moaned against his hungry, voracious lips, unable to deny him. Her legs parted slightly and he knelt between them, pushing them wide as he settled atop her. His fingers teased her, thrusting into the slickness of her desire, the heat of his touch kindling the fire inside her. Instinctively she arched against his hand, yearning for more than he was giving her, and hating herself for letting him use her again.

Then he was lifting her, pressing inside her, the heavy weight of his sex filling her with mindless pleasure. Even as she deplored her wanton response to a man she couldn't trust, she grasped his buttocks and urged him toward the core of her, grinding her hips against his.

He drove into her again and again. It was fever, madness, and wanting. And something more. Something so precious it defied words. His face was contorted with terrible need, his cheeks hollow, his eyes dark and hungry. He took and took and yet he gave.

Caught up in a whirlwind of passion, Belle arched upward, her nails digging into his shoulders as the fever rose to an unbearable pitch, and then she exploded in climax. Sharp, volatile, debilitating. Lost in a haze of intense rapture, Casey shouted out his own climax in a fiery torrent of sensation.

She lay there beneath him, her arms holding him tightly, feeling him shudder as he poured himself into her. An eternity later he moved off her and held her close. Several more minutes passed before his breath steadied enough for him to speak again.

"Are you all right? I don't know what got into me. I'm not usually that rough. We're explosive together, Belle." He turned to kiss her and tasted salt. "Are you crying? I *did* hurt you." Remorse colored his words.

Belle shook her head. "You didn't hurt me. I'm angry and disgusted with myself. You touch me and I become a slave to your passion. My body embraces yours while my mind rejects you utterly. I'm so ashamed. You cost me my sòn."

"Your mind doesn't reject me, love. Deep down you know I wouldn't hurt you or Tommy."

Belle wanted to believe Casey, but she couldn't forget the underhanded way in which Tommy had been taken. He was abducted while Casey kept her occupied in his bed. "I know nothing of the sort. I can't help the way my body responds to yours. Trusting you isn't nearly as easy as responding to you sexually."

"It would be if you let yourself believe. I care for you, Belle."

"Don't. Don't say anything you don't mean. I can't bear it."

"I'm going to restore Tommy to you, I swear it."

Belle closed her eyes against the pain. Only a miracle would give her back her son. McAllister was against her, the law was against her; was there no justice in this world? Nothing had ever been easy for her. Meeting Naomi, loving Tom, and having Tommy had been the memorable highlights of her otherwise troubled life. From childhood to adulthood her life had been difficult. She had desperately needed to trust someone, and she briefly thought she had found that someone in Casey.

And she needed someone to love, someone who would love her back.

"If you were able to get Tommy away from his grandfather, then I might be able to trust you again, Casey."

"It's not going to be easy, but I've already started working on it. Just believe in me, Belle, that's all I ask."

She couldn't, not yet, maybe never. But it was comforting to be held in his arms, especially after the way those despicable men had terrorized her. If not for Casey, she might be dead now. Of her own free will her arms slid around his waist, tightening around him. If she could forget Casey's betrayal, she would take joy in this night. She would savor the closeness of Casey's hard body, his kisses, his hands and mouth arousing her, loving her.

Unaware of her confused thoughts, Casey pressed her closer, wanting her again, needing her. When he moved on top of her she moaned in acceptance, and when he kissed her she opened her mouth to the thrusting of his tongue. He came into her with one deep plunge. Solid, hard, full. He began moving in and out of her, deeply, frantically, riding her hard and deep, one pounding thrust after another. Sensation after sensation tore through her, hurling her into a chasm of blinding pleasure, and when she reached that climactic pinnacle, she called out his name.

She felt him go rigid, felt his seed pumping into her body, and then he went limp. Afterward, he pulled her into the curve of his body and went to sleep.

* * *

Casey awoke to find Belle gone. He leapt out of bed, cursing himself for having overslept. The sun was high in the sky and the waterfront was a beehive of activity. He wanted to rush after Belle but had no idea what he would say. He'd already bared his heart to her, made promises he wasn't certain he could fulfill, and there was nothing more to say. Action spoke louder than words and he hoped that making love to Belle last night demonstrated how deeply he cared for her.

When he finished his investigation of McAllister he'd be in a better position to make demands. And his first demand would be to allow Belle full or partial custody of her son. Until that day arrived, Belle would continue to close her mind to him even if she couldn't shut down her body's reaction to his loving.

Casey left the inn, intending to resume his search for incriminating evidence through dusty records in city hall. When he approached the telegraph office he ducked inside, inquiring if a telegram had arrived for him from Simon Levy. He had wired the lawyer upon his return to San Francisco and was expecting a reply. He worried excessively about Mark, and as soon as this mess with Belle and Tommy was resolved he intended to return to Arizona and renew his efforts on his brother's behalf.

A telegram had indeed arrived for Casey. And it was good news. At long last the missing witness had been found and Casey was needed in Yuma. Mark had been granted a new trial and Casey had two weeks in which to reach Arizona. He cursed fervently and hurried off to make arrangements for an immediate departure. The thought of leaving Belle when she needed him most tore him apart. Last night he had told Belle he cared for her, and he was just now beginning to realize that his feelings went deeper than mere caring. He loved Belle, and he loved Tommy. He wanted to be a part of their lives forever.

But until his brother walked out of Yuma Prison a free man he couldn't think about a future with Belle. Oh, God, it was so difficult, so damn painful. He was being pulled in different directions. His heart was pulling him one way and duty the other. As soon as Mark was acquitted, he vowed to return to San Francisco and keep his promise to Belle.

Belle packed her meager belongings and checked out of the hotel. The expense was draining her scant resources and she needed every penny she had saved to fight McAllister. She knew Naomi's house was always open to her, and decided to accept Naomi's offer to move back to the Pleasure Parlor.

Naomi greeted her with relief. Then she saw the dark swelling on Belle's face and paled. "My God, what happened to you?" She wrung her hands in dismay. "I was so worried, honey. The moment you left here yesterday I knew you were headed for trouble. But there was no dissuading you. I hope you're not mad because I told Casey Walker."

Wan Yo appeared then and took her suitcase, looking as pleased to see Belle as Naomi was. "Wan Yo worried, Missy Belle." He studied her bruised face and scowled.

"I'm fine, Wan Yo," Belle assured him. "Take my suitcase up to my old room, please. I hope you don't mind my moving back in here," she said to Naomi.

"You know better than that. What about the rest of your things?"

"The hotel is sending them over." She settled

down on the sofa with Naomi. Most of the girls were still sleeping, so they had the parlor to themselves. "About Casey, Naomi, you did the right thing. I did get myself into trouble. Thank God Casey arrived in time."

"Did you two make up?"

Belle flushed and looked away. "Not exactly. I don't know if I will ever trust him again."

"Wan Yo told me you were in Casey's room the night Tommy was abducted. Does that mean what I'm thinking?"

"Casey used me, Naomi, and like a fool I fell for his lies. I thought he cared for me."

"Maybe he does. Why is it so difficult to believe he didn't lead McAllister to Tommy?"

"Casey was in McAllister's employ. He was paid to locate my son. Tommy was abducted while I was . . ." her voice quivered, "in Casey's bed. The facts speak for themselves."

"Facts aren't always what they seem. If Casey didn't care for you, he'd wouldn't have gone looking for you last night. Tell me what happened. Did you actually go to the waterfront? Who hurt you?"

"I went, all right. I was a naive fool to think I could rely on my own wits. I was nearly raped by two men I encountered in a dockside saloon." She touched her bruised cheek and winced. "One of them struck me. I don't really recall what happened, or how Casey found me. I was unconscious and woke up in Casey's room much later."

"I'd say you've got some serious soul-searching to do, Belle. Wan Yo says Casey has intervened in your behalf more than once since you've met. That ought to count for something."

"I can't allow myself to become involved with a man, not with Tommy consuming all my thoughts and energies."

"So you spent the night in Casey's bed," Naomi surmised. Belle thought it amazing the way Naomi could get down to the heart of the matter in so short a time.

Belle averted her eyes. "I was injured; Casey insisted I rest in his room until morning."

Naomi stifled a smile. She had said all she was going to say on the subject. "You look exhausted. Go on up to your room and rest, I'll send a lunch tray up to you later."

Before Belle could reply to Naomi's suggestion, the clatter of the brass door rapper announced a visitor. Belle looked at the clock on the mantel and shrugged. "It's a mite early but I'm not one to turn away business."

A maid opened the door and Casey Walker stepped inside. He strode across the hall into the parlor. His gaze settled on Belle and did not waver as he briskly walked toward her. Belle felt the impact of his hot gaze and her knees nearly buckled beneath her. He looked so big and virile and handsome. And he had loved her with so much passion last night. She felt her flesh burning with the memory.

"I need to speak with Belle alone, Naomi," Casey said when he reached the two women. His gaze never left Belle's.

"It's up to Belle," Naomi said, looking askance at Belle.

"It's all right, Naomi, I'll talk to Casey."

"Go on into my office, it's more private there. My girls will be wandering downstairs soon."

Belle nodded and led the way into Naomi's

private office. "How did you know where to find me?" Belle asked once they were alone.

"I went to the hotel first. They told me you'd checked out. I knew there was only one place you'd go."

"I thought we said everything there was to say last night."

"Why did you leave without a word?" He studied her bruised face and was sorry he hadn't killed the two men that hurt her. "Are you all right?"

"I'm fine. I left because I didn't want to engage in another tireless round of arguments. Thank you for rescuing me."

Casey reached inside his jacket and pulled out Belle's reticule. "Here, you left without this. Your money is all there."

Belle's eyes widened in shock. "I thought the men got away with it last night." She hugged it to her breast. "Thank you, Casey, you don't know what this means to me. I didn't mention it last night because I thought it was gone. Is that all you wanted? To give me my purse?"

Casey ruffled his fingers through his hair as he stared at her. Belle wondered why he appeared so upset. "Is something wrong?"

"You could say that. I received a telegram. The missing witness has been found and I'm needed in Arizona. My brother has been granted a new trial and I need to be there for him."

Belle felt as if the rug had been pulled from beneath her. She studied her hands. "There is nothing keeping you in San Francisco."

Casey spat out a curse and roughly raised her chin until their eyes met. "Dammit, Belle! I don't want to leave but I have to." He cursed again. "I want to stay and help you, but I can't let my brother down. I'll be back, I promise."

"Of course." Belle's heart felt like it was breaking. Her body felt heavy and lifeless. Surely she didn't expect Casey to remain now that his job was finished, did she? "You don't owe me anything, Casey Walker. Your brother needs your support, go to him."

"Promise you won't do anything foolish while I'm gone," Casey pleaded, desperately needing assurance that she'd be safe until he could return to her.

Belle merely stared at him. He grasped her shoulders and shook her roughly. "Promise me, damn you!"

"I'll make no such promise. I'll do what I must for Tommy's sake."

Frustrated beyond bearing, Casey kissed her with searing fervor, again and again, until they were both breathless. He wanted to do more than kiss her, but this was neither the time nor the place. His stage left in less than an hour.

"I have to go, Belle. But I *will* return, and I *will* get Tommy back for you."

He kissed her again. Hard. Then he strode out the door without looking back.

Chapter 9

The days following Casey's departure were difficult ones for Belle. Naomi and Wan Yo were a comfort, but they couldn't help solve any of Belle's problems. Or ease her heartache. Tommy was out of reach and even Casey had deserted her. Casey's leaving shouldn't make her feel as if she'd been abandoned but it did, and she couldn't understand why. He had used her, betrayed her, and then abandoned her. Oh, she knew his brother needed him, but she still couldn't help feeling utterly alone and defenseless.

Belle didn't want to miss Casey. He had promised to return, but she was afraid to set too much stock in his words. It wouldn't be the first time he had lied to her. He had made her care for him then betrayed her trust. Despite knowing that, she had still allowed him to make love to her after he rescued her from that vile pair of Sydney Ducks. It had seemed so right, so wonderful at the time. Oh, God, she needed Casey. Just to know he was nearby . . .

But he wasn't nearby. McAllister still had Tommy and she had no one to rely upon but herself. Each day she left the Pleasure Parlor and walked to the McAllister house, hoping for a glimpse of Tommy. She had walked up and down the block so many times in the past several days she knew how many blades of grass grew between the cracks in the sidewalk. Twice a man called at the house and gained entrance. She had no idea who the man was, for she didn't get a good look at his face.

Once she thought she spied Tommy in an upstairs window but when she waved, the shadowy figure disappeared and she was no longer sure it was Tommy she had seen. One time the bodyguard came outside and chased her away from the front gate. She usually lingered in the vicinity until dark before trudging back to Naomi's.

Then one sunny day Belle saw Tommy leave the house with his grandfather, nursemaid, and bodyguard. They hurried the boy down the front walk and into a waiting carriage. Belle saw them from across the street and rushed heedlessly into the road to hail them. McAllister saw her and whipped the horses into a fine lather, nearly running her down in the process. Her bad ankle gave beneath her and she fell, calling out Tommy's name. He must have heard her, for his pale face appeared at the back window. He started to wave and then someone pulled him down so she could no longer see him.

Belle lay in the road, sobbing as if her heart were breaking. They couldn't do this to her. She was a good mother. She didn't deserve this kind of treatment.

"Are you hurt, lady?"

Belle looked up into the eyes of an elderly, poorly dressed man with thinning gray hair and piercing, almost colorless gray eyes. A concerned frown puckered his brow as he endeavored to help her to her feet.

"I'm not hurt, thank you," Belle said as she rose unsteadily to her feet and dusted off her torn skirt.

"Why did McAllister try to run you down?"

"You know him?"

The man's sallow face assumed a wistful expression and his eyes dimmed with memory. "Not anymore. He could have killed you. Why?"

"It's a long story. It's getting dark, I should go home."

"Can I help you?"

"I'll be all right, thank you, Mr . . ."

"Hopkins. Harry Hopkins. Are you sure I can't help you?"

"I'll be fine, it's only a short walk back home." She certainly didn't want Mr. Hopkins escorting her to Naomi's. What would he think?

She turned and limped away, looking back over her shoulder only once. Harry Hopkins was gone, having disappeared as mysteriously as he had appeared. During the walk home Belle came to a decision. She couldn't go on this way. She had to see Tommy.

Belle hoped to slip up to her room without being seen, but Naomi had been watching for her. She met Belle at the foot of the stairs and pulled her into her office.

"What the hell happened to you? Look at you, you're covered with dirt, and your dress is torn beyond repair." Her eyes narrowed. "Who hurt you?"

"I slipped and fell," Belle lied. She knew if Naomi learned the truth, she'd feel obligated to involve herself in this battle and McAllister could ruin the madam with little effort. Belle had to fight McAllister on her own.

"Sure, and I'm a society matron," Naomi said, rolling her eyes. "Why won't you let me help you?"

"There is nothing you can do. My father-in-law is a powerful man."

"When Casey comes back he'll find a way," Naomi said with firm conviction.

"*If* he comes back. He's lied to me before."

"Don't give up, honey, something good is bound to happen soon."

Belle sighed. "You're right, something *is* going to happen. I'm tired, Naomi, I'm going upstairs. You have duties and I'm keeping you from them."

Just then a commotion broke out in the parlor, and one of the girls burst through the door to report to Naomi. Naomi gave Belle an apologetic shrug and left in a flurry of petticoats. Belle peeked out the door, saw that the hallway was empty, and quickly closed the door. It wouldn't do for her to be discovered rummaging through Naomi's belongings. She went quickly to Naomi's desk, opened the top drawer on the left, and immediately found what she was looking for.

Lying atop a sheath of papers, the gun Naomi used when her bouncers needed help evicting troublesome customers gleamed wickedly in the dark recesses of the drawer. Handling the gun gingerly, Belle checked the chambers, saw it was fully loaded, and slipped it into her pocket. Then she quietly left the office, hurrying to her own room to make her plans.

While lingering outside McAllister's house, Belle had learned several helpful facts. The bodyguard made rounds twice a day around the perimeter of the property—at ten in the morning and seven in the evening—and the front door was usually left unlocked in anticipation of the bodyguard's return. After the evening rounds he locked the front door and then took supper in the kitchen. He wasn't seen again in the front part of the house for an hour or better, allowing Belle sufficient time to gain entrance and confront McAllister. All she had to do was choose a time when McAllister was home.

Belle waited until Saturday night, when customers began arriving at Naomi's earlier than on weekdays. By six o'clock Naomi was too busy to notice Belle leaving through the back entrance. The weight of Naomi's gun rested comfortably in her pocket. Wan Yo took note of her departure, but was so accustomed to seeing Belle leave at odd times of day and night that he paid her little heed.

Belle walked as fast as her lame leg would allow, arriving at the McAllister house shortly before seven o'clock. She crept around to the back and noted that McAllister's horse and carriage were in the carriage house, which meant he was home. So far so good, she thought as she made her way to the front of the house and positioned herself behind a flowering hibiscus to wait and watch.

Kellerman exited the front door right on schedule. He walked to the gate, looked up and down the street, checked the front windows, then walked around the side of the house to the back. Belle moved with alacrity the moment his back was turned. Her steps were surprisingly agile as she raced toward the front entrance. Suddenly she had second thoughts about the gun she carried. Breaking into a man's home with a loaded gun was both stupid and dangerous. Removing the gun from her pocket, she emptied the chambers onto the front lawn. Then she turned the doorknob and ducked through the front door. She never noticed the slouched figure watching from across the street.

Inside the foyer she frantically searched for a place to hide until Kellerman returned from his rounds and went to the kitchen for his supper. She found what she was looking for in a large statue located in a dark corner. She scooted behind it and pulled her skirts around her scant seconds before Kellerman reentered the house and locked the door behind him.

The sound of Kellerman's heavy steps rang in her ears as he plodded past her down the hallway. Belle peeked out from behind the statue as Kellerman opened a door, poked his head inside and called out, "All's secure, boss. I'm going to take my supper now."

Belle heard a muffled reply but not the words. Not that it mattered. She knew McAllister was home and now she knew where to find him. She waited until Kellerman's footsteps could no longer be heard before leaving her hiding place. The foyer was cast in shadows both menacing and welcome as Belle tread quietly toward the door behind which she expected to find her ruthless father-in-law.

Before her courage failed her, she turned the knob and entered the room. She closed the door quietly behind her and stood in the shadows, staring at T.J. McAllister.

"Back already, Kellerman? Did you forget something?" McAllister asked without looking up from the evening paper he was perusing.

"It's not Kellerman and you've got something that's mine."

McAllister started violently. "How did you get in? Where is Kellerman?"

"Eating, I would assume. As to how I got in, where there's a will there's a way."

"Well you can just twitch your little butt out of here. This is Saturday night, you should be at Naomi's turning tricks."

Belle blanched. "You must really hate me."

"You can't begin to know how much. Get out of here."

"I want Tommy."

He gave a bark of laughter. "You can't have him."

Belle shoved her hand into her pocket and felt the weight of the gun. "You're wrong. You and I are going upstairs to get him right now."

"You've got guts, I'll give you that much, but you're beginning to bore me, Miss Parker."

She curled her fingers around the gun and slid it out of her pocket. "Maybe this will persuade you."

McAllister stared at the gun, then at Belle, and realized she was dead serious. "What do you intend to do with that?"

"You'll find out if you don't let me see Tommy," she threatened. "I'm desperate. I have no life without my son."

McAllister gave a nervous laugh. His gaze didn't waver from the gun in Belle's hand. "Put that thing down before you hurt someone."

"You have every reason to be afraid, Mr. McAllister," she warned. "You've taken everything from me, I have nothing to lose. Get up, we're going to find Tommy." Her finger caressed the trigger.

McAllister rose slowly. He considered Belle mad enough to shoot and wasn't taking any chances. Besides, she'd never get out of the house with the boy. And even if by some remote chance she did, she wouldn't get to the city limits.

Jubilant, Belle followed McAllister out the door. She didn't know what she would have done had McAllister refused to obey. She was desperate, but she could never kill another human being, that's why she had emptied the chambers of the gun beforehand. No matter how despicable T.J. was, he was still Tom's father and Tommy's grandfather.

"You're making a big mistake, Belle," McAllister said, glancing nervously over his shoulder at Belle. "You can't pull that trigger and you know it."

"I can and I will," Belle said with false bravado. "It would be so easy to kill you. Men like you are a menace to society." Belle couldn't believe she was saying such terrible things. It was so unlike her to make empty threats, but McAllister had driven her past reason. "Take me to Tommy and you won't get hurt."

The wild pounding of her heart drowned out the sound of footsteps creeping up behind her as she prodded McAllister toward the staircase. Caught up in a maelstrom of anticipation and yearning—she was so close to Tommy—Belle was completely focused on her son and sorely oblivious to her surroundings.

Suddenly she was turned violently and the gun wrested from her hand. Kellerman did not release his hurtful grasp as he handed the gun to McAllister. McAllister opened the chamber, saw it was empty and snorted in disgust.

"The damn thing isn't even loaded."

"You want me to send someone for the sheriff, boss?" Kellerman wanted to know.

Before McAllister could reply, Tommy appeared at the top of the stairs. His eyes lit up when he saw Belle and he flew down the steps before his nurse-maid could stop him. He started beating on Keller-man, who had Belle pinned against him.

"Don't hurt my mama! You're a bad man. Let my mama go!"

"Tommy." Belle sobbed out his name and he immediately went to her, his little arms hugging her waist fiercely. Then he turned to McAllister, his eyes blazing furiously. "I hate you, Grandfather!"

"What should I do with her, boss?" Kellerman repeated. "The bitch threatened you. I heard her. She belongs behind bars."

McAllister looked at the sobbing Tommy and couldn't get the boy's words out of his mind. He didn't want to live the rest of his life with his only grandchild hating him. "No, don't call the sheriff, she's harmless. Throw her out."

"Harmless, hell," Kellerman mumbled as he un-locked the door and pulled it open. Before he could toss Belle out he had to literally peel Tommy away from his mother.

Tommy screamed uncontrollably as Belle landed in the grass at the bottom of the front steps. McAllis-ter walked to the door and stared dispassionately at Belle. Tommy continued to scream long after he was dragged upstairs by his nurse.

Belle sprawled on the lawn, too stunned to move. She wasn't hurt badly, just bruised and humiliated, and so damn frustrated she wanted to lie there and die. Once again she had failed. It had been disgust-ingly foolish to think she could settle things this

way. Look where it had gotten her. Tossed out on
her ear and Tommy so upset she could still hear his
cries echoing through the night.

Gingerly she picked herself up, found she could
stand, albeit not without considerable pain, and
limped away. McAllister stood watching her from
the open doorway. He waited until Belle was out of
sight then tossed the gun into the shrubbery.

Belle was too upset and ashamed to tell anyone
about this fiasco tonight. She had planned to return
the gun before Naomi missed it, sparing herself the
humiliation of an explanation. Her plan had been
foiled by McAllister, and she had neither the gun
nor the bullets in her possession. Her shoulders
slumped in dejection, Belle trudged home wearily.

McAllister returned to his study. Tommy had
finally gone to sleep but McAllister had been deeply
disturbed by the boy's tears. He had come to love
the boy. Tommy was all he had left in the world, and
he wanted to give the child every advantage money
could buy. One day, when Tommy was older, he
would thank his grandfather, that much McAllister
knew, but until then the boy would have to learn to
get along without his mother.

"Any instructions for the night, boss?" Kellerman
asked, poking his head inside the study.

"Keep alert tonight. I'm sure there won't be any
further trouble, but I can't afford to take chances. I
didn't realize how determined that woman was."

"Sure thing, boss. Good night."

Kellerman locked the front door, checked all the
windows in the front of the house, then went to the
back of the house, repeating the process. Before he
reached the back door, he was distracted by a
kitchen maid who had caught his eye some time

ago. She was alone, the kitchen empty but for the flirtatious girl. When she gave Kellerman a provocative smile and twitched her hips at him, the brawny but not-too-bright bodyguard forgot everything but the aching bulge in his trousers. Grasping the girl, he kissed her hard. When she didn't object he kissed her again with gusto. After a few clumsy caresses he bent the girl over the kitchen table, flipped up her skirts, and thrust himself into her.

For the next two hours he pounded his desire into the willing girl he'd lusted after since spying her in McAllister's kitchen. Both he and the girl were pleasantly exhausted when they parted. The maid took the back stairs to her quarters, and Kellerman went to his own room. The kitchen door had been forgotten and remained unlocked.

Sometime later a shrouded figure let himself in through the rear entrance. He moved silently through the kitchen and down the hallway. He seemed to know exactly where he was going, for he moved unerringly toward McAllister's study. He opened the door noiselessly and stepped inside.

He saw McAllister sitting in his chair before the hearth, his head resting on his chest in slumber. Though his steps were nearly soundless on the thick carpet, McAllister must have sensed a presence for he opened his eyes just as the intruder raised a gun to his head.

"You!"

That was the last word McAllister ever spoke. The gunshot reverberated sharp and deadly through the stillness of the night. The assassin didn't wait to see if he'd killed his prey, there was no need. The blood and gore splattered on the wall behind McAllister was proof enough. Dropping the gun on the floor, the killer turned and quickly pried open the window, flinging himself through it and onto the ground below. The drop was a short one and he rolled once, gained his feet and sprinted off into the dark night.

Kellerman awakened to the sound of a gunshot exploding in the night. Several minutes passed before his dazed mind realized what it was that he had just heard. It occurred to him that he hadn't been vigilent enough. He found McAllister's body slumped over in his chair, and his brains splattered nearby.

"The damn bitch," he cursed as he headed out the door to summon the sheriff.

Belle slept late and arose feeling battered and bruised. While bathing she found several places on her arms and legs that had been scraped bloody. She supposed she had gotten them when she was thrown bodily from McAllister's house. There was even a raw place on her face that she wouldn't be able to hide from Naomi. She sighed despondently and turned her thoughts to Tommy. That one glimpse of him had been worth the small injuries she had suffered. Her heart ached when she recalled how he had clung to her and begged his grandfather not to hurt her.

She couldn't imagine what had gotten into her last night. Taking the gun from Naomi and brandishing it before McAllister had been stupid and utterly self-defeating. What did she hope to gain? Even if the gun was unloaded it was still considered a weapon. Since she no longer had the gun she'd just have to explain to Naomi what she had done and listen to the lecture that was bound to follow.

Naomi was waiting for Belle in the parlor. The madam took one look at the scratches marring Belle's face and arms and threw up her hands in defeat. "Where were you last night? Look at you! What did McAllister do to you?"

"It was my fault, Naomi, I shouldn't have . . ."

Her words were halted in mid-sentence by a racket at the front door. "Open up, it's the law!"

"Oh, Lordy," Naomi said, rolling her eyes. "Whose wife complained about us this time?"

Usually the law didn't bother her as long as her girls caused no problems and no one was murdered on the premises. But every now and again the wife of one of her customers complained and a deputy came by. It was little more than a formality, one Naomi usually solved with dispatch.

Naomi sighed heavily. "I'll get rid of them. Stay here, we haven't finished our discussion."

She went to the door, opened it and put on her most engaging smile. "Good morning Deputy Clancy, Deputy Roth. What can I do for you? It's a little early, but I can roust out a couple of my girls if you'd like to . . ."

"We didn't come for that. They pushed Naomi aside and strode into the parlor.

"Why are you here? Has some do-gooder complained about us again? Whatever it is, I'm sure there is a good explanation."

Clancy looked beyond Naomi at Belle. "You've done nothing, Naomi. We're here to place Belle Parker under arrest."

Naomi gasped and clutched at her throat. Her head swiveled around to look at Belle, who had turned deathly pale. "What has Belle done?"

Clancy walked into the parlor, grasped Belle's

wrists, and snapped on a pair of handcuffs. "Come along quietly, miss."

Numbness, disbelief, fear, all those emotions and more rendered Belle utterly speechless. Not so Naomi.

"What has Belle done?" She crossed her arms over her ample breasts and glared at Clancy and Roth. "You're not taking Belle away unless I know what crime she's being charged with. Surely it's not serious enough to warrant you taking her away in handcuffs like some dangerous criminal."

"Some people consider murder a very serious crime. T.J. McAllister was a prominent man in San Francisco. His murder is going to rock the city."

Belle's legs bucked beneath her and she would have fallen if Naomi hadn't placed a supportive arm around her.

"My father-in-law is dead?" Belle repeated shakily.

"His brains were blown out last night," Roth pointed out crudely. "With Miss Parker's gun."

"No! I didn't kill him!" Something terrible had happened and Belle didn't know what to make of it. She was confused, angry, and so frightened she was shaking visibly.

"That's nonsense," Naomi scoffed. "Belle doesn't own a gun, never did. I don't think she could use one even if she had one."

Clancy nodded to Roth, who pulled a small revolver from his jacket pocket and displayed it before Belle and Naomi. Naomi's eyes widened, recognizing it immediately. She sent Belle an oblique look, raising an immediate outcry from Belle.

"No, Naomi, I would never do such a thing!"

"Do you recognize the gun, Miss Parker?" Clancy asked. "According to witnesses it is the same gun you threatened Mr. McAllister with last night before he had you thrown out of his house for trespassing."

Belle stared at the gun then quickly looked away. "I didn't kill anyone. My father-in-law took the gun away from me and that's the last I saw of it. Besides, it wasn't loaded."

Clancy gave her an incredulous look. "If what you say is trué, how did it come to be used for the murder?"

"Perhaps it's not the same gun Belle brought with her to McAllister's house," Naomi offered.

"That's for the judge to decide. There are witnesses who saw and heard Miss Parker threaten Mr. McAllister. A conviction is almost certain. Come along, Miss Parker, the lieutenant wants to question you."

"Naomi, I didn't do it, I swear!" Belle cried. Until now the seriousness of the charge hadn't really begun to sink in. But this wasn't some horrible joke, this was real. These men actually believed she had killed her father-in-law.

Suddenly the thought of Tommy alone in the big house with no one to protect him set her heart to pounding. "Wait!" she cried, balking when the deputies tried to steer her out of the house. "What about Tommy? What will happen to my son now?"

Clancy shrugged. "You'll have to ask the judge that question at your hearing. Come along quietly, we don't want any trouble."

"Try not to worry, honey," Naomi said, wringing her hands. "The sheriff will recognize his mistake and let you go."

"Find out what happened to Tommy," Belle begged as she was dragged from the room and out the door. "Help me, Naomi. Oh, God, help me."

Belle was thrust into the paddy wagon waiting at the curb. The sound of the door slamming in her face had a ring of finality to it. She stared dazedly out the small barred window, shock numbing her mind and her body. She was being charged with a murder she didn't commit, and no one but Naomi cared. If only Casey were here, she thought, her mind staggering beneath the weight of that statement. She shouldn't want Casey so desperately, not after the way he had betrayed her. If not for Casey, she wouldn't be in this predicament. She and Tommy would still be in Placerville, living in anonymity. But no matter how hard she tried to disavow her feelings for Casey, her need for him was too strong to deny.

But she hated Casey, she told herself. She'd never trust him again. Hate and love. Both emotions were so closely related, it was difficult to tell where one stopped and the other began. They fed off one another. Love did not exist without hate; there was no heaven without hell. No good without evil. Since meeting Casey she had experienced all those emotions. She still hated, still distrusted, still wanted the one man she could love.

Belle was taken to a small cell to await Sheriff Rogan. Her back ached from sitting stiffly on the stool, and her wrists and hands were still numb from the handcuffs, which thankfully had been removed. She was almost relieved when the sheriff appeared. He stood over her in an intimidating manner, which did nothing to bolster Belle's confidence.

Rogan wasted no time with preliminaries. "You can save both yourself and me a lot of trouble by confessing, Miss Parker."

"My name is Mrs. McAllister, and I have a marriage license to prove it," Belle returned shortly. "I did not kill my father-in-law, so how can I confess to something I didn't do?"

Rogan cleared his throat. "There are witnesses willing to testify in court that you broke into McAllister's home last night and threatened him in their hearing. He had you thrown bodily from his house. You had to be angry enough to kill. Admit it, there was bad blood between you. The gun that killed McAllister is similar to the one you carried last night, in fact, it *is* the same gun, isn't it, Mrs. McAllister? You broke into his house and killed him."

He had thrust his face so close to hers she could smell tobacco smoke on his breath and count the tiny hairs growing out of his nose.

He gripped her shoulders hurtfully. "Confess, Mrs. McAllister, and save us all a lot of anguish."

"No, I didn't do it, I swear!" Belle cried, twisting from his grasp. "You can't make me confess to a crime I didn't commit. All I'm guilty of is trying to frighten Mr. McAllister into letting me see my son. The gun wasn't even loaded. I dumped the bullets before I entered the house."

"If that's the way you want it, Mrs. McAllister, then so be it. But you should know that the grounds were searched and no gun or bullets were found. Clancy," he barked, summoning his deputy.

The door opened immediately, admitting Officer Clancy. "Take Mrs. McAllister to her cell. We'll let the judge decide if there is enough evidence to bring her to trial."

Three days later Belle stood before the judge, listening to Kellerman explain how she had broken into the house and threatened McAllister. Even the nursemaid was brought forward to testify to Belle's guilt. Belle blanched when they repeated almost word for word the threats she had issued to their boss. During the hearing, the bad blood that existed between her and her father-in-law was outlined in detail by McAllister's lawyer. The same man who had drawn up the papers in which McAllister had disinherited his son, and more recently petitioned the judge for custody of Tommy on McAllister's behalf.

When Belle was finally allowed to speak, her claim of innocence was scoffed at. The judge had already made up his mind to hold her over for trial. The charge was first-degree murder.

Adding to Belle's grief was her concern over Tommy's welfare. When she voiced that concern, the judge ruled that Tommy would be sent to an orphanage. He would reside at Saint Francis until a new guardian was appointed.

Chapter 10

~~~
   ∽◯◯∽
~~~

Casey waited outside the gate of Yuma Territorial Prison for his brother to appear. He had arrived in Yuma in time for the trial and briefing by Mark's lawyer. The witness to the shooting had been a traveling salesman passing through town, who hadn't even known he was wanted to testify in Mark's trial. A timid man, the drummer had become frightened after witnessing the shooting and hopped the next stage out of town.

He'd learned he was being sought after reading an ad placed in newspapers and flyers throughout Arizona, and in large cities located all over the West. The reward mentioned convinced Duell Brickley to return to Yuma. Plenty of opportunists in search of a fast buck had showed up in answer to the ad, but the barkeep where the fatal game and shooting occurred identified Brickley as the missing witness. Casey thanked God he'd had the money to offer as a reward, but he still felt a twinge of guilt for the way it had been obtained. Not even the fact that he hadn't betrayed Belle to McAllister served to ease his conscience.

Casey was anxious to return to San Francisco. Since his arrival in Yuma an uneasiness had settled over him. Call it a premonition, call it a warning, whatever it was Casey knew it involved Belle and Tommy. He felt it now, a heavy weight pressing against his heart. His fears were confirmed that morning when he had received a mysterious telegram from Naomi. It said little except that Belle needed him, and it was imperative that he return to San Francisco as quickly as possible.

Casey thought of Belle and their tumultuous parting a few weeks ago, and wondered if she had forgiven him yet. Not likely, he decided. Until Tommy was with her again she'd never let Casey into her life. He had forced a response from her body but her mind was dead set against him. She had been so desperate he prayed she hadn't done anything foolish in his absence.

Suddenly Casey heard a metallic clang that could mean only one thing, and his thoughts returned to the present. This was the day Casey had been waiting for. The day Mark was to be released from prison. Casey saw him now, standing outside the gate, looking pale and wan, but free, oh, God, free at last. Casey's smile widened as he dismounted and slapped Mark on the back. Then he hugged him exuberantly. Once Mark realized he was standing outside the gate, and that the guards in the tower were paying no attention to him, he whooped jubilantly and returned Casey's hug with equal vigor.

"Let's get back to the hotel," Casey said, handing Mark the reins of the horse he had rented in town. "We need to make plans for the future."

The short ride back to town was accomplished mostly in silent appreciation as Mark drank in the sights and sounds of nature and freedom. He breathed deeply of the clean air, remarked on the clear blue of the sky and majesty of the mountains. Casey smiled to himself, never having heard Mark wax poetic about anything in his life, except maybe a beautiful woman.

Back in their hotel room Casey began pacing. "Something's on your mind, Casey, what is it?" Mark asked. "You haven't mentioned the case you were working on in San Francisco. Is it resolved?"

"Not by a long shot," Casey said, stopping before Mark. "I have to return. The sooner the better, and I want you to come with me."

Mark smiled, displaying a dimple in his chin identical to Casey's. "Why? I promise not to get into trouble again. I learned my lesson, brother."

"There is nothing here for you, Mark. We sold the house Pa left us to pay for your lawyers. You've no job, no money to speak of . . ."

"I have a couple hundred dollars saved. I lost my job at the newspaper office but there are other jobs to be had out there. Why must you return to San Francisco?"

"Sit down, Mark. If you're considering coming with me it's only right that you know. Here, read this," he said, removing the crumpled telegram from his pocket and handing it to Mark.

Mark read the telegram with a growing curiosity spreading across his face.

"Who in the hell is Naomi?"

"The madam of a popular brothel."

Mark gave Casey a wicked grin. "And Belle?

Don't tell me she's one of Naomi's stable of girls. I've never known you to get involved with whores. Is she part of this case you're working on?"

"In a way. I was paid a generous bonus by a wealthy wine grower to find his grandson. Belle is the boy's mother. She had disappeared with her son after her husband's death."

"You found them, I take it. To my knowledge you've always found your man . . . or woman. So what happened? I assume there is more to it than you're telling me."

"McAllister described Belle as a whore who tricked his son into marriage. He claimed she was a hard-hearted, cold-blooded mercenary and an unfit mother. It didn't take long to track Belle down. She was nothing like McAllister described."

"Sounds interesting. Go on."

Casey left out nothing, including the guilt he felt for making love to Belle while her son was being abducted. "The note McAllister's men left was meant to punish me for taking his money and refusing to deliver his grandson. His men followed me to Placerville and found Tommy anyway. It's my fault for not being more careful. I should have covered my tracks and not taken McAllister for granted. I misjudged him."

"If Belle was the loving mother you described, I suppose she was devastated to lose her son."

"You can't begin to know how much. We both tried to seek a compromise with McAllister, but he had been given sole custody of the boy and refused to allow Belle visitation rights. Before I left I asked Belle not to do anything foolish. To trust me to find a solution. But she doesn't trust me. She believes I betrayed her. She hates me, Mark, and that hurts."

Mark searched Casey's face, realizing just how devastated his brother was by Belle's rejection and his part in creating it. It was unlike Casey to become personally involved in a case. "If Belle hated you like you say I'm surprised she'd let you make love to her." His astute observation made little impression on Casey.

"I was too experienced for her. I seduced her both times. And now this telegram." He waved it in front of Mark. "I'm leaving on the next stage and I'd like you to come with me."

"You care about this woman, don't you, Casey? This goes far deeper than simply wanting to help her."

Casey began pacing again. "I've never felt this way about a woman, Mark. Did I mention Belle is lame? She was injured as a child and didn't receive proper treatment for her injury. But her deformity doesn't diminish her beauty. She's truly lovely, in both body and spirit. I've always been a cynic when it came to . . . to matters of the heart, but my feelings for Belle are too unsettling to ignore. All I know is that Belle is in trouble and I'm not there to help her. It's killing me. I have to help her. I need to learn if what I feel for her is real or merely a passing fancy."

Mark gave Casey a cocky grin. "You're not the type to indulge in passing fancies, brother. Your tale intrigues me. How could I not go with you when you've tickled my imagination so thoroughly? I want to meet this Belle and decide if she's worthy of my brother. This time it's my turn to help a brother in trouble. I know you can't have much money left after paying my lawyers and the witness, but if we pool our money we can find comfortable quarters in

San Francisco while I look for a job. I can see you
need me, Casey, and I want to be there for you."

The stage rolled to a stop and discharged its
dusty, tired passengers at the Wells Fargo depot.
Casey and Mark were the last to step down. They
made their way to a modest hotel, reserved two
rooms, then went directly to a bathhouse to clean
up. An hour later, they were on their way to
Naomi's Pleasure Parlor, freshly bathed and shaved
and wearing clean clothes. Neither Casey nor Mark
had eaten, but Casey promised Mark a substantial
meal after he had spoken to Belle and discovered
the nature of the trouble she had gotten herself into.

A maid answered the door and ushered the men
inside. The parlor was already buzzing with activity
and Mark eyed the girls appreciatively as Casey
located the madam across the room, talking to one
of the customers. Naomi spied Casey almost at the
same moment he saw her. Naomi excused herself
and made her way unerringly to Casey.

"Thank God you're here. I'm so worried about
Belle."

Alarm raced through Casey. He could tell by the
panic in Naomi's eyes that things were even more
serious than he had suspected.

"Where is Belle?"

"It's a tragedy, that's what it is," Naomi wailed.
"I feel so damn helpless."

Casey gnashed his teeth in frustration. He
grasped the madam's shoulders and gave her a not-
so-gentle shake. "Dammit, Naomi, tell me what
happened."

"They took her away. She didn't do it, Casey, I'd
stake my life on it."

"Who took her away? You're not making sense."

"Belle is in jail, awaiting trial for murder. I've hired a lawyer but the defense is shaky at best. There are witnesses who saw and heard Belle threaten McAllister."

Casey blanched. "Are you saying that McAllister is dead and Belle is charged with his murder?" Christ! He'd just gone through this with his brother. "That's absurd."

"Come into the office," Belle said, "it's too public here." She cast a furtive glance at Mark, then looked askance at Casey.

"This is my brother, Mark," Casey said. "Mark, meet Naomi."

Naomi nodded absently, too upset for polite greetings.

"Go with Naomi, Casey," Mark said when he noted the madam's impatience to get Casey alone. "I'll wait out here." He scanned the parlor, his gaze settling on a curvaceous blonde with a girlish face standing by the piano. "I've been in jail a long time," he continued, "maybe I'll just . . ."

Naomi noted the direction of Mark's gaze and gave a throaty laugh. "That's Sweet Sue. Tell her I said to show you a good time, it's on the house."

Casey didn't wait around to see if Mark took Naomi up on her generosity for the madam literally dragged him into her office. The minute the door latched behind them, Naomi broke down, her face contorted in anguish.

"Belle took my gun, Casey. I didn't even know she had it. She broke into McAllister's house and threatened to kill him unless she was allowed to see Tommy."

Casey groaned in dismay. "Why didn't she wait? I told her I'd come back and help her."

"She doesn't trust you, Casey, you know that. She blames you for losing Tommy. In a way you can't blame her. You *did* work for McAllister."

"You know I didn't lead that bastard to Tommy," Casey snarled.

"I believe it, but try convincing Belle. But none of that matters now," Naomi said, wringing her hands. "We've got to do something to help Belle. You should see her, Casey, she's given up. It's downright pitiful. I try to see her every day, bring her clean clothes and little delicacies she doesn't get in jail. But it's as if she doesn't care what happens to her anymore."

The sharp pain inside Casey was the feeling of his heart breaking. He wanted to rush to the jailhouse, tear the place apart with his bare hands, and set Belle free. "Tell me everything, from the beginning."

Naomi related everything she knew, including what Belle had told her during their brief visits. When she finished, he whirled on his heel and headed for the door, his face grim with determination.

"Where are you going?"

"To see Belle."

"You can't. Visiting hours ended at six o'clock. The sheriff won't let you in to see her."

A sudden, disturbing thought occurred to Casey. "What happened to Tommy?"

Naomi directed her gaze at the floor. There was a catch in her voice when she said, "He's been placed in St. Francis Orphanage until the court sees fit to appoint a guardian. He's a mighty rich little boy. I tried to talk the judge into awarding custody to me until the murder is resolved one way or another but," she shrugged expansively, "you know who and what I am. The judge wouldn't hear of it."

"Christ!" The word exploded from Casey in a rush of pure anguish. "No wonder Belle is unresponsive when you visit her. She's been put through hell. Knowing that Tommy is in an orphanage must be tearing her apart. Try not to worry, Naomi, I'll get to the bottom of this. We both know Belle isn't capable of murder. I'm a damn good detective, it's time I lived up to my reputation. But first, there is something I *can* do for her and Tommy. I pray Belle will agree."

Mark was nowhere in sight when Casey returned to the parlor. He didn't wait around. Mark was a big boy, he could find his way back to the hotel without his help. Obviously Sweet Sue was taking Naomi's words to heart and was showing Mark a damn good time. It was just as well, Casey thought. He had a whole lot of thinking and planning to do before he saw Belle tomorrow.

Belle shifted restlessly on the hard cot, unable to find a comfortable position. She had slept little since she had been charged with murder and thrust into the tiny cell to await trial. At first she had counted the days, but she no longer had the will or energy to do even that. Most days she lay listlessly on the cot or sat with her back propped against the wall, staring at nothing in particular, recalling happier days when she, Tom, and Tommy had been a happy family.

What she tried not to remember was Casey, a man she could love so easily. She'd known when he left that she'd never see him again. He had taken what he wanted from her then betrayed her to McAllister. He was no different from the worst wretch that frequented Naomi's place. And yet . . . he had made her *feel* for the first time since Tom's death. And he made her want. It was that wanting that was making her hurt so much now.

Worse yet was the knowledge that sweet, innocent Tommy was living among strangers, probably thinking she had abandoned him. Belle didn't try to stop the tears that flowed freely down her pale cheeks. Nobody cared whether she cried or smiled. No one, with the exception of Naomi and Wan Yo, cared whether she lived or died. Truth to tell, she no longer cared herself. She was as good as convicted anyway. The lawyer Naomi had hired told her there was virtually no chance of an acquittal and she had no reason to believe otherwise.

Belle sighed and stared at the bar of light slanting through the window, mesmerized by the specks of dust floating aimlessly in the glow. Soon the deputy would carry in her breakfast, she supposed, but she lacked an appetite for food. She just wanted to lie there and drift, like those specks of dust, carried hither and yon without reason or volition.

Casey arrived at the sheriff's office in a fever of impatience. He had woken at dawn and would have rushed off then if it hadn't been too early for visiting hours. He had forced himself to swallow a hasty breakfast, hardly tasting or even aware of what he ate. Then he woke **Mark** up and told him what he planned to do.

At first Mark was openly skeptical of Casey's

plan. But when he saw the simplicity of it he wholeheartedly endorsed it. Everything depended on Belle and her acceptance of Casey's idea.

The first thing Casey did was to impress the sheriff by flashing his credentials. "Not only am I here as a close and personal friend of Mrs. McAllister, but as a Pinkerton detective. The lady is innocent, Sheriff, and I'm going to prove it. I'd like to see her now."

"You can see the lady but you're wasting your time. She's guilty as sin."

"Why don't you let me judge that for myself? I'm a relentless investigator. Ask Allan Pinkerton if you don't believe me. I know Belle McAllister, and she isn't capable of committing murder."

The sheriff's eyes narrowed in speculation. "You know her, eh? How well?"

Casey fixed him with an icy glare. "Not that it's any of your concern, but Mrs. McAllister and I are engaged to be married." The lie fell easily from his lips. Casey was surprised at how naturally he'd just pronounced Belle his fiancée.

"Engaged," Sheriff Rogan sputtered. "That's the first I heard of a fiancée."

"It's true, nonetheless. I visited McAllister several times to plead Belle's cause."

"Where were you when the murder was committed?"

"In Arizona, working on a case. I arrived back in town on yesterday's stage. Enough talking, I want to see Belle."

"Through that door and down the hallway. She's the only one back there now. Our other prisoner was released last night."

Casey didn't wait around for further directions. He was through the door like a shot. He found Belle in one of the three cells, lying hollow-eyed and unresponsive on the bunk, staring at the ceiling. She neither turned in his direction nor acknowledged his presence, though he knew she had heard him. It was almost as if she were . . . dead. Sickening rage welled up inside him and he wanted to kill the person who had done this to her. Because he couldn't let her see him this way, he remained silent until he forced his anger under control. Only then did he call out her name.

"Belle." Nothing. "Belle, it's Casey. Talk to me, love."

Belle frowned but did not answer. She knew she was having another hallucination. At various times during her incarceration she'd heard voices speaking to her, and seen both Tommy and Casey in her dreams. She knew better than to let her imagination run away with her again.

"Belle, please look at me. I've come to help you. My brother is free now. I've brought him back with me."

That remark garnered Belle's attention. What Casey just said was something her imagination couldn't know. She turned her head slowly, her eyes glazed as they settled on Casey's broad-shouldered form. Her expression remained unchanged.

"So you did come back."

"Did you doubt it?"

Belle shrugged. "It doesn't matter."

"Snap out of it, Belle," Casey ordered harshly. "We've got work to do if we're going to clear you of this murder charge."

"Go away. I'm beyond help."

Casey was at his wit's end. Naomi had warned him about Belle's apathy, but he hadn't wanted to believe it. She had lost all hope. Her eyes were empty. Nothing remained but a lifeless shell of flesh and bone.

"Tommy is in an orphanage," Belle rambled on. "He's frightened and alone and I can't help him." She had no more tears left, she was utterly wrung out. "Sometimes I can hear him crying for me in the night." She looked at him then, and Casey was shocked by the great purple shadows beneath her eyes. "I'm going to die in prison. I'll never see Tommy again."

"That's not true. About Tommy, I've got a plan, Belle, but you have to agree."

"He's going to be six soon, did you know that? I wonder if they'll celebrate his birthday at the orphanage."

"Dammit, Belle, don't slip away from me now!" Casey all but shouted. "This isn't like you. You're a fighter. Where's the spirit that I have come to admire?"

Belle's attention shifted and she lifted herself from the bunk. Casey was shocked at how gaunt she had become. He could see her collarbone poking out beneath the material of her dress. Her cheekbones were stark against the paleness of her face, and her once vibrant hair lay limp and lusterless against her head. She stepped to the bars, curling her fingers around them, her face mere inches from Casey's.

"My spirit was destroyed by a man I thought I could trust."

Casey reached out and dragged his finger slowly down the curve of her cheek. He wanted to pull her into his arms and comfort her, but the bars prevented intimacy. "I never wanted to hurt you, love."

Belle had the most compelling urge to lean her cheek into the cradling warmth of his hand. To gaze into his eyes and tell him she trusted him. She could not.

Reaching through the bars, Casey grasped her arms and pulled her close, until he could reach her lips with his mouth. He touched them briefly in the gentlest of kisses.

"You can trust me, Belle. I'm the only hope you have of getting out of here and I'm going to do my level best to make it happen. I have a plan. I've thought a lot about this and I'm convinced it will work. If you agree, Tommy can be out of the orphanage in a day or two."

Something flickered in Belle's eyes and her attention sharpened. Her eyes were indeed the windows of the soul, Casey thought, for in them he saw the chaotic turmoil of her innermost thoughts and feelings. Where despair once dwelled, he recognized the beginnings of hope.

"How can you do that?" Her voice was raw with desperation, and a fair amount of disbelief.

"I told you I had a plan. But I need your cooperation."

"I'll do anything for Tommy, you know that."

"Anything, Belle? Even murder?" He hated himself for asking but it had to be done. Everything had to be out in the open between them. Even if she had killed McAllister he wouldn't abandon her. The old man had driven her to it.

Belle drew back in horror. "You think I killed my father-in-law, don't you?"

"No, I don't. Why don't you tell me what happened, then I'll tell you my plan."

Belle retraced her steps to the bunk and sat down, staring at her hands. Her voice was monotone and so low Casey had to strain to hear her. She told him everything that happened, from the moment she took Naomi's gun until she was thrown bodily from McAllister's house.

"And you didn't go back later?" Casey asked.

"No. I went right to bed."

"No one saw you?"

"No, no one. It's hopeless, Casey. You may be a good detective but you'll never solve this mystery."

"I'm not going to give up, Belle. I started investigating McAllister's past before I left San Francisco and have a couple good leads. The man wasn't without enemies."

Belle raised her eyes and their gazes collided. Hers was hesitant and dubious, his steady and confident. For the first time in weeks she felt something other than helplessness, despair, and frustration. His quiet assurance was encouraging.

"I've told you all I know, now it's your turn. How do you plan on getting Tommy released from the orphanage and who will take care of him once he's out? Naomi would be happy to . . ."

"Naomi has already tried," Casey reminded her, "and the judge refused to release Tommy into her custody." His hazel eyes grew intense as he spoke to her. "Listen carefully, love, and I'll tell you what we're going to do. I say we, because I need your cooperation."

Drawn by his words, Belle returned to the bars, grasping them so tightly her knuckles turned white.

Casey covered her hands with his, and Belle felt strength and courage flow into her. She didn't question why, she just accepted.

"I'm going to petition the court for custody of Tommy."

Belle's hopes plummeted down to her feet. "What kind of plan is that? No judge in the country would award custody of a young boy to you. You can't even claim remote relationship. For all they know you could be an opportunist after Tommy's inheritance."

Now comes the difficult part, Casey thought as he studied Belle's flushed face. "I would be related to Tommy if we were to marry. I'd be his stepfather."

"No!" Belle objected before giving the suggestion proper consideration.

"Don't be hasty, love. Think about it. Tommy knows me, he'd be safe. I'd even bring Wan Yo to the house to be with him. Mark is with me, he'd help look after Tommy."

"You'd be marrying a dead woman," Belle said. Her claim startled him. "I may as well be dead," she clarified, "with a long prison term facing me. You just went through that with your brother, remember? Why would you put yourself through it again?"

Casey grinned, revealing the deep dimple in his chin. "I suppose it's partly because of the detective in me. Then again," he said growing serious, "it could be because I care for you and Tommy."

"And Tommy's inheritance," Belle said caustically, unwilling to believe Casey would go through a bogus marriage just to help Tommy.

"I don't give a damn about Tommy's money," Casey argued. "He's a fine boy, any man would be proud to claim him. Dammit, Belle, don't reject this out of hand. Unless you want Tommy to remain in the orphanage and his estate to be managed by strangers, I suggest you give serious thought to my plan. And don't think you won't be out of here to help raise your son because you will. I swear it, Belle. I'll find the real killer if it's the last thing I do."

"Marriage," Belle whispered shakily. "After Tom died I never thought I'd marry again. Not like this, anyway. I appreciate your gesture, Casey, but I realize you're just trying to salve your conscience for betraying me to my father-in-law." She stared at him, her eyes glowing fervently. "But I've got to be practical and think of Tommy, don't I? Strange as it may seem, I'd rather have you raise Tommy than to leave him in the orphanage for strangers to raise.

"I'll agree with one stipulation," Belle said slowly. "If by some remote possibility I'm acquitted, I want your promise to let me dissolve the marriage."

"Belle, that's . . ."

"It's the only way I'll agree. I won't spend my life with a man I can't trust. A man who married me because of some guilt-driven need to ease his conscience."

Casey wanted to shake her until her teeth rattled. "Fine," he said tersely. "If that's the way you want it. I'll speak to the sheriff and make all the arrangements. We'll be married tomorrow morning. I'll also instruct your lawyer to prepare a petition to present to the judge. With any luck I'll bring Tommy to visit you in a few days."

Belle's eyes lit up. "I'd be truly grateful if you could do that, Casey."

"Not grateful enough to trust me when I say I'm not marrying you because of misplaced guilt," he charged. His voice was cool, his expression hard.

"Forget it," he growled when Belle opened her mouth to speak, "I don't want your gratitude. I'm doing this for Tommy, and because you don't belong behind bars. Once I find the real killer you can end our marriage in any way you please. Meanwhile, there are two weeks left before your trial and I've got a killer to find."

He whirled on his heel and strode away. Belle watched him leave, her heart thumping furiously. Casey had returned and she felt alive again.

Chapter 11

❝**Y**ou're *what?*❞ Naomi shouted when Casey revealed his plans to her.

"Belle and I are going to be married. I've already spoken to the sheriff and he expressed the same sentiments you just did. But since there is no specific law forbidding it, he's going to allow the ceremony. I located a minister willing to perform a wedding inside the jailhouse, and the ceremony will be held tomorrow morning."

"My God, you sure are full of surprises. Why? How can marrying Belle now possibly help her? What did you do, twist her arm? I can't imagine Belle agreeing to such an outrageous arrangement." She eyed him narrowly. "As long as Belle is in jail you know the marriage can be nothing but an arrangement."

"I know, and it's not as outrageous as you think if you consider it in terms of how it will help Tommy. He'll have a stepfather, a guardian who can take care of him. Belle's lawyer is already preparing a request for guardianship. In time I'll adopt Tommy legally. Belle was against it at first but I convinced her that it was for Tommy's good."

Naomi stared at Casey, her mouth agape, her eyes wide. "You're serious, aren't you? You must care for Belle a great deal to give up your freedom for her. It might not work, you know."

"It will work," Casey said vehemently. "It has to. And I fully intend to find McAllister's killer. I wouldn't be doing this if I didn't care for Belle."

"I'm just beginning to realize how much," Naomi muttered.

"I wish you could convince Belle of that. I'm just grateful she realizes Tommy will be safe with me. I'll need Wan Yo's help to care for the boy while I'm working on Belle's case, if that's all right with you."

"I'll cooperate in any way I can if it means obtaining Belle's freedom. Wan Yo, too. If the wedding is tomorrow there isn't much time. I'll find something nice for Belle to wear and bring it early so she'll be presentable for her wedding. How were her spirits when you left her?"

"I'd like to say I helped but I'm not sure. Her eyes weren't quite as lifeless as they were when I arrived, but she was far from her old self."

"That's a start, though."

"I've got work to do," Casey said as he turned to leave. "Meet me at the jailhouse at ten o'clock tomorrow morning."

Belle couldn't believe she'd agreed to Casey's bird-brained scheme. What did he hope to gain by marrying her while she remained behind bars? He'd explained that their marriage was for Tommy's sake and she had to believe it was so, not because he was eager to get his hands on Tommy's inheritance. Dare she believe him? Belle wondered despondently. She had to in order to remain sane throughout this ordeal. She was going to prison for a very long time, she knew that. There was no suspect save her. Casey was deluding himself if he thought he could find the real killer.

Sleep had eluded Belle last night and this morning her meager breakfast had lodged in her throat. Could this possibly work? she asked herself, not for the first time. Envisioning Tommy in an orphanage was excessively painful. Would Tommy be better off with Casey? Belle knew Tommy thought the world of Casey and at one time she felt Casey returned Tommy's regard. But since learning that Casey had been employed by her father-in-law, she was no longer certain Casey felt anything for either her or Tommy. Detectives were notoriously hardhearted.

Unfortunately Casey had given her little choice in the matter. His arguments in favor of their marriage had been valid and, deep in her heart, Belle had to believe Tommy would prosper in Casey's care. If she didn't think that she would go insane with worry.

The sound of approaching footsteps brought Belle's thoughts back to the present. Had Casey arrived already? Then she saw Naomi and sagged in relief. She wasn't ready for Casey yet.

"You look like hell, honey. Haven't you slept at all since you've been in this godforsaken place? This is your wedding day. I've come to cheer you up."

Naomi's rough bravado was just what Belle needed this bleak morning. "We both know why Casey is marrying me. He's guilt-ridden over his part in all this. I do believe, however, that he's genuinely fond of Tommy. If I didn't believe that I couldn't go through with this farce."

"Nonsense," Naomi said crisply. "I think you've misjudged Casey. He's an honorable man. He didn't know you when he took the job with McAllister and accepted his money. You've got to believe that. Now, enough of that negative thinking. Casey is working damn hard to free you. Here," she said, handing her a bundle through the bars. "I've brought you a dress and some ribbons for your hair. Make yourself pretty for your bridegroom, honey. I'll keep watch at the door so no one enters while you're changing."

Belle did the best she could with what Naomi had brought her and what little she had available in the cell. She washed and dressed in the attractive sky-blue gown and even threaded the matching ribbons in her hair. Some wedding day, she thought dully, with metal bars acting as a barrier between her and Casey. She had married Tom in a brief, clandestine ceremony, but at least he had loved her.

Casey arrived with his brother and the minister a short time later. Mark proved to be a charming rascal, with an engaging smile so like Casey's it was uncanny. After introductions were made, Casey motioned for the others to back away so he could speak to Belle in private.

"Are you all right, love? You look beautiful." He thought she looked ethereal and fragile in her blue dress and hair ribbons, and he wanted to envelop her in his arms, to protect her from harm, to rescue her from the ordeal of a trial. He had to be satisfied with marrying her.

"I know how I look," Belle replied tersely, "and it isn't beautiful."

"You haven't changed your mind, have you?"

She stared at him, thinking how handsome he looked. He had dressed up for the occasion. Broad shoulders stretched the fine material of his black suit, and beneath his crisp white shirt she imagined the heat and hardness of his tanned flesh. Shiny black boots and a string tie completed his wedding finery.

"I'd do anything for Tommy. I just want your promise that you'll take care of him no matter what happens to me."

"You have it," Casey said, hurt that she still distrusted him. "Wan Yo will help. And Naomi can see him as often as she likes. You've met Mark, he has a way with kids. But I don't know why you're talking like this. You're going to be around to take care of Tommy yourself."

"I'm a realist, Casey. I'm as good as convicted."

Casey spat out a curse. She sounded so defeated, so unlike herself, he wanted to shake her until her teeth rattled. Unfortunately there were so few clues leading to another killer he felt nearly as frustrated as Belle.

"Let's get on with the wedding," he said, motioning the others forward.

At Casey's signal they approached the cell. Mark and Naomi were to stand as witnesses. The reverend cleared his throat. Suddenly the sheriff appeared from the outer office, jangling his keys.

He shoved the wedding party aside and unlocked the cell door. "Never let it be said that Sheriff Rogan stands in the way of true love. I'll hang on to your

guns, Walker, while you stand beside your bride."
He laughed without mirth. "Don't expect a wedding
night. That's going a little too far."

Casey's jaw clenched as he unbuckled his gunbelt
and handed it to the sheriff. "You, too," Rogan said
as Mark prepared to enter behind Casey. Mark
dutifully placed his holster and guns into the sheriff's hands.

Then the wedding party entered the tiny cell and
Casey took his place beside Belle. He grasped her
hand. It felt cold and small, the bones exceptionally
fragile folded within the warmth of his own large
hand. "Get on with it, Reverend."

Belle appeared too numb to feel or think during
the blessedly brief ceremony. She gave the right
answers at the right time, but afterward recalled few
of the words spoken by the minister. It wasn't until
Casey placed a gold band on her finger and kissed
her that Belle realized the ceremony was over. She
was now Mrs. Casey Walker.

After hearty congratulations all around, the wedding party filed out. Sheriff Rogan returned to lock
the cell, holding it open while he waited for Casey
to leave.

"I'd like a moment alone with my wife," Casey
said, staring the sheriff in the eye. "It's the least you
can do."

Rogan thought about it a moment, then nodded.
"Very well, but no hanky-panky. This is a jail cell,
not a honeymoon cottage."

Casey saw Belle's face whiten and his fists knotted in anger. He took a threatening step toward
Rogan, who quickly shut the door and locked it.
"Fifteen minutes, Walker." Then he turned and
strode away.

Casey returned his gaze to Belle, saw her stricken expression, and cursed the circumstances that had led to their marriage. It shouldn't be like this, he thought. Belle should be an eager, smiling bride, not this shell of a woman who looked as if she had just walked through fire. Did she have no idea how much he cared for her? He wasn't the kind of man who would marry a woman to satisfy his conscience. Nothing could have coerced him to marry Belle if he hadn't wanted her.

Placing an arm around her narrow shoulders, he led her to the bunk and sat her down beside him on the hard surface. "This isn't the end of the world, love. I wouldn't have married you if I didn't want to."

"You pity me. I don't want your pity. Or your guilty conscience."

He tilted her chin and kissed her. The kiss was long and slow, growing increasingly more heated as her lips warmed beneath his. His arms tightened, crushing her against him. She felt stiff and unyielding and he despaired of ever recapturing the passion he had once elicited from her. When he tried to pry her mouth open with his tongue, she remained remote, uninvolved. He finally gave up and released her.

"You didn't need to kiss me," Belle said tonelessly. "You didn't need to prove anything. We both know why you married me."

Casey sighed. "Are we back to that again? I've got a helluva lot to make up for, Belle, and one day I will. Right now there is Tommy to consider, and convincing the judge to appoint me his guardian."

Belle suddenly displayed more enthusiasm than

she'd shown since Casey walked into the tiny cell. "Do you truly think it's possible?"

Casey nodded slowly. "Your lawyer, Mr. Crowley, has an appointment with the judge this afternoon. He'll present the request for guardianship and our marriage license, and ask for a hearing."

"It means a great deal to me to know Tommy would be safe and happy. I don't care if you're doing this through guilt or pity, as long as you take care of Tommy while I'm in prison."

"Dammit, Belle! You're not going to prison." He shook her hard then pulled her against him, kissing her so thoroughly she almost believed him. Almost but not quite.

"Time's up." Sheriff Rogan fitted the key in the lock and swung the cell door open, inviting Casey to leave.

Casey stood reluctantly, bringing Belle to her feet with him. "Don't give up," he said, squeezing her hands. "There are still two weeks remaining before your trial."

The door clanged shut behind Casey, and Belle's world shrank to the cramped confines of the cell. The vigor and enthusiasm Casey had brought with him into the cell had vanished when he left. The ring on her finger proclaimed her Casey's wife but she felt only emptiness. They had married for the wrong reasons. His was guilt, and hers was need. Had love been involved it could have been a joyous occasion.

Belle's lawyer greeted Casey with a hearty handshake. "Congratulations on your marriage, Mr. Walker."

"Thank you, Mr. Crowley. We have our work cut out for us, don't we?"

Crowley glanced away and cleared his throat noisily. "I haven't been able to assemble much of a case in your wife's defense. Hopefully you'll be able to turn up something before we go to trial. But I do have a bit of good news," Crowley said on a cheerful note.

"You've spoken to the judge?" Casey asked expectantly.

Crowley beamed. "Indeed I did. He'll see you in his chambers tomorrow morning at precisely ten o'clock."

"Much obliged," Casey said. "Anything else I should know?"

"Not really. Until another suspect turns up we've nothing to work with. Have you spoken to Kellerman and the nursemaid yet? I understand they and McAllister's servants are still living in the mansion."

"I'm on my way there now," Casey said. "See you tomorrow in the judge's chambers."

Kellerman answered Casey's knock, and would have slammed the door in his face if Casey hadn't shoved it open with his booted foot. "I have some questions for you, Kellerman. About the night T.J. McAllister was killed."

"I told the sheriff everything I know."

"Are you sure? McAllister isn't here now to pay you for your silence. You'll be turned out of this house very soon and maybe you won't even get the money McAllister owed you. All I'm asking is a few minutes of your time."

"Make it fast, I ain't got all day."

Casey asked Kellerman a few routine questions, the answers to which he already knew. Finally he asked, "What happened to the gun you took away from Belle? Belle said she saw you give it to McAllister when you tossed her out. She claims the gun wasn't loaded. Is that true?"

Kellerman clamped his lips together and glared at Casey.

"When you're called on to testify at the trial you'll be asked that question, and you'd better tell the truth or you could end up behind bars for giving false testimony. Come on," Casey wheedled, "what can it cost you to tell the truth?"

"No one asked me if the gun was loaded," complained Kellerman.

"I'm asking you now."

"What business is it of yours?" He gave a nasty laugh. "McAllister was right, you were f . . ."

Casey's temper exploded. Without warning his fist shot out, slamming Kellerman in the mouth. Kellerman staggered backward, wiping blood from his mouth with one hand while reaching for his gun with the other.

Casey was the faster draw. "Don't you ever mention my wife and that word in the same breath, is that clear?" His finger caressed the trigger.

One look at the menacing gleam in Casey's eyes persuaded Kellerman to drop his hand to his side.

"Are you ready to tell me what you know now?"

Kellerman nodded, his gaze never straying from Casey's weapon. "I gave the gun to McAllister."

"And . . ."

Kellerman licked his lips. "He threw it into the bushes."

It was not enough. "Before or after Belle left the premises?"

Kellerman paused for the briefest of seconds. "After. The woman had already picked herself up and limped off down the street."

"Did Belle watch McAllister throw out the gun? Did she see where it landed?"

"How in the hell would I know? It was dark out."

Casey's eyes glowed with quiet menace. "You can do better than that."

"I didn't see her look back, that's all I can say."

"Very good. Now, was the gun loaded?" Casey knew this was a tricky question. Kellerman could always deny knowledge of it. The sheriff had already said no bullets were found on the ground outside the residence. He had to rely on Kellerman's fear of reprisal if he lied.

"No." Kellerman said in a low growl.

"I didn't hear you. Was the gun loaded?"

"No! McAllister checked the chambers and seemed real put out when he found them empty."

"Let me get this straight," Casey said carefully. "McAllister tossed the unloaded gun in the bushes after Belle left the premises. So in effect, anyone could have picked that gun up and used it to kill McAllister."

Kellerman bristled indignantly. "Are you blaming me?"

"No, I'm just trying to prove my wife's innocence."

"Are you really married to McAllister's daughter-in-law?"

"We were married this morning. I have no more questions for you, except one. Were you one of the men who kidnapped Tommy?"

"Yeah, but we didn't hurt the boy," Kellerman protested. "McAllister said he was granted custody of the boy because his mother was a whore."

Casey scowled but did not belabor the point. "And the letter you left? Was it McAllister's idea?"

Kellerman nodded. "I didn't know what was in it. I was just following the boss's orders."

"That's all the questions. Don't leave town, you'll be called upon to testify. Is Miss Grundig around? I'd like to talk to her next."

"Yeah, I'll get her."

Hilda Grundig was a prune-faced old maid still loyal to McAllister even after his death. She wholeheartedly concurred with Kellerman's description of what took place the night of the murder.

By the time Casey returned to his hotel room he felt the heavy weight of failure. He had learned little beyond what he already knew. He found Mark waiting in his room and launched into an explanation of what he had accomplished, which was damn little.

"At least you'll know tomorrow if marrying Belle paid off where Tommy is concerned," Mark remarked. "I hope the judge is a sympathetic one."

"I'm counting on it, but that's not the only reason I married Belle. I really do care for her. Convincing her of it is another thing."

Mark searched Casey's face. "There are different degrees of caring. You wouldn't turn your life upside down for a woman you merely cared for. Admit you love the woman, Casey."

Casey walked to the window and stared down into the dark street. "I do love Belle. But she'll never believe it. She believes I'm suffering from a guilty conscience. She doesn't want my pity. She wants to end the marriage if she is found innocent."

"Belle doesn't know you very well, does she?" Mark remarked. "Will you let her end the marriage if she is spared prison?"

"Belle *is* innocent, Mark. If she still wants her freedom she can have it. But first I'm going to do everything in my power to change her mind."

Mark laughed. "The lady doesn't stand a chance."

Casey met lawyer Crowley in the judge's chambers the following morning at ten o'clock. Judge Winters nodded curtly and asked them to be seated.

"I have already read your request for guardianship of young Tommy McAllister, Mr. Walker. The marriage between you and the boy's mother was rather sudden, wasn't it?"

"Unusual but not sudden, Judge," Casey said earnestly. "Belle and I would have married eventually." Not exactly true but close. "Unfortunately T.J. McAllister interfered before we had time to let nature take its course."

"Yes, I recall," the judge said sternly. "I granted Mr. McAllister custody of his grandson on the grounds that the boy's mother was unfit to raise him."

"All those allegations were untrue, your honor. McAllister was a bitter old man who wanted revenge against a woman he disliked because he never considered her good enough for his son. Belle is a wonderful mother. She loves Tommy and Tommy loves her. The boy has a family now, he doesn't belong in an orphanage with people he doesn't know."

"Saint Francis is a respectable institution. The boy is being well cared for and his properties managed by trustees appointed by the court." He gave Casey a hard look. "Are you an opportunist looking for a quick buck? If you are, you're wasting the court's time."

"I don't give a damn about the money," Casey barked. "I'm concerned for Tommy's welfare. I work for Allan Pinkerton. I'm a damn good detective. I'm not some con artist trying to scam the boy out of his inheritance." He reached into this pocket and retrieved his credentials. "These ought to prove who I am."

Judge Winters studied Casey's credentials and raised his eyebrows. "Very impressive. But before I can act on this there is one person I need to consult with. Please wait in the outer office and send in my secretary."

Casey rose reluctantly, feeling as if he hadn't done enough or said enough to convince the judge. "I love the boy, judge, and I love his mother."

"Quite an admission for a hard-boiled detective," the judge said, stifling a smile. "Do as I say and I promise an answer before the day is out."

"Now what?" Casey asked Crowley as he paced the judge's outer chambers. The judge's secretary had already conferred privately with the judge and left on some mysterious errand.

"We wait," Crowley said. "Judge Winters is a hard man but a fair one. Whatever he has in mind will doubtlessly determine the outcome of your custody hearing."

"God, I hate this," Casey said, stabbing his fingers through his hair. Then he started pacing, imagining Belle's disappointment should he fail.

He'd been so confident his plan would work he hadn't let himself consider failure. But now it hung over his head like an ugly, dark cloud.

Casey lost all track of time. He started violently when the door opened and the judge's secretary beckoned to him. "Where in the hell did you come from?" Casey asked tersely.

"I returned through the back exit. You may go in now." He held the door open. "Only Mr. Walker," he added, when Crowley rose to accompany Casey.

Curious about what this was all about and anxious to learn the fate of his custody hearing, Casey strode into the room with somewhat less confidence than he had when he'd arrived an hour or so ago. Suddenly he heard a shout and a whoop and felt a small body careen into him.

"Casey! I knew you'd come. Where have you been? Take me with you, Casey, I want to see Mama."

Casey scooped Tommy up in his arms and hugged him tightly. The boy felt less sturdy, more fragile than the last time Casey had seen him. His eyes were deeply shadowed and his mouth turned down in a pout that hadn't been there before.

"Did you know Grandfather was dead?" the little boy asked, trembling. "That's why I was taken to the orphanage. Sister Michael said Mama killed Grandfather but I know she didn't. Mama wouldn't hurt anyone."

Judge Winter watched the exchange carefully, his expression thoughtful. "Sit down, both of you."

Casey took the nearest chair, placing Tommy on his lap.

"So, Tommy," Judge Winter began, "you seem to know this fellow. How do you feel about him?"

"Casey is my friend," Tommy declared stoutly. "He helped me and Mama when we lived in Placerville. We moved to Placerville after my papa died, did you know that?"

The judge nodded solemnly. "So I'd heard. You have a new papa, Tommy."

Tommy's eyes widened. "I do? Who is he? Why hasn't he come to the orphanage to see me?"

The judge nodded permission to Casey. Casey tilted Tommy's chin so he could look into his face. "I'm your new papa, Tommy. I married your mama yesterday. I'm asking the judge to let you live with me until . . ." he gave the judge a meaningful glance, "your mother is released from jail."

Tommy's eyes glowed warmly. "Can I, Judge? Can I go with Casey? The orphanage is all right but . . . I miss Mama and I miss Casey. I'm glad Casey's my papa." He hugged Casey exuberantly, leaving little doubt of his sincerity.

"I need to speak further with Mr. Walker, son," Judge Winter said. "Take the boy into the outer office, Mr. Walker, and give him over to my secretary's care until we're finished. And ask your lawyer to join us."

A few minutes later Casey perched on the edge of his chair, waiting to hear the judge's decision. Lawyer Crowley chose to stand.

"Obviously the boy cares for you," Judge Winter began. "And he trusts you, any fool can see that. Nothing I've heard thus far suggests you're anything but a responsible citizen. I have determined that Tommy would fare better living with his stepfather than at the orphanage."

The breath Casey had been holding exploded

from his chest. Crowley gripped his shoulder and smiled.

"Can I take Tommy with me now, Judge?" Casey wanted to know. He had won! He couldn't wait to tell Belle.

"It's not that simple," Judge Winter said. "Where will you take the child? He needs a home environment, especially since he is without a mother's influence at the present time."

"I hadn't thought that far ahead," Casey admitted sheepishly.

"I have. The McAllister house already belongs to the boy. I suggest you now make it your home. Your lawyer and I can work out the details, but in effect you will be caretaker of Tommy's assets as well as the boy's guardian. Mr. Engle at the bank can brief you on the financial aspects, and you'll be free to draw monies on the estate in moderation. Then there is the very lucrative wine business—"

"Whoa," Casey said. His head was spinning. "I didn't expect all this. The trustees . . ."

"What's wrong, Mr. Walker, aren't you up to the challenge? Did you think you could just claim Tommy and walk out of here, leaving all the responsibility to others? I could always change my mind, you know."

"I'm sorry, Judge," Casey said, "I just didn't realize the extent of McAllister's empire. I don't know a damn thing about the wine business."

"I understand the business has an excellent manager. I'm sure he'll advise you how to proceed."

The enormity of the responsibility Casey had just accepted began to sink in. "So," he summarized, "let me get this straight. Tommy's assets will become my responsibility and we're to live in the McAllister house. Am I also free to hire and fire at will? I don't particularly want to retain those servants devoted to McAllister, given his feelings toward my wife."

The judge nodded. "You may do as you see fit regarding employees or expenditure of money. The trustees will monitor large transactions and audit the books periodically to make sure that you're acting in Tommy's best interest. As I mentioned before, your lawyer can work out the details with the trustees."

"What happens if my wife is found innocent and released from jail? I'd prefer that she be given control of Tommy's assets."

Judge Winter gave Casey a look that told him exactly what he thought of the remote possibility of Belle being found innocent. "As Mrs. Walker's husband and Tommy's guardian, you'll still be required to handle Tommy's affairs. Any other questions?"

It wasn't the way Casey had planned things. He had never considered anything beyond the initial stage of getting custody of Tommy and removing him from the orphanage. He hadn't had time yet to think about basics, like where they would live. His main concern had been to ease Belle's mind about Tommy's welfare. He feared that he had bitten off more than he could chew. Running a winery was no simple task, and would take precious time from his efforts to find McAllister's killer. Somehow he had to make things work.

"No questions, your honor. Mr. Crowley can handle the legal aspects."

"Very well, you are free to go. I am sure Tommy will be eager to hear the news."

"You go on, Casey," Lawyer Crowley said. "There is a ton of legal paperwork to see to. I'll bring the papers around to the McAllister house later for your signature."

Casey was in a daze when he left the judge's chambers. He was a father. The prospect of fatherhood was daunting, especially when it involved a five-year-old boy. Yet at the same time he was elated. He couldn't wait to see Belle, to watch her face light up when she saw her son. He hoped it was the beginning of a slow journey that would ultimately earn her trust.

"Casey, what did the judge say?"

Casey's thoughts skidded to a halt when Tommy barreled into him. He scooped Tommy up and lifted him high in the air, eliciting excited giggles from the boy. "The judge says I'm your new papa. I don't want to take your dead papa's place in your heart, but I hope you can find room in there for me."

"I don't have to return to the orphanage?"

"No, never again. You and I will be living in your grandfather's house with Uncle Mark and Wan Yo."

"What about Mama?" Tommy asked eagerly.

"She'll be there, too," Casey promised, wishing he could guarantee that vow. He'd made little headway toward finding proof that anyone besides Belle killed McAllister. "How would you like to see your mother?"

Tommy's face lit up. "Really? Oh, yes, please, Casey. Can we go now?"

Casey gave the little boy a warm smile. "You bet, son."

Chapter 12

Belle sat listlessly on her bunk, staring at the wedding ring Casey had placed on her finger yesterday during their brief wedding ceremony. She had married a man she barely knew and had no reason to trust. Belle realized instantly how confused and contradictory her thoughts were. On one hand she didn't trust Casey, on the other, she obviously trusted him enough to raise her son. Even she recognized the irony of her thoughts.

Casey hadn't visited Belle yet today and she wondered if he had succeeded in his bid for custody of Tommy. She didn't expect miracles. Nothing had gone right in her life except for meeting Naomi and marrying Tom. She gazed at her wedding ring again, recalling the kisses Casey had tried to coax from her following the ceremony. She touched her lips, feeling them warming with the memory and wondering what *really* had made him marry her. She knew it wasn't love, since he had agreed to allow her to end their marriage if she was found innocent. She gave a snort of laughter at that ridiculous notion. She was excessively naive if she thought a jury would find her innocent.

Belle glanced at her wedding ring again and couldn't help wondering if she and Casey would have married eventually if he hadn't betrayed her. There were so many things to admire about Casey. Her body remembered his lovemaking. His tenderness had moved her and his sincerity at the time had seemed so real. She was so torn where Casey was concerned she no longer knew what she felt for him.

Love. Absolutely not, she thought. Well, maybe she had fancied herself in love with him at one time, but no longer. She knew he was loyal to his family by the way he had fought for his brother's freedom. His loyalty to Mark was one of the reasons she had agreed to the marriage. It was an admirable quality, one she hoped would work in Tommy's favor.

The sound of footsteps pulled Belle from her mental musings. She rushed to the bars and felt a rush of warmth when she saw Casey striding toward her. He wasn't alone. He carried Tommy in his arms, and Belle was nearly overcome with joy when she saw her son.

"Tommy! Oh, my God, Tommy!" Tears flowed down Belle's pale cheeks as she reached out to touch her son.

Tommy's arms stretched through the bars to hug his mother, and they clung to one another with almost desperate urgency. When the first tide of emotional upheaval had washed over them, Belle turned her solemn gaze to Casey.

"Does this mean the judge made you Tommy's guardian?"

"It does. I've been appointed Tommy's guardian and overseer of his estate," Casey added wryly. "I got more than I bargained for."

Belle stared at him. Did that mean Casey had permission to spend Tommy's money as he saw fit? Is that what he'd been after all along?

Casey must have read her thoughts for he said softly, chillingly, "You're wrong, Belle." Suddenly Casey had had enough. He was so damn sick of her accusations and so tired of trying to prove his worth, that he no longer cared what she thought. He'd continue his efforts to find McAllister's killer, and he'd care for Tommy because he truly loved the boy, but he was through trying to prove his worth to a woman who didn't love him and never would.

Casey had made a good living as a detective before Belle came into his life. Once he'd established Belle's innocence she could do as she pleased.

"I . . . I didn't mean . . ." Belle knew she had hurt Casey and felt a stab of guilt.

"I know what you meant. I'll leave you and Tommy alone for a spell and return for him later. We're staying in your father-in-law's home. It's Tommy's home now, and as good a place as any to live. You can decide what you want to do with the house after you are freed."

Casey turned and walked away. Before Belle could call him back or offer a proper thank you, Tommy was clamoring for her attention.

Casey, Mark, and Tommy moved into the McAllister mansion after Tommy's visit with his mother. Wan Yo joined them later, happy to be reunited with his young charge. The first person to be dismissed was Miss Grundig. The two maids were next to go.

Each was given severance pay and a bonus. Kellerman had already moved into other quarters. The cook, who was Chinese and whom Wan Yo knew, was allowed to remain. Mark was placed in charge of hiring sufficient staff to run the place, and Wan Yo was given complete control of the household.

The following day Crowley came by with papers for Casey to sign, making the guardianship legal. Casey visited the bank shortly afterward and was briefed by Mr. Engle concerning Tommy's inheritance. Casey left the bank in a daze, thinking he should have remained a simple detective with nothing to complicate his life save solving cases.

Still upset with Belle, Casey decided not to visit the jailhouse, assigning Mark the task of taking Tommy to visit his mother.

If Belle was surprised to see that Mark had brought Tommy instead of Casey, she was too happy to see her son to remark on it. Mark lounged against the wall, listening to the conversation between Belle and her son.

"I didn't like the orphanage, Mama. I don't ever want to go back. Casey said I didn't have to."

"You're fond of Casey, aren't you, Tommy?"

"He's my new papa," Tommy said proudly. "Wan Yo moved in with us. And Casey fired that old nurse. She smacked me when I told her I didn't want to stay with Grandfather."

Tears sprang to Belle's eyes. "I want you to be a good boy for Casey, Tommy. It might be a long time before Mama can come home."

Tommy searched her face. "Casey said you'd be home soon and I believe him."

Belle could have cheerfully strangled Casey for giving Tommy false hopes. "I just want you to be prepared if Casey is wrong. Just remember that I love you."

Mark felt moved to speak in Casey's defense. "Casey doesn't say anything he doesn't mean, Belle. He's working very hard to gather the evidence to set you free. If you recall, he refused to accept my guilty verdict. I'm living proof of Casey's determination."

"I respect your loyalty, Mark. I'd expect no less from Casey's brother. But we both know I'm doomed. Unlike your case, there is no witness to testify to my innocence."

She wanted to ask where Casey was, but didn't. She knew she had angered him yesterday and couldn't blame him for avoiding her. She truly was grateful to Casey. She didn't know why she continued to harbor doubts about him, after he had done so much for her and still continued to work in her behalf. She supposed it was because she wouldn't be in this position in the first place if Casey hadn't led McAllister's men to her.

"Don't give up," Mark encouraged. "Casey will get you out of this."

After promising to return again the next day, Mark and Tommy left the jailhouse. Belle waved them off with a misty smile.

Casey spent the following days poring over old newspapers and documents pertaining directly to T.J. McAllister's business dealings. He found one piece of information that intrigued him. The winery wasn't McAllister's first venture into the business world. Years earlier McAllister bought one-third interest in a gold mine. Eventually it produced a fortune before playing out. McAllister's two partners in the venture were Harry Hopkins and Arnold

Jones. Hopkins had sold his interest to McAllister and disappeared before the rich vein had been discovered. Jones had died in a mine accident, and McAllister had purchased Jones's share from his widow.

Later that week Casey's anger had cooled sufficiently for him to visit Belle without losing control.

"Have you been enjoying your visits with Tommy?" He searched her face and found his answer. "Yes, I can see you have."

"I . . . didn't thank you properly. I truly am grateful, Casey. I wouldn't have agreed to this marriage if I didn't believe you'd take good care of Tommy."

"Yeah, the lesser of two evils," Casey said with a hint of sarcasm. "I'm through trying to prove myself to you, Belle. A man can be pushed only so far and I've reached my limit. Once you're free I won't stick around where I'm not wanted. I've come to ask a question of you. Did you ever hear Tom mention either Harry Hopkins or Arnold Jones?"

Belle repeated the names. "Hopkins does sound familiar but I don't think I ever heard Tom mention anyone bearing those names. Is it important?"

"It could be. I've run across the names a time or two in my investigation and they aroused my curiosity. I have a nose for these things. Send for me immediately if you think of something or remember the names in connection with McAllister. I'd best get on with my investigation, I have another lead or two to follow."

"It doesn't look good, does it? My trial is in seven days and you have found nothing to prove I didn't kill my father-in-law."

"You give up too easily and have too little faith.

I'm not going to let you go to prison." Turning abruptly, he stalked off.

Prison. The word brought a rush of fear and the bitter taste of bile to her mouth. She clutched her stomach, trying to keep from spewing out its meager contents. She'd heard vile things about prison, and how women prisoners were treated. Maybe Casey was right. Maybe she did give up too easily. Perhaps she should have more faith in her husband. *Husband.* It was difficult to think of Casey as her husband, and more reasonable to consider him as the man she had married for Tommy's sake. The sickness building inside Belle finally erupted and she reached the slop bucket without a moment to spare.

The longer Casey dug into McAllister's past the more he became convinced that Harry Hopkins was the key to the case. He had too much experience in the field of investigation not to trust his gut feeling about such things. With less than a week before Belle's trial, he had no idea where to look for the man, or if he was even in San Francisco. The first thing he did was place an ad in the newspaper, requesting one Harry Hopkins to contact him at the address of the late T.J. McAllister, stating that it was a matter of life and death. While he waited for a response, he and Mark each took different streets and made the rounds of cheap inns and boarding houses in the area.

It was during this time that Belle recalled where and when she had encountered Hopkins, and she told Mark when he brought Tommy for his daily visit that she needed to see Casey. Casey arrived at the jailhouse a short time later.

"Mark said you remembered something," Casey said, staring at her with an intensity that made Belle's throat go dry.

The reason for Casey's scrutiny was due to the fact that Belle looked unwell. Her pasty complexion alarmed him. He hadn't seen her in days and she appeared to have lost weight. His concern turned to fear. Could she have caught something in this pest-ridden place? "What's wrong? Are you sick? You should have said something. I would have sent a doctor around to look at you."

"It doesn't matter anymore. Perhaps jail food doesn't agree with me. I haven't been able to keep much of it down lately."

Casey's concern increased. He *had* to get Belle out of here before she wasted away. "Mark said you remembered something about Harry Hopkins."

"After you returned to Arizona I took to lingering outside at the McAllister house, hoping for a glimpse of Tommy. One day I saw Tommy leave the house and get into a carriage with his nurse and his grandfather. I ran beside the carriage, calling Tommy's name. The carriage didn't stop and I was hurled to the ground."

"The bastard," Casey bit out, smacking the clenched fist of one hand against the open palm of the other.

"A man appeared from nowhere and came to my aid," Belle continued. "He said his name was Harry Hopkins, and that he used to know my father-in-law."

"I knew it!" Casey all but shouted. "Did he say where he was staying? Did he mention . . ."

"He didn't say anything else," Belle interrupted.

"I thanked him and he left as suddenly as he had appeared. I don't know where he came from but I got the impression that he was there for a purpose."

"It's been a month since T.J. was murdered. If Hopkins knew anything about McAllister's death he would have come forward. Unless . . ." Casey grew thoughtful as some of the pieces of his investigation fell into place.

"What do you think it means?" Belle tried not to show her disappointment. After all, what could she expect? Harry Hopkins wasn't a suspect, merely an acquaintance from McAllister's past. Casey wasn't a miracle worker.

"I don't know, but I intend to find out." He didn't want to give her hope where none existed.

"I don't expect anything to come of this, I just thought you should know," Belle said.

Distracted by this small breakthrough, Casey nodded absently. "I have to go, Belle. There is a lot of work to be done yet before your trial."

He would have liked to kiss her but knew Belle wouldn't welcome his attention. She'd made it abundantly clear from the moment Tommy had been abducted that she didn't want him, didn't trust him, and felt nothing for him. And she looked so ill he feared kissing her would add to her distress. His kisses hadn't always upset Belle, he recalled. At one time she had enjoyed them.

He turned to leave, feeling sadness and regret at the sorry state of their relationship.

"Casey!"

He stopped and looked back over his shoulder, waiting, hopeful, needing to hear the words he longed for.

"Tommy appears happy with you. No matter

what happens between us I'll always be grateful for that."

Bitter disappointment made his voice gruff. It wasn't exactly what he had hoped for. "Not grateful enough to forgive me for something that's not entirely my fault." Then he whirled on his heels and left.

Belle wanted to call him back but something stopped her. What was the use anyway? A long prison term was inevitable and her marriage to Casey would soon be even more of a farce than it already was. The terrifying thought of prison life brought a spurt of nausea into her mouth and she reached for the slop bucket again.

The next day Casey found Harry Hopkins. He had taken a room at a rundown boarding house close to the waterfront. Casey had arrived at dinner time and the landlady had pointed Hopkins out as he sat at the table with his fellow boarders. Jubilant over his success, Casey waited until the meal was concluded before asking the landlady to inform Hopkins he had a visitor waiting in the parlor. When Casey finally faced Hopkins, his gut told him he had found his murderer.

It would have helped had Hopkins looked more like a killer, Casey thought. Hopkins was of medium height, too thin to be considered healthy, and had a sickly gray complexion. His shoulders were bent beneath the cheap material of his jacket, and in both posture and looks he appeared to be at least sixty-five years old.

"Who are you?" he asked uncertainly. "I don't know many people in San Francisco anymore. I've been away."

"Sit down, Mr. Hopkins," Casey invited. "My name is Casey Walker. I'm a private investigator."

Hopkins looked startled. "What do you want with me?"

"The answer to a few questions. To begin with, did you know T.J. McAllister?"

Hopkins sank into the nearest chair. "I did at one time."

"Did you know he'd been murdered?"

"Read it in the papers."

"And are you aware that a young woman has been charged with the murder?"

"What are you getting at?"

"The young woman isn't guilty."

Hopkins wrung his hands nervously. "That's a shame. But what's that got to do with me?"

"You were McAllister's partner once, I thought you might have some insight into the killing."

"That was a long time ago. We shared ownership of a mine. Arnold Jones was the third partner. That was before McAllister went into the wine business." His voice turned bitter. "The mine produced enough gold to give him a start in a venture that made him a rich man."

"What about you, Mr. Hopkins? What did you get out of the mine? I understand you sold your share to McAllister. What happened to Jones's share?"

Hopkins shrugged. "Jones was killed in a mine accident shortly before I sold out. No one knows how it happened. I got none of the profit from the mine because I sold out before McAllister struck it rich. So did Jones's widow."

"Why don't you tell me about it? Evidently this has been festering inside you a long time. Maybe you were bitter enough to kill him," Casey suggested.

Hopkins sent Casey a wary look. "Don't put words in my mouth, mister. I ain't guilty of nothing. No one can prove I killed McAllister. Besides, you don't understand."

"Make me understand."

It had been a long time since Hopkins had found a sympathetic ear. Since being cheated out of half the profits of the mine, he'd spent the best years of his life prospecting the mountains and dreaming about getting even with McAllister for cheating him out of his due. When he realized he was dying, a condition confirmed by a doctor, he'd come back to San Francisco to die. As for McAllister, Hopkins had stayed up more nights than he could recall planning ways to get even, but he was so sick, so damn tired. . . .

"Our mine wasn't producing enough to feed one man, let alone three," Hopkins explained. "But I felt we were on the verge of hitting pay dirt. McAllister disagreed. He wanted to call in experts to evaluate our holding. I agreed, and even paid half the costs for the fancy experts McAllister hired.

"The findings weren't good. The experts found no evidence of a big vein and expressed grave doubts that the mine would yield anything of great value. I was devastated. I'd put my heart and soul into that mine. When McAllister offered to buy me out, I jumped at the chance to move on to greener pastures. It wasn't until years later that I learned McAllister struck it rich a month or so after I moved on, and it occurred to me that the bastard paid those experts to give a false report."

"I don't blame you for being bitter."

"The vein was good while it lasted. It played out after a year or two, but it gave McAllister the money he needed to buy land and grow grapes to produce wine, which was becoming a lucrative business in California." He gave a caustic laugh. "Me? I was left out in the cold. Now I'm old and sick and the money no longer means anything to me."

"My wife said she encountered you outside the McAllister mansion before T.J's death. What were you doing there?"

"Was that little lady your wife? McAllister damn near ran her down in the street. I was merely passing by."

"My wife has been charged with McAllister's murder. Her trial is in a few days."

"Too bad," Hopkins muttered, refusing to meet Casey's eyes. "What does any of this have to do with me?"

"Plenty, if you're man enough to admit it. Did you kill T.J. McAllister, Mr. Hopkins? A woman's life is at stake."

Hopkins' denial came swiftly. Casey didn't believe him. "I didn't kill McAllister. You got no call to accuse me of murder. I'm sorry for the little lady but I got my own life to live. The doc says I'm dying and I want to live my last days in peace."

"I'm sorry, Mr. Hopkins, but that doesn't change the fact that an innocent woman will be sent to prison if you don't come clean." Casey was furious. His gut told him Hopkins was guilty but he had no way of proving it. "Belle has a small son, think how lonely he'll be without his mother."

"I've said all I'm going to say," Hopkins declared, retreating before Casey's fury. "I just want to die in peace."

"You may die in peace but you'll go straight to hell."

Casey's quiet words shot terror straight to Hopkins' heart. A cry of denial left his lips as he fled from Casey's intimidating presence. Casey let him go but he wasn't through with the man, not by a long shot. He intended to confront Hopkins every day until the trial and appeal to his conscience until he confessed.

The next day Casey discovered just how far Hopkins was willing to go to escape his relentless pursuit. Casey learned that Hopkins had left the boarding house, bag and baggage, in the dead of the night. With only two days remaining before the trial, Casey held virtually no hope of finding him again. Telling Belle her last hope of being freed had fled with Harry Hopkins wasn't going to be easy. Failure was a difficult pill to swallow.

Belle remained stoic when Casey told her about Harry Hopkins. It wasn't as if she'd actually believed Casey would find a way to keep her from going to prison. She realized he was just trying to keep her spirits up and really didn't blame him. Actually, she felt nothing save the churning nausea that seemed to grow worse daily. She sat on the edge of the bunk, listening without really hearing about a man who might possibly have murdered T.J. McAllister.

"Belle, have you heard nothing I've said?" Casey asked, trying to pierce through her apathy.

"I heard. Harry Hopkins didn't look like a killer to me."

Casey searched her face. "What's wrong, love, are you ill?"

"I haven't been able to keep anything in my stomach and I feel wretched."

His brow creased in concern. "I'll send a doctor to see you right away."

"No, don't bother. There's no time. The trial is tomorrow. I just want to get it over with. Perhaps whatever is wrong with me is God's will. Maybe I'm dying."

"Dammit, Belle, a little nausea never killed anyone. Damn these bars," he cursed, viciously rattling the bars.

Sheriff Rogan heard the noise and came to investigate. "What's all the racket about?"

"Unlock the cell door, Sheriff, my wife is ill."

Rogan peered at Belle through the bars. "She does look a mite peaked but it's nothing to get upset about."

"Damn you!" Casey cried, his voice raw with emotion. "What can it hurt to let me comfort my wife?"

"Regulations . . ."

"The hell with regulations! Are you going to open the cell door, or am I going to have to get a court order?"

"Oh, very well," Rogan said. It was easier to cave in than deal with the surly detective. He unlocked the door and held out his hand for Casey's guns. Casey removed his gunbelt and shoved it into Rogan's face. "Ten minutes, Walker."

Casey knelt beside Belle, taking her cold hands in his. Then he felt her forehead, finding it cool and clammy. "Where do you hurt?" he asked worriedly.

Belle stared at him with empty eyes. "I . . . there isn't any pain. It's just this infernal nausea and a strange feeling I can't explain."

Relief shuddered through Casey. "It's a normal reaction for a woman in your situation. It's a wonder you haven't cracked before now under the strain."

Belle pulled her hands away. "Please don't tell me I'm going to be found innocent, because I know better. The only thing I'm concerned about is Tommy's welfare."

"I'm surprised you'd trust me with your son."

Belle glanced down at her hands, then up at Casey. Her expression was pained, her voice low and filled with unbearable anguish. "I have no one else. It's either you or the orphanage."

"God!" The word, something between a plea and expletive, exploded from his chest as he shot to his feet. It hurt like hell to know that Belle thought of him on the same level as the Devil. It hurt even worse knowing that he loved her when she cared for him not at all. He was a fool to fall in love in the first place. He'd spent years dodging women with marriage on their mind, and it was ironic that he should fall for a woman who didn't want him.

"Will you be all right?" Casey asked, changing the subject to something safer than his frayed feelings. "Are you sure you don't want a doctor?"

"Positive. Could you bring Tommy around tomorrow before the trial? I'd like to see him one last time before . . . Will you?"

Casey couldn't help himself. He reached for Belle, bringing her into the circle of his arms. He wanted to kiss her but her head was buried against his chest. "Somewhere there's a killer out there, Belle, and one day I'll find him. You have to believe that."

"I can't even think right now. My stomach is churning, and the thought of prison is so frightening I'm not sure I'll be able to bear it."

"It won't be for long, I swear it."

"Why do you care so much? You're Tommy's guardian, until he reaches his majority you're free to spend his money as you see fit."

Casey's arms dropped and he stepped away. "My God, you're right, you're not thinking clearly. Are you sure you don't want a doctor? The trial tomorrow is bound to be an ordeal."

Belle shook her head, so confused where Casey was concerned she no longer knew what to think. She'd all but driven him away and still he continued to work in her behalf. Why couldn't she throw herself into his arms and let him comfort her for what might be the last time? She would have if she wasn't so ill. If Casey didn't leave soon she was going to embarrass herself in front of him. Then Sheriff Rogan came and Casey had to leave.

Casey left reluctantly. He had wanted desperately to comfort Belle but feared rejection. He knew she was under nearly unbearable stress and wasn't herself, but being spurned time and again was humiliating.

"I'll see you tomorrow," he said, trying to imbue her with courage. "We'll all be there, Naomi, Wan Yo, Mark, and I. Don't count your lawyer out yet. He still has a few tricks up his sleeve."

"Good-bye, Casey," Belle whispered, aware of the finality of those simple words. It was going to take a miracle to get her out of this, and neither Casey nor Mr. Crowley were magicians.

Chapter 13

Belle spent the remaining hours before the trial vomiting into the slop bucket. She was pale and ill when she walked into the courtroom. She paused in the doorway, grateful to see Naomi sitting in the front row. Neither Mark nor Casey was present, and she couldn't fault them for choosing not to show up. This was a cut-and-dried case and unlikely to last long enough to warrant her husband's presence.

The bailiff gave her an ungentle shove and she stumbled forward. Her lame ankle gave way beneath her, and she would have fallen if the bailiff hadn't grasped her arm and steadied her. She limped to the defendant's table and sat down beside Crowley. She had conferred with her lawyer often during the last days before the trial, but she'd had nothing to add in her own defense that hadn't already been said, and Crowley had no new developments to report.

Belle's gaze strayed to the jury box again and again. Twelve men sat staring at her as if she were some freak in a sideshow. And she saw something else stirring in the depths of those twelve pairs of eyes. She saw her own conviction. Without hearing a single witness, they had tried and convicted her of a violent crime. Some of the men she recognized as friends of T.J. McAllister. Others she had seen at Naomi's place at one time or another. But all twelve had one thing in common. They thought her guilty of murder.

Belle vaguely recalled standing when the judge entered the courtroom. Kellerman was called to the stand first to testify. His testimony proved extremely damaging. Crowley cross-examined, bringing out the fact that the gun Belle brought into McAllister's home wasn't loaded. Then the prosecutor returned and got Kellerman to admit that Belle could have doubled back, retrieved the gun, loaded it and sneaked into the house through the back door, which Kellerman sheepishly admitted having left unlocked.

Testimony from Miss Grundig concurred with Kellerman's, and was even more condemning and judgemental. Acquittal looked hopeless and Belle resigned herself to a guilty verdict. Dimly she wondered why Casey had chosen to absent himself from the trial. He was probably suffering guilt for lying to her. All that nonsense about wanting her trust and not allowing her to go to prison was nothing but false words and empty promises. She began to doubt her own wisdom. Marrying Casey and placing her son into his keeping had been rash and foolish. As the testimony continued, Belle's thought process completely shut down.

* * *

Casey wasn't going to give up, not even on the day of the trial. He had to find Hopkins. He still felt Hopkins was the key to the case. He and Mark left the house before dawn, split up and conducted a search of the dives and boarding houses along the waterfront. When the time set for the trial arrived, Casey bemoaned the fact that he couldn't be with Belle, but figured she wouldn't miss him anyway, given the way she felt about him. And continuing the search was far more important than giving Belle moral support.

Then, the miracle actually happened. Casey found Harry Hopkins in one of the most disreputable saloons on the waterfront. He was hunched over a mug of ale, his eyes half closed, his face the color of ashes. Casey sat down in the chair opposite him.

Hopkins looked up. "You found me," he said without rancor. "Thought you might. I didn't kill McAllister. Thought about it often enough but I didn't do it."

"A young woman is going to prison if you don't confess."

"I'm sorry. She looked like a nice gel. McAllister must have treated her like hell, just like he treated his partners."

Casey grew desperate. "I can't prove you did it, Hopkins, but I'm appealing to your decency and honor."

Hopkins winced as if in pain and clutched his stomach. He did indeed look like a man courting death. "You must love the gel a great deal." He grew thoughtful and his words rambled aimlessly. "I never loved a woman like you love your wife. I never had time. I was always on the move, searching for that rich vein. Once I struck it rich I was gonna find me a woman to love and settle down. It never happened. I owe my wasted life to that cheating skunk McAllister."

"All the more reason for you to kill him. Time is running out for Belle, Hopkins."

"She has a child, you say?"

"Yes, a small son who needs her." For the first time in days Casey felt the dawning of hope.

Hopkins jerked the mug of ale up to his mouth and quaffed deeply while staring at Casey over the rim. "Did I tell you I'm dying?" he asked after he set the mug down.

"I believe so. I'm sorry, but that doesn't give you license to kill."

"Why are you so sure I did it, sonny?"

"There are no other suspects. Belle didn't do it and you had ample cause to want McAllister dead."

"Got it all figured out, ain't ya?"

"I believe so. All I need is your confession in court, in front of witnesses."

Hopkins looked even sicker and paler, if that was possible.

"How am I supposed to have killed McAllister?"

Casey sent him a disgruntled look. "Did your memory fail you? You used a gun. The same gun Belle used to threaten McAllister earlier that evening. McAllister took it away from her and threw it into the bushes beside the house. You retrieved it later, shot your old partner, and left through the window."

"Got him in the heart, huh?"

Casey stared at him curiously. "You blew his brains out. Don't you remember?"

The frail old man smiled cryptically. "Served him

right. Sometimes my mind plays tricks on me. Signs of age, I reckon.''

Casey fidgeted nervously. Time was running out. If he didn't persuade this tricky character to confess to murder, Belle would be wrongly convicted. Casey could always use force, he supposed, but it wouldn't be nearly as effective as Hopkins appearing of his own accord and claiming guilt for McAllister's murder.

Hopkins stared into his beer, mulling over Casey's words and picturing in his mind the little gel wrongfully accused of murder. He imagined Belle's son, crying for his mother, and he thought of Casey, who obviously loved his wife and would do anything to keep her from going to prison. Then he considered his own life. Dying, no friends to speak of, no relatives and nothing to look forward to. What little money he'd had ran out days ago, and finding work in his condition was out of the question.

He could always beg handouts like the other bums roaming the city, but no matter how broke he'd been in the past he'd never had to resort to begging.

"What will happen to me if I confess?"

"You'll probably have a hearing and be sent to prison or . . ." His words dangled ominously.

"If I live that long," Hopkins mumbled. He finished off the last of his ale and rose abruptly. "We'd best get going if we're gonna save that little gel.''

Casey shot to his feet, wanting to shout with joy. Urgency brought him back to reality. "I only pray it isn't too late.''

* * *

Belle watched the proceedings dispassionately. She knew the verdict would be anticlimactic. Everyone in the courtroom, including the jury, had decided beforehand that she was guilty. She had declined to testify and Crowley hadn't forced the issue. She just couldn't go through all that again. She'd be questioned on her past, which had already been thoroughly explored and vilified in turn by the prosecutor. And she'd have to admit that she'd been in bed with Casey while her son was being abducted by his grandfather's henchmen.

"Where is your husband?" Crowley asked anxiously. "I planned on calling on him to testify."

Belle shrugged, trying not to care. "It doesn't matter one way or another whether Casey testifies. Nothing is going to sway the jurors."

"He's your husband, he should be here." Crowley's voice was thick with disapproval.

Belle bowed her head and tried not to think about Casey. He had promised to bring Tommy to see her before the trial and hadn't. One more reason not to trust men. Her distrust of males started with her own father and hadn't improved during the years she lived with Naomi. Her father had dragged her from town to town, leaving her to fend for herself while he gambled away their livelihood. He had neglected her to the point of forgetting he even had a daughter. Many a night she had gone to bed cold and hungry, wondering when and if he'd come home. Finally he hadn't.

Casey's betrayal was just one more reason not to trust another man. Tom had been the only man she'd ever trusted and it had taken months to come to that decision. Marrying Casey had been the lesser of two evils where Tommy's welfare was concerned, one she hoped she'd not live to regret.

"The judge is about to give instructions to the jury," Crowley whispered into Belle's ear. Belle tensed but said nothing.

Suddenly the courtroom door burst open and Casey strode in. Following in his wake was a man Belle recognized as Harry Hopkins. A frail, ill, Harry Hopkins.

"What's the meaning of this?" the judge blustered. "We're in the middle of a trial here."

"I think you'll be interested in hearing what Harry Hopkins has to say, Judge." Casey reached behind him and pulled Hopkins forward. "Tell him, Hopkins. Tell the judge and jury what happened the night T.J. McAllister was killed."

Harry Hopkins located Belle in the crowd and sent her a tremulous smile. "I killed T.J. McAllister, Your Honor. He cheated both me and our third partner, Arnold Jones, out of what's rightfully ours. I've waited a long time to even out the score."

"You do realize what you're saying, don't you, Mr. Hopkins? This is a court of law. You haven't been sworn in, but the jury and witnesses heard every word you just said."

Momentary panic flashed across Hopkins' thin face. Then he composed his features and nodded his understanding. Once again his gaze sought Belle's, finding his reward in her obvious relief and joy.

"I killed McAllister," Hopkins repeated. "This little gel had nothing to do with it. I found the gun in the bushes, sneaked in after the lady left and blew out McAllister's brains."

Pandemonium reigned as the spectators in the

courtroom went wild. A bailiff came forward to take possession of Hopkins and he went along meekly. Meanwhile, Casey searched frantically over the heads of the spectators for Belle. He finally spotted her, standing alone at the defendant's table, looking confused, stunned, and ill. She seemed to stagger a bit and Casey pushed his way through the milling crowd to get to her. He cried out in dismay when he saw Belle start a slow spiral to the ground and shoved people out of his way to get to her. He reached her scant seconds before she hit the ground. He carried her from the courtroom amid bedlam.

Belle squeezed her eyes tightly shut, afraid to open them. The bed was too soft, the room too warm. It had been so long since she'd felt the comfort of a real bed she just wanted to lie there and dream a while longer. She knew the harsh realities of her situation would return once she opened her eyes. She stretched her limbs and gave a breathy little sigh. She even forced a smile, thinking how absurd her dream was for a woman facing a long prison term.

"Belle. Open your eyes."

Now she was hearing voices. What next?

"Come on, Belle, I know you're awake."

Slowly Belle opened her eyes. The mist before them cleared and she saw Casey sitting on the edge of the bed. Bed! Not a bunk but a bed. Remembrance came rushing back to her. Just before the jury had been sent out to reach a verdict, Casey had arrived in the courtroom with Harry Hopkins. And Harry Hopkins had confessed to McAllister's murder. How could that mild man kill anyone?

"Where am I?"

Casey watched her warily. "You're home. I brought you here after you fainted."

"I've never fainted in my life!" Suddenly her eyes narrowed. "Whose home?"

"Yours and Tommy's. The house and everything that goes with it belongs to Tommy. I've merely been the caretaker until your release."

She pushed herself up into a sitting position and Casey fluffed the pillows behind her. "What you need right now is rest. And something to eat. I've asked to have a meal sent up for both of us. It should arrive shortly."

"Where's Tommy?"

"He's with Wan Yo and Naomi. They wanted us to have some time alone. We *are* newlyweds," he reminded her. "Wan Yo will bring him back to-morrow."

"I want to see Tommy now. I've been without him too long."

"One more night won't hurt. Are you up to talking?"

"I suppose so." At least her nausea had passed for the moment. Her expression grew anxious. "I don't have to go back to jail, do I?"

"Never again," Casey vowed.

"Did Harry Hopkins really murder my father-in-law?"

"I believe he did. So does the judge."

Dimly Belle recalled meeting Harry Hopkins's gaze in the courtroom. She didn't believe his were the eyes of a cold-blooded murderer. She remembered how he had helped her after T.J.'s carriage had nearly run her down, and how solicitous he had

been of her. Deep in her heart she didn't believe
Harry Hopkins capable of murder. But clearly Casey
did.

She touched his arm, wanting to express her
misgivings, and Casey mistook her gesture for
something else. Desperate for a crumb of affection
from her, he thought she was reaching out to him.
He moaned helplessly as he pulled her into his arms
and bore her down with him onto the bed. He
kissed her with desperate fervor, tasting her lips and
thrusting his tongue into her mouth, exploring it
with unleashed passion. This was what he had been
waiting for, yearning for. One small sign from Belle
that she forgave him for his part in this godawful
mess.

Belle moaned out a protest, but Casey was too
inflamed to think it anything but encouragement for
him to continue. A soul-stealing sweep of his
tongue against the tender insides of her lips sent
heat swirling through her. Why was he doing this to
her now, when she was vulnerable and confused?

Frantically he fumbled with the buttons on her
blouse, pulling it free of her skirt and discarding it.
Their mouths were still fused as he unfastened her
skirt and drew it down her legs, tossing it aside to
join her blouse. One large hand moved over the tops
of her breasts, and with a few deft motions her
corset and shift were stripped from her, then her
petticoats and drawers.

When he finally lifted his mouth from hers she
was breathless with need and too disgusted with
herself to admit it.

"You don't know how often I dreamed of this
moment," Casey whispered against her lips. "To see
you free again and in my arms where you belong."

Belle made a feeble attempt to squirm out of his arms but Casey only held her tighter. "I don't belong in your bed," she protested. "You promised I could end this marriage."

Difficult as it was, Casey forced himself to practice patience. "I lied. We are married for the duration whether you like it or not. Tommy needs a father and he trusts me even if his mother doesn't. Why can't you give us a chance, Belle? Have you no forgiveness in your heart? Is it just me or all men you don't trust?"

Belle flushed and looked away. Casey had come too close to the truth. Trusting hurt. Her father had taught her that. She stirred beneath him, wanting to escape despite her aroused body but unable to find the will. What if she forgave him and he betrayed her again, like her father, like all the men she'd known with the exception of Tom?

"What is it, Belle, what aren't you telling me?"

"Just leave me alone."

"I want to make love to my wife."

His fingers slid down her throat. Then his hands were on her bare shoulders, drawing her against his fully aroused body. "I've not forgotten how it was between us, how it's always been. You can't hide your body's response. You felt something."

Belle shook her head wildly but her eyes gave her away. She *had* felt something. "I felt nothing!" she lied. "You seduced me. You made it possible for your cohorts to abduct Tommy. Lust-driven, that's what I'd call our last coupling."

For the space of a heartbeat anger leaped in Casey's eyes. But it was gone in an instant, replaced by a dark, sultry determination that frightened Belle. "If you truly believe that, at least give me a chance to prove you wrong. Give me the wedding night we never had. I kept my promise, I didn't let you go to prison. Does that count for nothing?"

Even as he spoke his hands claimed her breasts, his head began to lower. Belle opened her mouth to tell him she was grateful for his tenacity, but the sweet pressure of his lips stopped her words. At first his kiss was hard, his lips unyielding. Anger and disappointment churned within him. Belle's stubbornness had nearly defeated him. But his anger was short-lived.

Belle was surprised when Casey's hard mouth went soft and pliant. At first she kept her lips clamped tightly shut. But he was endlessly patient, endlessly coaxing . . . endlessly determined. Her lips parted fractionally.

"That's it, love, open your mouth. A little more . . . ah . . . just a little more . . ." Several minutes passed before Belle realized he had removed his shirt, and that his bare chest was molded intimately against hers.

Belle panted into his mouth and their breaths mingled deep in the back of her throat. A dark, sweet thrill swept through her. Belle moaned, helpless against his masculine allure. Then his trousers were gone and she felt all of him against her—the incredible breadth of his shoulders, the muscular hardness of his chest, the swelling heat and potency of his loins, and the taut length of his thighs.

She felt overwhelmed by the extent of power this man—her husband—wielded over her. No man deserved that kind of power. Tom had loved her and she him, but she had never allowed him to hold the awesome power to move her that Casey possessed.

Even as a child she had hidden an inner part of herself from her father, for it was the only part of her he couldn't reach and therefore disappoint.

His tongue entwined with hers, an erotic mating that sent heat and moisture to the tender spot between her legs. His fingers toyed with her nipples until they stood taut and tingling, aching for the hot brand of his mouth. She tried to deny the feelings coursing through her, tried to recall that this man had brought her to the brink of disaster, but the hot lashing of his tongue against her aching nipples made coherent thought impossible. It was a sensation like warm liquid being poured over her.

And then the sensation of his hair-roughened chest brushing slowly over her breasts brought a tormented gasp to her lips. He slid slowly down her body, his tongue blazing a fiery path across the satin plane of her stomach. Down . . . down . . .

Suddenly Belle realized where he was heading and she gasped in understanding. "Casey! Dear God . . . what . . ."

He gazed up at her. "Did you and Tom never . . . ?"

"No! Please . . ."

He pressed against her inner thighs with the breadth of his shoulders until he felt her thighs give way. "Relax, love, I won't hurt you. I want to please you . . . all of you . . . in every way."

For Casey there was no conscious thought. There was only the incredible, nearly obsessive need to pleasure her, to possess her in every way a man could possess a woman. Her hands fluttered helplessly against the muscular tautness of his arms as he lowered his head and tasted her, his breath a heated rush of wildly erotic fire against her dewy flesh. He groaned. She was hot and tasted tangy-sweet.

His tongue flicked against her sleek, wet recesses, again and again, teasing, circling, tormenting and exploring. Her fingers knotted his hair. She arched against him and panted, her needy cries filling the air, driving him to a frenzy. His blood pounding a primitive beat, he gave her what she so guilelessly sought.

His tongue pressed high and full against her swollen core, against the dewy pearl of sensation, wringing a convulsive shudder and a cry from her lips. Despite his nearly bursting manhood, he waited until she quieted before levering himself over her. She opened her eyes, all smoky and dazed, and stared at him as his lean fingers separated soft, downy fleece and then pink, moist folds. With a triumphant cry he plunged deep, embedded tight within her heated center. He withdrew, all hard and hot and glistening. Belle watched in awe as he came inside her again, driven and powerful. Thrust and withdrawal became wild and frenzied, performed against the welcoming wetness of her sheath.

He felt his seed rising, felt its burning path sear him, a mere heartbeat away from spilling himself. Beads of perspiration popped out on his forehead as he fought for control. He wanted Belle to find pleasure again before seeking his own fulfillment.

He seized her lips, his kiss raw and hungry. He felt her breath, hot and wild against the back of his throat, and caught her cries inside his mouth. He thrust harder, deeper, faster in answer to her silent plea. Suddenly he tore his mouth from hers and gave a hoarse shout as he felt himself rushing toward climax.

"I can't wait! Hurry, love, please . . ."

Belle gasped for air, fearing she would drown in the sea of bliss. Then she felt Casey tense, felt him grow huge and pulsing inside her, and she let his passion carry her to splendor. She cried out his name and convulsed around him. Casey dug his fingers into her buttocks and pulled her closer as he drove upward, once, then again. With a hoarse shout of triumph, he exploded powerfully as his body emptied. He hunched above her for long minutes, fighting for breath, his forehead pressed to hers, savoring the moment and the woman beneath him.

Belle couldn't think, could only feel. This man had intruded into her life, made it a living hell, then stolen her heart. To make matters worse, she had married him, making him a part of her and Tommy's life. Would he disappoint her again? she wondered. The answer was obvious. He was a man, wasn't he? Most men had no hearts, no compassion. Of course she appreciated Casey's efforts to find T.J.'s killer, but she was well aware that he had done so out of guilt, not love.

"What are you thinking?" Casey asked as he settled down beside her.

"I'm thinking how easy it was for you to seduce me."

Casey's brow furrowed. "I made love to you and you responded. Surely you must feel something for me. You trusted me with your son, remember."

"I had no choice."

"I know, I'm the lesser of two evils," Casey

muttered dryly. Casey hovered on the edge of anger. What did he have to do to get Belle to admit she cared for him? "You don't think much of me, do you?"

She felt the heat of his gaze sliding down her nude body and reached for the sheet. Once she was decently covered she gazed into his hazel eyes and tried to recall his question. At length, she said, "I've no reason to trust any man and you haven't changed my mind. Tom was the exception."

Casey was sick of hearing about Tom, that paragon of virtue. He knew he could never measure up to Belle's dead husband however much he tried.

"Did you respond to Tom like you do to me? Did Tom make you cry out and writhe like a wanton beneath him? Did he make your blood sing and your body soar?" She stared at him. "I know how I make you feel, Belle. I can feel your excitement, taste your passion. It pools inside you like sweet honey."

Belle felt the warmth of his words flow over her, inside her, and promptly denied he made her feel any differently than Tom had. "Of course Tom made me feel those things!" she hotly proclaimed.

Yet she knew she lied. Making love with Tom had been comfortable and pleasant, but certainly no earth-shattering experience. And she resented Casey for making her feel things Tom had not. She felt like a traitor to Tom's memory. Tom had married her against his father's wishes and paid for it with his life. All in the name of love. She didn't deserve to feel the kind of passion Casey aroused in her.

"Liar." He caressed her breasts. He could feel her heart thumping against his hand and smiled cynically. "Deny it all you want. You want me as much as I want you."

In one hand Casey gathered the rich silk of her hair and with the other he pulled her against him. She felt his arousal and caught her breath, surprised that he was aroused again so soon. Tom had never taken her twice with scarcely a breather in between. "What are you going to do?"

"I'm going to make love to my wife. Then we're going to eat something and go to sleep."

"You can't! It's too soon. Tom never . . ."

"Dammit, Belle, I don't want to hear what Tom did or didn't do. Tom is dead. I'm tired of hearing about your former husband. I'm the man in your bed. When I make love to you I don't want to be compared to another."

Abruptly Belle realized how Casey must feel being constantly compared to Tom. She couldn't help it. Tom had been the only man she had ever trusted. Tom had given her Tommy.

"I don't . . . I didn't mean . . ."

He kissed her long and deep, swallowing whatever reply she had intended to make. She squawked in surprise when he lifted her high and set her atop him. She was open and straddling him; Casey could feel the moist heat of her against his loins.

"Take me inside you when you're ready, love," he urged in a hoarse whisper.

When she hesitated he raised his head and took her nipple into his mouth, tugging it with his lips and laving it with his tongue. He moved freely from one breast to the other, until passion returned and she trembled with the force of it.

"Now, love, now," he gasped as he lifted her

buttocks and urged her down upon his turgid manhood.

Belle shook her head no even as she guided him to the portals of her glistening sex. He entered her slowly then pushed her down hard to take all of him. She cried out in sheer joy, then gave herself up to the heat and passion consuming her. She came in a rush as he thrust forcefully inside her. Moments later he followed her to paradise. She fell asleep lying on top of him.

Belle awoke with a start. She stretched out her hand and found the place beside her on the bed empty. The room was dark but for a shaft of moonlight spearing through the window. She saw Casey immediately, standing before the hearth, poking at the dying flames. He was gloriously nude and Belle's admiring gaze swept over the incredible width and breadth of him. She followed the pattern of corded muscles across his back and down his legs and taut buttocks and her tingling fingertips remembered the strength of them. She stirred restlessly and Casey must have heard her for he turned and smiled at her.

"You're awake. I'm glad. You really should eat something."

He walked over to his discarded clothing and tugged on his pants. A maid brought a tray earlier but I told her to take it back to the kitchen. I didn't want to awaken you. I'll go get it."

Belle sat up in bed, pulling the sheet up to her chin. "I'm not very hungry."

"Nonsense. You're far too thin."

"That's because I haven't been able to keep much food down the last week or so."

A worried frown darkened Casey's brow. "I'll summon the doctor first thing tomorrow." She started to protest. "No, don't try to talk me out of it. I'll be right back." He turned and strode out the door.

While he was gone Belle thought about Harry Hopkins and how things had turned out. Somehow she couldn't imagine Harry Hopkins killing anyone. He'd seemed such a gentle man. Suddenly another name came to mind and her brow furrowed in concentration. Casey returned before Belle had time to complete the thought. He set the tray across her lap, lit a lantern, and pulled a chair close to the bed so he could join her.

Despite Casey's encouragement Belle merely picked at her food. She was weary, so very weary. She was troubled and confused over Harry Hopkins' confession and bewildered by her response to Casey sexually. There was no longer a reason to remain married to Casey. Tommy was her responsibility now and she could raise him without Casey's help.

After several bites she set down her fork and stared into space. Suddenly she blurted out the words that had been nagging at her since Harry Hopkins had confessed to McAllister's murder.

"He's not guilty, Casey. Harry Hopkins didn't do it."

Chapter 14

Casey dropped his fork and stared at Belle. "What in the hell are you talking about? You heard Hopkins. He confessed before dozens of witnesses. Of course he's guilty."

"You've got the wrong man," Belle persisted stubbornly. "Harry Hopkins is a gentle man. Look into his eyes, that ought to tell you something. I'm convinced he's not capable of murder."

Casey carefully set the tray aside. "If you didn't kill McAllister," he asked reasonably, "and Hopkins didn't, who did?"

"I don't know."

"Forget it, Belle. You're free. As far as I'm concerned the right man is in jail. You must be exhausted. You'll feel better after a good night's sleep."

Perhaps Casey was right, Belle thought as she hunkered down between the blankets and closed her eyes. A moment later she felt the mattress dip and the warmth of his body and realized he meant to sleep with her all night.

"What are you doing?"

Casey cocked a dark brow at her. "Going to bed. It's been a long day."

"A house this size should have several bedrooms. I'm sure you'd be more comfortable in one of them."

"You're my wife and I want to sleep beside you." He stretched out and reached for her.

Belle scooted to the edge of the bed. She supposed now was as good a time as any to discuss their marriage. "We both know why you married me. You did it for Tommy, because you felt responsible for his abduction. I'm free now. You're not bound by our hasty marriage vows. You can leave any time you wish."

Anger throbbed against Casey's temples. Did Belle feel nothing for him? How ironic. The first time he'd ever felt this way about a woman and she wants nothing to do with him. Perhaps Belle was right. Perhaps a quick separation and divorce was the logical thing to do. Unfortunately his heart rebelled.

He pushed himself off the bed and stood over her, his eyes hooded. "I'm going to stay and take care of Tommy whether you like it or not. I gave my word to the judge. If you don't want me in your bed, fine, but you can forget about a divorce. A few minutes ago I could have sworn you enjoyed being married to me." He shrugged expansively. "But then, I never did pretend to understand women. There is no shortage of willing women, I should have no problem finding one to satisfy me. Just remember, you're the one who sent me from your bed. I was perfectly willing to let my wife satisfy my needs. You may be right. Perhaps I *don't* need a wife."

At a loss for words, Belle watched him gather up his clothes and stride nude from the bedroom. She opened her mouth to call him back but the words caught in her throat. Allowing Casey into her heart would be disastrous. She had loved her father and he had neglected her and finally left her, as well as this earth. She had loved and trusted Tom and he had left her, too. Allowing herself to love Casey would bring her to utter ruin. When he left her, and he invariably would, the final humiliation would destroy her where McAllister had not succeeded.

Casey paused in the doorway. "I'll see that the doctor is sent for first thing tomorrow. Do you have a particular doctor in mind?"

"It's not necessary, I'm . . ." She knew what was wrong, had suspected she was pregnant for some days, but she wasn't certain she wanted Casey to know.

"No arguments, Belle."

"Doctor Peabody, then. He's seen Tommy through some minor illnesses and he's also Naomi's doctor. He's elderly and always treated the girls kindly."

"Very well, Doctor Peabody it is." Then he was gone, closing the door softly behind him.

Once back in his own room Casey's temper exploded. He hit the wall so hard with his fist he bloodied his knuckles. He'd learned the wisdom of controlling his anger early on, but this time he'd nearly succumbed. He realized that frightening Belle with his temper would not change her mind about him.

The single most important thing that kept Casey from packing and leaving was the knowledge that Belle enjoyed, no, *craved* his lovemaking. She had participated with unbridled passion tonight despite her initial reluctance. He had not forced her, he would never do that, and she had responded with an eagerness that thrilled him. It was enough to make him believe she cared for him more than she was willing to admit.

Resting in bed with his hands behind his head, Casey realized that Belle's life had not been an easy one. More than once she had mentioned being disappointed and hurt by her father. She even blamed her beloved Tom for dying and leaving her at the mercy of his father. The things she had seen and heard at the whorehouse contributed to her distrust of men. And learning that Casey worked for McAllister had been the final blow to her fragile ego. Belle believed that all men were users and takers, including Casey. Somehow, some way, he had to change her mind. Was he capable of gaining her trust? he wondered. Was he wasting his time loving a woman who didn't love him?

Casey's last thought before embracing sleep was that he should have sold his soul to the Devil before accepting T.J. McAllister's money.

Belle's stomach rebelled the moment she lifted her head from the pillow. She was grateful for the slop jar tucked under the bed, for she wouldn't have made it to the rather modern bathroom McAllister had installed in his mansion. She was still retching when Casey burst into the room. He had pulled on his pants but hadn't taken the time to fasten them. They gaped open, revealing a tantalizing vee of crisp, dark hair.

"My God, I could hear you vomiting from my room next door." He knelt beside her and held her head as she continued to dry heave. "This is serious," Casey said as he helped her back to bed. "Don't move. I'm sending for the doctor immediately and for a maid to help you until he arrives." He was through the door before she could form a reply.

The maid, a young girl with bouncy blond curls and pert features, stared at Belle with consternation. "What can I do to help, ma'am?"

"I'm feeling better," Belle said. "I'd like to bathe before the doctor arrives."

"Mr. Casey said you weren't to get out of bed. I'll bring water and towels and something to freshen your mouth." Her blue eyes twinkled. "I've seen my ma and sister like this. In a month or two you'll be right as rain."

"What's your name?" Belle asked, liking the little maid on sight.

"Betsy, ma'am. I'm new here. All the servants who worked for Mr. McAllister were let go except for Chen Lee, the cook."

"How many servants are there, Betsy?"

"Let's see now. There is Minnie the downstairs maid, Sally and Tia the kitchen helpers, and Pierson the butler. Wan Yo is acting as housekeeper until a proper one is hired. That's all the servants except for Sterns, who lives in the carriage house and has charge of the carriage and animals. When you're feeling yourself again you'll meet them all."

"I know, but right now I feel like I'll never be up to meeting them," Belle groused.

Betsy offered a shy smile as she stripped off Belle's soiled nightgown and provided her with a clean one. "I've never been married, but it must feel wonderful to be giving a fine man like Mr. Casey a child."

Belle wondered if the entire household knew she was increasing. Did Casey suspect? She supposed not since he would have said something. Her thoughts scattered when Casey entered the room with Doctor Peabody.

Doctor Peabody smiled benignly down on Belle, took her wrist out of habit, and checked her pulse. "Your husband tells me you've been ill. Got me out of bed and rushed me here without my breakfast."

"I'm sorry," Belle whispered contritely. "It's really nothing." Having a child was nothing unusual. She'd had Tommy and survived.

"Don't listen to her, Doctor," Casey countered. "She's been vomiting regularly. Food doesn't agree with her. She assumed jail fare was the culprit, but I think it's more serious than that."

Casey thought he heard the doctor chuckle but couldn't be sure. He frowned. This was no laughing matter. "What could be wrong, doctor?"

"I won't know until I examine your wife, Mr. Walker. And I can't do that until you leave me alone with my patient."

Casey sent a lingering glance at Belle then reluctantly left the room. But he didn't go far. He paced the narrow hallway just outside the closed door.

Doctor Peabody pulled a chair up beside the bed and studied Belle's wan features. "Well, my dear, let's see what ails you, shall we? Tell me your symptoms."

"I know what ails me, Doctor. I'm expecting a child. The symptoms were all there for me to recognize."

Doctor Peabody gazed at her from beneath bushy gray eyebrows and cleared his throat nosily. "I never believed you killed your father-in-law. I've known you a long time, Belle, and you've been a gentle and loving young woman. I'm happy to see you married to a good man again. Mr. Walker will make a fine father for Tommy and the new babe. Now, about those symptoms, why don't you tell me about them?"

Belle spoke in hushed tones, recounting the numerous times in the past few weeks she had been ill in the mornings and lost her breakfast. After a few more pointed questions and an embarrassing examination, Doctor Peabody confirmed Belle's suspicions.

"Two months along, is my guess," the doctor said, snapping his bag shut. "I'll leave a bottle of tonic to build up your strength until the nausea abates. Once it passes I predict you'll be eating everything in sight, and when it's time you'll deliver a healthy baby."

Suddenly Belle burst into tears. "I can't have this baby, Doctor."

"There, there, my dear. You're clearly distraught. It's not as bad as all that. I understand your fear. You've only been married a short time, but you aren't the first woman to bear her husband a child in seven months or less. You *are* married and that's all that counts. I'd best be on my way, I've got sick patients to see."

"I'd appreciate it if you'd let me tell my husband in my own way," Belle said on a tremulous sigh.

She wondered how she was going to apprise Casey of his impending fatherhood and if he would accept it. They hadn't discussed children since theirs wasn't a normal marriage, and she worried excessively about his response. He seemed fond of Tommy. Perhaps she should take it as a sign that he wanted children of his own.

Maybe she shouldn't tell him, Belle considered. Once he returned to the Pinkerton Agency he'd probably forget all about her. She'd already told Casey she didn't want to continue this marriage but he hadn't seemed impressed by her declaration. Damn his guilty conscience. Pity and guilt were no substitute for love. She didn't want a man who didn't love her.

Doctor Peabody bustled through the bedroom door, nearly colliding with Casey, who was still pacing the hallway. Casey stopped abruptly and barred the doctor's way.

"Well? How is my wife? Is her illness serious? Whatever it takes, I want her cured."

This time there was no mistaking the doctor's throaty chuckle. "It's out of my hands, Mr. Walker."

Casey felt the blood drain from his face. "Are you saying . . . ? No! She's too young!"

"Now, now, don't get excited. Your wife isn't going to die. She'll be right as rain in a few months. She wanted to be the one to tell you." He tried to walk around Casey, but Casey was having none of it.

He grasped the doctor by the collar and pulled him back. "Oh, no you don't! Tell me what's wrong with my wife and tell me now."

Doctor Peabody threw up his hands in defeat. "You're a determined man, Mr. Walker. Very well, but you must promise not to tell your wife I told you. It always spoils the surprise and it's more personal coming from the wife."

"What in the hell are you talking about? Just tell me what's wrong with Belle."

"You're going to be a father, Mr. Walker. In something less than seven months. But remember," he said, wagging his finger in warning, "you didn't hear it from me. Just make sure your wife takes her tonic."

Dazed, Casey leaned against the wall and took several deep breaths. A father! He'd often thought about having children of his own, but had never met a woman he cared enough about to marry. Until Belle. He wondered how she felt about bearing his child. Was she happy? Somehow he doubted it. At least now there was no question over ending their marriage.

Casey never thought he could feel this happy about anything. He couldn't seem to wipe the smile off his face. It just grew wider.

"You seem mighty happy for someone with a sick wife, brother," Mark accused. He had seen the doctor leave and had taken the steps two at a time, anxious to learn from Casey the outcome of the doctor's visit.

Casey could not stop grinning. "I'm about as happy as a man could be right now, brother. I'm going to be a father."

"Well, I'll be damned. I always said you were a lucky stiff. You didn't waste any time getting Belle with child. Kind of anticipated the wedding night, didn't you?" His mischievous grin was infectious, and Casey threw back his head and laughed.

"It doesn't matter when we had our wedding

night as long as a wedding followed. I just hope Belle is as thrilled as I am." He looked at the closed bedroom door with trepidation. "Wish me luck, brother."

"You have it but you won't need it. Go to your wife."

Belle couldn't stop crying. A baby. She couldn't have a baby, not now. She had scant moments left in which to decide whether or not to tell Casey. She could probably keep her secret for another few months, plenty of time for Casey to grow weary of playing at being a husband and move on. She expected him to move on anyway. It was the way men operated. Belle's dismal thoughts ended the moment Casey walked through the bedroom door.

Casey sat down on the edge of the bed and clasped Belle's hand, his face carefully composed. The doctor had warned him not to spoil the surprise and he wasn't going to, even if he had to bite his tongue to contain his happiness.

"How are you feeling, love?"

In that split second Belle made a decision, unwise though it might be. "Did Doctor Peabody say anything to you?" Casey shook his head in a negative manner. "He said I was suffering from stress and exhaustion," Belle lied. "I should be fine in a few days so you have nothing to worry about."

Casey stared at her through narrowed lids. "Are you sure that's all?"

She forced a smile. "Of course. Why would I lie?"

"Why indeed? Your eyes are red, have you been crying?"

"I suppose. It's a natural reaction to all that's happened to me."

Why was she lying? Casey wondered. Her tears clearly weren't tears of joy. The next thought struck him forcefully and he reeled back in dismay. Belle might as well have thrust a sword into this heart. She didn't want his child. She needed time to come to grips with the fact that she was pregnant. He wanted to throw her lie back in her face, but decided to play out her little game to the bitter end. How long did she expect to continue this charade? Sooner or later nature would reveal her condition.

Casey was angry and hurt. Everything he'd done in the past several weeks had been for Belle's and Tommy's sake. He'd put his entire life on hold while he searched for McAllister's murderer. He had given Belle his name and pledged his protection, did she expect him to leave just because she thought she no longer needed him? Evidently that's exactly what she expected. If Belle wanted to play games he would play along as long as it suited him. But the first time she did anything to harm his child the game ended.

"Rest as long as you like, Belle. That's the best medicine, I suppose. And take the tonic the doctor left. It's supposed to build your strength. If you need me I'll be at the winery. I haven't had time to go out there yet and it's been more or less running without leadership. The manager is a good man, I understand, but even he needs direction. The trustees of the estate placed me in charge of Tommy's holdings until he reaches his majority, and I'm not going to let them deteriorate for lack of attention."

Belle breathed a sigh of relief. Casey believed her. She would wait and see how long he stuck around before deciding if and when to tell him about the baby. Time would tell.

"Casey, before you leave, have you given any thought to what I said last night about Harry Hopkins?"

"If you're referring to the fact that you don't believe he's guilty, as far as I'm concerned the right man is in jail." He bent down and brushed a cool kiss across her lips. It was difficult to forget that Belle had been crying over an unwanted pregnancy. And even harder to reconcile to the fact that she had deliberately denied being pregnant.

The coolness of Casey's kiss lingered on her lips and Belle compared it to the heated, passionate kisses they had shared last night. Was he cooling to her already? Perhaps it was best that it happened now, before she learned to love him more than she did already did. If that were possible.

Belle felt so much better that she was up and dressed when Wan Yo brought Tommy home later that morning. Their reunion was poignant, tender, and exuberant. Tommy clung to his mother with a desperation that brought tears to Belle's eyes. Everything, it seemed, brought tears to her eyes these days. It was a very long time before Belle could convince her small son that she would never leave him again. Once convinced, he allowed Wan Yo to lead him off to play.

Belle was exploring the house that was now her home when Naomi arrived. She appeared in a state of agitation, obviously upset over something. Naomi hugged Belle tightly, then congratulated her heartily.

"Thank God you had the good sense to marry Casey," Naomi said as she sank into the nearest chair. "If not for him you'd still be in jail. The man cares for you a great deal, Belle. And for Tommy, too."

Belle perched on the edge of the sofa, her face a study of contradictions. "Casey was driven by guilt, not love for me or Tommy."

"For God's sake, Belle, give the man some credit. He worked tirelessly in your behalf. He's your husband, do you feel nothing for him? This marriage could be a good one if you let it."

Belle stared down at her hands. "I doubt that Casey will be around long enough to develop lasting attachments."

"Still don't trust him, huh? Are you sleeping with him?" Naomi asked bluntly. Belle's flaming cheeks was all the answer Naomi needed. "You can't fool me, honey. I know you. You wouldn't bed any man unless you loved him. Does Casey know you love him?"

Belle's head shot up sharply. "No! And don't you dare tell him. I don't want his pity. I've got everything I need right here. Tommy, a house, and money." Instinctively her hand splayed over her stomach, arousing Naomi's curiosity.

"Is there something you're not telling me, honey?"

Belle looked startled. "No, nothing." Her answer came quickly, too quickly, Naomi thought. "Well, there is one thing that bothers me, Naomi. I don't think Harry Hopkins killed McAllister. Casey thinks I've lost my mind but I can't help feeling as I do. I . . . I'm going to visit Mr. Hopkins in jail today. Maybe he'll tell me the truth. I met him before, you know. He seemed such a kindly man."

"Don't rock the boat, honey," Naomi advised. "The man confessed, what more do you want?"

"I want to know why he confessed. If he isn't guilty he shouldn't be sent to prison or"—she gulped convulsively—"hung for murder. Casey said he'll probably be sentenced soon."

"I'm advising you to forget Hopkins, Belle."

Naomi's stern warning fell on deaf ears. Belle was already planning her visit to Harry Hopkins.

"There's something else I'd like to talk to you about," Naomi added. "I took on a new girl. I did so with misgivings because she wasn't the type I usually hire. But the poor thing seemed so desperate I couldn't say no. Her name is Greta. She claimed to be experienced but I finally got her to admit she'd had only one previous sexual encounter. With a man she fancied herself in love with. She left her father's home with the man. Unfortunately the bounder abandoned her after he stole her virginity and her money.

"Last night was her first working night. A customer named Hank Jones took a liking to her and took her upstairs. I thought she could handle him but I was mistaken. At the last minute she got cold feet and refused to service him. Jones beat her quite severely. Doc Peabody patched her up and she'll be all right, but I don't have the heart to toss her out on the streets. She's no whore and never will be.

"The girl refuses to return home. Her father is a preacher and she doesn't want to shame him more than she already has. She's young, Belle, but smart. I thought it was about time Tommy had a governess."

"That poor girl," Belle sympathized.

"I reported Jones to the sheriff and hopefully the man will spend a night or two in jail."

"You're a good woman, Naomi, always taking in

strays. I'd fight anyone who says you aren't. Send Greta around. If she's as smart as you say, I'm sure Tommy will benefit from her instruction. And I'd be glad for the company. This is a household of males."

"Then it's settled," Naomi said, rising. "And honey, now that you live up here with the rich, I don't think it's wise for me to visit you again. I don't want our friendship to sully your reputation."

Belle gave her a disgruntled look. "I had no reputation to begin with. You're the only one who stuck by me when everyone else had me guilty of murder. I'll see you anytime I damn well please. If you won't come here, I'll come to you."

Naomi shook her head, inordinately pleased but still skeptical. "You're a stubborn woman, Belle. I certainly can't stop you from coming to my house. You're welcome anytime. But shouldn't you ask your husband first if he wants you to visit a house of ill-repute?"

"I doubt Casey will stick around long enough to care," Belle said softly.

"He might surprise you, honey. Well, I've got to go. I'll send Greta around later. If it doesn't work out I'll try to think of something else for the girl."

Naomi left in a tantalizing swirl of frothy white petticoats and scarlet satin skirts.

Later that afternoon Belle put Tommy down for his nap and prepared to go out. Wan Yo offered to accompany her but Belle declined. She preferred that he stay with Tommy. If Harry Hopkins didn't kill McAllister, then the person who did was still roaming the city and could present a danger to those she loved. Belle knew she wasn't thinking straight but somewhere in the tangled mass of her wild imaginings was a reasonable explanation. She just hadn't figured it out yet. If Casey wouldn't help it was up to her to make sure an innocent man wasn't hung for a murder he didn't commit.

Sheriff Rogan refused to allow Belle access to the prisoner when she arrived at the jailhouse. "Haven't you had enough of this place, Mrs. Walker? Does your husband know you're here?"

Belle refused to leave. When the sheriff could quote no law forbidding a visit with the prisoner, he grudgingly allowed Belle ten minutes. He escorted Belle to the cell and waited nearby while Belle spoke in low tones to Harry Hopkins.

"What are you doing here?" Hopkins asked when he saw Belle standing on the other side of the bars.

Belle thought the poor man looked more ill than he had the day before. "I'm here to satisfy my curiosity," Belle said in a hushed voice. "I'm going to ask you a question, Mr. Hopkins, and I want a truthful answer. Why did you lie? Why did you confess to killing Mr. McAllister when you didn't do it?"

Hopkins stared at Belle in consternation. "You're loco, lady. Of course I killed old T.J. For your own sake you've got to believe that."

"But you didn't do it, Mr. Hopkins. Did my husband talk you into confessing? Did he threaten you?"

"That young man was mighty persistent but he didn't threaten me. Look here, little lady, I'm dying. I knew you couldn't have killed the bastard so I thought I'd do one good deed before meeting my maker."

"But it's not fair!"

"Life is rarely fair. But ya gotta make the best of it. You got your whole life ahead of ya. McAllister hurt you just like he hurt me and Jones. I didn't kill him but I'm not sorry he's dead. That husband of yours is one determined man. If my confession served to bring you and your son and husband happiness, then I will die a contented man. Who's to say I wouldn't have killed McAllister if I had gotten to him first?"

"Do you have any idea who killed my father-in-law?"

"Old T.J. must have had numerous enemies. I haven't been in town long enough to name them."

"Why were you watching his house?"

"I admit I walked past the mansion a few times, trying to get up the nerve to confront the bastard, pardon my language, ma'am."

"I'm going to try to convince my husband to find the real killer," Belle promised. "He's got to listen to me."

"Good luck, ma'am. I ain't afraid to die, if that's to be my fate. I ain't got long to live anyways. Thank you for caring, little gel. If I had a daughter I'd want her to be just like you."

"Time is up, Mrs. Walker."

Belle started violently, surprised to find the sheriff standing behind her. Had it been ten minutes already? "Good-bye, Mr. Hopkins. Try to keep your spirits up."

"What's your connection with that man?" Rogan asked curiously.

"No connection. I just wanted to hear from his lips why he killed my father-in-law."

"Did he tell you? I'd be interested in finding that out myself."

"We hadn't gotten around to that yet. Good-day, Sheriff." She left Rogan staring after her with his mouth hanging open and his curiosity unappeased.

When Belle arrived home, she found Greta waiting for her in the parlor. Tommy had woken and he and Greta were conversing quietly.

"I see you've met my son," Belle said, smiling at Greta's bowed head. "I'm Belle Mc . . . Walker. Naomi told me all about you."

Greta looked up at Belle and flushed. "And you still want me to be your son's governess?"

Belle got her first good look at Greta's face and her hand flew to her mouth. The girl had been severely battered. Her face was bruised and swollen until its original contours were all but obscured by purple and black blotches. Her eyes had been blackened and her bottom lip was swollen to twice its size. "Oh you poor thing!"

"Miss Greta fell, Mama," Tommy said. "Isn't it awful? But the doctor told her she'd be all well soon. Naomi sent her to be my governess."

"If you'll have me, Mrs. Walker, after . . ." Greta's voice cracked with nervousness. "I'll understand if you don't think I'm appropriate for your son's governess."

Noting Tommy's rapt attention, Belle said, "I'll bet cook has cookies and milk for you in the kitchen, son. Go get your snack while I speak with Miss Greta."

Tommy ran off, and Belle took Greta's hands and led her to the sofa. "Sit down and tell me about yourself. Noami told me a little but if you're going to be my son's governess I'll need to know more."

Greta cleared her throat and looked Belle in the eye. "Despite what you know about me I'm not a whore."

"What is this all about?" Casey strode into the parlor. He had heard Greta's words and his curiosity was aroused.

Belle jumped to her feet. "This is between me and Greta."

Casey studied Greta with slow perusal, wincing at the sight of her battered features. "If this is a household decision then I damn well better be included. Especially in view of what I heard when I entered the room."

Just then Tommy bounded back into the room and grasped Casey's hand. "Casey, have you met my new governess?"

Belle sent Casey a bright smile. Casey frowned furiously. Poor Greta wished for the floor to open up and swallow her.

Chapter 15

Belle wished she'd had more time to talk to Greta before Casey came home, but there was no help for it now but to introduce her. "Casey, this is Greta. Naomi recommended her for Tommy's governess."

Casey was clearly startled. Since when was the madam an expert on governesses? He pitied the severely beaten girl, but she'd need more qualifications than that before he'd agree to bring her into the household. Her pale blond hair was piled atop her small head and she was dressed in a demure, peach-colored gown with a high, round collar. She was small and neatly fashioned. Her figure was pleasing but that was all he could tell about her appearance. Her face was too hideously swollen and discolored to tell if she was even remotely pretty.

"This is my husband, Casey Walker," Belle continued as she introduced Greta to Casey.

Greta held out a small, white hand to Casey. Casey shook it without compunction. "Are you qualified to work as a governess, Miss . . . ?" Suddenly he realized he hadn't been given a last name.

"Collins. Greta Collins." Her voice quavered nervously. If the Walkers didn't hire her she had no place else to go. "My parents insisted I be given an education. I attended a finishing school and am qualified to teach young children the basics of education."

"My wife says Naomi recommended you." He hesitated but felt compelled to ask, "Have you known Naomi long?"

Belle cleared her throat, forestalling Greta's answer. Tommy seemed to be hanging onto every word. "Tommy, find Wan Yo and tell him to take you to the park. There is plenty of time for a romp before dinner."

Once Tommy was gone Casey turned his gaze back to Greta, waiting for her answer.

"I met Naomi when she took me in a few days ago."

Casey's next questions were more pointed. "Are you one of Naomi's stable of girls? Did one of your . . . er . . . customers beat you?"

Greta turned a dull red beneath the bruises.

"Casey! Don't badger Greta," Belle cautioned.

"It's all right, Mrs. Walker, your husband has a right to know. I worked for Naomi one night but couldn't go through with it. The man who paid for my services beat me when I refused to accommodate me. Naomi brought me here. She said I didn't belong in her house."

Casey's features softened but he still wasn't satisfied. Tommy was a young, impressionable child. A governess could influence his life in countless ways and should be above reproach. "What caused you to seek employment with Naomi? Why did you leave your parents' home?"

Belle hated the way Casey was probing into Greta's past. Just as she had been condemned for living with Naomi, Casey was judging Greta unfairly. "Casey, isn't it enough that Naomi recommended Greta?"

"I'm afraid it isn't, Belle. Tommy's welfare is at stake. We don't want him placed in the care of someone inappropriate."

Greta rose to leave. "Perhaps I should go. It was wrong of me to . . ."

"No! Stay," Belle said, glaring at Casey. "Naomi's word is good enough for me."

"Allow me to be the judge of what's good for my family," Casey said tightly. He turned back to Greta. "Would you care to answer my question?"

Greta stared at her hands. "I ran away with a man I thought I loved. My parents didn't approve of him. But since I was of age I listened to my heart instead of their good judgment. I withdrew my small inheritance from the bank and left my family home with the man I thought would be my husband. He took my money and my virginity and left me penniless in San Francisco."

"So you sought work in a brothel. You could have gone home," Casey contended.

"You don't know my father. He's a preacher and very strict. He would have not have taken me back into his home. I had no self-esteem left. I thought working in a bordello was all that I deserved." She lifted her gaze to Casey. Her eyes were blue and spoke eloquently of her utter defeat. "Perhaps I was right after all. I have fallen from grace and should accept my fate. If Naomi won't take me back I'm sure I will find a place in another bordello."

"That won't be necessary," Belle said, taking

Greta's hands in hers. "You are young and were taken advantage of, and no blame can be attached to that. You were wrong to seek employment in a bordello but you've paid for your mistake. Men can be pigs. You didn't deserve the beating you received. There is an empty room next to Tommy's, I'm sure you'll be comfortable there. Wan Yo can retrieve your belongings from Naomi's later."

"There you are. Are you discussing something important or can I join in?"

Mark had returned from the winery, eager to discuss his day. He had found the workings fascinating and wanted to ask Casey if he could return to the winery on a daily basis to learn all aspects of the business. He spied Greta and came to an abrupt halt.

"Oh, I'm sorry, I didn't know you had company."

Greta turned slowly, giving Mark the full benefit of her ravaged features. Mark gasped, paling beneath his tan. "My God! Tell me who did that to you, miss, and I'll make him sorry he still walks the face of the earth."

"I feel the same way, brother," Casey said. "This is Greta Collins, Tommy's new governess. Miss Collins, this is my brother, Mark Walker."

After introductions were made, Belle showed Greta to her room. Casey walked to the liquor cabinet and poured himself a brandy. "Join me, Mark," Casey invited.

"What happened to that poor woman?" Mark asked, accepting a dram of brandy from Casey.

"It's a long story."

"I've got time."

"I don't know the whole story but I'll tell you what I do know." He then related everything Greta had told him. "I was reluctant to hire the woman but you know Belle."

"I wonder what Greta looks like beneath those bruises," Mark mused.

"Don't get any ideas, Mark. I won't have any hanky-panky going on beneath this roof. Except for her one mistake, Miss Collins seems like a decent woman."

"She is," Belle said, reentering the room. "She's a victim of a man's lust and has paid dearly for her mistake."

"Belle is right," Mark agreed, slapping his brother on the back. "I'll leave you two alone to work this out."

The moment Mark was gone, Belle rounded on Casey. "You had no right talking to Greta the way you did! Tommy is my son, not yours, and I'd never do anything to hurt him. Hiring Greta should have been my decision, not yours."

Casey's temper dangled by a slim thread. Then he saw a maid peeking around the corner and realized that whatever was said in the parlor would be repeated among the servants. "Not here." Grasping her hand, he pulled her up the stairs and into their room, slamming the door behind him.

"When we married I accepted responsibility for the family," Casey said.

Belle's chin slanted upward. "Responsibility is a forever thing. I don't expect you to remain around long enough to undertake that kind of commitment."

"I'm not leaving, Belle."

There was a momentary flicker in Belle's eyes. "But I assumed . . ."

"Until I tell you I'm leaving, I suggest you accustom yourself to having me around." His eyes narrowed. "Shouldn't you be in bed? I thought the doctor told you to rest."

Casey waited in vain for Belle to tell him about the baby, and when she failed to do so disappointment made his voice harsh. "From now on you'll rest in bed every afternoon until your natural color returns and you regain your former stamina. If you won't take care of yourself, I reckon it's up to me to do it for you."

Casey reacted so fast Belle had no time to protest. Sweeping her from her feet, he placed her in the center of the bed. "Rest until dinner. Lord knows you didn't get much sleep last night."

Belle fumed in silent rage. He didn't have to remind her that she had spent the night in his arms, being loved and loving him in return.

When Belle continued to remain mute about their child, Casey stomped from the room. Love hurt when it was not returned. He wondered how long Belle would keep her little secret. She was going to be damned surprised to find him still here when she bore their child. Maybe by that time she would realize he had no intention of leaving her, Tommy, or their expected baby.

As far as Casey was concerned, his detective work had ended with his marriage. Casey had already repaid the three thousand dollars he had borrowed from Allan Pinkerton. He had also written a letter to his employer explaining his situation and resigning his position.

Greta joined them for dinner that night. The conversation was dominated by Mark. His enthusiasm for the wine business and all its various stages, from the initial harvesting of grapes to the final production of wine, was catching. He waxed eloquent about all he had seen that day at the winery and announced his intention to learn the business.

When Mark tried to engage Greta in conversation, she answered shyly and in monosyllables. She kept her head bent, ashamed to show her bruised countenance, and excused herself immediately following the meal. Mark stared after her, his expression thoughtful.

"I'd still like to get my hands on the bastard who hurt her," he said harshly.

"Get in line," Casey said dryly. "What are your plans tonight, Mark?"

"Thought I'd go out, perhaps stop in at Naomi's later."

"Mind if I tag along?"

Mark sent Casey a sidelong glance, wondering what he was about. Casey was a newlywed, for godsake. And an expectant father. Evidently all wasn't well between him and Belle. "Sure, come along, if it's all right with Belle."

Belle's head jerked upright. "Casey doesn't need my permission to carouse. It's what men do, isn't it?"

"It doesn't have to be like that," Casey said quietly.

"Of course it does. If you'll excuse me, I promised Tommy a story before bedtime."

"Trouble in paradise?" Mark asked once they were alone. "Did the baby make no difference in your relationship?"

"Belle isn't aware that I know about the child. I'm waiting for her to tell me. If you must know, I'm at my wit's end where my wife is concerned. She's convinced I'll leave her and Tommy, and that I can't be trusted. Don't let on that you know about the child. If I'm not supposed to know, then you can't either.''

"This is too complicated for me," Mark contended. "But if you still want to join me, be ready in an hour."

Sleep eluded Belle. She remembered Casey's words about finding a woman to satisfy him and imagined him with Sweet Sue, or Ellie, or any one of Naomi's girls. It shouldn't hurt so much, but it did. If Casey wanted to earn her trust he was going about it the wrong way, she reflected. She just thanked God Casey wasn't like the pig who hurt Greta. If Greta had been a whore, Belle still would have taken her in. Perhaps not as Tommy's governess but in some capacity in the household. Every woman deserved a second chance.

The hall clock was striking midnight when she heard Casey's footsteps on the stairs. She held her breath when he paused at her door, and let it out in a shaky sigh when he continued on to his room. The previous night she had slept in Casey's arms. Now he was returning from another woman's arms and the pain was unbearable. Belle was mired in confusion. She wanted Casey and hated herself for needing him. She loved him yet didn't trust him.

Belle finally fell asleep, her hand splayed across the place where her child grew inside her. Casey's child.

Casey paced the length of the room and back. He hadn't gone to Naomi's after all. He had left Mark on Naomi's doorstep and continued on to the nearest saloon. He tossed down several beers, watched a girlie show on stage, and allowed one of the dancers to sit on his lap. He had politely refused her whispered invitation for something more intimate and wandered off to join a poker game.

No matter how hard Casey tried to drown his problems, drinking only seemed to magnify them. He was going to be a father and his wife refused to acknowledge her pregnancy. He knew Belle was unhappy about her pregnancy, that she wanted neither him nor his child. When liquor lost the ability to dull the pain of Belle's rejection, Casey had returned home. He had paused briefly before Belle's door then continued on to his own room, where he now paced in silent misery.

Abruptly Casey stopped pacing and quietly let himself out into the hall. Belle was his wife, dammit, and he had every right to be with her. Her door opened noiselessly beneath his fingertips and he stepped inside. Beams of moonlight filtered through the window, bathing the room in a silvery glow. Casey's gaze stopped at the bed where a slender figure lay curled beneath the covers. He padded to the bed on bare feet, threw off the robe he had donned when he'd undressed earlier and slid into bed beside his wife.

Belle didn't awaken. A breathy sigh slipped past her lips as she went willingly into Casey's arms. She slept there in contentment all night. She awoke the following morning to find Casey staring at her as if he could see through to her very soul. She jerked back in surprise.

"What are you doing here?"

"This is where I belong."

She wrinkled her nose and lashed him with a

look of contempt. "You smell like a cheap whore. The least you could do was wash off the other woman's scent before climbing in bed with me."

"There was no other woman."

Belle turned away in disgust. "Keep your secrets. I don't want to know about your women." She started to rise, but the moment her head left the pillow she turned white and dove for the slop jar. Casey leapt from bed and held the jar steady while she heaved into it. When she finished, he helped her to lie down again and fetched water and a cloth.

"How long is this supposed to last?" he asked as she rinsed out her mouth and washed her face.

Belle went still. Casey didn't know, did he? "Not too much longer. The tonic the doctor left should help."

He waited for her to tell him about their child and when she didn't, he said, "Stay in bed today. Wan Yo will bring your meals and Greta can see to Tommy."

"I can't."

"You can't?" he asked incredulously.

"There is something I have to do."

"Perhaps I can do it for you."

Belle was silent a long time, wondering how much to tell Casey about her decision to find McAllister's real killer. "Perhaps you can help if you can tear yourself away from all the women clamoring for your attention."

"Belle." His voice was low, but hard as steel. "Get this straight once and for all. I'm not leaving you. I don't have another woman . . . yet," he added ominously, "and I damn sure can't help you if I don't know the problem."

Belle pulled herself into a sitting position, found

she could control the nausea churning inside her, and felt encouraged to continue. "I went to see Harry Hopkins yesterday."

Of all the things Belle could have said, that was the least expected. And the most likely to upset Casey. "You what! Good God, Belle, are you crazy? The man's a killer."

Casey's outburst didn't seem to faze Belle. "He didn't do it, Casey. He told me so himself."

"I'd deny it myself if I thought I'd hang for it."

"I believe him. You're a detective. Find the man responsible before it's too late."

"I already found the right man. Why would Hopkins confess if he wasn't guilty?"

"He did it for my sake. He's a kindly man."

"He's a stranger. He hardly knows you, why should he offer his life in exchange for yours?"

"He said he's dying anyway, and he didn't believe I killed my father-in-law. He knew I had a son who would miss me if I was sent to prison."

Casey shook his head. "You're too gullible for your own good, love. The man has you hoodwinked."

"Then you won't help?"

"I would if I thought it wasn't a waste of my time."

"Very well, I'll do this on my own."

Casey tensed, recalling Belle's condition. "What exactly are you going to do?"

"Find a killer, of course."

"Then I have nothing to worry about where you're concerned, because the killer is already behind bars." He regarded her somberly. "Is there anything else we need to discuss?"

Tell me, Belle, tell me now, Casey silently implored.

"Do you intend to sleep in my bed tonight? And the next night? And the next?"

"Why are you being stubborn about this?" Casey charged.

"About what? Our sleeping together?"

No, about the baby, Casey thought, but did not say. "I'll sleep in your bed and make love to you whenever I get the urge. You're the most exasperating woman I've ever known."

"What about those other women you mentioned? The ones who can satisfy your needs better than I? The ones whose perfume you're wearing?"

"You haven't driven me that far yet," Casey said by way of warning.

Belle believed him. Or perhaps it was that she *wanted* to believe him. He still hadn't explained the perfume to her satisfaction, but she let it pass.

"Are you going to obey me and stay away from the jailhouse?" Casey asked, toying with a bright strand of her hair. It felt like silk between his fingers, and he loved the rich sable color spilling over his hand. He brought it to his lips, kissed it and placed it behind her ear.

Belle watched him warily, all too aware of the power he held over her emotions. His kisses rendered her witless, and if she wasn't careful she might inadvertently let slip about the baby. She wasn't ready for that truth yet.

"I'm going to do what I think is right," Belle replied. "I'm willing to bet the killer is still in town." She gave him a little shove. "Don't you have work to do this morning?"

"Nothing is more important than tending to my wife."

"Why do you keep pretending ours is a real marriage?"

"What will it take to convince you it *is* a real marriage?"

Love, Belle wanted to say. "If you don't know, I'm not going to tell you."

"Shall I show you?"

He didn't wait for her answer. His arms went around her, bringing her beneath him on the bed. He held his body slightly above her so as not to hurt her as he lowered his head and fused his mouth to hers. He kissed her long and hard, feeling her mouth soften and open beneath his and rejoicing in her surrender. She might not love him, but her body recognized his as her soul mate.

He touched her breasts and she arched violently against him, whimpering beneath her breath. Pregnancy made her breasts exquisitely sensitive, and Casey took advantage of it by manipulating her nipples with his fingers and tongue.

"Can marriage get any more real than this?" Casey challenged as she moved restlessly against him, seeking him with her body if not her mind.

"You're taking unfair advantage," Belle panted as his hands sought the moist, silken petals between her legs. "Please stop."

"You don't really want me to stop." His lips slid downward, leaving a trail of fire across her skin. Then his mouth was *there*, between her thighs, the pleasure nearly painful as his tongue scraped across the nub of swollen flesh he found there. His tongue, shrewd and clever, laved her expertly, then plunged deep inside her.

Belle arched off the bed, a guttural cry ripping out of her chest. She began to spiral upward toward release, rocking back against the bed, her fingers digging into his shoulders.

Casey felt her slide into ecstasy and moved upward over her. "No, not yet. Together, love. We'll do this together."

Bracing himself above her on his forearms, he rubbed the ripe tip of his manhood against her slick sex. Belle whimpered. He was torturing her. When Casey bent and laved her sensitive nipple with his tongue, she shattered. Screaming his name.

In the midst of her climax, Casey thrust inside her. Fast. Hard. Belle sobbed as her pleasure intensified. Casey's thrusting increased, became wild.

"Oh, my God!" he cried. Then his mouth found hers. She returned his kiss as his body spasmed and trembled against hers. He made a strangled sound and emptied himself inside her.

Belle felt Casey's weight shift as he lifted himself off her. She closed her eyes, adrift in a sensory fog, willing herself not to look as he rose from the bed and went to the wash basin. A few minutes later she heard him approach the bed and she opened her eyes. He was staring down on her, regarding her through hooded lids. She had this strange feeling that he was waiting for her to say something. When she remained mute she felt the tattered edges of his disappointment reach out to her. What did he want her to say? What was he waiting for?

"Don't ever tell me this marriage is an empty one because I just proved otherwise."

She felt her cheeks flaming. She said nothing.

His regard was intense, probing. It was also enigmatic. Belle could not decipher his thoughts and wasn't sure she wanted to. Finally he turned away and began dressing.

"Mark and I are going back to the winery today," he informed her coolly. "Mark is proving indispensable. His interest in the winery is something I hadn't expected. Perhaps I'll make him manager of the operation once he's learned the ropes. If that's all right with you."

"Since I have little knowledge of that kind of operation, I have no objection. I do intend to acquaint myself soon with all the facets of Tommy's inheritance."

"Talk to Mr. Engle at the bank, he's trustee of the estate."

Belle regarded him curiously. Casey had gone from passionate lover to polite stranger in a matter of minutes.

"Is there anything else you'd like to tell me, Belle?" Casey encouraged. He was fully dressed now and eyeing her dispassionately.

"You're not angry about Greta, are you?"

Disappointment flickered briefly in Casey's eyes. "No, but you're going to have to quit taking in strays." He turned to leave. "Stay in bed today, Belle. And eat something substantial. After heaving this morning your stomach must be touching your backbone."

Belle decided to follow Casey's advice, up to a point. She was feeling fine now and devoured a huge breakfast while a beaming Wan Yo stood over her, nodding his approval.

"Missy eat for two now," the old man said.

Belle's fork clattered into her plate. "What! How do you know?"

"Wan Yo not stupid, missy. Baby come. Wan Yo happy for missy and master."

"You haven't said anything to Casey, have you?"

Wan Yo gave her a reproving look. "Not my place, missy, but master not stupid, either."

After bestowing those words of wisdom, Wan Yo left to tend to duty. Greta entered the dining room while Belle was sipping her coffee.

"Tommy is eating in the kitchen with Wan Yo," Greta said shyly. "I thought this was a good time to discuss my duties."

"Perhaps you should take it easy for a few days," Belle suggested kindly. She wondered if Greta had been beaten about her body as well as her face, but didn't want to ask embarrassing questions.

"I'd prefer to begin my duties immediately," Greta said. "Tommy is an adorable child. I'm sure we'll get along famously."

"Very well. I do have some books for his lessons, but you're to purchase anything else you need and charge it to my husband. In addition to room and board you'll receive a salary of one hundred dollars a month."

"One hundred dollars! That's far too much," Greta protested.

"I insist," Belle said. "You will have weekends free but your weekdays must be devoted to Tommy."

Tears of gratitude slid down Greta's cheeks. "I don't know what to say."

"Taking care of my son will be thanks enough. How old are you, Greta, if I may be so bold as to ask?"

"Twenty-one. Is that a problem? Did you want someone older?"

Belle smiled. "You'll do just fine. Why don't you

eat breakfast with Tommy? I have an errand or two to run."

Belle's errands consisted of visits to Mr. Engle at the bank and Harry Hopkins at the jailhouse. She was stunned by what she learned from Mr. Engle. Tommy would never want for a thing as long as he lived. His grandfather had left him wealthy beyond belief. She was somewhat surprised at how effortlessly Casey had taken control of Tommy's vast estate. While grateful for his business acumen, she was nonetheless wary of the amount of authority he wielded, but Engle seemed pleased that Casey had willingly assumed responsibility for Tommy and his empire.

The visit to the jailhouse was enlightening in one respect yet disheartening in another. The sad part was that poor Harry appeared to be wasting away. They conversed for a few minutes, and in the course of the conversation Harry told her the cell next to him was occupied by a man named Hank Jones. Belle remembered Naomi telling her that Hank Jones was the man who had beaten Greta. On the way home Belle recalled something else. Something Casey had mentioned while trying to prove her innocence.

T.J. McAllister's third partner was a man named Arnold Jones. It could be a coincidence. Jones was a common enough name. But intuition told Belle there was a connection between Hank Jones and Arnold Jones. In that respect the visit to the jailhouse had been enlightening.

Chapter 16

$\sim\!\!\infty\!\!\sim$

A week later Harry Hopkins was sentenced to die. Confessed killers were shown little mercy. He was to hang in two weeks. A gallows was being constructed on the empty lot across from the jailhouse. Belle visited Hopkins following his sentencing. The old man seemed resigned to his fate. Not so Belle.

"I'm sorry," Belle lamented. "But I have an idea. Do you recall the man who occupied the cell next to yours? What happened to him?"

"You mean Hank Jones? He was fined ten dollars for beating up one of Naomi's girls and set free."

"Wasn't one of the partners in the gold mine named Jones?"

Hopkins scratched the bald spot on his head and peered at Belle through rheumy eyes. "I reckon he was, but I don't see the connection. Arnold Jones would be nearly as old as I am had he lived. Jones is a common name."

"Tell me about Arnold Jones," Belle urged. "Help me, Harry, I'm trying to save your life."

Harry gave her a gentle smile. "I appreciate your

concern, Belle, but it's no use. I confessed, remember? It ain't gonna be that bad. I'll probably cheat the hangman and die in this here bunk."

"Humor me, Harry. Tell me about Arnold Jones. Where did you meet? Was he a friend of T.J. McAllister's?"

Hopkins stared off into space, thinking back twenty years. "We met in a saloon over a poker game one night. A miner by the name of Rusty Steinbeck needed money. He'd lost heavily at the tables and offered to sell the deed to his mine for cash money. Neither McAllister nor Jones nor myself had enough cash to buy the mine, but by pooling our money we found we could manage it. So we formed a partnership. That's how it all began."

"How did Jones die?"

"Cave-in. He was in a new tunnel. Said he smelled gold. A ton of rock fell on him. We never even tried to dig him out. Still there, for all I know."

"When was that, Harry? Before or after you sold out to my father-in-law?"

Harry's mind traveled backward in time, trying to pinpoint the exact time of the cave-in that took Jones's life. "I reckon it happened shortly after the surveyor told us the mine was worthless, and McAllister offered to buy us out. I was more than agreeable but Jones refused. He said the mine held gold and he was going to find it. That cave-in ended all his dreams."

"What happened to Jones's share? Was it divided between you and McAllister?"

"Naw. Jones had a family back East. Left a widow and young son. They inherited his share. McAllister wrote the widow a nice letter, told her the mine was worthless and sent her a draft to cover Jones's share. She accepted McAllister's money, though truth to tell the sum was a mere pittance compared to the gold McAllister pulled out of the mine later.''

Belle grew excited. *Jones had a son!* It could mean everything or it could mean nothing. ''Did you ever hear from the son or widow?''

''Naw. Like I said before, I didn't stick around. Didn't learn McAllister struck gold until months later. I don't see how all this is gonna make any difference in what happens to me,'' Hopkins said. His voice was thready and weak; he was completely tuckered out from talking.

''I don't know,'' Belle said, ''but it gives me something to go on. Get some rest, I'll return soon.''

Belle lingered to talk to the sheriff before leaving the building.

''I don't know why you're wasting your time coming here, Mrs. Walker. Haven't you better things to do?''

''I'm convinced Harry Hopkins is innocent, Sheriff.''

''It's a mite late for that, ma'am. Why don't you go on home and see to your family?''

''There is a killer loose in your city, Sheriff,'' Belle said with asperity. ''Do you remember Hank Jones, the man who beat up one of Naomi's girls? Find him and you might be surprised at what you learn.''

Sheriff Rogan gave her a look of utter disbelief. ''Are you accusing Hank Jones of murder? You don't even know the man. I think all this has made you a tad loco, Mrs. Walker. I got rounds to make and I know you've got things to do.''

He held the door open for her. Belle had no

choice but to leave. It looked like Harry Hopkins was going to die on her account, and it nearly tore her apart.

Casey left his office and walked down the street toward the Lucky Nugget saloon. He needed a drink. He knew Harry Hopkins had been sentenced to hang and worried over Belle's response to the sentence. She was so convinced the man was innocent it was beginning to rub off on him.

His lips curved upward into a smile, recalling Belle's chagrin when he'd continued to sleep with her each night. He didn't make love to her every night, but just holding her in his arms made him happy. When he did make love to her, it didn't take long for her to warm to his kisses and caresses. In the end her own passion took over and her pleasure was as exuberantly vocal as his.

But no matter how long he waited, how badly he wanted Belle to tell him about their baby, she remained stubbornly mute on the subject. Her stomach was still flat and showed no signs of pregnancy. It was her ultra-sensitive breasts that gave away her condition. Not only were they sensitive to his slightest touch, but they had become fuller, her nipples larger.

Lost in his contemplation of Belle's ripening body, Casey suddenly realized he had reached the Lucky Nugget. Two things happened at the same time. Sheriff Rogan hailed Casey from across the street, and a man approached the swinging door from the inside, saw the sheriff hurrying in his direction and ducked away from the door. He was a youngish man, no more than thirty-five. His reddish hair and beard were in need of cutting and his clothing was rumpled and stained. His eyes were downright mean. One knew immediately that crossing this man was dangerous. He hovered just inside the swinging doors, out of sight but close enough to eavesdrop on the sheriff and Casey.

"Sheriff Rogan," Casey greeted affably, "is there something on your mind?"

"Yeah, Walker, something *is* on my mind. It's that wife of yours. Can't you keep her home where she belongs? I'd advise you to keep her barefoot and pregnant so she can't meddle."

Casey gave him a wry smile. What in the hell had Belle done now to upset the sheriff? "My wife is free to go where she pleases."

"Yeah, well it doesn't please me to have her visiting my jail every day. She's a damn nuisance, Walker, with her accusations and suppositions. Now she claims a man named Hank Jones killed McAllister. Granted, Jones is an ornery bastard, but she can't go around accusing people of murder without proof."

"That's exactly what you did, Sheriff, when you jailed Belle for McAllister's murder," Casey charged.

"That's different," Rogan grunted, not quite meeting Casey's eyes. "Tell your wife to stay away from the jailhouse and to keep her accusations to herself. If Mr. Jones gets wind of them, he might get ugly. I haven't heard he's left town so I reckon he's still around."

Flattened against the wall inside the saloon, Hank Jones had heard everything. A few months ago he'd learned that old man McAllister had cheated his father out of a fortune, and he'd come to San

Francisco to confront his father's old partner. McAllister hadn't been frightened of him and had refused to part with the money that rightfully belonged to his father. Now McAllister was dead and could no longer make him a rich man, but his daughter-in-law and grandson could. Women were weak, they frightened more easily than men. Old McAllister was probably burning in Hell now, sorry he'd not heeded Hank Jones or given in to his demands. Jones was smiling when he headed back to the bar and ordered another drink.

Casey fumed in impotent rage as he watched the sheriff march off down the street. He no longer wanted a drink. He wanted to go home and put an end to Belle's meddling. Hank Jones was the man who'd beaten Greta and he was taking no chances with his wife's life. Belle had more to protect now than her own beautiful neck.

Belle had reached home in a despondent mood. There was only one way Harry Hopkins could be saved. Casey was a good detective. She needed to convince him of Harry's innocence and implore him to investigate Hank Jones. And it had to be done within the space of two weeks.

Casey wasn't home yet when Belle returned, but Mark was. She found him and Greta seated side by side on the parlor sofa. Their heads were together and they appeared quite taken with one another. They sprang apart guiltily when Belle entered the room and cleared her throat.

"Oh, Belle, we didn't hear you come in," Greta said, flushing. "Tommy is in the kitchen with Wan Yo, I haven't been neglecting him. We just finished our lessons for the day."

"No need to explain," Belle said distractedly.

"Problems?" Mark asked. "Can I help?"

"It's . . ." She started to tell him, then thought better of it. "Nothing."

It suddenly occurred to Belle that Greta and Mark had become more than just friends in a very short time. She should have noticed it before now but she'd been too involved with Harry Hopkins. She didn't begrudge either of them their happiness. Both had suffered reverses in their lives and had earned the right to happiness. She wished she and Casey could find that same kind of happiness.

Belle wanted to tell Casey about the baby and almost had on several occasions. But the words wouldn't come. True, Casey seemed content with his life here, but for how long? How long before he yearned for the excitement and danger of his previous occupation? How long before he tired of making love to her and sought variety in the arms of other women? Perhaps he already had.

"I'll go find Tommy," Greta said in the uncomfortable silence that ensued during Belle's mental musings.

"I'll come with you," Mark said, hurrying off after Greta.

Belle sighed. Had her morbid mood chased them off? She hoped not. Constantly wondering when Casey was going to announce his departure was extremely nerve-racking. Especially coming on the heels of Harry Hopkins's death sentence.

As if she'd conjured up his image, Casey walked into the room. "There you are. I was hoping to find you alone. There is something we need to discuss and it won't wait. Please sit down."

Here it comes, Belle thought with resignation. *He's*

going to tell me he's leaving. She perched on the sofa and stared at her hands.

"I understand you went to the jailhouse to see Harry Hopkins today."

Belle's head shot up in surprise. "Who told you?"

"The sheriff stopped me on the street a little while ago. He suggested that I keep you barefoot and pregnant so you won't meddle where you don't belong." He searched her face for her reaction. She paled somewhat but said nothing in response to his remark.

"The sheriff is as pig-headed as you are. Why won't anyone listen to me?"

"Are you referring to that garbage you've been spewing about Hank Jones? I know you're angry at the man for hurting Greta, but murder? Come on, love, be serious. Jones is a vicious man and I don't want you hurt."

Belle gnawed the soft underside of her lip. This wasn't at all what she'd expected Casey to say. Daily she'd waited for him to announce his departure. When he made love to her at night and looked at her strangely afterward, she expected him to tell her good-bye. Had she been wrong about Casey?

"Listen to me a minute, Casey, then tell me I'm wrong," Belle argued. "The name of McAllister's third partner in the gold mine was Arnold Jones. Harry Hopkins told me all about him. He refused to sell his share to McAllister because he believed they would hit pay dirt. He died in a cave-in shortly after refusing to sell out. Harry had already sold his share, and T.J. bought the remaining share from Jones's widow after he told her the mine was worthless. Jones had a wife and son back East.

"It seems more than coincidental that Hank Jones

should arrive in town at the time of McAllister's murder," Belle continued. "A man who would ruthlessly beat a helpless woman wouldn't hesitate to kill a man in cold blood."

Suddenly Casey began to listen to Belle, really listen. If what Belle said was true, she could be asking for a heap of trouble. Accusing a man like Jones of murder was certain to anger him. Voicing her suspicions to the sheriff placed her in danger, whether her accusations were true or not.

Yet he couldn't help admiring Belle's spunk and determination. "You'd make a damn good detective, Mrs. Walker."

Belle's face lit up. "You believe me? Oh, Casey, I . . ."

"Whoa, I didn't say I believed you. I admit your story has merit, and I promise to check out Hopkins' story and look into Jones' background. But you have to promise me something in return."

"If I can," Belle said, intrigued by the concern she saw in Casey's eyes.

"Stay away from the jailhouse and don't go outside unless accompanied by either Mark or myself."

"But I promised Harry . . ."

"I'll take care of it, love. If anything happened to you I don't know what I'd do."

He brought her hands to his lips and kissed each wrist. But that wasn't enough. He pulled her against him and felt her heart beating a wild tattoo against his chest.

She regarded him through misty eyes, as if seeing him for the first time.

"What is it, love? Why are you looking at me like that?"

"I . . . I thought you were going to tell me something else when you said we needed to talk."

"What did you think I was going to say?"

"That you were leaving. I've been waiting, you know, wondering how long it would be before you missed the excitement and danger of your previous work. And the women, of course."

"Have I sought another woman since meeting you?" Casey asked, anger making his voice gruff. "How many times have I told you I'm not leaving? How many times will it take before you believe me?" Suddenly the anger building inside him could no longer be contained, and he confronted her with the words he'd wanted to say since learning Belle was pregnant with his child. "You're carrying my child. Do you think I'd leave you now?"

Belle went still. *He knows!* How did he find out? When? Is that why he'd stayed this long? Was he remaining with her merely for the sake of their child? Please, God, she didn't want him that way.

"How long were you going to keep it from me, Belle?" Casey blasted. "You must think I'm stupid not to notice the little changes taking place in your body. I sleep with you every night. I know your body as intimately as I know my own.

"Take your breasts, for instance." He touched her right breast and stroked her nipple. She jerked in response. "Sensitive, aren't they? That would have given me my first clue had I needed it. But I knew you were expecting my baby shortly after you did. I browbeat the doctor into telling me what was wrong with you. I was that worried."

Belle sucked in a shallow breath. "Why didn't you tell me?"

"I could ask you the same question. What did you

hope to gain by keeping me in the dark? The child you carry is mine, for godsake! Did you think I wouldn't want it?"

"I didn't know. I wanted to make sure you were going to be around for awhile before I told you. Can you blame me? I don't trust any man. Everyone I've ever loved left me. First my mother, then Father, then Tom."

Casey's expression softened. "Are you saying you love me?"

"Hell no! I'll never allow myself to admit to loving a man again. If you're going to leave, do it now."

Casey grit his teeth in frustration. "I told you, I'd never leave a woman who's carrying my child."

"Am I supposed to thank you? Sorry, Casey, I want more than that. You only want me for our child's sake."

"Where in the hell did you get that idea? If that was the case, why would I come to your bed every night when there are plenty of other women willing to accommodate me? I swear, Belle, I've never known a more irritating female."

He rose abruptly. "I've got work to do. Don't leave the house. Someone has to think about our child if you won't." Sending her an exasperated look, he charged from the room before he said something he'd regret.

I did it again, Belle thought dimly. *I made Casey angry when all I really wanted was to throw myself in his arms and stay there forever.* Why did she continually aggravate him to the point of intense anger? Was she testing him? Why was she deliberately trying to drive him away, when all she wanted was his love?

At least she'd gotten through to him where Harry Hopkins was concerned, she thought with grim satisfaction. She had planted the seed of Hank Jones's guilt and Casey could take it from there. Not that she intended to stay home while Casey did all the investigating. She hadn't actually promised she'd remain home so she felt no obligation to do so. There were a few things she could do herself to help Harry. One was to bring him nourishing food during his last days. Another was to ease his loneliness.

Casey realized he had allowed fury to get the best of him again. But damn, he couldn't help it. He'd waited with more patience than he thought possible for Belle to tell him about the baby, and when she'd calmly stated that she'd expected him to tell her he was leaving, he'd blurted out knowledge of their child. Then his temper had made him lash out at her.

One positive thing had come out of their confrontation. He no longer had to hide his knowledge of the baby. Belle had damn well better start taking care of herself or he'd know the reason why.

Casey arrived at the telegraph office a short time later. He composed a telegram to Allan Pinkerton requesting information on Hank Jones. If anyone was privy to information about known outlaws, it was Allan. While he waited for an answer there were other things he could do. He set off to talk to both Harry Hopkins and Hank Jones.

Finding Hopkins was easy. He wasn't going anyplace except to the gallows. During the lengthy interview Casey became convinced that the old man hadn't killed McAllister. It was obvious to Casey that Hopkins had confessed to save Belle, and he wondered why he hadn't seen it sooner. Before taking his leave, he promised Hopkins that he'd do his best to try to find the real killer. But unfortunately time was running out.

Locating Jones proved more difficult. The man seemed to be avoiding all the popular watering holes and dives in town. Casey's carefully worded inquiries got him exactly nowhere. All he received for his trouble were blank stares and silence.

That night Casey avoided Belle's bed. He sat in the study tossing back snifter after snifter of McAllister's choice brandy, brooding in stony silence. If it wasn't for the baby, he'd pull up stakes and get the hell out of here. Belle didn't want him. She had Tommy, she had money, she'd never want for anything. What in the hell could he give her that she didn't already have?

Love? Hell! She didn't want his love. Protection? She could buy that. She sure knew how to knock down a man's ego. He wondered why she let him make love to her if she expected him to catch the next stage out of town? Probably because she needed what he could give her, he thought uncharitably.

"Do you mind company or would you rather drink alone?"

Casey raised his eyes to Mark, who was leaning negligently against the door frame.

"Come in, brother, if you can stand the company. I'm in a foul mood tonight."

Mark sauntered into the room and took a seat opposite Casey. "Are the lovebirds at it again?"

"I just can't figure that woman, Mark. She manages to chew me up and spit me out without conscious effort. She angers and bewitches me at the same time. There are times I'd like to strangle her. But more often I just want to make love to her. She makes me crazy, Mark."

"Thank God it's you and not me," Mark said with a grin.

"Enough of my problems. What about you, Mark? Are you sorry you came to San Francisco?"

"Not a bit. The making of wine is an intriguing process. I'm learning fast, you know."

"I know. That's why I've decided to place you in charge of the production end of the business. I certainly can't handle everything myself. You'll find the salary generous, enough for you to set up your own household if you wish. Not that I want you to leave. You're welcome here as long as you like. I'm sure Belle feels the same as I do."

"Thanks, Casey. Still taking care of your little brother, just like Pa wanted, aren't you? That stint in prison made me grow up. Pa would be proud of me now."

"He was always proud of you."

"No, he worried about me. He was proud of you. I accept the job. And if you don't mind, I'd like to stay on here for a while longer."

"A blond-haired beauty wouldn't have anything to do with your staying, would it?"

Mark flushed. "You've probably noticed I'm more than a little fond of Greta. She returns my regard but she thinks she's not good enough for me. Hell, Casey, she's not a whore. She earned a severe beating for refusing to bed a man for money. As for the other matter, any naive girl can be led astray by a fancy man spouting false promises."

"If you really want Greta I have no objection. Hell, how can I tell you how to conduct your life when I can't even handle my own wife?"

"Is it that bad?"

"Worse. Belle is aware that I know about the baby. She didn't want to tell me because she still believes I am going to leave her and Tommy. Nothing I say or do will convince her that I'm here to stay. Especially now that I'm going to be a father." His last sentence was spoken with consummate pride.

"You'll be a good father, Casey. I'm sure Belle will realize it and come to her senses."

"I hope I can hold out that long," Casey muttered darkly.

"Good night, brother. I can't sit around jawing with you all night. Some of us have to work for a living."

"I reckon I should hit the sack, too. I've got some investigating to do tomorrow. Belle said some things tonight about Harry Hopkins and a man named Hank Jones that made sense. I wired Allan Pinkerton for information."

"Want to tell me about it?"

"Not now. It's late. Good night, Mark."

Casey failed to follow his own advice. Instead of going to bed he stared into the dying fire for another hour. He was close to dozing off when he heard footsteps pass just outside the closed door and continue on up the stairs. They were furtive footsteps, but Casey's keen hearing and trigger reflexes held him in good stead. He removed his boots and crept to the door, easing it open on silent hinges. He thanked God for the servants' diligence in keeping them well oiled. What he saw froze the blood in his veins. A shadowy figure dressed in unrelieved black was creeping up the stairs, his footsteps all but silent on the carpeted treads. Casey turned back to the study for a loaded derringer he kept in the desk drawer and returned to the foyer. The man had reached the top landing now and turned unerringly toward the master bedroom. Casey saw him clearly. Light from the lamp left burning in the upstairs hallway cast his shadow against the wall.

Gun in hand, Casey crept up behind him. The intruder reached for the doorknob. Casey called out a challenge. The intruder turned and fired wildly at Casey. Casey returned the fire, but poor lighting and his constant movement made the intruder a difficult target. Casey heard Belle scream and warned her to remain in her room. He gave the same advice to Mark, Tommy, Greta, and Wan Yo.

Mark had no intention of obeying. The first exchange of gunfire brought him scrambling out of bed and reaching for his own weapon. He opened the door to his room and poked his head into the hallway. His eyes widened when he saw the intruder standing between him and Casey.

"We've got him trapped, Casey," he called out. "Are you all right?"

"I'm fine. Be careful, Mark."

The intruder spat out a curse when he realized he was in trouble. He had expected everyone to be sleeping and had walked unsuspecting into a hornet's nest. He cast about for an escape, saw the lamp, and acted instinctively. Grasping the lamp by its base, he dashed it to the floor. It sputtered a moment then burst into flame.

Mark and Casey started forward at the same time. A small section of the carpet caught fire, and if it wasn't contained the entire upper floor would go up in flames. Obviously the intruder was desperate. Mark and Casey sprinted toward the fire with one thought in mind. The intruder reacted at the same time.

The intruder and Casey passed one another on the staircase, going in opposite directions. The man shoved past Casey, not stopping until he reached the front door. Casey glanced over his shoulder in time to see him rush out the unlocked door. Casey grunted in surprise. He was certain he'd locked that door before retiring to the study earlier that night. But there was no time for reflection now. Barefoot and wearing long johns, Mark was already fighting the blaze with a blanket he had pulled from his bed.

Belle could no longer stand the suspense of not knowing if Casey was all right. She had heard the gunshots, heard Casey shout for her to remain in her room, and her heart thumped wildly against her breast as she waited . . . and waited. She heard scuffling outside the door and smelled smoke. Fear for Casey overcame her panic and she threw open the door. She saw a dark figure rushing headlong down the stairs, and she saw flames licking down the hallway.

She released her breath in a shaky sigh when she saw Casey at the top of the staircase, apparently unharmed. He raced toward the fire, ducking into their room on the way. Words were unnecessary as he seized the water pitcher from the commode and ran back into the hall, where he dumped the entire contents onto the flames. The fire sputtered then died a natural death.

"Is everyone all right?" Casey called out.

Wan Yo hobbled into the hallway, followed by

Tommy and Greta. The servants on the third floor had heard the commotion and were creeping down the stairs. Casey saw them and told them all was well and that they should return to their room.

"We're all fine," Greta said, searching Mark for signs of injury. "What was that all about?"

"I wish I knew," Casey muttered. "Did anyone see his face?"

"It was too dark," Mark said, "but he was big. How did he get in?"

"Through the front door," Casey explained. "I know I locked it so he had to have a key. Get all the locks changed tomorrow, Mark. Wan Yo, see that all the locks on the windows are intact." Both men nodded. "I'll search the ground for clues first thing tomorrow. Everyone go to bed now, the danger is over."

"I will stand guard tonight," Wan Yo said as he moved down the stairs. "You and missy go to bed."

"I'll stay with Tommy," Greta offered.

"Take Belle to bed, Casey," Mark advised, "she looks done in."

The hallway was empty now but for Belle and Casey. Belle had said little during the past ten minutes, and Casey wondered if she was in shock.

Belle was the first to speak, her eyes never leaving his face. "Are you sure you're all right?"

"I was going to ask you the same thing."

"I'm fine. I was worried about you. I heard gunshots."

"It was too dark to see clearly but I don't think I hit him." He guided her into her room and closed the door behind them. "Go to bed, love, you need your rest."

"Who do you think it was?"

"I don't know, but he seemed to know exactly where he was going. He had a key to the front door. Perhaps a former employee was looking to rob us."

"I don't think so," Belle said slowly. "There's more to it than that."

"I'll take care of it. Go to bed." He turned to leave.

"Casey, don't leave me! Stay with me tonight. I need you."

She was trembling. Casey swept her into his arms and carried her to bed.

Chapter 17

"**Y**ou want me to stay with you?" Casey asked, both surprised and pleased. Belle had never asked him to stay with her before. He placed her in the center of the bed, then stood back and searched her face for a glimmer of her thoughts.

"I was afraid for you. I don't want anything to happen to you," Belle said on a quivering sigh.

"You were afraid for me?" A slow smile lifted the corners of his lips. "Do you realize what you're saying?"

Belle nodded, abruptly realizing how desperately she'd miss this man if he left her. And he might if she continued to treat him with suspicion instead of the love he deserved. "I need you tonight, Casey.

"If all it took was a shock to bring you to your senses, I would have created one a long time ago."

"I'm sorry . . . I don't want to be alone tonight."

Casey suffered a jolt of disappointment. He should have known better than to expect more. She was frightened. It wasn't as if she wanted him. "Is that all?"

"Will you stay?" Belle asked, skirting his question.

Casey let his breath out slowly. "Of course." Belle scooted to the far side of the bed as Casey began undressing. He slid beneath the covers nude, but he made no move toward Belle.

Belle couldn't blame Casey for not wanting to touch her. She knew he expected her to express more than a need for his comfort but some perverse demon inside her resisted. What would happen if she told him she loved him? she wondered. Would he become frightened and leave? Or would he express his own love? Did she want to risk rejection? She knew he wasn't going to leave her now that there was a baby. Why couldn't she be satisfied with that? Because it wasn't enough, she told herself.

"Hold me, Casey," Belle pleaded. She still hovered at the edge of shock. Tonight had been a frightening experience. What if something had happened to Casey?

Casey knew Belle spoke from fright and shock but he could no more keep his arms from embracing her than he could stop breathing. He pulled her close, inhaling deeply of the soft, flowery scent that clung to her hair and skin.

"Nothing will happen to you or our child while I'm here to protect you, love."

She cuddled close to him. "I know. I've always felt safe with you."

Casey was inordinately pleased by Belle's admission. It wasn't what he'd hoped for but it was enough for now. "Go to sleep, love. You've had quite a fright for a pregnant lady."

"I'm not sleepy. Make love to me, Casey."

Casey went still. Belle had never asked to be

made love to before. Had shock done something to that stubborn reserve she'd always imposed upon herself? As much as he wanted her, he couldn't take advantage of her fragile emotions.

"That's not what you really want, love."

"Dammit, Casey, I know what I want and I want to feel you over me, around me, inside me. Flesh to flesh, mouth to mouth. I want to be totally consumed by you until I can no longer think. Please, Casey, love me."

"You make me crazy, sweetheart. I'd love you every day of your life if you'd let me. Are you sure? I've never been certain you truly wanted me. I was experienced enough to make you want me, but that's not the same as knowing you desire me in the same way I desire you."

The words Belle wanted to say lodged in her throat. Instead she showed him by action how much she wanted him. She groped for his manhood and stroked his thick length to the root. Casey went rigid, letting her small hand handle him in any way that pleased her. She was slowly driving him toward ecstasy and he groaned with the need she was creating inside him. When she lowered her head and opened her mouth to him, he cried out her name. Her mouth was hot and wet and he felt a powerful climax building inside him. He allowed her free reign a few moments more then pulled her away and tucked her beneath him.

"Now it's your turn," Casey said in a low, sexy growl.

He proceeded to torment her sweet body with his mouth and hands until she begged him to come inside her. Grasping her hips, he thrust full and deep into her soft warmth and stroked them both to shimmering splendor. When it was over, Casey couldn't recall when he'd been so thoroughly sated, so perfectly at peace. When he raised up to ask Belle if she felt the same, he was disappointed to find she had fallen asleep. He sighed regretfully, wondering if she had turned to him only out of fear and shock and if he'd ever know the truth.

The following morning Casey arose before Belle had awakened and made a thorough search of the grounds. He found several footprints, but nothing to indicate the identity of the intruder. Mark saw to the changing of the locks on the doors and Wan Yo reported that the locks on all the windows were intact. Casey and Mark went into the study after breakfast to discuss the break-in the night before.

"What do you think?" Mark asked curiously.

"The intruder had no interest in the study, where the safe and money were likely to be found. He went directly upstairs to the master bedroom. It was almost as if he knew exactly where he was going."

"Do you think it was one of the discharged servants?"

"It's possible, but I don't think so. The only one who might match the size of our intruder is Kellerman, and there is no reason for him to hurt Belle."

Mark scooted to the edge of his seat and leaned forward. "Do you actually think the intruder wanted to hurt Belle?"

"Call it a hunch, but that man meant harm to either Belle or myself. Maybe both of us."

"Damn! For what reason?"

"I think it might be Hank Jones but I can't be sure. I've got my work cut out for me if I'm going to find the culprit. Stick around the house today, will you, Mark? Make sure my stubborn wife stays out of trouble."

"That's a tall order, brother. I'll do my best."

Casey found Kellerman in a squalid brothel on Kearny Street. Casey dragged the man out of a whore's bed and held a gun to his head while he posed his questions. Without weapons to bolster his courage, Kellerman spilled his guts. He admitted that he had sold the key to the house, which he had kept after McAllister's murder, to a man named Jones, with whom he had struck up a conversation one night in a saloon. He had also provided Jones with a description of the inside of the house.

Casey's dire threats gleaned no more information and he left Kellerman to his whore, warning him that it would be unhealthy for him to remain in town. Kellerman got the hint. He was gone before sundown. That still didn't solve Casey's problem. Evidently Jones had gone into hiding for he had literally dropped out of sight.

Mark refused to allow Belle out of the house during Casey's absence and Greta made certain she obeyed his orders. Belle wanted to visit Harry Hopkins and assure him that they hadn't given up, that Casey was trying to find the real killer. She worried excessively about Harry's health. If not for her, Harry would not be in jail now. But if he hadn't falsely confessed to the crime she would most likely be in prison, or maybe worse. Juries had been known to sentence women to death.

That night, when Casey joined Belle in bed, he told her that he had found Kellerman, and revealed what Kellerman had said.

"So Hank Jones had a key to our house," Belle

said, shivering with the thought. "Why would he want to hurt us?"

"My guess is that we're getting too close to the truth about McAllister's death. Once Harry Hopkins is hung for the murder he figures he's off the hook. Until then he's going to do everything he can to keep us from digging into his past. Don't worry, love, I'm not taking any chances where you or my child are concerned."

Casey didn't make love to her that night, but Belle was content to lie in his arms and listen to the thumping of his heart.

The next day Casey reported the break-in to the sheriff then resumed his search for Hank Jones. To Belle's delight Mark was unexpectedly called away to the winery late in the afternoon. While Greta was busy with Tommy's lessons, she was able to sneak away unnoticed with a basket of nourishing food for Harry Hopkins. Sheriff Rogan was not in his office when she arrived at the jailhouse, but the deputy complied with her request to visit the prisoner.

Harry Hopkins smiled wanly at Belle through the bars. "You shouldn't have come."

"I've brought hot soup and freshly baked bread. Jail food didn't agree with me and it probably doesn't with you, either." She passed a jar of soup and two thick slices of warm, buttered bread through the bars.

Harry sipped the soup and sighed. "It does taste better than the fried potatoes and beans I was served for lunch. Thank you."

She watched him eat, wishing she could do more. When he finished, he passed the empty soup jar to her.

"Casey is still looking for Hank Jones," Belle said. "Our house was broken into last night. Casey believes Jones is responsible. Someone means us harm and we have no other enemies that I know of."

"I wish you'd let well enough alone," Harry said softly. "I'm dying anyway, a little neck stretching isn't going to hurt anything."

"How do you know you're dying?" Belle asked fiercely.

"Look at me. How can you doubt it? I visited a doctor a spell back and he told me there was a cancer growing in my stomach. He gave me a few months to live. Fessing up to the crime you were charged with was the most selfless thing I've ever done. I can die happy, knowing I done one good thing in my life."

"I won't let you die, Harry, I won't!"

"Those words mean more to me than you can guess. It's been a long time since anyone cared whether I lived or died."

"I care, so does Casey."

Harry gave her a gap-toothed smile. "Best you get yourself home, little gel. It's nigh on to suppertime." He glanced out the barred window behind him, concerned over the lengthening shadows. "Your husband will be worried about you."

Belle was startled to see that it had grown dark during the length of her visit. Casey would be livid if he arrived home before she did and found her missing. Perhaps he was already out looking for her.

"I'll try to return tomorrow. Don't worry. If you have to die it's going to be in bed." Her bravado didn't fool Harry. He had already resigned himself to death, and the view of the gallows through his tiny window confirmed his fate.

Belle hurried through the darkened streets. Had a hack been available she would have taken it, but they were predictably scarce when needed. Then she heard the rattle of wheels and breathed a sigh of relief as a hack came lumbering into view. Truth to tell, after last night's break-in she was nervous about walking home in the dark. Belle stepped from the curb and hailed the driver. The hack ground to a halt. The driver stepped down from the box and opened the door. Belle barely gave him a second glance, except to note that his hat was pulled low over his eyes and he wore a colorful plaid jacket.

"Where to, lady?"

Belle gave the address on Telegraph Hill and settled back against the cushions. The hack clattered off down the street. After fifteen minutes or so, Belle realized it was taking an inordinate amount of time to reach Telegraph Hill and she glanced out the window. Dismay turned to fear when she realized nothing in the passing scenery was familiar. In addition to that, the hack had picked up speed and seemed to be racing down the street at a breakneck pace.

Sticking her head out the window, Belle screamed for the driver to stop. She might as well have been screaming to the wind for all the good it did. The driver didn't even look back as he whipped up the horses. The ground sped by at an alarming rate. For the space of a heartbeat Belle considered jumping. But the thought died quickly when she realized she couldn't risk the life of her child. She hung on for dear life and prayed that whoever was behind this scurrilous deed would realize his mistake and release her unhurt.

Don't panic, she told herself. There could be a

logical explanation to all this. And then it came to her. *Hank Jones!* He was the only person with a reason to kidnap her.

Suddenly the hack clattered to a halt. Before Belle could wrench the door open the driver jumped from the box, flung open the door, and dragged Belle out. She resisted fiercely but her strength was nothing compared to that of her abductor.

"Who are you? Where are you taking me?"

The man said nothing. He merely tightened his hold on her and dragged her toward a clapboard shack nestled against a hill in a copse of trees. He opened the door and threw her inside. Belle stumbled but caught herself, and watched in terror as her abductor lit a lamp, threw off his hat, and leered at her.

"You! So I was right. You're Hank Jones. I saw you when I visited Harry Hopkins in jail. You're the man who hurt Greta."

"Your memory is good, lady," Jones snarled. "Greta is the name of that whore I roughed up, ain't it? She should have given me what I paid for. She's a damn tease. Got me all hot and hard then changed her mind."

"You beat her viciously," Belle charged.

"She had it coming. No one cheats Hank Jones and gets away with it. McAllister learned the hard way not to cross me. Though it happened a long time ago, I just recently learned he was responsible for my father's death, and told my mother the mine was worthless so she'd sell Pa's share to him."

"I was right! You killed my father-in-law!"

Jones glared at her. "So what? No big loss. The man was a liar, cheat, and murderer."

"Killing McAllister makes you as evil as he was.

You could have gone to the authorities with your suspicions. And what about poor Harry Hopkins? He's as innocent of murder as I was."

Jones laughed gleefully. "That was right neighborly of Hopkins to confess. Either way, I'm in the clear. If Hopkins hadn't confessed, you would have been convicted of the murder. I was in the courtroom the day of your trial. I saw how eager the jury was to convict you."

Belle started toward the door. "I'm leaving. You disgust me."

Jones was surprisingly fleet of foot for a man his size. He reached the door before Belle and thrust her aside. "You ain't going nowhere."

"What do you want from me?"

"You and that kid of yours inherited money that belongs to me. I would have snatched the kid but he's too well-guarded."

"You want money?"

He grinned, eyeing her with slow relish. "That's part of it. I want your husband to leave me alone and stop poking into things that are none of his business. Hopkins will swing in another few days. Walker has got to stop investigating a murder that has already been solved.

"And another thing," Jones said, eyeing her lewdly. "That old bitch at the whorehouse wouldn't let me through the door when I got hankering for a woman and returned. No other whorehouse is open to me, either. No woman will let me touch her after I was jailed for roughing up that whore. Somebody owes me, and since you're handy . . ." He started toward her, tearing off his jacket and working the buttons on his shirt.

Terrified, Belle retreated. "Touch me and you won't get a cent of McAllister's money."

He paused, his expression thoughtful. "McAllister owes me. He killed my father."

His hesitation gave Belle hope. "Hurting me will gain you nothing. How do you know McAllister killed your father?"

"I didn't know until after Ma died recently. I found an unopened letter from Pa in her belongings. It was the last letter written to her before his 'accidental' death. The letter was caught in a narrow space behind a drawer. I have no idea why Ma never opened the letter, or how it became lodged behind the drawer, but I suspect she was too grief-stricken after Pa's death to read it. She probably misplaced it and never found it. It fell to the floor when I pulled out the drawer, looking for money and valuables."

Jones failed to explain that he had left home at the age of fifteen, shortly after his father's death, to take up a life of crime. He had been angry with his mother for selling his father's share of the mine to McAllister and refusing to part with any of the money. During the following twenty years Jones could count on one hand the times he had visited or kept in touch with his mother. After he learned of her death recently, he'd returned home, hoping his miserly parent had left him an inheritance. He'd found nothing substantial save the letter.

Seeing that Jones was lost in memories, Belle remained silent, edging farther away from him. She started violently when he resumed speaking.

"Pa wrote that if he should suffer an unfortunate accident, we should suspect McAllister of foul play. He said that McAllister was angry with him for refusing to sell his share of the mine. Pa felt that McAllister was trying to cheat him and Hopkins. I came all the way to San Francisco to confront McAllister and demand my dues, but the bastard laughed at me."

"So you killed him," Belle said. "That made you no better than he, if what you say is true. What did you gain by committing murder?"

Jones sneered. "Satisfaction, lady, satisfaction. McAllister as much as admitted he cheated both Pa and old man Hopkins. He told me I could prove nothing, that my letter was twenty years old and the law would turn a deaf ear at my claim. But I got even. And now you're going to give me everything that's due me."

He met her across the room and cornered her against the far wall, trapping her within the span of his arms as he braced them on either side of her. "You're a pretty little thing. Prettier than Greta. You ain't gonna make me hurt you, are you?"

Belle tried to duck beneath his arm but he pressed her against the wall with the weight of his body. She felt like a trapped rabbit. His body was hard and heavy against hers and his fetid breath made her gag. Fear lanced through her. She recalled Greta's bruised body and battered face, and knew Hank Jones was a brutal man.

"There is only one way you can get any money from the estate and that's through either me or my husband. Casey will hunt you down no matter where you go, if you hurt me."

Belle's words gave her a small amount of comfort. It occurred to her that Casey would protect her and Tommy with his life. She'd just been too stubborn to acknowledge the depth of Casey's feelings for her.

Or admit her own for him. If she ever saw Casey again, the first thing she'd tell him was that she loved him.

Jones stared at Belle, his lust barely contained. Not the brightest of men, he did realize that Casey Walker wasn't a man to be trifled with. He knew it wouldn't be long before the detective found enough evidence to clear Hopkins despite the old man's confession. But now that Jones had leverage in the person of Walker's wife, he could demand that Walker drop the investigation and ransom his wife for McAllister's money. Taking his pleasure with the little slut wasn't worth his life, or the money he'd get for her return, if he decided to return her after he had the money safely in his hand. But if he wasn't careful he'd have the entire Pinkerton Agency breathing down his neck, and he couldn't afford that.

"You win for now, lady," Jones said, backing away. "But your man better do as I say or your life ain't worth shit." He shrugged into his jacket and jammed his hat on his head, glaring at Belle with obvious malice.

Belle had to lock her knees in order to keep them from collapsing, so great was her relief. "Where are you going?"

"You gonna miss me?" He leered at her. "Don't worry, lady, I ain't going far. I'm gonna contact your man and tell him you'll stay healthy as long as he does like I say. Don't try to escape," he warned. "The windows are shuttered and I'm gonna bar the door from the outside. If the candle burns down there's another beside it. I ain't gonna starve you, either. I'll bring some grub back with me."

Belle held her breath as Jones slammed out the

door. The moment the door closed behind him she rushed forward. She was too late. She heard the bar slide into place and began screaming and pounding on the door in a fit of irrational panic. What if Jones decided not to return? Her body wouldn't be found for months, maybe years, in this secluded place. And her babe would die with her. What would Casey think when she failed to return? How long would he look for her before giving up?

Casey returned home shortly after dark. He'd had a busy but rewarding day. He'd received a telegram in answer to his inquiry into Hank Jones' past. The message was enlightening. Hank Jones had earned a reputation in the Midwest as a habitual criminal. Until now he'd not strayed west of the Mississippi. There was a poster and reward out on him for his capture. He was wanted for killing a man during a bank robbery. Casey had already spoken to the sheriff, who had promised to keep an eye out for Jones. He couldn't wait to tell Belle what he'd learned.

Casey bounded up the front steps, eager for the sight of his wife. Before he reached the landing the door was flung open. Greta stood on the threshold. She was wringing her hands, clearly distraught. Casey's heart skipped a beat.

"What is it, Greta? Is it Tommy? Where is Belle?"

"I didn't even know she'd left the house," Greta wailed. "Mark was unexpectedly called to the winery to inspect a piece of equipment that had broken down, and I was going over lessons with Tommy."

Beads of cold sweat broke out on Casey's forehead. He grasped Greta's shoulders, shaking her to calm her down. "Has something happened to Belle?"

"That's just it, I don't know. She went out and should have returned long before now. Why did she leave without saying anything?"

Anger exploded inside Casey. "Damn her! She probably went to the jailhouse without my permission. I'll go get her. When Mark gets home . . ."

"Did someone mention my name?"

"Oh, Mark," Greta sobbed as she launched herself at Mark. He barely had time to mount the stairs and catch her in his arms.

"What's going on here?" Mark asked, alarm evident in his voice.

Casey's face was grim. "That's what I want to know. Belle left the house earlier and hasn't returned."

"Good Lord! I wouldn't have left if I thought she would go out the minute my back was turned. Why are we standing here talking? Do you have any clues?"

"I suspect Belle went to the jailhouse," Casey allowed. "But she'd have returned before now."

Suddenly the metallic scrape of the gate latch brought three heads swiveling around to view the newcomer. A ragged street urchin stood just inside the gate, looking as if he was ready to bolt.

"Are either of you gents Mr. Casey Walker?"

Casey stepped forward. "I'm Casey Walker. What can I do for you, son?"

"I got a note for you, mister. The man said to deliver it personally into your hands. He gave me a whole dollar." He offered Casey a folded sheet of paper that bore his grimy fingerprints.

"Don't let him leave yet, Mark," Casey barked as he plucked the note from the youngster's hand. His own hands were trembling as he read it.

"Let me go!" The boy resisted violently as Mark held him in place. "I ain't done nothing."

"Good God!" Casey's face went white beneath his tan. "The bastard! I'll kill him if he's hurt Belle."

"What is it?" Mark's voice was sharp with concern.

"Hank Jones has Belle. He wants me to stop my investigation of McAllister's murder. If I don't, he'll hurt Belle. He's asking ten thousand dollars in gold for her safe return. He's going to contact me later, with instructions on where to leave the money. He also says I'm not to try to find him or go to the sheriff. If I do he won't be responsible for Belle's safety."

Mark spat out an oath. "The man is a brutal killer. Look what he did to Greta. We've got to find Belle, Casey."

Casey glanced down at the youngster struggling in Mark's grip. He knelt before the boy and grasped his thin shoulders. "Where did you get this note, son?"

The boy was shaking with fear. "I don't know nothing, mister. The man just came up to me on the street and offered me a dollar to carry a note. He gave me the address and I ran all the way. You gotta believe me, mister."

"I believe you, son," Casey said in a more reasonable tone, "but I want you to tell me everything you remember about the man. Was he tall or short? Fat or thin? Did you see where he went when he left? Was he riding or walking? Try to remember, it's important."

Casey's mild tone somewhat eased the boy's fears. "The man was big but I couldn't see his face. He wore a hat and plaid jacket."

"What color hat?"

"Black, I think."

"And the jacket? What color plaid?" Casey was grasping at straws and knew it.

"The jacket was red and green plaid," the boy said with confidence. "I remember 'cause my friend has one just like it."

At least that was something to build on, Casey thought as he formed the next question in his mind. "Was he mounted or on foot?"

"Neither. He was driving a carriage. A big one. It was black."

"Which way out of town was it headed?"

The boy thought a minute then said, "I don't know. I didn't think it was important."

Casey shot to his feet, his face grim, his eyes cold as ice. He dug in his pocket for money and pulled out a five-dollar bill. He handed it to the boy. "Here, son, you've been a big help."

The boy snatched the money and darted away. His "Thanks, mister," floated to Casey through the darkness.

"What are we going to do?" Mark asked. "Surely you're not going to wait until Jones contacts you again, are you?"

"I failed, Mark," Casey lamented. "I promised Belle I would protect her and Tommy. How could I let this happen? I'm going to find the bastard and kill him for daring to lay hands on my wife."

Mark didn't doubt him for a moment.

Chapter 18

Belle hovered on the edge of despair. She had searched the tiny hut thoroughly but had found nothing that would serve as a weapon. Nor had she found a way to escape. The door was barred and the windows were shuttered. She had already lit the second candle, and if Hank Jones didn't return soon she'd be sitting in total darkness.

Had Jones contacted Casey? Belle wondered. She doubted there was anything Casey could do but wait on Jones to dictate the terms of her release. *If* Jones actually intended to release her, that is. Belle didn't trust Jones. An evil man like him would have no qualms about taking money from Casey then killing her out of spite.

Don't think like that, she told herself. Tommy needed her. She couldn't die before telling Casey she loved him. Why had she waited until now, she lamented, when she'd loved Casey for so very long? Learning that Casey had worked for T.J. McAllister made trusting him difficult. It was late in coming but Belle finally realized how much Casey cared for her and Tommy, and she prayed she'd live long enough to tell him what a fool she'd been to reject him.

Jones returned the rented carriage to the livery, retrieved his horse, and rode back to the hut. The note had already been delivered to Casey Walker, he'd made sure of that, and he was smart enough to realize that the urchin he'd paid to deliver it would have noticed the carriage, so he'd promptly returned it. Jones was taking no chances. To his knowledge there was no way anyone could identify him or follow him to the hut.

In that he was wrong. Casey and Mark were even now searching for a large man wearing a plaid jacket. Since neither man had ever seen Hank Jones, the colorful plaid jacket was their solitary link to finding him.

Casey made the rounds of livery stables, inquiring about a man wearing a plaid jacket who had recently rented a carriage. He hit pay dirt at Stemple's Livery.

"Have you seen a big man wearing a plaid jacket?" Casey asked. "He might have rented a large black carriage."

"He was here, mister. What's he done?"

"He's a dangerous criminal. I don't have time to explain, but I'm a private detective. Do you know where he was headed after he left here?"

Kurt Stemple scratched is stubbly chin and stared at Casey. "Private detective, you say? Wish I could help ya, mister, but Mr. Smith didn't say where he was going after he brought back the carriage and retrieved his horse."

"Mr. Smith? Is that what he called himself?"

"Yeah. Hank Smith. Said he wasn't going to be in town long. Had some kind of business deal pending."

Casey's jaw tightened. "Do you recall in which direction he was headed when he left here?"

"Sorry, mister, I didn't notice. Another customer came in about then and I had to go out back to the wagon yard."

"What kind of horse was he riding?"

"A sorrel gelding. Big fella, nice lines." He thought a minute. "Say, there is something you might be able to use. Just before Smith left I noticed that the sorrel's left shoe was cracked. Ought to leave an easy trail to follow. I wanted to put on a new shoe but Smith said he didn't have time."

"Thanks, Mr. Stemple, you've been a big help."

"I hope you catch your man," Stemple called after Casey.

"I will," Casey returned over his shoulder. "You can bet on it."

Unfortunately Casey wasn't as certain as he sounded of finding Jones in time to prevent him from hurting Belle. What he'd learned from Stemple wasn't much to go on. He felt so damn helpless. He had failed Belle. Been unable to protect her like he'd promised. He'd never forgive himself if anything happened to Belle or the babe she carried, and he wondered if Belle blamed him for his failure.

Casey left the livery and paused on the sidewalk, wondering what to do next, when Mark hailed him from across the street.

"Casey! Wait there for me! I saw him."

Hope soared within Casey's heart. He waited impatiently while Mark dodged traffic to reach him.

"I've been looking all over for you," Mark panted.

"I saw Jones. Or a man wearing a plaid jacket who could be Jones."

"For godsake, man, where is he?" Casey cried, grasping Mark's shoulders in a desperate bid for information.

"I just caught a glimpse of him riding north out of town. He was astride a sorrel gelding. It's almost too dark now to track him, we'll have to wait till morning."

"Damn!" Casey cursed the darkness as well as his own helplessness. "I can't bear the thought of Belle in the hands of that bastard. What if he . . ."

"He won't," Mark said, cutting off Casey's sentence. "You've got to think positively. Belle is smart. She'll find a way to keep Jones from hurting her."

"Granted, Belle's resourceful," Casey allowed, "but she's pregnant for godsake! I swear I'll kill him if he so much as touches her. I can't wait till morning, Mark. I'm going to leave now, and when I can no longer follow his trail I'll camp and wait for first light."

"I'll come with you."

"No, someone has to stay to look out for Tommy and Greta. Wan Yo is too old to be of much protection. Besides, Jones might send another message and someone has to be here to receive it."

"I'll do whatever you think best," Mark replied, clearly disappointed. Casey was capable, even deadly, when the need arose, but it wouldn't hurt to have someone protecting his back. Perhaps he should use his own judgment in this, Mark decided.

An hour later Casey rode north out of town. It didn't take long to find the tracks of a horse with a defective left shoe. When he came to a fork in the road, darkness prevented him from distinguishing

Jones' tracks from others. Casey made camp a short distance from the road, and spent a miserable night worrying about Belle and making a mental list of all the things he loved about her.

Casey did not consider Belle's limp a disfigurement. It was so much a part of her and so inconsequential that it detracted nothing from her natural beauty. To him her body was perfect. Her slight deformity made her all the more dear to him. He couldn't believe that Belle considered herself unattractive because of her lameness. Nothing could be farther from the truth. He had thought her beautiful from the onset of their relationship and he knew other men did, too. Her feelings of inferiority were a product of her own mind.

Casey knew that Belle had been in love with her husband and despaired that she could ever feel for him in the same way. Tom had married her against his father's wishes and given her Tommy. It saddened Casey to know that he could never compete with Belle's dead husband, despite her enthusiam for his loving. At least she responded to him on one level, Casey reflected on a happier note.

Abruptly Casey's thoughts took him in another direction. What if Jones hurt Belle? Would he be able to live with himself if that happened? Sleep was a long time coming but Casey finally dozed off.

The room was bare but for a rickety table. Lacking a chair, Belle sat on the floor with her back to the wall facing the door, hugging her knees to her chest. The candle was sputtering out and soon she'd be shrouded in total darkness. She shivered, wondering if Jones would return soon and praying he would not. He was a vicious man, one who attacked women without provocation. Poor Greta had suffered his wrath and bore the scars of his unprovoked beating.

Sleep wasn't an option. There was no way Belle intended to close her eyes this night. She had to be awake and alert when Jones returned. To keep her mind from dwelling on her hopeless predicament, she thought of Casey. Casey made her feel loved and beautiful when she knew she was far from perfect. Her misshapen ankle and limp had made her the brunt of many cruelties. Especially during her years with Naomi. Not all the girls were kind and some of them had ridiculed her clumsinesses.

But Casey had thought her beautiful from the beginning, Belle remembered. Her limp meant less than nothing to him. He had massaged her lame leg many times and found nothing repulsive about it. He made love to her with consummate tenderness and the right amount of aggressiveness. Together they were wild and wonderful. She had always liked making love with Tom but with Casey loving was addictive. He made her body glow. She felt reckless and frenzied in his arms, and he made her want to feel that way again and again.

Belle's thoughts skidded to a halt when she heard a rider approach the hut. She stiffened, her gaze on the door, waiting for Jones to barge inside. She didn't have long to wait. A few minutes later she heard the scrape of the wooden bar and saw the door burst open. Jones stepped inside and slammed the door behind him.

He carried a gunny sack, which he set down on the rickety table. He rummaged inside for a fresh candle, lit it and placed it in the holder. Then he turned and leered at Belle.

"I'm glad you made yourself comfortable, it's going to be a long night. Hungry?"

Belle shook her head. Her stomach was roiling dangerously.

"Suit yourself. I'm starved." He took a hunk of bread, a wedge of cheese, and a bottle of whiskey from the sack and hunkered down on the floor beside her. Belle scooted away. He grinned at her but did not stop her. He ate quickly, gulping from the bottle between mouthfuls. He burped loudly when he finished eating and continued to drink from the bottle. He rested his head against the wall, his eyes narrowing on Belle. He offered her the bottle. "Let's celebrate."

Belle shook her head, wishing he would drink himself into oblivion and forget her. She should have known better.

"Your man got my note," he said between swigs.

"Did you tell him where to find me?" Belle asked.

He laughed harshly. "You think I'm stupid?"

"I'll send him another message after the hanging, instructing him where to bring the gold. Once I have the ransom maybe I'll set you free and maybe I won't."

His words sent terror racing through her veins. "What do you hope to gain by holding me prisoner? Take your gold and run. Casey is a detective, he'll find you. I'll only slow you down."

"Who says I'm going to take you with me? It would be easier just to get rid of you. I'll amuse myself with you until the old man swings for murder. When I leave San Francisco it will be alone, if you get my drift. Of course," he hinted, "if you please me I might change my mind." He reached for her. "Show me how you're gonna change my mind."

Belle leaped to her feet. "Don't touch me!"

He lurched after her, swearing when he grasped air. He was drunker than he thought. "Oh, I'm gonna do more than touch you, lady. I know how to make a woman willing."

"With your fists," Belle charged injudiciously as she backed away from him.

"Stand still!" he growled as she slipped from his grasp a second time. "I don't aim to chase you around this room."

He lurched forward, Belle darted away. But she wasn't fast enough. His hand caught her skirt. She wrenched it free. He wasn't prepared for her resistance, and when she jerked her skirt out of his hands he stumbled backward, lost his balance, and fell against the table. The candle skittered across the table, dropped to the floor, and sputtered out, pitching the room into darkness. Belle seized the moment. She ran to the door, jerked it open, and rushed outside into blessed darkness.

Cursing her lameness, Belle ran as fast as her crippled leg would allow into the thick forest of pine trees growing on the hillside behind the hut. She heard Jones stumbling after her and ran faster. He crashed through the underbrush, his curses turning the air blue. She darted one way then changed directions, widening the gap between them. Belle grew frantic. There was nothing but narrow tree trunks and darkness to conceal her from Jones.

"Come back!" Jones shouted, shattering the silence. "When I catch you I'm gonna make you sorry you ran away. Do you hear me? If you think that whore looked bad when I got through with her, it's nothing compared to how you're gonna look."

His words were slurred but Belle took his threat seriously. Breathing hard, she climbed up the hill, refusing to be caught like a rabbit in a trap. The pace she set for herself was grueling. Her breathing became ragged as she picked her way up the hill. Pain shot up her lame leg; dry brush and twigs tore at her skirts and ripped into her face. She tasted blood when a branch cut her lip. She had to go on. She had to find a hiding place until Casey found her.

It was amazing how completely she believed in Casey given how she had distrusted him a short time ago. She knew Casey would come for her, she just wasn't sure when. Until he did it was up to her to keep from becoming Jones's victim. But her leg, oh, God, her leg was nearly numb with pain. Finally it buckled and she went down in a tangle of petticoats. She began rolling head over heels down the hill, gaining speed as she rolled. She feared for her babe and protected her stomach as best she could with her arms. She came up hard against a tree trunk and stopped abruptly. Her breath emptied from her lungs and she blacked out.

"Where in the hell are you?" Jones bellowed from somewhere above her. When she didn't reply he bounded down the hill after her. Belle held her breath as he passed within feet of her without spotting her, thanks largely to her dark clothing.

"I'll find you, bitch," he muttered as he headed back toward the hut. "Just as soon as it's light enough to see where I'm going. You can't go far on a gimpy leg."

Belle regained her wits slowly, aware of intense

pain in every part of her body. Her arms still hugged her belly and she prayed that God had spared her child. Then she realized that the pain wasn't coming from her middle. She was on the verge of pinning it down when she blacked out again.

Casey arose from a fitful sleep at the first hint of dawn. He drank from a nearby creek and chewed on jerky while he saddled his horse. Pink was tingeing the eastern sky when he returned to the dusty trail and picked up Jones's tracks. Luck was with him. Since no rain had fallen overnight, he found them easily. He tracked Jones to a place where he turned his mount off the trail onto a narrow lane. His lips flattened into a mirthless grin as he followed.

Belle awoke in a daze. She was chilled to the bone and realized she must have lain on the damp ground for hours, but daylight hadn't arrived yet. She tried to move and found she could drag herself without too much pain into an upright position. Her hands flew to her stomach, vastly relieved when she felt the barely discernable bulge where her child lay in her womb. But when she tried to stand, her leg collapsed beneath her. She lay on the ground, tears of frustration trailing down her pale cheeks. Then she heard Jones crashing through the underbrush in search of her, and panic seized her. Spying a clump of bushes nearby, she scooted into them, ignoring the prick of thorns and scrape of dead branches on her tender skin.

Once again her dark clothing saved her, as Jones failed to see her huddled in the shadows as he scoured the hillside. Poised on the horns of dilemma, Belle couldn't decide whether to make her way to the cabin or to remain hidden. Her leg was badly bruised and dragging herself across rough ground didn't appeal to her. In the end she decided to stay where she was and trust that Jones wouldn't find her.

As darkness turned to dawn, Belle realized that her hiding place wasn't as secure as she had first assumed. The bushes in which she had sought cover seemed far more sparse in broad daylight than they had in the dark. Casting her gaze about for safer concealment, Belle saw nothing but scrawny scrubs and tall pines, so she opted to remain where she was. Thirsty and hungry, she hunkered down into a bed of pine needles and waited for a miracle.

Instead of a miracle, a bobcat emerged from the trees and ambled toward her. Belle froze, too panic-stricken to move. The bobcat sniffed the air, caught her scent, and moved unerringly in her direction. Belle knew little about bobcats so she allowed her instincts to guide her. She rolled into a ball and played dead. She heard a low growl close to her ear, smelled the acrid stench of his breath, and knew the cat had found her. She sucked in her breath and held it, fearing this was to be her last day on earth. Being mauled by a bobcat wasn't her idea of a miracle.

Belle tried not to panic when the bobcat batted at her with a sharp-clawed paw. She nearly screamed aloud when she felt his claws rip through her dress and dig into the tender flesh of her back. She felt a rush of warm blood and forced herself not to move. After a few minutes the bobcat tired of the game and wandered away. Belle's relief was so intense she was insensate to her pain. She already ached in so many

places a few more made little difference. At least
Jones hadn't found her yet and perhaps he
wouldn't. If she could hold out until dark, God
willing she could slip away.

Casey followed the sorrel's tracks along a winding path. He reined to a halt a short distance from a
secluded hut that was all but invisible against a
wooded hillside. He dismounted, tethered his horse
to a branch, and crouched at the edge of the woods.
Every instinct told him that Belle was nearby, but he
knew better than to rush headlong into a situation
that could result in death. Belle's life and that of his
child were at risk should he fail.

He waited and watched a good half hour, until his
nerves were stretched taut and he could no longer
stand the suspense of waiting. He had to know if
Belle was safe and he had to know now. He could be
doing something positive instead of wasting precious time.

Creeping across the clearing to the front door,
Casey drew his weapon and prepared to enter. He
kicked open the door and burst inside. The room
was empty. Moving cautiously through the sparsely
furnished room, Casey saw signs of recent occupan-
cy. Bread crumbs and scraps of cheese were scattered about the floor beside an empty gunny sack.
An abandoned whiskey bottle lay nearby, its contents sadly depleted. It was the lingering fragrance
of lilacs that convinced Casey that Belle had been
here. It was the same scent Belle used in her bath.
He would never forget the arousing fragrance on her
skin when he made love to her.

Where had Jones taken Belle? Casey wondered in
a fit of panic. Why had they left the hideout?

Something had driven Jones and Belle from the hut, and Casey racked his brain for an answer. Nothing inside the hut gave Casey the tiniest clue so he wandered outside to look around. The hard-packed dirt around the hut yielded a multitude of footprints. Casey studied them carefully, encouraged when he saw a set of small prints that could only belong to a woman. A lame woman who put more pressure on one foot than the other. They led up into the hills.

Casey felt his first stirring of hope. According to the signs, Belle had managed to escape the hut and had headed for high ground. Since Jones was nowhere to be seen Casey assumed Jones was hard on her heels. Casey prayed that Jones hadn't found her yet. Fragile hope flowered in his breast. He had to get to Belle before Jones found her. His face set in grim lines, he started up the hill.

Jones pushed through the tangle of underbrush, cursing his rotten luck. He'd been tramping up and down the hillside and through the woods for hours, and still hadn't found his prey. He had started back down the hill now, thinking he'd missed her on his way up, and was determined to search every bush along the way. He'd nearly reached the bottom when he heard a low growl and saw a bobcat sniffing around a clump of bushes. Jones backed away slowly until he was upwind of the animal. He watched from a safe distance as the bobcat clawed at something in the bushes. After a few minutes the bobcat lost interest and bounded off.

Jones waited until he was certain the bobcat wouldn't return before going to investigate. He smiled when he saw Belle curled into a ball, her back oozing blood from the bobcat's claws.

"Well, well, what have we here? You should have stayed in the hut instead of trying to escape me. Look at you. You're one helluva mess, lady. Get up! I'm not taking any chances this time. I've got some rope back at the hut."

Belle slowly uncoiled and stared up at Jones. She was numb with pain, dazed, and in shock. She couldn't have stood even if she'd wanted to. "I can't," she whispered hoarsely. "My leg won't hold me up."

Jones spat out a curse. "Bitch! I don't care about your leg. If you don't get up now, I'm going to make you sorry you left the hut and caused me so much trouble."

Belle tried to rise but her leg buckled beneath her. She cried out in agony. "I can't."

Grasping her arm, Jones started to drag her down the hill.

"Take your filthy hands off my wife." The quietly rendered words made them all the more deadly.

"What the hell!" Jones's hands dropped away from Belle as he spun to face Casey.

"Casey!" Belle sobbed out his name. Never had she been so glad to see anyone in her life. "Thank God you've come."

"Are you all right?" Casey asked harshly. "What about the baby? Say the word and I'll kill the bastard."

"No, don't kill him!" Belle cried. "His confession will free Harry Hopkins. I'm . . . all right, and as far as I can tell, so is our baby."

"Can you walk?" Casey asked.

"I don't think so. I injured my leg when I rolled down the hill."

Assuming Casey was preoccupied with Belle, Jones tried to make a dash for it. Casey was more alert than Jones thought. He fired over Jones's head and ordered him to stop. Jones skidded to a halt and Casey shoved him against a sturdy sapling.

"Damn, I left my rope with my horse," Casey muttered. He glanced at Belle and was immediately alarmed by her pallor. He cursed again. "I need my rope to secure Jones to a tree so I can get you back to town, love."

"Use strips from my petticoat," Belle offered.

"Here," Casey said, handing her his gun. "Keep this trained on Jones while I do the tearing. If he moves an inch, shoot him."

Casey's expression turned grim when he finally got a good look at Belle. Her clothing was torn, and she was a mass of scrapes and bruises. He wanted to take her in his arms and comfort her, but he didn't dare relax his vigil until Jones no longer presented a danger to them. Casey had yet to see Belle's mauled back. If he had he would have cheerfully beaten Jones to within an inch of his life.

"How far did you fall?" Casey asked as he ripped her petticoat into strips.

"I don't know. I must have blacked out."

"Is that how you got all these bruises?"

"I suppose."

Casey cursed fluently. "Did Jones hurt you?"

Jones sent him a sullen look. "I didn't touch her. I would have returned her safely after I got my money. All I wanted was what McAllister cheated my pa out of."

"Did that include murder?" Casey asked as he approached Jones with the strips of cotton. "Back up against that tree."

"You ain't gonna leave me here to die, are you?"

"I'd like to, but there's an innocent man who will die for a murder he didn't commit if I do. I'm turning you over to the sheriff."

Casey bound Jones securely to the tree, fastening his wrists and feet together and lashing them to the trunk. Then he wound extra strips around his neck and middle until there was no possible way Jones could escape.

"I'll come back for you later," Casey said, stepping back to examine his handiwork.

"What about wild animals?" Jones asked fearfully.

"You'll just have to take your chances. I've got to get my wife to a doctor. If she loses our baby your life is forfeit."

"Shit! A baby," Jones muttered. "Just my luck."

"How do you feel?" Casey asked of Belle. She'd been through hell and he had failed to protect her. He pried the gun from her hands and returned it to his holster. "Hang on, love. I'll have you back to town in no time. Let me check first to see if your leg is broken and needs setting."

Lifting her skirt, Casey gently probed Belle's injured leg, relieved to find no broken bones. "I'm not a doctor but I can find no broken bones, love. It's badly bruised and you may have sprained an ankle, but hopefully the rest of your injuries are minor." He lifted her into his arms. "I'm going to have to carry you to my horse."

He heard her sudden intake of breath and feared

he had hurt her leg. He was still unaware of the wounds she had suffered to her back and she didn't tell him.

"Put your arms around my neck," he instructed. "I'll try not to jostle you too much."

Belle nodded, burying her face against his chest so he couldn't tell by her expression how badly she hurt. She managed to remain conscious through pure dint of will. When they reached the bottom of the hill, they found Mark waiting for them.

"Do you need help, brother?"

"Mark! I thought I told you to stay in town."

"Since when have I ever done anything you said? I followed your trail, thinking you might need help, but I see you have things well in hand." He studied Belle carefully. "Is she all right?"

"I won't know until we reach town and the doctor has seen her."

"What about the baby?"

"Belle says all is well, but I won't be content until the doctor pronounces them both sound."

"Take me home," Belle said, hugging him tightly. "I need to see Tommy. He must be worried about me."

"What can I do to help?" Mark wanted to know. "Did Jones get away?"

Casey sent him a wry grin. "You know me better than that. I left Jones bound to a tree. Now that you're here you can take him to town and turn him over to the sheriff. Tell Sheriff Rogan I'll be in soon to press charges. Be sure Rogan knows Jones is responsible for McAllister's death." He told Mark where to find Jones and advised him to bring a rope. Mark gave him a jaunty salute and bounded up the hill.

"I'm going to set you on my horse," Casey told Belle when they reached the place where his mount was tethered. "We're not far from town. I know you're in pain, love, but try to concentrate on Tommy, and how happy he'll be to see you."

"Casey, I have to tell you something first."

"Later, love. Nothing is more important than getting you home safely." He'd noticed blood on her clothing and feared she was seriously injured.

"This is more important. I love you, Casey Walker. I love you with all my heart and soul."

Chapter 19

~⚬○⚬~

Casey cradled Belle against his heart all the way to San Francisco. She had fallen asleep shortly after uttering those magical words Casey never expected to hear.

She loved him.

He still couldn't believe it. He tasted the sweetness of Belle's words on his lips and savored them. If she never said them again, he would always remember this day. Casey's greatest fear was that Belle had been in shock when she uttered those words and hadn't realized what she'd said. Or that he had imagined them. Perhaps she'd said them out of gratitude. That didn't bear thinking about.

They had just entered the city when Belle stirred restlessly in his arms and started to awaken. Casey tightened his hold on her. "We're almost home, sweetheart. That's Telegraph Hill in front of us. Is the pain bad?"

Belle regarded him solemnly. His face was so dear to her she wanted to go on looking at him forever. It took a near-disaster for her to realize she couldn't live without this man. She knew now that he wasn't going away, that he would remain with her and Tommy and their new babe as long as a breath remained in his body. He would protect them and love them always, and she had been a fool to doubt him.

"The pain isn't so bad when you're holding me," she said, giving him a wobbly smile. "I love you, Casey. Never let me go."

She said it again! Casey couldn't stop grinning. He hadn't imagined it. Belle *did* love him. "You ought to know by now I'll never let you go. If I was going to leave, I would have done so long ago. I love you, Belle. I've loved you from the moment I saw you and realized you weren't the kind of woman McAllister described. No more talking now. We're home."

Belle remain alert until the moment Casey lifted her down from the horse. No matter how carefully he handled her, the pain proved too much as she cried out and lost consciousness again. She didn't see Greta, Tommy, and Wan Yo rush from the house and surround them, or hear their worried voices as they questioned Casey.

"What's wrong with Mama?" Tommy asked as Casey carried Belle into the house.

"She's going to be fine, son," Casey said, praying it was so.

"What can I do?" Greta asked worriedly. "She's so pale."

"She's in shock. Send one of the servants for the doctor."

Greta hurried off to do as she was bid, while Wan Yo scurried before Casey to open doors and pull the covers back on the bed. It wasn't until Casey placed

Belle on the bed that he was able to examine the blood stains on Belle's clothing more closely. He stared at the red blotches in dismay, fearing that she had more severe injuries than those which he had inspected. No wonder she was so pale.

Greta returned to the bedroom, saw Casey staring at her blood-stained clothing, and asked, "What did Jones do to her?"

"I don't know. Did you send for the doctor?"

"He should be here shortly. Someone is bringing hot water and antiseptic."

Tommy clung to Wan Yo, his eyes swimming in tears. "Why is Mama so still? What's wrong with her?"

"You have to trust me, Tommy, when I say your mother is going to be fine," Casey said earnestly. "The doctor will be here soon to make her well. I think it best that you go with Wan Yo now." He sent the Chinaman a speaking glance. "I'll send for you when your mother is more herself."

"Wan Yo will take care of Tommy, Mister Casey," Wan Yo said as he led the reluctant child away.

"Help me get Belle's clothes off," Casey said to Greta after a servant arrived with hot water and antiseptic, set it on the night table, and left. Casey gently turned Belle on her side so he could reach the fastenings on the back of her dress and froze. The material was shredded and blood-soaked. "Oh, my God!"

Casey paled when he saw the torn flesh on Belle's back. He'd suspected she'd suffered a grave injury but wasn't prepared for this. He carefully peeled away the layers of material until the wounds were bared.

"How in the hell did this happen?" he wondered

aloud as he dipped a cloth into the water and pressed it to her wounds. "No wonder she was in so much pain." He cursed fluently. "I should have killed Jones."

He had just finished bathing Belle's wounds when the doctor bustled into he room. He pushed Casey aside so he could get to his patient.

"How did this happen?" Doctor Peabody asked.

"I don't know." Casey then launched into an explanation of Belle's abduction. "Do you think Jones could have used a whip on her?"

Peabody shook his head. "No, it appears like she's been mauled by an animal. I'll need to douse it with a strong antiseptic and put in a few stitches. If infection doesn't set in, she should heal without leaving too many scars."

He worked quickly and efficiently, not pausing until the bandage was in place. Then he treated the minor cuts and abrasions on Belle's arms and face. Finally he examined her lame leg. Casey sighed audibly when Peabody pronounced it badly wrenched but not broken. When he finished he asked everyone to leave the room so he could perform an internal examination to determine if any harm had been done to the babe Belle carried.

Casey paced the hallway, waiting for the doctor to finish with his examination. After what seemed like hours, Peabody opened the door and motioned Casey inside.

"She's awake," the doctor said as he returned to his patient. "I know you're both anxious about the baby. As far as I can tell, the child is firmly entrenched. Belle told me she took a nasty fall. I'd say this child is determined to be born. If Belle hasn't miscarried by now, she probably won't.

Nevertheless, she should stay in bed a week or two to be on the safe side."

All the while the doctor spoke Casey sat on the edge of the bed, holding Belle's hand. He didn't ever want to let go of her.

"I'll leave something for pain and a salve for her back," Peabody said as he gathered up his paraphernalia and prepared to leave. "Send for me at the slightest sign of infection. Right now the best thing for your wife is rest."

"Thank you, doctor. Greta will see you out." The door closed softly and Casey returned his regard to Belle. He squeezed her hand. "Do you want to tell me about it, love?"

"There's not much to tell. I know I shouldn't have gone out alone after being warned not to, but I wanted to see Harry. The poor man is so very ill. Time ran away with me. It was dark when I left the jailhouse. I wanted to hire a hack but none was available. I was relieved when one finally turned in my direction, and I hailed it."

"It must have been Jones," Casey bit out. "He'd probably been waiting and watching for just such an opportunity."

"I didn't realize anything was amiss until it occurred to me that it was taking too long to reach home. By then the hack was speeding down the road too fast for me to jump out."

"Did you learn why Jones killed McAllister?"

Belle nodded. "It's a strange story but true nonetheless." Then she related everything Jones had told her, including the letter he had found in his mother's belongings.

"You're right, it's just farfetched enough to be true. How did you escape him?"

"It was easy. Jones was drinking heavily. He grew groggy and unsteady on his feet. When he came after me, I shoved him off balance, ran out the door, and fled into the hills. The pace proved too strenuous for my lame leg. The pain was nearly unbearable. I must have blacked out for a short time. When I came to, I heard Jones crashing through the underbrush. It was dark, he passed me by without seeing me."

"How did he find you? And what happened to your back? The doctor thought you had been mauled by an animal."

"I must have blacked out again. When I awakened it was still dark, but dawn was closing in fast. The bobcat found me shortly after that. I played dead. He mauled me but eventually lost interest and wandered off. Jones found me then and you know the rest."

"I was out of my mind with worry when that street urchin delivered the note from Jones. Mark and I set out to find you. A bit of luck and a little detective work led me to that abandoned hut. I should have done a better job protecting you. I'm going down to the sheriff's office soon to press charges against Jones. The bastard will hang for his crimes this time."

"What about Harry Hopkins?"

"Once Jones confesses, Hopkins will be set free." He forced a taut smile to his lips. "And I promise you he'll confess."

"Casey, I . . ." She yawned hugely, suddenly exhausted. But she wanted to make certain Casey understood what she'd tried to tell him before. She wanted to tell him she loved him again and again, until he tired of hearing it.

"Enough talk," Casey said, aware of her fatigue. "I promised Tommy he could see you after the doctor left and I'm sure he's anxiously awaiting my summons."

"Wait," Belle said as Casey rose to leave. "I just want to tell you that I knew you'd find me. I never doubted that. My greatest fear was that I'd lose our baby. The doctor said it could still happen."

Casey knelt beside the bed and kissed her gently on the lips. "You're not going to lose the baby, love," he said, splaying his hand over her belly. "He's still inside you. His tiny heart is beating strongly."

She bit her lip. "But if I do . . ."

"Then we'll make another when the doctor says you're ready. Shall I call Tommy now?"

Belle gave him a misty smile. "I love you, Casey Walker. By all means, call Tommy. I can't wait to see him."

Casey left mother and son to their tearful reunion, his heart pounding with joy. All of his life he'd been a loner. Of course he'd always had Mark. But Mark was a grown man and hadn't really needed him. Casey's life had been mostly one of work and loneliness. But no longer. He had a family now. A wife he loved beyond reason, a son he'd proudly claim as his own, and a much-anticipated baby he had created with Belle.

A short time later Casey left the house and went directly to the sheriff's office. Mark should be back with Jones by now and there were things the sheriff needed to know about the killer.

Casey found Mark and Sheriff Rogan deep in conversation when he arrived at the jailhouse.

"Casey, how is Belle?" Mark asked with obvious concern "Has the doctor seen her yet?"

"Belle is as well as can be expected under the circumstances," Casey replied. "She took a nasty fall and was mauled by a bobcat. No woman should have to endure the terror Jones subjected her to."

"The baby . . ."

"She hasn't lost it . . . yet. We have every hope that all will be well. Did Jones give you any trouble?"

Mark grinned. "Not much. Without his guns he's a coward. He's locked up safe and sound."

"Your brother was trying to explain the situation, Walker," Sheriff Rogan said, "but now that you're here you can take up where he left off. Why did Jones abduct your wife?"

"Sit down, Sheriff, this is going to take a while."

"I've got time."

"It all started years ago when T.J. McAllister cheated his two partners in a mining venture. He led them to believe the mine was worthless and offered to buy them out. Harry Hopkins took McAllister up on his offer and lit out for greener pastures, but Arnold Jones didn't believe McAllister. McAllister arranged an 'accidental' death for Jones and then turned around and bought Jones's share of the partnership from his widow for a mere pittance. Hank Jones is Arnold's son. After his mother's recent death, Jones discovered a sealed envelope which contained a letter written years ago by his father. The letter implicated McAllister in his death. Hank decided to come to San Francisco and demand retribution from McAllister. But McAllister wasn't about to part with any of his money."

"So Hank Jones killed McAllister with your wife's

gun," Rogan surmised. "He must have been watching the house closely."

"Exactly. But Jones wasn't satisfied that McAllister was dead. He wanted money. I assume that's why he remained in town. When Harry Hopkins confessed to the murder, he felt he was in the clear and began to explore ways to get money from McAllister's heir. Things started going awry when Belle got the notion into her head that Hopkins was innocent."

"Why in the hell did Hopkins confess if he was innocent?" Rogan wanted to know.

"He took a liking to Belle. He was dying and knew it. He wanted to do one meaningful thing in his lifetime, and saving Belle appealed to his sense of honor."

"Evidently Mrs. Walker wasn't satisfied. She came to me and openly accused Hank Jones of murdering her father-in-law. I thought she was deranged."

"Belle was more insightful than any of us," Casey admitted. "Jones broke into our house, intent upon killing Belle, hoping it would stop my investigation of the murder. When Jones' assassination attempt failed, he abducted Belle. He sent me a note demanding a ransom."

Rogan whistled in appreciation. "Now I know why you're considered one of Pinkerton's best detectives. Finding your wife was one of the best pieces of work I've ever encountered."

"Jones confessed," Mark said at the first lull in the conversation.

Casey was stunned. "He did? In front of the sheriff?"

"I told you he was a coward," Mark smirked. "He sang like a bird to the sheriff." Mark rubbed his bruised knuckles. "Probably figured he'd rather take his chances with a jury than with me or you. Damn smart of him."

Casey clapped Mark on the shoulder. "I don't want the details. It's enough that the bastard confessed." He turned to Rogan. "Is Hopkins free to go?"

"Just as soon as I complete the papers. Frankly, I didn't expect him to live long enough to face the hangman. He's a tenacious old codger, though. I'll give him that. Too bad he doesn't have a family. Seems a shame to turn him loose to die alone."

"He has a family, Sheriff," Casey returned. "I'm taking him home with me."

Rogan's brows shot upward. "That's mighty generous of you. I'll go get him."

A few minutes later Harry Hopkins stood before Casey and Mark, clearly confused. "What's this all about, Mr. Walker? The sheriff said I'm free to go."

"That's right, Harry. We know you didn't kill McAllister. The real killer has confessed. Hank Jones is in jail where he belongs. I'll tell you all about it on the way home."

"Home? You know I ain't got no home, Mr. Walker."

"You do now, Harry. You're coming home with me. Belle would skin me alive if I let you disappear from her life."

Shaking with emotion, the old man walked out of the jailhouse a free man. He was sick, possibly dying, and bent with age, but his weathered face glowed with joy. When he passed the gallows he kept his eyes carefully averted. He needed no grim reminder that his life could have ended violently the day after tomorrow.

Wan Yo and Harry Hopkins got along famously. Now Tommy had two surrogate grandfathers and a surrogate grandmother in Naomi. Harry rallied somewhat after being released from jail and seemed to prosper. At least for the time being. Everyone was aware that the old man was dying but hoped it wouldn't happen for a long time.

Belle remained in bed for ten days before Casey let her up to test her leg. The doctor had removed the stitches from her back and pronounced it healing well with no sign of infection. The baby still grew inside her and Belle felt confident that she was no longer in danger of miscarrying. As for her leg, it would always be weak and she'd always be lame, but it no longer pained her. When the doctor suggested that she exercise her weak leg, she was giddy with happiness. She was thoroughly sick of lying abed and couldn't wait to join her family at meals . . . and be a wife to Casey again.

Since her abduction he had treated her like a piece of fragile glass, even sleeping on the daybed in their room so as not to hurt her. But Belle wasn't about to let that continue. The doctor had just left and she intended to surprise Casey with her excellent health. She had the doctor's blessing to resume normal marital activities and couldn't wait to tell Casey. She'd missed him dreadfully. Missed having his body next to hers at night. Missed feeling him inside her, loving her the way only he could do.

And there were things they needed to discuss. Casey had been so busy with the winery and other related business that they'd had precious little time together lately. Not that she lacked for company. It seemed as if her room was always crowded with visitors. Tommy, Greta, Mark, Naomi, Wan Yo, and Harry. She thrived on their attention, but it wasn't their attentiveness she craved. She wanted Casey. And now that she was well, she wanted him in every way a woman wanted the man she loved.

Casey couldn't help staring at Belle throughout the meal that night. It was the first time she'd been out of bed to join them since her abduction, and he worried that she was a trifle premature in thinking she was significantly recovered from her ordeal. He had even insisted on carrying her down the stairs. She certainly looked well, he thought. She was wearing a midnight blue dress that brought a glow to her amber eyes and made her skin appear translucent. She looked fragile enough to break if he touched her.

Casey couldn't recall when he'd wanted to caress a woman as desperately as he did Belle. But he wasn't going to do anything to harm either Belle or his child. He would wait until after the birth of their babe to make love to her if necessary. Lord, he hoped he didn't have to!

"You look wonderful tonight, Belle," Greta said encouragingly.

Belle directed her reply to Casey. The smile she gave him was filled with promise. "I've never felt better in my life. Casey said Hank Jones has been tried, found guilty, and will hang for his crime the day after tomorrow. In a way I feel sorry for him. T.J. did cheat his family out of what was due them."

Casey groaned in dismay. "Your soft heart is

going to get us into trouble one of these days. McAllister was a manipulative bastard but he didn't deserve to be murdered. If you're finished eating, I think you should go to bed. This is your first day up and I don't want you suffering a relapse."

"Very well," Belle agreed with a sassy grin that should have warned Casey. She held out her arms. "Will you carry me?"

"My pleasure," Casey said, trying not to appear too eager. He lifted her easily, handling her as if she were made of delicate porcelain.

"Good night, everyone," Belle called over Casey's shoulder as he carried her from the room.

Belle clung to him, resting her head against his chest, inhaling his fresh, masculine aroma. When they reached their room he set her carefully on her feet. "Should I call your maid to help you undress?"

"Not tonight. Perhaps you could act the ladies' maid this once." She turned her back and lifted her hair so he could reach the fastenings on the back of her dress.

Casey stifled a groan. Didn't Belle know what she was doing to him? He grit his teeth and lifted shaking hands to the hooks holding her dress together. One by one he released them, swallowing convulsively when a provocative expanse of delicate curves was revealed in the opening.

"Can you manage on your own now?" Casey asked. Proceeding further would sever the last slim thread of his control. "I need to discuss something with Mark before he retires for the night."

Belle turned to face him and the bodice of her dress slipped past her shoulders and down her arms. Grasping the skirt, she slid it down her hips until it formed a puddle around her feet. She wore no corset, for the confining garment would have irritated her healing wounds. She smiled up at Casey, her charms seductively displayed in a diaphanous shift that ended at her knees.

Casey's heated gaze followed the outline of her breasts and hips, past the hemline of her shift, all the way down to her ankles then back up to her breasts. The taut peaks, larger now in pregnancy, poked temptingly against the thin material. His gaze slid downward again, his body reacting violently to the glistening sable triangle between her legs. Just gazing upon her was pure torture.

Belle noted Casey's reaction and smiled inwardly. "I don't want you to leave, Casey. We haven't had any time alone since . . . since Jones abducted me. There is so much we need to discuss. So much I need to explain to you."

She grasped his hand and led him to the bed. Casey resisted, but finally succumbed to her urging and sat down beside her. "You don't need to explain a thing."

"I do. I've loved you for a very long time, Casey, but was afraid to admit it. I've never forgotten that everyone I loved left me. My mother, my father, Tom. They were all so young. I felt guilty, thinking it was somehow my fault my loved ones deserted me. I feared you'd leave me just like they did."

"Sweetheart, I understand. You didn't know me when I arrived in Placerville. You naturally mistrusted strangers, especially with McAllister hot after Tommy. I insinuated myself into your life at a time when you were vulnerable. At first I just wanted to get close to you, to learn for myself the kind of woman you were. It wasn't long before I realized McAllister had lied to me about you. You weren't a whore. You were a loving mother who worked hard to support her son. That's when I fell in love with you."

"I should have trusted you when you claimed you didn't betray Tommy to his grandfather. But all I felt was guilt for being in your bed when Tommy was abducted. My whole world disintegrated when I allowed you to seduce me and I lost Tommy. You were my betrayer. I hated myself almost as much as I hated you."

"I loved you even then."

Belle studied her hands. "I guess I knew that, but I was so afraid. Then when you went to Arizona I was sure you'd never return. That's why I didn't tell you about the baby when you did come back. I kept expecting you to leave."

"I'm here to stay, you ought to know that by now."

She nodded solemnly. "I know. I'm so grateful you put up with me for so long. I want to spend the rest of my life making you happy."

"You already have."

"Kiss me, Casey."

"I don't think that's wise."

"The doctor gave his blessing. My leg is stronger and our baby is thriving. I need you, Casey. Make love to me."

Casey shot to his feet. "It's too soon."

She reached for him, urging him back to her. "I need you."

"Are you sure? Perhaps we should wait."

"Do you want to wait?"

"Good God, no! I want you so desperately I'm shaking." He held out his hands. "Look how I'm trembling."

She grasped his hands and brought them to her breasts. "Touch me, Casey."

She murmured incoherently as his hands cupped her breasts through her chemise. Delicious spirals of delight coursed through her. She gave a low moan deep in her throat as he lowered her onto the bed.

His fingers were sure and gentle, his eyes full of loving promise as he brushed kisses across her eyelids, her cheeks, the sensitive hollow of her throat. His mouth was warm and sensuous, the movement of his fingertips upon her flesh pure fire.

Sweet, sweet torture. Belle's blood sang through her veins; her heart beat so rapidly she feared it would burst through her chest. Reaching up between them she tugged at his shirt, telling him without words what she wanted. She wanted to feel the warmth of Casey's firm flesh against hers. She wanted them both naked.

Casey raised slightly and tore off his shirt, ripping off buttons in his haste. Then he removed Belle's shift and tossed it aside. Without rising he removed his shoes and stockings and kicked off his pants. Now as naked as she, he smiled down at her. She was so lovely. So warm and giving. He inhaled the sweet scent of her hair, letting the satiny strands trail through his fingers.

Belle ran her hands over the firm flesh of his shoulders and chest, admiring the glowing sheen of his skin, the breadth of his shoulders, the hardness of his bronzed flesh. The harsh intake of his breath as she pulled him down to her told her without words that her touch affected him as profoundly as his did her.

"I love you," Casey whispered as he lowered his head and licked the crest of one impudent breast.

His mouth closed over the hard nipple even as his hand tormented its twin.

Her body was so hot, so soft, so willing. He loved the way she arced and writhed beneath the expert torment of his lips and hands. He felt his own body swelling, growing, felt the massive ridge of hard muscle between his legs clamoring for satisfaction.

"Touch me, love," he whispered against her mouth.

She obeyed instantly, curling her hand over the huge ridge of his warm manhood. His hand flew to hers, holding her palm tightly against his erection. He moved her hand slowly up and down until she learned the rhythm. Suddenly she stopped and gave him an impudent grin. Then she lowered her head and opened her lips to him.

Sweat beaded on his temples. "God," he gasped, flinging his head back as splendor splintered through him. When he could take no more, he gently pushed her away. "Enough. I want to adore you, every wonderful, dewy inch of you." Then he knelt between her legs and lowered his head.

His mouth was hot and moist against her intimate flesh, his tongue a fiery sword, thrusting and arousing. Belle felt something darkly primitive, utterly consuming rushing through her and cried out Casey's name.

Casey rose up above her, his expression raw and intense as he watched her face in the throes of ecstasy. Her climax triggered his own grinding need. He growled with pleasure as he joined his body to hers in a long, smooth plunge, seating himself deep within her. He thrust and withdrew, again and again, always mindful of her condition, curbing his wildness without sacrificing their pleasure.

Belle felt the tension inside her building as she rose to meet Casey's thrusts. Desire grew hotter, brighter with each successive thrust, until they found themselves consumed in an inferno of blazing ecstasy. Their cries rose in harmonious accord, wrapping them in joyous splendor, fading away to perfect contentment.

"How do you feel?" Casey asked worriedly when he regained his breath.

"Wonderful," Belle murmured on a sigh. "You're wonderful."

"Never lose that thought, sweetheart. I shouldn't have lost control like that. I didn't hurt you, did I?"

"You could never hurt me. You're a gentle man. You're going to make a wonderful father. Tommy already adores you."

Casey fell silent. After a moment of introspection he said, "Belle, about Tom. I know I will never take his place in your heart. I understand how you felt about him and I respect your memories of him. I want to make a place all my own in your heart. I know you'll never love me like you did Tom and I'll try to contain my jealousy."

Belle was astounded. How could Casey believe she didn't love him as much as she had loved Tom? Undeniably she had loved Tom dearly. He had been kind and gentle and comfortable. But with Tom she had felt none of the wildness, none of the madness of loving a man like Casey. Loving Casey was like being caught up in a hurricane. The turbulent, gut-wrenching journey into the center was a dangerous prelude to the rewarding calm that followed. Loving

Tom had been like sailing a peaceful sea ruffled by balmy breezes. She'd felt pleasure but none of the tumultuous upheaval of Casey's frenzied loving.

"You've no cause to be jealous," Belle whispered. "Never think I'm comparing you to Tom. There is no comparison, Casey. Tom was Tom, and I'll always love him for his good qualities. But you are my destiny. Sometimes the tumultuous emotions you wrest from me are frightening. I'll never love anyone like I love you."

Belle's words thrilled Casey. Not for the first time he thanked God for sending him to McAllister. Without McAllister he would never have found a love to cherish.

Chapter 20

⌒ᏋᏆᏋ⌒

Belle awoke the following morning feeling as if everything was right in her world. Her baby was thriving and Casey loved her. She was no longer alone. She had Casey, Tommy, and her friends around her. For the first time since Tom's death she felt as if she had a complete family again. Belle glanced at Casey, saw he was still sleeping, and snuggled close to him. Even in sleep he must have felt her warmth, for he pulled her into the curve of his body and sighed contentedly.

Murmuring happily, Belle closed her eyes and dozed off again. Scant moments had passed, or so it seemed to Belle, when a loud pounding awakened her.

Casey reacted to the disturbance instantly, trained by his years of living dangerously. He was out of bed before Belle stirred herself to move.

"What is it?" Belle asked, wide awake now.

"I don't know," Casey said, pulling on his pants. "Who is it?" he called through the panel.

"It's Mark. I'm sorry to awaken you but the sheriff

is here. Something happened that you should know about."

"Be with you in a minute," Casey replied as he searched in his wardrobe for a shirt with all its buttons attached. He smiled at the memory of his buttons rolling on the floor in his eagerness to remove his shirt last night.

"What could the sheriff possibly want?" Belle asked as she watched Casey pull on his stockings and boots.

"I'll find out soon enough. Wait here, I'll return as soon as I know anything."

"I'm coming with you," Belle insisted.

"Very well. Come downstairs when you're dressed. I don't want to keep Rogan waiting."

A few minutes later Mark and Casey descended the staircase together to join the sheriff. "What's happened?" Casey asked Mark.

"It's Jones. I'll let Rogan tell you."

Casey's face was grim when he entered the study where Sheriff Rogan waited. "What's wrong, Sheriff?"

"Jones escaped last night," Rogan said, his face nearly as grim as Casey's. "We're forming a posse. Will you join us?"

Casey cursed fluently. "How in the hell did you let him get away?"

"My deputy was on duty last night. I took the night off. I'm not required to work night and day, you know," he said defensively. "Deputy Jenkins brought in a drunk late last night. Jones appeared to be sleeping when Jenkins passed his cell. On his way back from locking up the drunk, he paused at Jones's cell to check on him. The bastard grabbed Jenkins through the bars and choked him until he blacked out. Jones stole the keys from Jenkins and escaped from his cell. He locked the deputy inside before he took off."

A muscle in Casey's jaw twitched. "When did you find out?"

"This morning when I went to relieve my deputy. I put the word out that I was forming a posse. Jones stole a horse from the livery and is armed. I'd guess he's headed for the border."

"Damn! Give me half an hour. I'll meet you at the jailhouse."

"Where are you going?" They turned in unison as Belle walked into the room. "What happened?"

"Hank Jones escaped last night," Casey said. "I'm joining the sheriff's posse. He thinks Jones is headed for Mexico."

"Count me in," Mark said. "I want the bastard to pay for what he did to Greta."

The sheriff nodded. "Bring food and gear for a week. We should catch up to him by then. I'm leaving my deputy in charge here."

The sheriff left a few minutes later. Mark hurried off to gather their gear, leaving Casey and Belle alone.

"Do you have to go?" Belle asked worriedly. "I have a bad feeling about this."

"I don't really think Jones left town," Casey confided. "I want to give the appearance of leaving in case Jones is watching, but as soon as it's feasible I'll double back to wait and see if my hunch is right. I don't want to leave you alone, even for a minute, but I want the bastard caught and punished for what he did to you."

"Are you sure he didn't leave town?"

"No, but the sheriff thinks he did."

Twenty minutes later, Casey was ready to leave. He smiled tenderly at Belle and pulled her into his arms. She strained against him, raising her lips for his kiss. He obliged eagerly, outlining her lips with his tongue before sealing them in a kiss that stole her breath and left her wanting more. But there was no time for a longer farewell. He kissed her one last time, hard, his grip nearly painful, as if he was loathe to part with her.

"I won't leave you alone long," he whispered against her lips. "I'll be nearby." Then he was gone.

As the day progressed, Belle couldn't dispel the alarming premonition that something was amiss. Before Belle returned to her room later that morning to rest—she still wasn't fully recovered from her ordeal—Greta approached to ask if she could take Tommy to the park.

"Only if you take Wan Yo and Harry with you," Belle contended. "Make sure they're armed. The sheriff seemed convinced that Jones was headed for the border, but one can't be too careful."

"Would you like to come with us?" Greta invited. "I'm going to pack a lunch and make a day of it. It's so pleasant out but for a few wispy clouds, and if it rains it won't be till later."

"I'm not up to a picnic yet," Belle contended. "You go and have a good time. I think I'll just take a nap while you're gone."

"Perhaps Harry or Wan Yo should remain here with you."

"No, I'll be fine," she said, aware that Casey would return soon. "Tommy needs a diversion. I'll see you at dinner tonight."

Belle stood in the doorway waving to the happy

group as they walked off down the street. The day was exceptionally fine and Tommy was in high spirits. An outing would do him good. Belle turned back into the house. She knew Casey wouldn't let anything happen to her but something struck a disturbing chord in her. It was more than a premonition, it was like a strong warning that something was going to happen.

"Mrs. Walker, might I speak with you a moment?"

Startled, Belle spun on her heel, relieved that it was only one of the maids. "Oh, Betsy, you frightened me. What can I do for you?"

"I'd like the day off if it doesn't cause a problem. My mother took sick yesterday, and there is no one to take care of the little ones. My older sister promised to tend her but she won't arrive until tomorrow."

"I think we can do without you for one day. Run along. Minnie can see to your chores."

"No, ma'am, she can't. That's the problem. This is Minnie's day off, she won't be back until morning. There's just cook, and he went to the market this morning."

"I think we can fend for ourselves for one day. Go help your mother, she's the one who needs you."

"Thank you, ma'am," Betsy said, bobbing her head. "I'll be back bright and early tomorrow morning."

The house was quiet, too quiet, Belle thought as she walked through the deserted rooms. Being alone in the big, rambling mansion made her nervous. She couldn't ever recall feeling so out of sorts before over nothing.

The thump, thump of the brass door knocker

jolted Belle from her reverie. Caution made her peek out the side window before answering the summons. When she saw Naomi standing on the threshold, she flung open the door with a glad cry.

"If I'd known I'd get this kind of welcome I'd have come sooner," Naomi joshed as she stepped inside and closed the door behind her. "I heard about the posse. Just wanted to stop by and see if you're all right."

Naomi had been a frequent visitor during Belle's recuperation and Belle was grateful for her caring. "I'm fine. Come inside and have some tea. We'll have to go to the kitchen and fix it ourselves, since I'm the only one in the house right now."

"You're alone? What was Casey thinking to leave you alone? Where are Greta and Wan Yo? Where's Harry? Are there no servants in attendance?"

Belle laughed. "Greta and Wan Yo took Tommy on a picnic. Harry went with them. The servants are . . . occupied elsewhere. And Casey won't be gone long."

"No tea, honey, I can't stay long. I have several errands to run before the customers start arriving for their usual pleasures. The girls are all silly, can't trust any of them to run things in my absence. I just wanted to make sure you're all right. And I thought I'd check on Harry." She fluffed her hair and gave Belle a wink. "He's a feisty old codger. Once he fattens up a mite, he won't be half bad to look at."

Belle grinned. "Why Naomi, are you sweet on Harry?"

Naomi laughed off Belle's inquiry. "You know me. Are you sure you'll be all right? How is the baby?"

"We're both fine, stop worrying. I was preparing to take a nap when you arrived. I didn't get much sleep last night."

Naomi gave her a knowing grin. "That randy husband of yours keep you up all night, did he? Don't let that one get away, honey. You sure are crazy about that man, aren't you?"

Belle blushed clear down to her toes. Was she so transparent? "You know me well, don't you, Naomi?"

"I should. You've been my joy all these years." She wiped away a tear. "I'll leave you to your nap, honey. Send someone around if you need me. And tell Harry to come and see me." She kissed Belle on the cheek and sailed out the door.

Belle smiled after her with true fondness. She couldn't have picked a better mother had she chosen Naomi herself. The tenderhearted madam had given her the best life she could, given the circumstances of their environment. Much better than the life her own father had provided for her.

Before she went upstairs for her nap, Belle made certain the front door was locked. Then she recalled that the cook had left by the back door to do the marketing, and decided to lock that door too. The instant she entered the kitchen she knew a moment of fear. Something dark and foreboding filled the room. She shivered, trying to shake off the feeling. But it remained, potent and frightening. Hurrying to the door, she turned the key in the lock, then rested her forehead against the panel, her breath coming in short, jerky puffs of air.

What was wrong with her? she wondered. Was the baby making her fanciful? She was locked in the house, nothing could hurt her. Casey promised he wouldn't leave her alone long. Feeling better, she walked on shaking legs through the kitchen.

"Hello, bitch."

Belle screamed. The sound was cut off abruptly when clawing fear closed her throat. She couldn't believe her eyes. Hank Jones was standing near the pantry, where he'd obviously been hiding. His leering countenance was a frightening reminder of the terror he had put her through.

"You're supposed to be on your way to Mexico," Belle managed to gasp out.

"That's what I wanted everyone to think. I doubled back. I hid behind some rocks when the posse passed on their way out of town. I had unfinished business right here in San Francisco. I need money. Lots of it. And you've got it."

"I'm not alone," Belle lied, drawing upon an inner courage she didn't know she possessed.

Jones gave a bark of laughter. "I ain't stupid. I been watching the house. They all left, even the cook. You're alone, lady, and I want money."

"H—how much?"

"Ten thousand dollars."

Belle blanched. "We don't keep that kind of money in the house. I'll need to go to the bank."

"Fat chance. I don't trust you out of my sight. I know there's a safe in the house. I saw it once when I came to the house to try to wheedle money out of McAllister. I figured he owed it to my father."

"I don't know the combination."

"Then you damn well better find it if you know what's good for you," Jones said, grasping her shoulders and shoving her into the hallway. "Move, bitch."

Belle stumbled toward the study on wooden legs. She couldn't conceive of Casey keeping that much money in the house. Although she knew the combination of the safe, she had never found the need to use it.

As Belle moved in front of Jones, he eyed her slim figure speculatively. "Are you really breeding?"

"Yes," Belle answered tersely. She wondered if he held any special feelings for motherhood. He didn't.

"You don't look it." He gave her a lewd grin. "I never done it with a pregnant woman."

Belle paled. She'd rather die than have him defile her. Where was Casey? Why hadn't he returned yet?

They had reached the study now and Belle stopped just inside the door. Jones swung her around to face him and placed a grimy paw on her stomach. He seemed intrigued by her condition.

Belle slapped his hands away, sickened by his touch. It made her want to retch. "Keep your filthy hands off me!"

"You're right. That will come later. Money first. Open the safe," he growled, shoving her into the study. "After the money is in my hands I'll feel a helluva lot better." He eyed her with slow relish, fingering his crotch. "Maybe I'll even find time to get rid of this," he said, humping his loins forward in an obscene gesture.

Trying not to panic, Belle averted her eyes from the disgusting display. "I have no idea how much money is in the safe."

"It better be enough," Jones muttered, giving her a vicious shove toward the safe. Belle stumbled against the desk, crying out in pain when the sharp corner jabbed into her thigh.

"You sure are a clumsy bitch. You must be damn

good in bed for your husband to put up with a cripple like you."

Ignoring his cruel words, Belle limped to the safe, hunkered down on her knees, and fiddled with the combination. Her fingers were shaking so she failed to open it on the first try.

"What's wrong?" Jones growled. "Ya didn't forget it, did you?"

"N . . . no. This is the first time I've attempted to open the safe."

He nudged her in the side with the tip of his boot. "Try again. Hurry."

Belle flexed her fingers and tried again. The sooner she got it open, the sooner Jones would leave. The money was nothing. She'd give him twice that amount to be rid of him. Being alone with a killer was terrifying, but in a way she was glad everyone was gone so Jones couldn't hurt them.

"There, I've got it," Belle cried as she pulled the safe door open.

"Out of my way," Jones said, shoving her aside in his eagerness to get to the money inside.

"Sonuvabitch!" His expression was thunderous as he scattered papers and personal items on the floor. "There ain't hardly enough money here to get me out of town. A measly few hundred dollars and a small sack of gold dust. How am I supposed to get to Mexico on that?"

"I'm sorry, that's all there is."

"What about jewelry?"

"I have none."

"Don't give me that shit. All women have jewelry." He prodded her with the gun. "Upstairs, be quick about it. You better hope I find something valuable up there."

Picking herself up from the floor, Belle limped up the stairs, reaching through space and time to send silent plea to Casey. *Please hurry back, Casey. I need you. You've never failed me when I needed you, and I've never needed you more.*

Everyone except Casey seemed to be of the opinion that Jones was headed for Mexico, but so far they'd found no evidence suggesting Jones was ahead of them. Casey decided it was time to double back. He'd given Jones plenty of time to think he had ridden with the posse instead of just making it look that way in order to set Jones up.

"What's wrong, brother?" Mark said as he rode up beside Casey.

"I'm turning back, Mark. I never intended to leave Belle alone for long. If Jones remained in town as I suspect, he saw me leave with the posse, just like I'd planned. I'm going to double back and wait for him at the house. My gut tells me Belle needs me."

"Your instincts are usually good. I'd trust them no matter what. Do you think Jones is dumb enough to return to your house?"

"Frankly, I don't put anything past him. He'd have no reason to remain in San Francisco. Unless . . ." He sawed on the reins. His horse danced to a halt. "I'm going back. Now!"

Mark reined in beside him. "I'll come with you."

"No. Tell the sheriff I'm turning back. I have to follow through on my hunch."

Mark looked alarmed. "You don't think . . ."

"I wish I could explain but I can't. I just have this urgency to return home. Belle needs me, I can feel it in my bones. Perhaps it has nothing to do with Jones. Maybe it's the baby. Whatever it is, I promised to be there for her." He wheeled his mount around and rode hell-for-leather toward San Francisco.

"You sure as·hell weren't lying when you said you had no jewelry," Jones muttered as he rummaged through Belle's bureau drawers. In Casey's bureau he had found a pair of gold cufflinks, which he promptly pocketed, but for the most part the pickings were slim.

"You'll find little of value here. Take what you have and leave before my family returns."

"I saw them leave with a picnic basket. As for your man, he joined the posse on a wild goose chase." He laughed raucously. "He won't be back for days. That leaves you and me, lady." He leered at her. "You owe me for these slim pickings."

Belle retreated, her mind numb with fear. She had to say something, anything to divert his thoughts. "There's silver downstairs in the pantry. Take the silver, take the paintings, take anything you want, just leave me alone."

"I want *you*, bitch. I'm gonna finish what we started back at the cabin." He grasped the neckline of her bodice and ripped downward. The material gave easily, revealing a generous portion of skin and the rounded tops of her breasts.

Suddenly Belle recalled the loaded gun Casey kept in the drawer of the nightstand. She'd never shot a man before, but she would if it meant saving her life and that of her child. She edged toward the table, but before she reached it Jones grabbed her and threw her onto the bed.

"That's where all women belong," Jones sneered, "on their backs."

Belle's fear turned to anger as Jones removed his belt and snapped it several times between his huge hands.

"Bastard! Don't you dare touch me."

"That whore from Naomi's squealed like a pig when I beat her with my belt. I want to see how loud you can holler. Beating a woman gives me pleasure. Nearly as much pleasure as bedding her."

"Despicable pervert," Belle hissed, rolling to the opposite side of the bed then leaping up. "Do you think I'd lie there meekly and let you beat me? Or rape me?"

Her defiance seemed to amuse Jones. He laughed mirthlessly. "You got spunk, lady, but I'll beat it out of you." He stalked her around the bed, snarling viciously as he reached for her. Belle anticipated his move and threw herself across the bed, rolling to the opposite side.

Elated, she saw that Jones no longer stood between her and the door. Lunging forward, she reached the door and flung it open, groaning in frustration when her lame leg gave way beneath her. She sprawled through the door, landing on her back in the hallway.

With a cry of triumph, Jones was on her in an instant, pinning her to the floor with his body. "Got ya now, bitch." He shoved up her skirts, cursing when he became entangled in her petticoats. His curses cut through the silence of the empty house. What else could go wrong? He was about to find out.

Casey arrived home and let himself in the front door with his key. Finding it locked somewhat eased his fears. His imagination must be working overtime, he thought as he paused in the foyer. Surely Jones wouldn't make his move this soon, would he? The house was secure and all was quiet. Too quiet, he decided as he made his way toward the kitchen to ask the cook where everyone had gone. He passed the study, saw that it was empty, and continued on. He took two steps and stopped abruptly. Something was wrong, terribly wrong.

Retracing his steps to the study, he realized immediately what had bothered him. The safe was gaping open and the floor beneath littered with papers. Alarm bells went off in his head. Then he heard a noise and moved stealthily toward it. He paused at the foot of the steps to listen. He heard the noise again, and this time there was no mistaking the sound. The voice he heard was male and harsh and vaguely familiar, and did not belong to a member of his household.

Fear lanced through Casey. His heart was pounding so hard it sounded like thunder in his ears. His hunch had been right. Jones hadn't left town, but Casey hadn't expected him to make his move so soon. He palmed his gun and started up the stairs.

Suddenly the bedroom door flew open and Belle spilled out onto the floor. A man followed, flinging himself on top of her. Casey's blood froze when he recognized Hank Jones.

Jones was untangling himself from Belle's skirts when he became aware of Casey pounding up the staircase. Spitting out an oath, he fumbled for his gun, rose to his feet, and pulled Belle up with him, encircling her neck in a stranglehold.

"What are you doing here, Walker? You're supposed to be with the sheriff's posse."

"That's what I wanted you to think. And you were supposed to be in jail awaiting execution."

"Yeah, but I ain't."

"And I'm not with the posse. Let go of my wife."

"I don't think so. She's coming with me and you're not going to do a damn thing about it. If you make one move, I'll plug her."

"Let her go, Jones. She's breeding."

"That's your problem. Mine is getting out of town with my skin intact. Your wife is my safe passage. Back up, we're coming down the stairs."

Suddenly the front door opened then slammed shut. "Mama, I'm home! It looked like rain so we came back early."

Belle cried out in anguish when she saw Tommy bounding up the stairs. She felt Jones' grip tighten around her neck. "Tommy, go back! Run!"

Tommy recognized Casey standing on the stairs, saw no reason to turn back, and kept coming. "I beat the others home, Mama. I ran all the way." He sounded proud of his accomplishment. Then he saw Belle in Jones' grip and skidded to a halt beside Casey. "Who is that man? Why is he holding Mama? Is he going to hurt her?"

"Go back downstairs, son," Casey said evenly, so as not to frighten the boy.

"Do as Casey says," Belle urged. "I'll be all right."

Astute for his age, Tommy knew exactly what was going on. "You're a bad man," he told Jones. "I won't let you hurt Mama."

Tiring of the game, Jones shoved Belle forward, wringing a cry of pain out of her when her leg twisted beneath her.

"You're hurting Mama," Tommy accused furiously. His little face reddened with anger.

Fearing for both Tommy and Belle, Casey tried to find a vulnerable spot on Jones that wasn't being shielded by Belle. He couldn't risk hurting Belle, so he was forced to wait until he could get a clear shot.

Tommy's thoughts were less complicated. He knew a bad man was hurting his mother, and it was up to him and Casey to save her. His mouth clamped tightly, his hands clenched into fists, and he darted past Casey before Casey could stop him. Small and fleet of foot, he scooted behind Jones before Jones realized what was happening, and plowed into his legs from behind. Jones's arm went flying upward, and with it his gun. His knees buckled beneath him. His hold on Belle slackened and Belle struggled free, stumbling forward into Casey's arms. Casey caught her handily, shoved her behind him, and turned to confront Jones.

Casey nearly panicked when he saw that Tommy was on the move again. Before Casey could shout a warning, Tommy shoved Jones hard from behind. Already off balance, Jones crashed to the floor. His hand landed scant inches from his gun. Scooping it into his hand, Jones squeezed off a shot at Casey. The bullet went wild, slamming into the wall.

"Get back, Tommy," Casey called as he took aim at Jones. Tommy obeyed without question, darting into an open doorway. Casey's aim was straight and true. The bullet lodged between Jones' eyes, killing him instantly.

Tommy peeked around the bedroom door, his eyes bulging, his face pale. Belle darted around Casey and gathered his shaking body into her arms. "That was a very brave thing you did, darling," she told him. Her voice trembled with emotion. "But also very foolish."

"The bad man was hurting you, Mama."

"You should have let Casey take care of it," Belle contended. "You know he wouldn't let anyone hurt me."

Casey listened to the exchange, nearly moved to tears by the trust Belle had placed in him. After a rather inauspicious beginning, Belle had come to love and trust him without reservation. His heart was full to overflowing.

Greta, Wan Yo, and Harry stood at the foot of the stairs, having returned while the drama was unfolding. All three bounded up the stairs now, full of questions and concern. They had not interfered earlier for fear Belle or Tommy would be hurt. They had heard some of what happened and Casey explained the rest.

"Tommy is the hero," Casey said, smiling fondly at the boy. "But I may still tan his hide for endangering his life. When I saw him darting toward Jones, I lost ten years off my life."

"I feared you wouldn't return in time," Belle said, grimacing with distaste at the dead body.

"I almost didn't. I'm sorry, Belle. I didn't think Jones would act so soon. Gut instinct told me it was time to return home, that you needed me. Take Tommy downstairs, love. Wan Yo, Harry, and I will get rid of the body." He gave her a quick kiss then turned her toward the staircase.

Belle was waiting alone for Casey in the parlor. She ran into his arms the moment he stepped into the room.

"It's all over now, sweetheart," Casey soothed. "Jones is dead. He won't ever hurt anyone again." He held her at arm's length, his hands curling protectively around her shoulders. "He didn't . . . you aren't . . ."

"No, you arrived in time. Jones wanted money. When he didn't find enough in the safe, he wanted jewelry. When he found none, he became angry and abusive."

He pulled her against him and kissed her hard. "It's all behind us now, love. We have our whole lives ahead of us."

"What about your job?" Belle asked. "Are you going back to work for the Pinkertons?"

"Those days are over. My job is here, taking care of my family and protecting Tommy's assets. Mark wants to stay, too. He and Greta are becoming close and he's happy at the winery. It wouldn't surprise me to see Mark and Greta wed before long."

"Greta is crazy about Mark. Even Harry appears to be holding his own." Belle sighed happily. "I'm hoping the doctor's diagnosis was wrong. Did you notice how taken he is with Naomi? I learned today that she's equally enamored of him."

"Are you playing matchmaker, love?"

"Perhaps. I'm suddenly blessed with a large family. It's the most wonderful feeling. When our baby is born our life will be complete. Do you want a boy or girl?"

"I want a baby," Casey said. "But since you asked, I already have a son, a girl would be nice."

"I love you, Casey Walker."

"I love you, Belle Walker. Let's make a vow right now. Let's promise one another to repeat those words before we go to sleep each night. For the rest of our lives."

They did. For the rest of their lives.